MOON
FLIGHTS

Other books by Elizabeth Moon:

The Deed of Paksenarrion (available as an omnibus edition)
  Sheepfarmer's Daughter
  Divided Allegiance
  Oath of Gold

The Legacy of Gird (available as an omnibus edition)
  Surrender None
  Liar's Oath

The Planet Pirates (with Anne McCaffrey) (available as an omnibus edition, with *Death of Sleep* by Jody Lynn Nye)
  Sassinak
  Generation Warriors

Remnant Population

The Serrano Legacy
  *Hunting Party**
  *Sporting Chance**
  *Winning Colors**
  (* available as an omnibus edition titled *Heris Serrano*)
  Once a Hero
  Rules of Engagement
  Change of Command
  Against the Odds

The Speed of Dark

Vatta's War
  Trading in Danger
  Marque and Reprisal (UK title: *Moving Target*)
  Engaging the Enemy
  Command Decision

Short fiction collections
  Lunar Activity
  Phases

ELIZABETH
MOON

MOON
FLIGHTS

With an Introduction
by Anne McCaffrey

NIGHT SHADE BOOKS
San Francisco

First Edition

Trade Hardcover: 978-1-59780-109-6
Limited Edition: 978-1-59780-108-9

Night Shade Books
Please visit us on the web at
http://www.nightshadebooks.com

In memory of my grandfather, Edwin James Jamerson, who loved stories and storytelling and was a storyteller himself, of the cracker-barrel-and-whittlin' school.

CONTENTS:

INTRODUCTION
BY ANNE MCCAFFREY

What a treat! To write an introduction for a writer whom I hold in high esteem. All her books are on my "comfort shelves."

I think it was Bill Fawcett who first introduced me to Elizabeth Moon for her book, *Sheepfarmer's Daughter,* the first volume of The Deed of Paksenarrion. Then, when I was looking for another collaborator to finish the Planet Pirates trilogy, I took him up on his suggestion of using EMoon—as she is respectfully known as in Dragonhold. Having read the first novel, I was certainly more than interested and she proved interested in writing *Sassinak.* With her background of service in the Marines—not that anyone regarding this tall slender woman with long black hair coiled on her pate would ever think she'd been a captain in the Marines. But she was willing to write with me and I was delighted. We actually met about then, at an Atlanta Dragoncon. We both felt that we must have known each other in some distant incarnation, as we were comfortable with each other very quickly. I certainly admired her work. I gave her a basic summary of what I thought the novel should contain and where I wanted to go with it. WOW! She took it and ran.

So, she got the trilogy up to the final book and she did most of *Generation Warriors.* She phoned me one morning, from the depths of Texas, to ask if she could put in an opera about the tragedy of the heavyworlders. I told her to run with it and the sequence is enough to stop your heart and start your tears, tragic and beautifully handled. I could even like heavyworlders after that. What started out as a notion to mind to have a planet that stayed in the Mesozoic Age—and thus dinosaurs survived—was a fun sort of script and we did have fun with it. Jody Lynn Nye wrote the really hard one, *The Death of Sleep,* and then we all got in the act.

So now you have a collection of stories from this imaginative and highly inventive author and I get the chance to urge you to read it. Which I most certainly do…not that you'll need much nudging for you will recognize her name and probably have read her Heris Serrano series or the latest fun run of hers, Vatta's War. With great pride and pleasure, I add that her magnificent *The Speed of Dark* quite rightly won the Nebula Award with which science fiction writers compliment their colleagues. A powerful and gripping story of how one young man fights the handicaps of autism and makes his own way in a "normal" world. As the lad has told me, "normal" is a setting on your washing machine. Not only has that book been honored but she also wrote *Remnant Population,* which is very much a sneak-up-on-you, which I recall cackling about for the sheer mischief she created for her main characters and winds it all up with an ending every author would like to have achieved. I still find myself reading it, just for the fun of the ending. Wish I could write like that.

EMoon has been a not frequent enough guest at Dragonhold as much because we are both "into" horses as being science fiction writers. Her novel *Hunting Party*, set on a planet that is devoted entirely to the chases of the inedible by the unspeakable, earned her an invitation to join a proper English hunt for a day. She asked could she stay over with me on her way back. She had also been complaining about not finding a horse in Texas who jumped. (Well, ALL Irish horses jump!) So I suggested that she stop here first and I would see that she had a ride or two on a proper hunter horse. She did so, which was serendipitous because, as some of us here feared, the English hunt put her up on an old racehorse. She had neither steering nor brakes and how she stayed on at the speed she was going to keep up with the pack is another tribute to her expertise and determination. Fortunately before her arms and legs gave out, others were changing to second horses, and she was quite within hunt manners to end the session without disgracing herself, S-F, Texas or the Marines.

So, dive into this collection with the assurance that you will have your mind set at ease, your ears scratched and your eyes pleasured and maybe learn something new in the process. That's what good writing's all about…teaching the reader something new or an aspect to something familiar that they hadn't quite considered before.

Well done, EMoon!

Anne McCaffrey
Wicklow County, Ireland
June 2007

IF NUDITY OFFENDS YOU

When Louanne opened her light bill, she about had a fit. She hadn't had a bill that high since the time the Sims family hooked into her outlet for a week, when their daddy lost his job and right before they got kicked out of the trailer park for him being drunk and disorderly and the kids stealing stuff out of trash cans and their old speckled hound dog being loose and making a mess on Mrs. Thackridge's porch. Drunk and disorderly was pretty common, actually, and stealing from trash cans was a problem only because the Sims kids dumped everything before picking through it, and never bothered to put it back. The Sanchez kids had the good sense to pick up what mess they made, and no one cared what they took out of the trash (though some of it was good, like a boom box that Carter Willis stole from down at Haley's, and hid in the trash can until Tuesday, only the Sanchez kids found it first). But when Grace (which is what they called that hound, and a stupid name that is for a coonhound, anyway) made that mess on Mrs. Thackridge's front porch, and she stepped in it on the way to a meeting of the Extension Homemaker's Club and had to go back inside and change her shoes, with her friends right there in the car waiting for her, that was *it* for the Sims family.

Anyhow, when Louanne saw that $82.67, she just threw it down on the table and said, "Oh my God," in that tone of voice her grandma never could stand, and then she said a bunch of other things like you'd expect, and then she tried to figure out who she knew at the power company, because there was no way in the world she'd used that much electricity, and also no way in the world she could pay that bill. She didn't leave the air conditioner on all day like some people did, and she was careful to turn off lights in the kitchen when she moved to the bedroom, and all that. All those things to keep the bill low, because she'd just bought herself a car—almost new, a real god buy—and some fancy clothes to wear to the dance hall on weekends, now that she was through with Jack forever and looking for someone else. The car payment alone was $175 a month, and then there was the trailer park fee, and the mobile home payments, and the furniture rental… and

3

ure light bill was supposed to stay *low,* like under thirty dollars.

It occurred to Louanne that even though the Simses had left, someone else might have bled her for power. But who? She looked out each window of her trailer, looking for telltale cords. The Loomis family, to her right, seemed as stable and prosperous as any: Pete worked for the county, and Jane cooked in the school cafeteria. No cord there. The Blaylocks, on the left, were a very young couple from out of state. He worked construction; she had a small baby, and stayed home. Almost every day, Louanne had seen her sitting on the narrow step of their trailer, cuddling a plump, placid infant. Directly behind was an empty slot, and to either side behind.... Louanne could not tell if that ripple in the rough grass was a cord or not. She'd have to go outside to see for sure.

Now, if there's one sure way to make an enemy at a trailer park, it's to go snooping around like you thought your neighbors were cheating on you somehow, and before Louanne got into that kind of mess, she thought she'd try something safer. Back when Jack was living there, she wouldn't have minded a little trouble, being as he was six foot three and did rock work for Mullens Stone; but on her own, she'd had to learn quieter ways of doing things. Like checking up close to her own power outlets, to see if she could spot anything funny coming off the plugs.

She was still in the heels and city clothes she wore to work (secretary over at the courthouse: she made more money than either of her parents here in Behrnville), which was not exactly the right outfit for crawling around under things. She took off the purple polyester blouse, the black suit skirt (the jacket hung in her closet, awaiting winter), the dressy earrings and necklace, the lacy underwear that her mother, even *now,* even after all these years, thought unsuitable. And into the cutoffs, the striped tank top, and her thongs.

Outside, it was still blistering, and loud with the throbbing of her air conditioner, which she'd hung in the living room window. She opened the door of her storage shed that Jack had built her, a neat six-by-six space, and took down her water hose from its bracket. The outside hydrant wasn't but six feet from her power outlet, and with a new car—new for her, anyway—nobody'd wonder about her giving it a wash. Especially not on such a hot day.

She dragged the hose end around behind her trailer, and screwed it onto the faucet, letting her eye drift sideways toward the power outlet. Sure enough, besides her own attachment, another plump black cord ran down the pipe and off into the grass. But where? Louanne turned the water on as if a car wash were the only thing on her mind, and sprayed water on her tires. They did look grungy. She flipped the cutoff on the sprayer and went to get a brush out of her storage shed. About then, Curtis Blaylock drove in and grinned at her as he got out of his car.

"Little hot for that, ain't it?" he asked, eyeing her long, tanned legs.

"Well, you know... new car...." Louanne didn't meet his eye, exactly, and went back around the end of the trailer without stopping to chat. Becoming a father didn't stop most men from looking at everyone else. She scrubbed at the tires, then sprayed the car itself, working around it so she could look everywhere without seeming to. That ripple in the grass, now... it seemed to go back at an angle, and then... lot 17. That was the one. A plain, old-fashioned metal trailer with rounded ends, not more than a twenty-seven- or thirty-footer. She thought she could see a black cord lifting up out of the grass and into its underside.

She finished the car, put her hose and brush back into the storage unit, and went back inside. Through the blinds in her bedroom, she could see a little more of lot 17. A middle-aged pickup with slightly faded blue paint sat beside the trailer. Lot 17's utility hookups were hidden from this angle. Louanne watched. A man came out... a big man, moving heavily. Sweat marks darkened his blue shirt; his face looked red and swollen. He climbed into the pickup, yelled something back at the trailer, then slammed the door and backed carefully into the lane between the rows. The trailer door opened briefly, and someone inside threw out a panful of water. Louanne wrinkled her nose in disgust. White trash. Typical. Anyone that'd steal power would throw water out in the yard like that instead of using the drain. It was probably stopped up anyway.

Louanne got herself a sandwich and a beer from her spotless refrigerator, and settled down on the bed to watch some more. A light came on as the evening darkened; against a flowered curtain, she could see a vague shape moving now and then. About nine or so the pickup returned. She heard its uneven engine diesel awhile before stopping. It was too dark to see the man walk to the door, but she did see the flash of light when the door opened.

Her light, she thought angrily. She'd paid for it. She wondered how long they left it on. Eighty-two dollars minus the maybe twenty-seven her bill should be, meant they were wasting over fifty dollars a month of her money. Probably kept the lights on half the night. Ran the air conditioner on high. Left the refrigerator door open, or made extra ice... stuff like that. She flounced off the bed and into the living room, getting herself another beer on the way. She didn't usually have two beers unless she was out with someone, but getting stung for someone else's electricity was bad enough to change her ways.

Thing was, she couldn't figure out how to handle it. She sure wasn't going over there in the dark, past nine at night, to confront that big, heavy man and whoever else was in there. That would be plain stupid. But on the other hand, there was that bill.... She couldn't afford to have her credit rating ruined, not as hard as she'd worked to get a decent one. She thought of just pulling the plug out, maybe at two in the morning or so, whenever their light went out, and cutting off the plug end. That would sort of let them know they'd been found, but it wasn't the same as starting a fight about it. On the other hand, that didn't get the bill paid.

Louanne put the can of beer down on a coaster— even if the tabletop *was* laminated, there was no sense in getting bad habits. Someday she'd own a real wood dining room table, and pretty end tables for her living room, and she didn't intend to have them marked up with rings from beer cans, either—and eased back into her darkened bedroom to look between the blinds. The light was still on behind the flowered curtain. It wasn't late enough yet. She went into her bathroom and used the john, then checked her face in the mirror. Her eyebrows needed plucking, and she really ought to do something about her hair. She fluffed it out one way, then another. The district judge's secretary had said she should streak it. Louanne tried to imagine how that might look… . Some people just looked older, grayer, but Holly Jordan, in the tax office, looked terrific with hers streaked. Louanne took out her tweezers and did her eyebrows, then tried her new plum-colored shadow. That might do for the dance hall on Friday.

But thinking of the dance hall on Friday (not Ladies Night, so it would cost her to get in) made her think of that electric bill, and she slammed her makeup drawer shut so hard the contents rattled. She was not going to put up with it; she'd do something right after work tomorrow. She'd make them pay. And she wouldn't cut the cord tonight, because if she did that, she'd have no proof. When they got up and didn't have lights, all they'd have to do would be pull the cord in, slowly, and no one could prove it had been there. On that resolve, she went to bed.

The blue pickup wasn't there, which she hoped meant the big man wasn't there, either. She had chosen her clothes carefully—not the city clothes she wore to work, in case things got rough, but not cutoffs and a tank, either. She wanted to look respectable, and tough, and like someone who had friends in the county sheriff's office… . And so, sweating under the late-afternoon sun, she made her way across the rough, sunburnt grass in a denim wraparound skirt, plaid short-sleeve blouse, and what she privately called her "little old lady" shoes, which she wore to visit family: crepe-soled and sort of loafer-looking. There was an oily patch where the pickup was usually parked. That figured. So also the lumps of old dried mud on their trailer steps, when it hadn't rained in weeks. Anyone who'd throw water outside like that, and steal power, wouldn't bother to clean off a step. Louanne squared her shoulders and put her foot on the bottom step.

That's when she saw the notice, printed in thick black letters on what looked like a three-by-five card. "If nudity offends You," it said, "Please do not ring this Bell." Right beside the grimy-looking doorbell button. Just right out there in public, talking about nudity. Louanne felt her neck getting even hotter than the afternoon sun should make it. Probably kept the kids away, and probably fooled the few door-to-door salesmen, but it wasn't going to fool her. Nobody went around without clothes in a trailer park, not and lived to tell about it. She put her thumb firmly on the button and pushed hard.

She heard it ring, a nasty buzz, and then footsteps coming toward the door. Despite herself, her palms were sweaty. Just remember, she told herself, that you don't *have* $82.67, and they owe it to you. Then the door opened.

It wasn't so much the nudity that offended her as the smell. It wasn't like she'd never smelled people before.... In fact, one of the things that made her so careful was remembering how it was at Aunt Ethel and Uncle Bert's, the summer she'd spent with them. She wasn't squeamish about it, exactly, but she did like things clean. But this was something else. A sort of heavy smell, which reminded her a little of the specialty gourmet shop in the mall near her sister Peggy's house in north Dallas—but reminded her a lot more of dirty old horse hooves. Bad. Not quite rotten, but not healthy, either; and the bare body of the woman staring at her through a tattered screen door had the same look as the smell that wafted out into the hot afternoon.

Louanne swallowed with determination and tried to fix her eyes on the woman's face ... where she thought the face would be, anyway, hard as it was to see past the sunlit screen into the half-light where the woman stood. The woman was tall—would be taller than Louanne even if she stood on the ground—and up above her like that, a step higher, she looked really big, almost as big as the man. Louanne's eyes slid downward despite herself. She was big, with broad shoulders gleaming, slightly sweaty, and big—Louanne dragged her gaze upward again. She saw a quick gleam of teeth.

"Yes?" the woman said. Even in that word, Louanne knew she wasn't local. "Can I help you?" The rest of the phrase confirmed it—she sounded foreign almost, certainly not like anyone from around Behrnville.

"You're plugged into my outlet," said Louanne, gritting her teeth. She had written all this out, during her lunch hour, and rehearsed it several times. "You're stealing electricity from me, and you owe me sixty dollars, because that's how much my bill went up." She stopped suddenly, arrested by the woman's quick movement. The screen door pushed outward, and Louanne stepped back, involuntarily, back to the gravel of the parking slot. Now sunlight fell full on the woman, and Louanne struggled not to look. The woman's face had creased in an expression of mingled confusion and concern that didn't fool Louanne for a minute.

"Please?" she said. She didn't even look to see if anyone outside the trailer was looking at her, which made Louanne even surer the whole thing was an act. "Stealing? What have you lost?"

A bad act, too. Louanne had seen kids in school do better. Contempt stiffened her courage. "Your cord," she said, pointing, "is plugged into my outlet. You are using *my* electricity, and I have to pay for it, and you owe me sixty dollars." She'd decided on that, because she was sure not to get what she asked for.... If she asked for sixty dollars, she might get thirty dollars, and she could just squeeze the rest if she didn't go out this weekend at all, and didn't buy any beer, or that red blouse she'd been looking at.

"You sell electricity?" the woman asked, still acting dumb and crazy. Louanne glared at her.

"You thought it was free? Come on, Lady... I can call a deputy and file a complaint—" Actually, she wouldn't ever do that, because she knew what would happen in the trailer park if she did, but maybe this lady who was too crazy or stupid to wear clothes or use a sink drain or take showers wouldn't know that. And in fact, the lady looked worried.

"I don't have any money," she said. "You'll have to wait until my husband comes home—"

Louanne had heard that excuse before, from both sides of a closed door. It was worth about the same as "the check's in the mail," but another billow of that disgusting smell convinced her she didn't want to stomp in and make a search for the cash she was sure she'd find hidden under one pillow or another.

"I want it tonight," she said loudly. "And don't go trying to sneak away." She expected some kind of whining argument, but the woman nodded quickly.

"I tell him, as soon as he comes in. Where are you?" Louanne pointed to her own trailer, wondering if maybe the woman really was foreign, and maybe in that case she ought to warn her about standing there in broad daylight, in the open door of her trailer, without a stitch on her sleek, rounded, glistening body. But the screen was closing now, and just as Louanne regretted not having gotten her foot up onto the doorsill, the door clicked shut, and the woman flipped the hook over into the eye. "I tell him soon," the woman said again. "I'm sorry if we cause trouble. Very sorry." The inner door started to close.

"You'll be sorry if you don't pay up," said Louanne to the closing door. "Sixty dollars!" She turned away before it slammed in her face, and walked back to her own lot, sure she could feel the woman's eyes on her back. She wasn't too happy with the way it had gone, but, thinking about it, realized it could have been worse. Who knows what a crazy naked woman might have done, big as she was? Louanne decided to stay in her visiting clothes until the man came home, and, safely inside her own kitchen, she fixed herself a salad.

She had to admit she was kind of stunned by the whole thing. It had been awhile since she'd seen another woman naked, not since she'd gone to work for the county, anyway. She saw herself, of course, when she showered, and like that, but she didn't spend a lot of time on it. She'd rather look at Jack or whoever. When she looked at herself, she saw the kind of things they talked about in makeovers in the magazines: this too long, and that too short, and the other things too wide or narrow or the wrong color. It was more fun to have Jack or whoever look at her, because all the men ever seemed to see was what they liked. "Mmmm, cute," they say, touching here and there and tugging this and patting that, and it was, on the whole, more fun than looking at yourself in a mirror and wondering why God gave you hips wide enough for triplets and nothing to nurse them with. Not that that was *her* problem, Louanne reminded herself, but that's how her friend Casey had put it, the last time they skinny-dipped together in the river, on a dare, the last week of high school.

But that woman. She could nurse anything, up to an elephant, Louanne thought, and besides that…. She frowned, trying now to remember what she'd tried so hard not to see. She hadn't been particularly dark, but she hadn't been pale, either. A sort of brown-egg color, all over, with no light areas where even the most daring of Louanne's friends had light areas… . You could tan nude under a sunlamp or on certain beaches, but you couldn't go naked all the time. But this woman had had no markings at all, on a belly smooth as a beach ball. And—odd for someone who smelled so—she had shaved. Louanne shook her head, wondering. Her aunt Ethel had never shaved, and Louanne had come to hate the sight of her skinny legs, hairy and patched brown with age spots, sticking out from under her shabby old print dresses. But this woman… the gleaming smoothness of her skin, almost as if it had been oiled, all over, not a single flaw…. Louanne shivered without knowing why.

She stood and cleared the table, washing her single dish quickly. She started to get a beer out, and then changed her mind. If that man did come, she didn't want to smell of beer. She looked out her bedroom window. Nothing yet. The sun glared off the gravel of the parking space and the lane behind it. She was about to turn away, when she saw the blue pickup coming. It turned into the space beside the trailer, and the big man got out. Today he wore a tan shirt, with dark patches of sweat under the arms and on the back. Louanne wrinkled her nose, imagining the smell. He looked sunburnt, his neck and arms as red as his face, all glistening with sweat.

He went in. Louanne waited. Would the woman tell him at once, or wait, or not tell him at all? She didn't want to go back there, but she would, she told herself. He couldn't do anything to her in daylight, not if she stayed out of reach, and Jeannie Blaylock was home, if she screamed. She saw the flowered curtain twitched aside, and the man's face in the window, looking toward her trailer. She knew she'd been careful how she set the blinds, but she still had the feeling he knew she was watching. The curtains flipped shut. Then the door opened, and he came out, his round red face gleaming. He shot a quick glance toward her lot, then looked down before he went down his steps. He opened the pickup door, leaned in, came back out, shut the door. Then he started toward Louanne's trailer.

Her heart was hammering in her chest; she had to take two long breaths to quiet herself. He was actually coming, almost right away. She hurried out to the living room and sat poised on the rented tweed sofa. It seemed to take a long time, longer than she thought possible, even trying to count the steps in her mind. Finally a knock at her door. Louanne stood, trying to control her knees, and went to the door.

Even a step down, he was as tall as she, a man Jack might have hesitated to fight. But he was smiling at her, holding out a grubby envelope. "Sorry," he said. His voice was curiously light for such a big man. "We didn't mean to cause trouble…. The money is here…." He held it out. Louanne made a long arm and took the envelope; he released it at once and stepped back. "The… the connection at our lot didn't work," he went on, looking slightly past her, as if he didn't want to see her. His voice, too, had a strange accent, something Louanne classified as foreign, though she couldn't have said if it was from the East Coast or somewhere farther away than that. "I have already taken our wire away," he said, glancing quickly at her face and away again. "It will not trouble you again…. We are sorry…. It was only that the connection did not work, and yours did."

The money in the envelope was twenties… more than three. Louanne looked at his gleaming red face and felt a quiver of sympathy. Maybe they hadn't known, if they were really foreigners. "You have to pay a deposit," she said. "To the power company, before they turn it on. That's why it didn't work."

"I'm sorry," he said again. "I didn't know. Is that enough? Are you satisfied?"

Greed and soothed outrage and bewilderment argued in her forehead. "It's all right," she found herself saying. "Don't worry." She wondered if she should give some of it back, but, after all, they had stolen from her, and it was only fair they should pay for it. Then her leftover conscience hit her, and she said, "It was only sixty, anyway, and if…."

"For your trouble," he said quickly, backing away. "So sorry…. Don't worry. If you are not angry, if you are not reporting this to authorities…."

"No," said Louanne, still puzzled. Foreigners afraid of the law? Illegal immigrants? He didn't sound Mexican. Drug dealers?

"No more bother," he said. "Thank you. Thank you." And turned and walked quickly away, just as Curtis Blaylock drove in. Curtis looked at the man walking off, and at Louanne standing there with the envelope in her hand, for all the world like a whore with her pay, and grinned.

"Trouble?" he asked in a silky voice. Louanne had to stop that right where it was, or she would have more problems than a big light bill.

"Foreigners," she said, allowing an edge in her voice. "He wanted to know where to find"—she peered at the envelope as if to read the address, and found herself reading what was written on it—"3217 Fahrenheit, wherever that is. Not in this town, I told him, and he asked me to look it up on the county records. Somebody must've told him I work for the county."

"Pushy bastard," said Curtis. "Why's he think you should look things up for him?"

"I don't know," said Louanne, wondering why men like Curtis had a knack for asking questions you couldn't answer.

"Well, if you have any trouble, honey, just give us a call."

Louanne didn't answer that, and Curtis went on into his trailer, and she went back into hers. It was real money, all right, all twenties, and there were five of them. She could smell a fainter version of the smell in the trailer on lot 17, but money was money. A hundred bucks. It was too much, and made her worry again. Nobody in their right mind would've paid the sixty, let alone more. She made up her mind to send some of it back, somehow. Probably the woman would take it; women usually did. She readjusted the blinds in her bedroom, so that no one could possibly see in, and had a cooling shower. And finally went to bed, wondering only briefly how the foreigners were getting along in their lightless trailer.

She overslept, and had to run for it in the morning, dashing out of the door, slamming into her car, and riding the speed limit all the way to work. It wasn't until noon, when she paid the bill at the power company with the twenties, tossed the crumpled envelope in the wastebasket by the counter, and put the change in her billfold, that she thought of the foreigners again. Something nagged her about them, something she should have noticed in the morning's rush, but she didn't figure it out until she got home and saw lot 17 as bare as a swept floor.

They were gone. They had left in the night, without waking her or anyone, and now they were gone.

All through the subsequent excitement, Louanne kept her mouth shut about the hundred dollars and the stolen electricity, and made the kind of response everyone expected to rhetorical questions like, Who do you suppose? and Why do you think? and Whoever could have guessed? She figured she was thirty or forty dollars to the good, and didn't see why she should share any of it with old Mrs. Thackridge, who had plenty already or she wouldn't own the trailer park. They all knew she'd talked to the man (Curtis being glad to tell everyone, she noticed), but she stuck to her story about him wanting an address she'd never heard of, and wanting her to look it up in the county records. And she said she'd thrown the envelope away after not finding any such place, and not caring much, either, and after a while they all let her alone about as much as before, which pleased her just fine.

But she did wonder, from time to time, about that foreign lady wandering around the country without any clothes on. Brown as an egg all over, and not a hair on her body, and—it finally came to her one day, as she typed up a list of grand jury indictments when the judge's secretary was off sick—and no *navel* on the smooth, round, naked belly. She shook her head. Must have been there; everyone has a navel. Unless she had plastic surgery. But why?

After a while she didn't think of it much, except when she was wearing the red blouse … and after a while she was going with Alvin, who didn't like her in red, so she gave the blouse to the other secretary, and forgot the whole thing.

GIFTS

In the fullness of spring, with flowers everywhere and the scent of them filling the nose, Dall Drop-hand, Gory the Tail's third son, quarrelled with his father and brothers, and went off to find adventure.

"You'll regret it," his father said.

"You'll come crawling back as soon as your belly gripes," said his oldest brother.

"You'll find out nobody wants a fool whose only talent is dropping things," said his second-oldest brother.

His younger brothers and two of his sisters merely jeered. But the last sister cried, and hugged him, and begged him to stay. The others watched, still laughing, and he turned away.

"Wait," she said. "I'll give you a parting gift."

"The only parting gift he needs is a kick in the pants," said his father. But he stood aside to let the girl scamper to her bed and pull out her treasure, a bit of wood carved in the likeness of a knife. She had found it lying loose among the leaves while nutting the year before. She ran back to her brother, and put it in his hand.

"Take this," she said. "You may need it."

It was only wood, and not very sharp, but hers was the only kind voice that day. "Are you sure, Julya?" he asked.

"I am," she said, standing straight as young children do, upright as a pine, and she flung her arms around him and kissed him. Then she stood back, and he was bound to go, a gawky lad of no particular beauty or skill, out into the world all alone, at the very season when food was shortest, for no one can live on flowers.

He walked off down the path that led to the ford, and stopped to drink deeply of that fast, cold water. He would have taken some in a waterskin, but he had no waterskin. Still it was spring, with water running fast in every brook and rill, and he was sure he would find water at need. Food was another matter. He had

13

no bow, no line for setting snares. In all this wealth of flowers, no fruit had set but wild plums, and they were green and hard as pebbles still. His eye fell on a ruffle of green leaves trembling in the moving water. They looked very much like the greens his mother grew in the back garden. He picked off a piece, and tasted it. Yes. The very same. He picked a handful, and stuffed them into his shirt and set off away from the stream, on a path that narrowed here to a foot's width from little travel.

By midafternoon, he had passed through the woods near the stream and come out into open country, fields grown up into tall grass and flowers that reached his waist. He had lost the path in that tall growth, and found it again by stumbling over its groove; now he walked slowly, letting his feet feel their way and hoping no snake lurked below, where he could not see through the lacework of white and yellow. In the distance, the land rose in billows to blue hills, but he could not tell how far off they were.

At sunfall, he was still in the fields, wading slowly through the flowers. He trampled out a circle his own length, with the groove of the footpath running across it, and sat down. The footpath made a little tunnel, forward and back, under the tall growth. If he'd been a small animal, he could have used it as a private road and traveled hidden. The thought amused him; he wondered what it would be like to be so small, to see the meadow as a forest. For him, the footpath would make a comfortable hole for his hip, when he lay down to sleep.

The leaves he'd gathered were a limp, unappetizing mess when he pulled them from his shirt, but he ate them anyway and tried not to think of his family at their supper. He lay down then, and sat up quickly as his sister's gift poked him in the side. He pulled it out and rubbed his finger along the rib of wood. There was still enough light to see that it gleamed a little, where his sister had rubbed it with fat, but not enough to see the design that his finger felt, something carved, not deeply, into it. He kissed the thing, blessing the sister who had given it—useless though it was, it had been her treasure—and lay down to sleep with it in his hand.

He woke in darkness, uneasy, at first not knowing where he was. His shirt had rucked up, baring his back to the chill spring breezes; he yanked it down one-handed but could not go back to sleep. Around him, over him, the grass and flower-stalks rustled in the breeze. So did something else; he sat up, eyes wide. Was that more than star-shadow, that dark movement on the trail? Meadow mice, probably, or the slightly larger field rats. A stoat? A fox?

Laughter ringed him in so suddenly that he felt a shock like cold water. They were all around him, tattered shadows in the starlight, holding weapons that already pricked his back, his sides. Weapons that glinted slightly in that faint light. Laughter stilled to uneasy silence.

"Mortal man, you trespass." That voice was high, higher than his youngest sister's, but very clear.

"I'm not a man," he said. His voice broke on the absurdity of that; he had told his father he was man enough, when his father called him boy once too often.

"Not a man?" the voice asked, mocking. Laughter rimmed the circle again, and again died. "And what, pray, art thou if not man? Art too tall for rockfolk, too uncomely for elvenkind, and having speech canst not be a mere beast, despite the smell…" More laughter.

He found his voice again. "I'm a boy." Most of the elder folk were kinder to children than adults; he would claim that protection if he could. Surely if his father considered him a mere boy, so also would beings far older than his father.

"I think not," the voice said. "I think thou art man grown, at least in some things…" The voice insinuated what things, and he felt himself going hot. "And since we found thee asleep athwart our high road, man-grown as thou art, I say again: mortal man, you trespass. And for your trespass, mortal man, you shall be punished."

The shift of tone, from common to formal and back again, jerked at his mind, confused him. He fell back on childhoods excuse. "I didn't know…"

"Did not know what? That this was our highway, or that it was forbidden to such as you?"

"Either—both. I was only trying to get away from home…" That sounded lame as a three-legged cow in the night, with sharp points pricking him.

"You drew a circle across our highway," the voice said. "You drew a circle and then lay athwart, your loins on the path, and you thought nothing of it? No loss to the world then, such an oaf as you."

"But a circle is holy," he said. "A circle protects…"

Hisses all around him, as sharp as sleet on stubble; his belly went cold.

"A circle with a line across it negates the protection of the circle," the voice said. "And when that line is our highway—you have made a grave error, mortal man, and you will indeed be punished. Away from home, you wanted to go? Away from home you shall go indeed, never to return…"

His fists clenched, in his fear, and in the heart hand his sisters gift bit into the insides of his fingers. But what use a little wooden knife-shape against the creatures here, whose sharp weapons were surely harder and sharper than wood?

He had to try. He shifted the knife forward in his hand, and the blade caught the starlight and flashed silver.

"Ahhhh… so you would fight?"

"I… just want to go," he said. He felt one of the weapons behind prick through his shirt, and jerked forward, away from that pain. The shadows in front retreated, as if that knife were a real weapon. He waved it experimentally, and they flinched away.

"Do you know what you bear?" the voice asked.

"It's a knife," he said.

"Thou art a fool, mortal man," the voice said. "Stay away from our highways; thy luck may change." The pricks at his side and back vanished; a huddle of dark shapes ran together, vanishing into the tunnel beneath the grass.

Dall stood up, his heart pounding. He could see nothing across the field but a blurred line where he had come from, his body pushing the grass and flowers aside, but nothing ahead. Yet now he knew the footpath was perilous, he could not go back to it. He did not know what those beings were. He never wanted to see them again.

From the line of his passage the day before, he struck out at an angle, pushing his way through the waist-high growth. As anyone who has ever tried it, he found walking in the dark more difficult than he expected. Where the surface of the flowers seemed level, the land below dipped and rose beneath his feet, here a hummock like a miniature hill just high enough to catch his toe, and there a hollow deep enough to jar his teeth when he staggered into it. He pushed on, careless of the noise he made and any hazards he might wake, until—witless with fatigue—he caught his foot on yet another hummock and measured his length in the tall growth, falling hard enough to knock the breath from his lungs. And there he slept, overcome by all that had happened, until the sun rose and an early bee buzzed past his ear.

In the morning, he could scarcely understand his panic of the night. He stood, stretched, and looked around him. His backward path was clear, a trampled line that twisted and turned like that of a fleeing rabbit. He thought he had gone straight, but by day he could see that he had not come half so far from the... the highway... as he hoped.

Remembering that, he looked again at his sisters gift. Clearly wood, carved to the likeness of a knife, and polished. In the low slanting light, he could see the incised design he'd felt before. He ran his forefinger over it, but nothing happened, and the lines themselves meant nothing to him. Whatever it was, it had driven away those... whatever they were.

He was hungry, but he often woke hungry at home, and nothing to eat until chores were done. He was thirsty, but he would come to water soon; all he had to do was go on. He looked around at the wide, green, flower-spangled world, and saw nothing he knew. He told himself he was happy about that. No father and brothers to bully him; no sisters to scold and laugh.

As morning wore on, hunger and thirst vied for his attention. Thirst won; by afternoon, he could think of nothing but water... and no water could he see, or sign of it. No friendly line of trees beside a brook or river... all around the grass lifted and flattened in the wind, billowing... the hills as distant as ever, flat and shimmery against the pale sky. He went on, into the lowering sun, hoping to get to the hills... surely he would find trees and water there.

Instead, he trod on something that yielded beneath his foot, and sharp pain stabbed his leg. With a gasp and cry, he threw himself away from whatever it was, and caught a glimpse of a long, sinuous body, checkered brown and yellow, as he landed hard on his side. He scrambled to his feet, but whatever it had been did not follow him. His leg burned and throbbed; the pain ran up and down his leg like scalding water. Groaning, he sat down again, and pulled up his trews. Two tiny dark holes a thumbwidth apart, and a rapidly purpling bruise around them. He felt sick and shaky. It must have been a serpent, but the little grass and water snakes near home had been smaller. They never bit anyone—of course he'd never stepped on one...

Suddenly his mouth was full of sour mucus; he spat, and blinked away tears. Poison. It was some kind of poison. His mother's mother, before she died, had said something about poison from evil creatures. Cut it out, she'd said, or cut it off. The wooden knife could not be sharp or strong enough, but it was all he had.

He touched the point of it to one of the fang-marks, but he could not make himself push it in... the pain was already beyond bearing, and how could he cause more. Thick yellow ooze came from the wound, running down over his leg like honey. He stared, blinked, and realized he felt better. The flow of liquid stopped. He moved the knife point to the other fang-mark, holding his breath... and again, the thick yellow oozed out, ran down his leg. His belly steadied back to the simple ache of hunger; his mouth was dry again. As he watched, the fang-mark closed over, leaving a dry pale dimple. The other one still gaped; he moved the knife tip back to it, and it too closed over.

Grass rustled; he jerked up, stared. Unwinking eyes stared at him from a narrow head on a long, coiled body. Another serpent, this one much larger. A pink forked tongue flickered out; he flinched, scooting backward, and held the knife forward. The serpent's head lowered.

Slowly, trembling, he clambered to his feet. He wanted to back away but what if there was another one...? Holding the knife toward the serpent, he dared a quick glance behind him.

At his back stood someone he had never seen, someone who had appeared... he almost forgot the serpent, in that astonishment, but the serpent moved, and that caught his eye. Slowly, without appearing to move at all, it lowered its coils until it lay flat to the ground, and then, too fast to follow, whipped about and vanished into the grass.

"You're very lucky," the person said.

Dall could say nothing. He shook his head a little in his confusion. How could a full-grown man, dressed in fine leathers and a shirt with a lace collar, and boots to the thigh, have walked up on him without making a noise?

"I surprised you," the person said. "As you surprised the serpent's child."

"I don't know you," Dall said. He could think of nothing else to say.

"Nor I you," the stranger said. "But it needs no names to befriend someone, does it?"

"I—I'm Dall," Dall said. He almost added *Gory the Tail's third son,* but didn't because he had left home and could no longer claim his father's name.

"And I am Verthan," the stranger said. "You're a long way from a village, Dall. Gone hunting a lost sheep?"

"No… I left home," Dall said.

"You travel light," the stranger—Verthan—said. "Most men setting out would take at least a waterskin."

"Didn't have one," Dall muttered.

"Then you're thirsty, surely," Verthan said. "Have a drink of mine." He unhooked from his belt a skin dyed scarlet, bound in brown.

Dall reached for it, his mouth suddenly dryer than ever, but then pulled his hand back. He had nothing to trade, nothing at all, and the deepest rule he knew was hearth-sharing. He shook his head and shrugged.

"Nothing to share? You must have left in a hurry." Verthan shook his head. "You've set yourself a hard road, lad. But you'll not go much farther without water—water you must have."

Dall felt the words as if they were a hot summer wind in the hayfield; he felt dryness reach down his throat to his very marrow.

"I'll tell you what," Verthan said. "Why not trade your knife? Come evening, if you'll travel with me, we'll come to a place where you can gather early fruits, and we can trade it back to you. How's that?" He held out the waterskin. Dall could see the damp surface of it; he could almost smell the water inside it; he could certainly hear it as the man shook it.

His hand jerked, as if someone had caught it from behind, and he felt the edges of the knife against the insides of his clenched fingers. The memory of the snake venom oozing out, and the sickness leaving… the memory of Julya's face, as she handed him the knife… He shook his head, mute because his mouth was too dry to speak.

Verthan's expression sharpened into anger, then relaxed again into humor. "You are not as stupid as you look," he said. Then, as wind blows a column of smoke, he blew away, and where he had stood a rustle in the grass moved off downslope.

Dall's knees loosened and he slumped down into the grass, frightened as he was of the grass and all that lived in it. He sat huddled a long time, hardly even aware of his thirst and hunger, while fear fled ice-cold up and down his veins.

Some while later, when fear had worn itself out, he became aware of something wet touching his hand. Too tired now to jump away, he looked. The wooden knife in his heart hand, blunt as it was, had poked a little way through the grass stems into the soil beneath. The wet soil, he now saw, for the base of the grass stems around it glistened with water, and his hand and the knife.

At once his thirst returned, fierce as fire, and he scrabbled at the place, digging with the knife. He could see it, he could smell it… when he had opened a space the size of his cupped palm, he pushed his face into it and sucked in a half-mouthful of water flavored with shreds of dry grass and dirt. He spat out the mud, and swallowed the scant water. The tiny pool refilled; he drank again, this time with less mud in his mouth. Again. Again. And again. Each a scant mouthful, but each restoring a little of his strength.

When he had drunk until he could hold no more, he sat up and looked again at his sister's gift. Through his mind ran the events since he'd left home—the attack of the little people, the snakes, the phantom of the air, his thirst. Each time the thing had saved him, and he did not understand how. It looked like something an idle boy might whittle from any handy stick of wood. He himself had no skill at carving, but he had seen such things: little wooden animals and people and swords. As far as he knew—which seemed less far than the day before—none of those were magical. And so… his mind moved slowly, carefully, along the unaccustomed paths of logic… this must not be what it looked like. It must be something else. But what?

By now the sun hung low over the hills. He looked around. He had no idea where to go, or how to avoid the dangers he now knew inhabited these apparently harmless meadows. Only the gift that had saved him… could it help him find his way?

He bent again to the tiny pool of water, and then stood, holding the knife as always in his heart hand. How could he tell it his need? His hand twitched, without his intention. The thought came into his mind that he had not needed to tell the knife what his need was before. He held out his hand, palm up, and opened it. The knife squirmed on his hand—he almost dropped it in a moment of panic—and the tip pointed the way he least expected, downslope and back the way he had come. Toward that perilous footpath. Even—if he thought about it—toward home.

He did not want to go that way. Surely, with the knife's help, he could go on the way he wanted, into the hills… he might find more dangers, but the knife would protect him. It might even feed him.

His hand fell with the sudden weight of the knife, and lost its grip; the knife disappeared into the tall grass.

Dall cried out, wordless surprise and fear, and threw himself into the grass, feeling among the springy stems for something stiff, unyielding, wooden. Nothing. He tried to unthink the thought he'd had, promising the thing that he would follow its guidance always, in everything, if it would only come back.

Always? The question hung in the air, unspoken by mortal voice, but ringing in Dall's ears like the blow of a hammer.

"I'm sorry," he muttered aloud. "Julya gave it to me, and she loved me…"

A gust of wind flattened the grass over his head; pollen stung his eyes. He turned to blink and clear them, and there it lay, on top of the grass he had flattened while sitting on it. He reached out gingerly, wondering if it would let him touch it, and picked it up.

No heavier than at first. No less plain wood than at first. It lay motionless in his hand and when he stood he was facing the way the blade had pointed.

"All right then," he said. "Show me."

With water enough in his belly, the worst of the day's heat past, and the sun and high ground behind him, he made quick progress down and across the slope. Now his feet found good purchase wherever he trod, now the wind at his back cooled him without burning his face.

In the last of the light, he came to a stream fringed with trees. Was it the same stream he had crossed at the ford near his home? He could not tell, in the gloom. The knife had led him between the fringing trees to a flat rock beside the water, and there he drank his fill again, and there he found ready to hand the green leaves he knew could be eaten safely. He fell asleep on the rock, warded on three sides by clean running water, and woke before dawn, cold and stiff but otherwise unharmed, the knife still in his hand.

He expected the knife to lead him back home, to return it to his sister Julya, but instead it led him upstream, and insisted (for its guidance strengthened as the day went on) that he stay within the trees beside the stream, and on this hither side. Because of the trees, he could not see the land around, but he knew it rose by the ache in his legs from climbing, always climbing, ever more steeply as the waters note changed from the quiet gurgle lower down to the high, rapid laugh as it fell over taller and taller rocks.

Near the stream he found a few early berries, gleaming red, and ate them, along with more of the greens. He pried loose a few clingshells from rocks and sucked out the sweet meat inside; he managed to tickle one fish in the noon silence, when the knife had made it clear (how he was still not sure) that he should rest by the stream awhile. Always he had water to drink, so by nightfall he was well content to sleep again, this time in a hollow between oak roots.

Midmorning the next day, following the stream ever higher, he came out of the woods into a wide bare land of low grass, with here and there tussocks of reeds and an occasional gnarled shrub. Now he could see over the land—see how the trees traced out the stream below in its twists and turns and joinings with others… see little columns of smoke far in the distance that might have come from farmhouse chimneys… see the great green sea of grass breaking on the hills' knees, washing up this high as grass that would not cover the top of his foot.

Upslope, where the stream leaped in silver torrents from rock to rock, the land heaped up in mounds as far as he could see, all the way to the pale sky. Off to his right a great rocky wall, blue-shadowed and white-topped, had risen as if from nowhere… far higher than the hills he'd seen from home.

You wanted adventure. Again that voiceless voice, those words with no breath, hung in the air. *Now will you follow? Or shall I take you home?*

Against the memory of home—sweeter now than it had been when he left—came the memory of that first night and day of terror, and then the pleasanter but still strenuous days of travel since. What finally determined him to keep going was the memory of Julya. She would be glad to see him come home, but she alone had believed he might do something… become something. For her he would keep going until he could bring her… something worth the gift she had given him.

"I'll go on," Dall said.

Silence. He scrubbed one leg with the other foot, and waited. The knife lay quiescent in his hand. That had not, he realized, been the question. It had been *follow or go home,* not *go on or go home.*

"I'll follow," he said.

The knife twitched, and Dall headed on up the steepening slope, following the knife and the cold rush of water.

Finally, legs trembling with fatigue, he staggered up yet another slope to find that the water gushed from a cleft in the rocks beside the thread of trail. Above him the slope broke into vertical slabs of rock, bare and forbidding in the evening shadows beneath a darkening sky. Dall looked back, where the land beyond sloped down again, down and down into a purple gloom that hid every place he had ever been. Did the knife expect him to climb those rocks? He was sure he could not. He looked around for someplace to sleep, finally creeping between two massive boulders each bigger than his family's hut, but an insistent breeze chilled him wherever he tried to curl up, and he could not really sleep.

He was awake, and just this side of shivering in the chill, when he heard the cry. He was on his feet, peering wide-eyed into the darkness, when he felt the knife twitch in his hand. "But it's dark," he said. "I can't see where I'm going." He thought perhaps the knife would glow, giving light for him to see. Instead, it pricked his fingers, a sharp sting.

Another cry, and hoarse shouts. Shaking with fear, Dall started that way, only to run into one of the rocks. He scrabbled back; his foot landed on loose rubble, and he fell, rocks rolling about him and down below, loud and louder. He slid with them, flung out his arms and tried to stop himself. He had scrambled up over a ledge… and now his legs waved in the cold air, his belly lay against a sharp irregular edge, his bruised, skinned fingers dug in.

He pulled himself up a little, panting with fear, and felt around with his use-hand for a better purchase. Then his foot bumped the rock below, and he remembered where the foothold had been. He let himself slide backward, into the air and darkness, and another rock fell from the ledge, bounced loudly below, and hit something that clanged louder than his mother's soup-kettle.

This time he heard, though he did not understand the words, the angry voice below. He pressed himself against the cold rock, shivering. But his heart hand cramped, and he had to move, and again rocks fell from under his feet, and he lost his grip on the rock, falling his own length in a rattle of small stones to land on something that heaved and swore, this time in words he'd heard before. Hard hands clamped on his bare ankle, on his arm, angry voices swore revenge and stank of bad ale and too much onion… and without thought his heart hand swept forward, and the hand on his ankle released it with a hiss of pain, and with another swipe the grip on his arm disappeared.

"Back!" he heard someone say, panting. "It's not worth it—" And there was a scramble and rattle and clang and clatter of rocks on stone, and metal on rocks, and shod feet on rocks and someone falling and someone cursing—more than one someone—all drawing away into the night and leaving him crouched breathless and shaking.

He drew a long breath and let it out in a sigh that was almost a sob. Like an echo of his own, another sigh followed, then a groan. He froze, staring into darkness, seeing nothing… he could hear breathing. Harsh, irregular, with a little grunt at each exhalation. Off to his left a little, the way the knife pulled at him now. He took a cautious step, his left foot landing on a sharp pebble—a quick step then, and his foot came down on something soft, yielding.

The scream that followed knocked him to the ground like a blow, his fear came so strongly. Once there he fell asleep all at once, heedless of his scrapes and bruises and the danger.

In the first cold light of dawn, the man's face might have been carved of the stone he lay on, flesh tight to the bone with care and pain. Dall stared at the face. Longer of jaw than his father's, it still had something of the same look in the deep lines beside the mouth, the deep-cut furrows of the brow.

Color seeped into the world with the light. That dark stain, almost black at first, was blood—bright red where it was new, the color of dirty rust where it had dried. The man's shirt had once been white, and edged with lace; now it was filthy, soaked with blood, spattered with it even where it was not soaked. His trews were cut differently than any Dall had seen, fitted closer to his legs, and he had boots—real leather boots—on his feet. They were caked with dried mud, worn at the instep, with scuffed marks on the side of the heels. The dangling ends of thongs at his waist showed where something had been cut away. Dall could smell the blood, and the sour stench of ale as well.

The man groaned. Dall shuddered. He knew nothing of healing arts, and surely the man was dying. Dead men—men dead of violence, and not eased into the next world by someone who knew the right words to say—could not rest. Their angry spirits rose from their bodies and sought unwary travelers whose souls eased their hunger and left the travelers their helpless slaves forever. Such tales Dall's grandda had told by the winter fireside; Dall knew he was in danger more than mortal, for he knew none of the right words to smooth a dying man's path.

He tried to push himself up, but he was too stiff to stand up and his ankle—he could just see, now, that it was swollen as big as a cabbage and he could feel it throbbing—would not bear his weight even as he tried to get away on hands and knees.

The man shifted in his blood-soaked clothes, groaned again, and opened his eyes. Dall stared. Bloodshot green eyes stared back.

"Holy Falk," the man said His voice was breathy but firm, not the voice of a dying man. He sounded more annoyed than anything else. He glanced down at himself and grimaced. "What happened, boy?"

Dall gulped, swallowed, and spoke aloud for the first time in days. "I don't know... sir."

"Ah... my head..." The man lay back, closed his eyes a moment, and then looked at Dall again. "Bring water, there's a good lad, and some bread..."

The incongruity made Dall giggle with relief. The man scowled.

"There's no bread," Dall said. His stomach growled loudly at that. "And I don't have a waterskin."

"Am I not in the sotyard...?" The man pushed himself up on one elbow, and his brows raised. "No, I suppose I'm not. What place is this, boy?"

"I don't know, sir." This time the *sir* had come easily.

"Are you lost too, then?"

"I—aren't you dying, then?"

The man laughed, a laugh that caught on a groan. "No, boy. Not that easily. Why did you think—?" He looked down at himself, and muttered "Blood... always blood..." then squeezed his eyes shut and shook his head. When he next looked up, his face was different somehow. "Look here, boy, I hear a stream. You could at least fetch some water from there... I have a waterskin..." He patted his sides, then shook his head. "Or I suppose I don't. It must've been thieves, I imagine. Were there thieves, boy?"

"I didn't see them," Dall said. Odds on this man was a thief himself. "I heard yells in the dark. Then I fell..."

Now the man's eyes looked at him as if really seeing him. "By the gods, you did fall—you look almost as bad as I feel. You saved my life," the man said. "It was a brave thing, to come down on unknown dangers in the dark, and take on two armed men, a boy like you."

Dall felt his ears going hot. "I… didn't mean to," he said.

"Didn't mean to?"

"No… I fell off the cliff."

"Still, your fall saved me, I don't doubt. Ohhhh…" Another groan, and the man had pushed himself up to sitting, and grabbed for his head as if it would fall off and roll away. "I don't know why I drink that poison they call ale…"

"For the comfort of forgetting," Dall said, quoting his father.

A harsh laugh answered him. "Aye, that's the truth, though you're over-young to have anything worth forgetting, I'd say. You—" The man stopped suddenly and stared at the ground by Dall's hand. "Where did you get that?" he asked.

Dall had forgotten the knife, but there it lay, glinting a little in first rays of the sun. He reached and put his hand over it. "My sister gave it to me," he said. "It's only wood…"

"I see that," the man said. He shook his head, and then grunted with pain. Dall knew that sound; his father had been drunk every quarter-day as long as he could remember. The man pushed himself to hands and knees, and crawled to the tiny stream, where he drank, and splashed water on himself, and then, standing, stripped off his bloody clothes. There was plenty of light now, and Dall could see the bruises and cuts on skin like polished ivory, marked as it was with old scars on his sides.

While the man's back was turned, Dall pushed himself up a little, wincing at the pain—he hurt everywhere—and picked up the wooden knife. If it could mend a serpent bite, what about a swollen ankle? And for that matter the bloody scrape some rock had made along his arm? He laid the knife to his arm, but nothing happened. Nor when he touched it to his ankle.

The man turned around while Dall still had the knife on his ankle. "What are you doing?" he asked sharply.

"Nothing," Dall said, pulling his hand back quickly. "Just seeing how bad it hurt if I touched it."

"Hmmm." The man cocked his head. "You know, boy—what is your name, anyway?"

"Dall Drop—Dall, son of Gory," Dall said.

"Dall Drop? That's one I haven't heard."

"My father calls me 'Drop-hand'," Dall said, ducking his head.

"Drop-*body*, if last night was any example," the man said, chuckling. Dall felt himself going hot. "Nay, boy—it's not so bad. Your dropping in no doubt scared those thieves away. Maybe it was all accident, but you did good by it. Let's see about your wounds…"

"They're not wounds," Dall said. "Just cuts and things."

"Well, cuts or whatever, they could use some healing," the man said. He looked around. "And none of the right herbs here. We'll have to get you down to a wood, and you can't walk on that ankle."

" 'M sorry," Dall muttered.

"Nonsense," the man said. "Just let me get the blood off this—" He took his wadded shirt back to the creek. Dall gaped. Was he going to pollute the pure water with his blood? But the man sat down, pulled off one of his boots, and scooped up a bootful of water, then stuffed his shirt into the boot and shook it vigorously. The water came out pink; he dumped the wet shirt on the ground, emptied the bloody water into a clump of grass, and did it again. That was bad enough, but at least he wasn't dipping the shirt itself in the water.

After several changes of water, he came back to Dall with the sopping mess of his shirt, wrung it out, and reached for Dall's foot. "This'll hurt, boy, but it'll help, too."

It did hurt; every movement of the foot hurt, and the wet shirt was icy. The man wrapped it around his ankle, and used the sleeves to tie it tightly. Dall could feel his bloodbeat throbbing against the tight wrapping.

"Now, boy, give me your hand."

Dall had reached out his hand before he thought; the man took it and heaved him up in one movement.

"You'll have to walk; I'm still too drunk to carry you safely on this ground," the man said. "I can help, though. Let me guide you."

"Sir," Dall said. His foot hurt less than he expected as he hobbled slowly, leaning on the man's shoulder. The other aches also subsided with movement, though his cuts and scrapes stung miserably.

It was a slow, painful traverse of the slope, down and across, even when they came to the thread of a path the man said he'd followed the night before. "Sheep are not men," the man said, when they came to the first drop in the path. He slid down first, and Dall followed. The man caught him before his bad ankle hit the path. That was almost all the man said, other than the occasional "Mind this" and "That rock tips."

The sun was high overhead when the path widened abruptly at the head of a grassy valley, where several sheep trails came together. Ahead, smoke rose from a huddle of low buildings. Dall could smell cooked food for the first time in days; his stomach growled again and he felt suddenly faint. He sagged; the man muttered something but took more of his weight. "Come on, boy—you've done well so far," he said.

Dall blinked and gulped, and managed to stand more on his own feet. The man helped him down the wider track to an open space where someone had placed a couple of rough benches around a firepit. No one was visible outside the buildings, but from the smell someone was busy inside them. The man lowered Dall to one of them, then bent to unwrap his ankle. "I need a shirt, boy, if I'm to talk someone into giving us food. And down here I should be able to find the right leaves for your injuries."

Dall's ankle had turned unlovely shades of green and purple; now his foot was swollen as well. The man shrugged into the wet, dirty shirt, and headed for one of the huts as if he knew it. Dall glanced around, and caught sight of someone peeking around a house-wall at him. A child, younger, smaller. He looked away, then looked back quickly. A boy, wearing a ragged shirt much like his own over short trews... barefoot as he was. The boy offered a shy smile; Dall smiled back. The boy came nearer; he could have been Dall's younger brother if he'd had one.

"What happened to you?" the boy asked. "Did he beat you?"

"No," Dall said. "I fell on the mountain."

"You need to wrap that," the boy said, pointing to his ankle. "Are you hungry?"

"I have nothing to share," Dall said.

"You're hurt. It's Lady's grace," the boy said. "Don't you have that where you come from?"

"Yes... I just..."

"I'll get something," the boy said, and was gone like a minnow in the stream, in an instant.

He was back in a moment, with a hunk of bread in his hand. "Here, traveler; may the Lady's grace nourish us both."

"In grace given, in grace eaten, blessed be the Lady." Dall broke the bread, giving a piece back to the boy, and looked around for the man. He had disappeared; an empty doorway suggested where he'd gone. Dall took a bite of bread and the younger boy did also.

The bread tasted better than anything he'd ever eaten, so much better that he forgot the pain in his foot, and his other pains. He could've eaten the whole piece, but he set aside a careful half for the man, in case no one shared with him.

But the man was coming back now, carrying a jug and another loaf. "I see you've made friends," he said.

"I saved you a bit," Dall said. "It's Lady's grace."

The man raised his eyebrows. "I suppose we could all use grace." He ate the piece Dall had set aside, then broke the loaf he carried. "Here—you could eat more, I daresay. And here's water."

Dall wanted to ask if this too had been given as Lady's grace, but he didn't. The man sat a few minutes, eating, and taking sips of the water. Then he stood. "I'd best be going to work," he said. "There's a wall to mend." He nodded at the far end of the village, where one wall of a sheepfold bulged out, missing stones at the top. Dall started to push himself up and the man shook his head. "Not you, boy. You're still hurt. Just rest there, and one of the women will be out to tend you shortly. She's boiling water for boneset tea for you."

That night Dall lay on straw, his injured ankle wrapped in old rags. Sleeping under a roof again after so many nights in the open made him as wakeful as his first nights on the trail. He could hear the breathing of others in the cottage, and smell them all too. He wanted to crawl outside into the clean night air scented with growing things, but that would be rude. Finally he fell asleep, and the next morning ate his porridge with pleasure. Cooked food was worth the discomforts of the night, he decided.

He and the man stayed in the village for six hands of days; the man worked at whatever chores anyone put him to, without comment or complaint. As Dall became able to hobble around more easily, he too worked. It was strange to do the familiar work he had grown up with, but for strangers. When he dropped something—less often than before—he waited for the familiar jibes, but none came. Not even when he dropped a jug of new milk and broke the jug.

"Never mind," said the woman for whom he'd been carrying that jug and two others. "Its my fault for giving you more than you could carry, and the handle on that one's been tricky for years." She was a cheerful dark-haired woman with wide hips and a wider smile; all her children were like her, and the boy who had first given him bread was her youngest.

One evening after supper, Dall had an itch down his back, and scratched at it with the point of the wooden knife. The man watched him, and then asked, "Where did you get that knife?"

"I told you—my sister gave it to me." Dall sighed with relief as the tip found the perfect itchy spot to scratch.

"And where did she get it?"

"She found it in the woods last fall; we were all out nutting together, and she was feeling among the leaves in between the roots, and there it was."

"By itself?"

"I don't know. I didn't see her find it. Why, what could have been with it?"

The man sat down, heavily. "Dall, I carved that knife myself, two winters gone. I had thrown away my sword—oh, aye, I had a sword once, and mail that shone like silver, and a fine prancing horse, too. I had a dagger yet, and while I was snowed in, that first winter of my freedom, I whittled away on the kindling sticks. Most I burnt, but a few I kept, for the pleasure of remembering my boy's skill. Then spring came, and when I set out again I tossed them in the stream one summer's day to watch them float away."

"So the knife is yours," Dall said.

"I threw it away," the man said. "Like my sword. And unlike my sword it has come back, in a hand that valued it more." He cleared his throat. "I just wondered… if any of the others were found. Some flowers—mostly rose designs, over and over—and one fairly good horse."

"I don't know," Dall said. "But if the knife is yours…" He held it out.

The man shook his head. "No, lad. I threw it away; it's yours now."

"But it's special," Dall said. "It saved me—" He rattled on quickly, sensing the man's unwillingness to hear, about the little people in the grass, and the serpent's bite, and the strange being that appeared from nowhere and vanished back into nowhere, and the water…

The man stared at him, open-mouthed. "That knife?"

"This knife," Dall said. He held it out again. "Your knife. You made it; the magic must be from you."

"'To ward from secret treachery, from violence and from guile, from deadly thirst and hunger, from evil creatures vile…'" The man's voice trailed off. "It can't be…" His fingers stretched toward it, then his fist clenched. "It can't be. It's gone; what's loosed cannot be caught again."

"That's silly," Dall said. He felt silly too, holding out the knife. "When we let the calf out of the pen, we just catch it and bring it back."

"Magic is not a cow, boy!" The man's voice was hoarse now; Dall hardly dared look at his face for the anger he expected to see, but instead there were tears running down the furrows beside his mouth. "I forswore it…"

And will the wind not blow? And will not the spring return? The man's head jerked up; he must have heard it too.

Dall took a small step forward, and laid the knife in the man's hand, folding the man's fingers around it. As he stepped back, he saw the change, as if the sun had come out from behind a cloud. Light washed over the man, and behind it the man's filthy old shirt shone whiter than any cloth Dall had seen. His scuffed, worn boots gleamed black; his mud-streaked trews were spotless. On his tired, discouraged face, a new expression came: hope, and love, and light. What had seemed gray hair, once clean, now gleamed a healthy brown.

And the knife, the simple wooden knife, stretched and changed, until the man held a sword out of old tales. Dall had never seen a sword at all, let alone such a sword as that.

Vows are not so easily broken, or duties laid aside. Dall had no idea what that was about, but the man did; his quick head-shake and shrug changed to an expression of mingled awe and sorrow. He fell to his knees, holding the sword carefully, hilt upright. Dall backed away; a stone nudged the back of his legs and he sat down on it. He watched the man's lips move silently, until the man looked straight at him out of those strange green eyes, eyes still bright with tears.

"Well, boy, you have done quite a work here."

"I didn't mean to," Dall said.

"I'm glad you did," the man said. He stood, and held out his hand. "Come, let me call you friend. My name's Felis, and I was once a paladin of Falk. It seems Falk wants me back, even after—even now." He looked at the sword, the corners of his mouth quirking up in what was not quite a smile. "I think I'd better find this wood where your sister found the knife I carved, and see if any of the other bits washed up there. Something tells me the road back to Falk may prove... interesting."

Dall took the proffered hand and stood.

"What about me?" he asked.

"I hope you will travel with me," the man said. "You saved my life and you brought me back my knife... my life, actually, as a servant of Falk. And surely you want the sister who found it to know that it saved you."

"Go *home?*" Dall's voice almost squeaked. He could imagine his father's sarcasm, his brother's blows.

"It seems we both must," Felis said. "We both ran away; the knife called us both. But neither of us will stay with your father, I'm sure. What—do you think a boy who has saved a paladin remains a drop-hand forever?"

In the days of high summer, when the trees stood sentinel over their shade at noon, still and watchful, and spring's racing waters had quieted to clear pools and murmuring riffles, Dall no longer Drop-hand returned to his home, walking across the hayfield with a tall man whose incongruous clothes bore no sweat-stains, even in that heat. Gory the Tall recognized Dall the moment he came out of the trees, but the man with the spotless white shirt and the sword he did not recognize. Dall's brothers stood as if struck by lightning, watching their brother come, moving with the grace of one who does not stumble even on rough paths.

That evening, in the long soft twilight, Felis told of Dall's courage, of the magic in the knife he'd carved, of his oaths and his need to return.

"Then—I suppose this is yours too," said the youngest girl, Julya. She fished out of her bodice a little flat circle of wood carved with rose petals and held it out to him. Dall could hear the tears in her voice.

Felis shook his head. "Nay, lass. When I carved the flowers, I thought of my own sisters, far away. If it has magic, let it comfort you." He touched it with his finger. Then the air was filled with the perfume of roses, a scent that faded only slowly. The girl's face glowed with joy; she sniffed it again and tucked it back into her clothes.

"And he really saved you?" Dall's oldest brother asked.

"I slipped and fell," Dall said.

"At exactly the right moment," Felis said, a wave of his hand shutting off the gibes Dall's brothers had ready. "I hope he'll come with me, help me find the rest of the carvings I must find before I go back to my order."

"But—" Gory the Tall peered through the gloom at his son and at Felis. "If he's not the boy he was..."

"Then it's time for him to leave," Felis said. He turned to Dall. "If you want to, that is."

He was home without blows and jeers; he had triumphed. If he stayed, he would have that to fall back on. Stories to tell, scars to show. If he left, this time it would be for such adventures as paladins find—he knew far more about real adventures now than he had… and he was no longer angry and hurt, with every reason to go and none to stay.

An evening breeze stirred the dust, waking all the familiar smells of home. At his back, Julya pressed close; he could just smell the rose-scent of the carving in her bodice. But beyond that, he could smell the creek, the trees, the indefinable scent of lands beyond that he had only begun to know.

"I will go with you," he said to Felis. And then, to his family, "And someday I will come home again, with gifts for you all."

POLITICS

Politics is always lousy in these things. Some guy with rank wants something done, and whether it makes any sense or not, some poor slob with no high-powered friends gets pushed out front to do it. Like Mac… he wants a fuzzball spit-polished, some guy like me will have to shave it bare naked and work it to a shine. Not that all his ideas are stupid, you understand, but there's this thing about admirals—and maybe especially *that* admiral—no one tells 'em when their ideas have gone off the screen. That landing on Caedmon was right out of somebody's old tape files, and whoever thought it up, Mac or somebody more local, should've had to be there. In person, in the shuttles, for instance.

You know why we didn't use tanks downside… right. No shields. Nothing short of a cruiser could generate 'em, and tanks are big enough to make good targets for anyone toting a tank-bashing missile. Some dumbass should have thought of shuttles and thought again, but the idea was the cruisers have to stay aloft. No risking their precious tails downside, stuck in a gravity well if something pops up. Tradition, you know? Marines have been landed in landing craft since somebody had to row the boat ashore. Marines have died that way just about as long.

Now on Caedmon, the Gerin knew we were coming. Had to know. The easy way would've been to blast their base from orbit, but that wouldn't do. Brass said we needed it, or something. I thought myself it was just because humans had had it first, and lost it; a propaganda move, something like that. There was some kind of garbage about how we had this new stealth technology that let the cruisers get in real close, and we'd drop and be groundside before they knew we were there, but we'd heard that before, and I don't suppose anyone but the last wetears in from training believed it. I didn't, and the captain for sure didn't.

He didn't say so, being the hardnosed old bastard he is, but we knew it anyway, from the expression in his eyes, and that fold of his lip. He read us what we had to know— not much—and then we got loaded into the shuttles like so many cubes of cargo. This fussy little squirt from the cruiser pushed and prodded and damn nearly got his head taken off at the shoulders, 'cept I knew we'd need all that rage later. Rolly even grinned at me, his crooked eyebrows disappearing into the scars he carries, and made a rude sign behind the sailor's back. We'd been in the same unit long enough to trust each other at everything but poker and women. Maybe even women. Jammed in like we were, packs scraping the bulkheads and helmets smack onto the overhead, we had to listen to another little speech—this one from the cruiser captain, who should ought to've known better, only them naval officers always think they got to give Marines a hard time. Rolly puckered his face up, then grinned again, and this time I made a couple of rude gestures that couldn't be confused with comsign, but we didn't say anything. The Navy puts audio pickups in the shuttles, and frowns on Marines saying what they think of a cruiser captain's speechifying.

So then they dropped us, and the shuttle pilot hit the retros, taking us in on the fast lane. 'Course he didn't care that he had us crammed flat against each other, hardly breath-room, and if it'd worked I'd have said fine, that's the way to go. Better a little squashing in the shuttle than taking fire. Only it didn't work.

Nobody thinks dumb Marines need to know anything, so of course the shuttles don't have viewports. Not even the computer-generated videos that commercial shuttles have, with a map-marker tracing the drop. All we knew was that the shuttle suddenly went ass over teakettle, not anything like normal re-entry vibration or kickup, and stuff started ringing on the hull, like somebody dropped a toolshed on us.

Pilot's voice came over the comm, then, just, "Hostile fire." Rolly said, "Shut up and fly, stupid; I could figure out that much." The pilot wouldn't hear, but that's how we all felt. We ended up in some kind of stable attitude, or at least we weren't being thrown every which way, and another minute or two passed in silence. If you call the massed breathing of a hundred-man drop team silence. I craned my neck until I could see the captain. He was staring at nothing in particular, absolutely still, listening to whatever came through his comunit. It gave me the shivers. Our lieutenant was a wetears, a butterbar from some planet I never heard of, and all I could see was the back of his head anyway.

Now we felt re-entry vibration, and the troop compartment squeaked and trembled like it was being tickled. We've all seen the pictures; we know the outer hull gets hot, and in some atmospheres bright hot, glowing. You can't feel it, really, but you always think you can. One of the wetears gulped, audible even over the noise, and I heard Cashin, his corporal, growl at him. We don't get motion sickness; that's cause for selection out. If you toss your lunch on a drop, it's fear and nothing else. And fear is only worthwhile when it does you some good—when it dredges up that last bit of strength or speed that we mostly can't touch without it. The rest of the time fear's useless, or harmful, and you have to learn to ignore it. That's what you can't teach the wetears. They have to learn for themselves. Those that don't learn mostly don't live to disagree with me.

We were well into the atmosphere, and dropping faster than my stomach liked, when the shuttle bucked again. Not a direct hit, but something transmitted by the atmosphere outside into a walloping thump that knocked us sideways and halfover. The pilot corrected—and I will say this about the Navy shuttle pilots, that while they're arrogant bastards and impossible to live with, they can pretty well fly these shuttles into hell and back. This time he didn't give us a progress report, and he didn't say anything after the next two, either.

What he did say, a minute or so later, was "Landing zone compromised."

Landing zone compromised can mean any of several things, but none of them good. If someone's nuked the site, say, or someone's got recognizable artillery sitting around pointing at the strip, or someone's captured it whole (not common, but it does happen) and hostile aircraft are using it. What landing zone compromised means to us is that we're going to lose a lot of Marines. We're going to be landing on an unimproved or improvised strip, or we're going to be jumping at low level and high speed. I looked for the captain again. This time he was linked to the shuttle comm system, probably talking to whatever idiot designed this mission. I hoped. We might abort—we'd aborted a landing once before—but even that didn't look good, not with whatever it was shooting at us all the way back up. The best we could hope for was an alternate designated landing zone—which meant someone had at least looked at it on the upside scanners. The worst—

"Listen up, Marines!" The captain sounded angry, but then he always did before a landing. "We're landing at alternate Alpha, that's Alpha, six minutes from now. Sergeants, pop your alt codes…" That meant me, and I thumbed the control that dropped a screen from my helmet and turned on the display. Alternate Alpha was, to put it plainly, a bitch of a site. A short strip, partly overgrown with whatever scraggly green stuff grew on this planet, down in a little valley between hills that looked like the perfect place for the Gerin to have artillery set up. Little colored lines scrawled across the display, pointing out where some jackass in the cruiser thought we ought to assemble, which hill we were supposed to take command of (that's what it said), and all the details that delight someone playing sandbox war instead of getting his guts shot out for real. I looked twice at the contour lines and values. Ten-meter contours, not five… those weren't just little bitty hills, those were going to give us trouble. Right there where the lines were packed together was just about an eighty-meter cliff, too much for a backpack booster to hop us over. Easy enough for someone on top to toss any old kind of explosive back down.

And no site preparation. On a stealth assault, there's minimal site preparation even on the main landing zones—just a fast first-wave flyover dropping screamers and gas canisters (supposed to make the Gerin itch all over, and not affect us). Alternate strips didn't get any prep at all. If the Gerin guessed where alternate Alpha was, they'd be meeting us without having to duck from any preparatory fire. That's what alternate landing sites were like: you take what you get and are grateful it doesn't mean trailing a chute out a shuttle hatch. That's the worst. We aren't really paratroops, and the shuttles sure as hell aren't paratroop carriers. Although maybe the worst is being blown up in the shuttle, and about then the shuttle lurched again, then bounced violently as something blew entirely too close.

Then we went down. I suppose it was a controlled landing, sort of, or none of us would have made it. But it felt, with all the pitching and yawing, like we were on our way to a crash. We could hear the tires blow on contact, and then the gear folded, and the shuttle pitched forward one last time to plow along the strip with its heatshield nose. We were all in one tangled pile against the forward bulkhead by then, making almost as much noise as the shuttle itself until the captain bellowed over it. With one final lurch, the craft was motionless, and for an instant silent.

"Pop that hatch, Gunny." The captain's voice held that tone that no one argues with—no one smart, anyway—and Rolly and I started undogging the main hatch. The men were untangling themselves now, with muttered curses. One of the wetears hadn't stayed up, and had a broken ankle; he bleated once and then fell silent when he realized no one cared. I yanked on the last locking lever, which had jammed in the crash, just as we heard the first explosions outside. I glanced at the captain. He shrugged. What else could we do? We sure didn't have a chance in this nicely marked coffin we were in. Rolly put his shoulders into it, and the hatch slid aside to let in a cool, damp breath of local air.

Later I decided that Caedmon didn't smell as bad as most planets, but right then all I noticed was the exhaust trails of a couple of Gerin fighters who had left their calling cards on the runway. A lucky wind blew the dust away from us, but the craters were impressive. I looked at the radiation counter on the display—nothing more than background, so it hadn't been nukes. Now all we had to do was get out before the fighters came back.

Normally we unload down ramps, four abreast—but with the shuttle sitting on its nose and the port wing, the starboard landing ramp was useless. The portside hatch wouldn't open at all. This, of course, is why we carry those old-fashioned cargo nets everyone teases us about. We had those deployed in seconds (we *practice* that, in the cruisers' docking bays, and that's why the sailorboys laugh at us). Unloading the shuttle—all men and materiel, including the pilot (who had a broken arm) and the wetear with the bad ankle—went faster than I'd have thought. Our lieutenant, Pascoe, had the forward team, and had already pushed into the scraggly stuff that passed for brush at the base of the nearest hill. At least he seemed to know how to do that. Then Courtney climbed back and placed the charges, wired them up, and came out. When he cleared the red zone, the captain pushed the button. The shuttle went up in a roiling storm of light, and we all blinked. That shuttle wasn't going anywhere, but even so I felt bad when we blew it… it was our ticket home. Not to mention the announcement the explosion made. We had to have had survivors to blow it that long after the crash.

What everyone sees, in the videos of Marine landings, is the frontline stuff—the helmeted troops with the best weapons, the bright bars of laser fire—or some asshole reporter's idea of a human interest shot (a Marine looking pensively at a dead dog, or something). But there's the practical stuff, which sergeants always have to deal with. Food, for instance. Medical supplies, not to mention the medics, who half the time don't have the sense to keep their fool heads out of someone's sights. Water, weapons, ammunition, spare parts, comunits, satellite comm bases, spare socks… whatever we use has to come with us. On a good op, we're resupplied inside twenty-four hours, but that's about as common as an honest dockside joint. So the shuttle had supplies for a standard week (Navy week: Old Terra standard—it doesn't matter what the local rotational day or year is), and every damn kilo had to be offloaded and hauled off. By hand. When the regular ground troops get here, they'll have floaters and trucks, and their enlisted mess will get fresh veggies and homemade pies… and that's another thing that's gone all the way back, near as I can tell. Marines slog through the mud, hump their stuff uphill and down, eat compressed bricks commonly called—well, you can imagine. And the next folks in, whoever they are, have the choppers and all-terrain vehicles and then make bad jokes about us. But not in the same joint, or not for long.

What bothered me, and I could see it bothered the captain, was that the fighters didn't come back and blow us all to shreds while all this unloading went on. We weren't slow about it; we were humping stuff into cover as fast as we could. But it wasn't natural for those fighters to make that one pass over the strip and then leave a downed shuttle alone. They had to know they'd missed—that the shuttle was intact and might have live Marines inside. All they'd done was blow a couple of holes in the strip, making it tough for anyone else to land there until it was fixed. They had to be either stupid or overconfident, and no one yet had accused the Gerin of being stupid. Or of going out of their way to save human lives. I had to wonder what else they had ready for us.

Whatever it was, they let us alone for the next couple of standard hours, and we got everything moved away from the strip, into a little sort of cleft between two of the hills. I wasn't there: I was working my way to the summit, as quietly as possible, with a five-man team.

We'd been told the air was breathable, which probably meant the green stuff was photosynthetic, although it was hard to tell stems from leaves on the scrub. I remember wondering why anything a soldier has to squirm through is full of thorns, or stings on contact, or has sharp edges… a biological rule no one yet has published a book on, I'll bet. Caedmon's scrub ran to man-high rounded mounds, densely covered with prickly stiff leaves that rustled loudly if we brushed against them. Bigger stuff sprouted from some of the mounds, treelike shapes with a crown of dense foliage and smooth blackish bark. Between the mounds a fine, gray-green fuzz covered the rocky soil, not quite as lush as grass but more linear than lichens. It made my nose itch, and my eyes run, and I'd *had* my shots. I popped a broad-spectrum anti-allergen pill and hoped I wouldn't sneeze.

Some people say hills are the same size all the time, but anyone who's ever gone up a hill with hostiles at the top of it knows better. It's twice as high going uphill into trouble. If I hadn't had the time readout, I'd have sworn we crawled through that miserable prickly stuff for hours. Actually it was less than half a standard when I heard something click, metal on stone, *ahead* of us. Above and ahead, invisible through the scrub, but definitely something metallic, and therefore—in this situation—hostile. Besides, after Duquesne, we knew the Gerin would've wiped out any humans from the colony. I tongued the comcontrol and clicked a warning signal to my squad. They say a click sounds less human—maybe. We relied on it, anyhow, in that sort of situation. I heard answering clicks in my earplug. Lonnie had heard the noise, too (double-click, then one, in his response), which figured. Lonnie had the longest ears in our company.

This is where your average civilian would either panic and go dashing down-hill through the brush to tell the captain there were nasties up there, or get all video-hero and run screaming at the Gerin, right into a beam or a slug. What else is there to do? you ask. Well, for one thing you can lie there quietly and think for a moment. If they've seen you, they've shot you—the Gerin aren't given to patience— and if they haven't shot you they don't know you're there. Usually.

It was already strange, that the Gerin fighters hadn't come back. And if Gerin held the top of this hill—which seemed reasonable even before we went up it, and downright likely at the moment—they'd have to know we got out, and how many, and roughly where we were. And since Gerin aren't stupid, at least at war, they'd guess someone was coming up to check out the hilltop. So they'd have some way to detect us on the way up, and they'd have held off blowing us away because they didn't think we were a threat. Neither of those thoughts made me feel comfortable.

Detection systems, though… detection systems are a bitch. Some things work anywhere: motion detectors, for instance, or optical beams that you can interrupt and it sets off a signal somewhere. But that stuff's easy enough to counter. If you know what you're doing, if you've got any sort of counterhunt tech yourself, you'll spot it and disarm it. The really good detection systems are hard to spot, very specific, and also—being that good—very likely to misbehave in combat situations.

The first thing was to let the captain know we'd spotted something. I did that with another set of tongue-flicks and clicks, switching to his channel and clicking my message. He didn't reply; he didn't need to. Then I had us all switch on our own counterhunt units. I hate the things, once a fight actually starts: they weigh an extra kilo, and unless you need them it's a useless extra kilo. But watching the flicking needles on the dials, the blips of light on the readouts, I was glad enough then. Two meters uphill, for instance, a fine wire carried an electrical current. Could have been any of several kinds of detectors, but my unit located its controls and identified them. And countered them: we could crawl right over that wire, and its readout boxes wouldn't show a thing. That wasn't all, naturally: the Gerin aren't stupid. But none of it was new to our units, and all of it could fail—and would fail, with a little help from us.

Which left the Gerin. I lay there a moment longer wondering how many Gerin triads we were facing. Vain as they are, it might be just one warrior and his help-ers, or whatever you want to call them. Gerin think they're the best fighters in the universe, and they can be snookered into a fight that way. Admiral Mac did it once, and probably will again. It would be just like their warrior pride to as-sign a single Gerin triad to each summit. Then again, the Gerin don't think like humans, and they could have a regiment up there. One triad we might take out; two would be iffy, and any more than that we wouldn't have a chance against.

Whatever it was, though, we needed high ground, and we needed it damn fast. I clicked again, leaned into the nearest bush, and saw Lonnie's hand beyond the next one. He flicked me a hand signal, caught mine, and inched forward.

We were, in one sense, lucky. It was a single triad, and all they had was the Gerin equivalent of our infantry weapons: single-beam lasers and something a lot like a rifle. We got the boss, the warrior, with several rounds of rifle fire. I don't care what they say, there's a place for slug-throwers, and downside combat is that place. You can hit what you can't see, which lasers can't, and the power's already in the ammo. No worry about a discharged power-pack, or those mir-rored shields some of the Gerin have used. Some Navy types keep wanting to switch all Marine forces away from slug weapons, because they're afraid we'll go bonkers and put a hole in a cruiser hull, but the day they take my good old Belter special away from me, I'm gone. I've done my twenty already; there's no way they can hold me.

Davies took a burn from one of the warrior's helpers, but they weren't too aggressive with the big number one writhing on the ground, and we dropped them without any more trouble. Some noise, but no real trouble. Lonnie got a coldpak on Davies, which might limit the damage. It wasn't that bad a burn, anyway. If he died down here, it wouldn't be from that, though without some time in a good hospital, he might lose the use of those fingers. Davies being Davies, he'd probably skin-graft himself as soon as the painkiller cut in… he made a religion out of being tough. I called back to our command post to report, as I took a look around to see what we'd bought.

From up here, maybe seventy meters above the strip, the scattered remains of the shuttle glittered in the sun. I could see the two craters, one about halfway along, and another maybe a third of the way from the far end. Across the little valley, less than a klick, the hills rose slightly higher than the one we lay on. The cliffs on one were just as impressive as I'd thought. The others rose more gently from the valley floor. All were covered with the same green scrub, thick enough to hide an army. Either army.

I told the captain all this, and nodded when Skip held up the control box the Gerin had used with their detectors. We could use the stuff once we figured out the controls, and if they were dumb enough to give us an hour, we'd have no problems. No problems other than being a single drop team sitting beside a useless strip, with the Gerin perfectly aware of our location and identity.

Brightness bloomed in the zenith, and I glanced up. Something big had taken a hit—another shuttle? We were supposed to have 200 shuttle flights on this mission, coming out of five cruisers—a fullscale assault landing, straight onto a defended planet. If that sounds impossibly stupid, you haven't read much military history—there are some commanders that have this thing about butting heads with an enemy strength, and all too many of them have political connections. Thunder fell out of the sky, and I added up the seconds I'd been counting. Ten thousand meters when they'd been blown—no one was going to float down from that one. "

"What kind of an *idiot…* ?" Lonnie began; I waved him to silence. Things were bad enough without starting that—we could place the blame later. With a knifeblade, if necessary.

"Vargas…" The captain's voice in my earplug drowned out the whisper of the breeze through stiff leaves. I pushed the subvoc microphone against my throat and barely murmured an answer. "Drop command says we lost thirty cents on the dollar. Beta Site took in four shuttles before it was shut out." Double normal losses on a hostile landing, then, and it sounded like we didn't have a secure strip. I tried to remember exactly where Beta Site was. "We're supposed to clear this strip, get it ready for the next wave—"

I must have made some sound, without meaning to, because there was a long pause before he went on. If the original idea had been stupid, this one was stupid plus. Even a lowly enlisted man knows it's stupid to reinforce failure, why can't the brass learn it? We weren't engineers; we didn't have the machinery to fill those craters, or the manpower to clear the surrounding hills of Gerin and keep the fighters off.

"They're gonna do a flyby drop of machinery," he went on. I knew better than to say what I thought. No way I could stop them, if they wanted to mash their machinery on these hills. "We're going to put up the flyspy—you got a good view from there?"

"Yessir." I looked across the valley, around at all the green-clad slopes. The flyspy was another one of those things that you hated having to take care of until it saved your life. "By wire, or by remote?"

"Wire first." That was smart; that way they wouldn't have a radio source to lock onto. "I'm sending up the flyspy team, and some rockers. Send Davies back down." Rockers: rocket men, who could take out those Gerin fighters, always assuming they saw them in time, which they would if we got our detection set up.

Soon I could hear them crashing through the scrub, enough noise to alert anyone within half a klick. The rockers made it up first, four of them. I had two of them drag the Gerin corpses over to the edge and bounce 'em over, then they took up positions around the summit. Now we could knock off the Gerin fighters, if they came back: whatever's wrong with the rest of Supply, those little ground-air missiles we've got can do the job. Then the flyspy crew arrived, with the critter's wing folded back along its body. When they got to the clearing, they snapped the wings back into place, checked that the control wire was coiled ready to release without snagging, and turned on the scanners.

The flyspy is really nothing but a toy airplane, wings spanning about a meter, powered by a very quiet little motor. It can hold an amazing amount of spygear, and when it's designed for stealth use it's almost impossible to see in the air. On wire control, it'll go up maybe 100 meters, circle around, and send us video and IR scans of anything it can see; on remote, we can fly it anywhere within line-of-sight, limited only by its fuel capacity.

Soon it was circling above us, its soft drone hardly audible even on our hilltop, certainly too quiet to be heard even down on the strip. We didn't know whether the Gerin *did* hear, the way we hear, but we had to think about that. (We know they hear big noises, explosions, but I've heard a theory that they can't hear high-pitched noises in atmosphere.) The videos we were getting back looked surprisingly peaceful. Nothing seemed to be moving, and there was only one overgrown road leading away from the strip. Garrond punched a channel selector, and the normal-color view turned into a mosaic of brilliant false colors: sulfur yellow, turquoise, magenta, orange. He pointed to the orange. "That's vegetation, like this scrub. Yellow is rock outcrops—" The cliff across from us was a broad splash of yellow that even I could pick out. "Turquoise is disturbed soil: compacted or torn up, either one." The strip was turquoise, speckled with orange where plants had encroached on it. So was the nearly invisible road winding away from the strip between the hills. So also the summit of the hill which ended in cliffs above the strip... and the summit of our own hill. Another outpost, certainly.

But nothing moved, in the broad daylight of Caedmon's sun. According to briefing, we'd have another nine standard hours of light. None of our scanners showed motion, heat, anything that could be a Gerin force coming to take us out. And why not?

It bothered the captain, I could see, when he came up to look for himself. Our butterbar was clearly relieved, far too trusting an attitude if you want to survive very long. Things aren't *supposed* to go smoothly; any time an enemy isn't shooting at you, he's up to something even worse.

"An hour to the equipment drop," said the captain. "They're sending a squad of engineers, too." Great. Somebody else to look after, a bunch of dirtpushers. I didn't say it aloud; I didn't have to. Back before he saved Admiral Mac's life and got that chance at OCS, the captain and me were close, real buddies. Fact is, it was my fault he joined up— back then they didn't have the draft. Wasn't till he started running with me, Tinker Vargas, what everyone called gypsy boy—gambler and horsethief and general hothead—that Carl Dietz the farmer's son got into any trouble bigger than spilled milk. He was innocent as cornsilk back then, didn't even know when I was setting him up—and then we both got caught, and had the choice between joining the offworld Marines or going to prison. Yet he's never said a word of blame, and he's still the straightest man I know, after all these years. He's one I *would* trust at poker, unlike Rolly who can't seem to remember friendship when the cards come out.

And no, I'm not jealous. It hasn't been easy for him, a mustang brought up from the ranks, knowing he'll never make promotions like the fast-track boys that went to the Academy or some fancy-pants university. He's had enough trouble, some of it when I was around to carefully not hear what the other guy said. So never mind the pay, and the commission: I'm happy with my life, and I'm still his friend. We both know the rules, and we play a fair game with the hand dealt us—no politics, just friends.

In that hour, we had things laid out more like they should be. Thanks to the flyspy, we knew that no Gerin triads lurked on the nearest two hilltops, and we got dug in well on all three hills that faced the strip on the near side. There was still that patch of turquoise to worry about on the facing hill, above the cliffs, but the flyspy showed no movement there, just the clear trace of disturbed soil. Our lieutenant had learned something in OCS after all; he'd picked a very good spot in a sort of ravine between the hills, out of sight beneath taller growth, for the headquarters dugout, meds, and so on.

Then the equipment carrier lumbered into view. I know, it's a shuttle same as the troop shuttle, but that's a term for anything that goes from cruiser to ground. Equipment carriers are fatter, squatty, with huge cargo doors aft, and they have all the graceful ease of a grand piano dumped off a clifftop. This one had all engines howling loudly, and the flaps and stuff hanging down from the wings, trying to be slow and steady as it dropped its load. First ten little parachutes (little at that distance), then a dark blob—it had to be really big if I could see it from here—trailing two chutes, and then a couple more, and a final large lumpy mass with one parachute.

"I don't believe it!" said the captain, stung for once into commentary. But it was—a netful of spare tires for the vehicles, wrapped around a huge flexible fuel pod. Relieved of all this load, the shuttle retracted its flaps, and soared away, its engines returning to their normal roar.

Already the lieutenant had a squad moving, in cover, toward the landing parachutists. I watched the equipment itself come down, cushioned somewhat by airbags that inflated as it hit. Still nothing moved on the hilltop across from us. I felt the back of my neck prickle. It simply isn't natural for an enemy to chase you down, shooting all the while, then ignore you once you've landed. We know Gerin use air attack on ground forces: that's how they cleaned up those colonists on Duquesne.

Yet ignore us they did, all the rest of that day as the engineers got themselves down to the strip from where they'd landed, and their equipment unstowed from its drop configuration and ready for use. One grader, what we called back on my homeworld a maintainer, and two earth-movers. The whole time the engineers were out there getting them ready, I was sure some Gerin fighter was going to do a low pass and blow us all away… but it didn't happen. I'd thought it was crazy, dropping equipment that had to be prepped and then used in the open, but for once high command had guessed right.

By late afternoon, the engineers had their machines ready to work. They started pushing stuff around at the far end of the strip, gouging long scars in the dirt and making mounds of gravelly dirt. The captain sent Kittrick and one platoon over to take a hill on the far side; they got up it with no trouble, and I began to think there weren't any Gerin left there at all. Half that group climbed the hill with the cliff, and found evidence that someone had had an outpost there, but no recent occupation.

We were spread out pretty thin by this time, maybe thirty on the far side of the strip, the rest on the near side, but stretched out. We'd rigged our own detection systems, and had both flyspys up, high up, where they could see over the hills behind us. What they saw was more of the same, just like on the topo maps: lots of hills covered with thick green scrub, some creeks winding among the hills, traces of the road that began at the landing strip. Some klicks east of us (east is whatever direction the sun rises, on any world), the tumbled hills subsided into a broad river basin. The higher flyspy showed the edge of the hills, but no real detail on the plain.

Meanwhile the engineers went to work on that strip just as if they *were* being shot at. Dust went up in clouds, blown away from our side of the strip by a light breeze. Under that dust, the craters and humps and leftover chunks of our troop shuttle disappeared, and a smooth, level landing strip emerged. There's nothing engineers like better than pushing dirt around, and these guys pushed it fast.

By dark they had it roughed in pretty well, and showed us another surprise. Lights. Those tires we'd laughed at each held a couple of lamps and reflectors, and the coiled wiring that connected them all into a set of proper landing lights controlled by a masterboard and powered from the earthmover engine. By the time everyone had had chow, the first replacement shuttle was coming in, easing down to the lighted strip as if this were practice on a safe, peaceful planet far from the war.

None of us veterans could relax and enjoy it, though. The new arrivals had heard the same thing I had—thirty percent losses on the initial drop, sixty shuttles blown. No report from anyone on what we'd done to the Gerin, which meant that the Navy hadn't done a damn thing... they tripled their figures when they did, but triple zilch is still zilch. So how come we weren't being overrun by Gerin infantry? Or bombed by their fighters? What were the miserable slimes up to? They sure weren't beat, and they don't surrender.

During the night, five more shuttles landed, unloaded, and took off again. Besides the additional troops and supplies, we also had a new commanding officer, a mean-looking freckle-faced major named Sewell. I know it's not fair to judge someone by his looks, but he had one of those narrow faces set in a permanent scowl, with tight-bunched muscles along his jaw. He probably looked angry sound asleep, and I'd bet his wife (he had a wide gold ring on the correct finger) had learned to hop on cue. His voice fit the rest of him, edged and ready to bite deep at any resistance. The captain had a wary look; I'd never served with Sewell, or known anyone who had, but evidently the captain knew something.

Major Sewell seemed to know what he was doing, though, and his first orders made sense, in a textbook sense. If you wanted to try something as impossible as defending a shuttle strip without enough troops or supplies, his way was better than most. Soon we had established a perimeter that was secure enough, dug into each of the main hills around the strip, each with its own supply of ammo, food, and water. Besides the original headquarters and med dugout, he'd established another on the far side of the strip. All this looked pretty good, with no Gerin actually challenging it, but I wasn't convinced. It takes more than a few hundred Marines to secure an airstrip if the enemy has a lot of troops.

Shortly after sundown, one of the squads from the first replacement shuttle found ruins of a human settlement at the base of a hill near the end of the strip, and had to get their noses slapped on the comm for making so much noise about it. Not long after, the squad up on that clifftop put two and two together and made their own find. Having heard the first ruckus, they didn't go on the comm with it, but sent a runner down to Major Sewell.

There's a certain art to getting information, another version of politics you might call it. It so happened that someone I knew had a buddy who knew someone, and so on, and I knew the details before the runner got to Major Sewell.

We'd known the strip itself was human-made, from the beginning. What we hadn't known was that it had been privately owned, adjacent to the owner's private residence. It takes a fair bit of money to build a shuttle-strip, though not as much as it takes to have a shuttle and *need* a shuttle strip. The same class of money can take a chunk of rock looking out over a little valley, and carve into it a luxurious residence and personal fortress. It can afford to install the best quality automated strip electronics to make landing its fancy little shuttle easier, and disguise all the installations as chunks of native stone or trees or whatever. The Gerin had missed it, being unfamiliar with both the world and the way that humans think of disguise. But to a bored squad sitting up on a hilltop with no enemy in sight, and the knowledge that someone might have hidden something… to them it was easy. Easy to find, that is, not easy to get into, at least not without blasting a way in… which, of course, they were immediately and firmly told not to do.

Think for a little what it takes to do something like this. We're not talking here about ordinary dress-up-in-silk-everyday rich, you understand, not the kind of rich that satisfies your every whim for enough booze and fancy food. I can't even imagine the sort of sum that would own a whole world, hollow out a cliff for a home, operate a private shuttle, and still have enough clout left to bribe the Navy in the middle of a desperate war. This was the sort of wealth that people thought of the military-industrial complex having, the kind that the big commercial consortia do have (whether the military get any or not), the kind where one man's whim, barely expressed, sends ten thousand other men into a death-filled sky.

Or that's the way I read it. We were here to protect—to get back—some rich man's estate, his private playground, that the Gerin had taken away. Not because of colonists (Did I see any colonists? Did anyone see any evidence of colonists?) but because of a rich old fart who had kept this whole world to himself, and then couldn't protect it. That's why we couldn't do the safe, reasonable thing and bomb the Gerin into dust, why we hadn't had adequate site preparation, why we hadn't brought down the tactical nukes. Politics.

I did sort of wonder why the Gerin wanted it. Maybe they had their own politics? I also wondered if anyone was hiding out in there, safe behind the disguising rock, watching us fight… lounging at ease, maybe, with a drink in his hand, enjoying the show. We could take care of that later, too. If we were here.

Sometime before dawn—still dark, but over half the night gone—the higher flyby reported distant activity. Lights and nonvisible heat sources over at the edge of the hills, moving slowly but steadily towards us. They didn't follow the old road trace, but kept to the low ground. According to the best guess of the instruments, the wettest low ground. I guess that makes sense, if you're an amphib. It still didn't make sense that they moved so slow, and that they hadn't come to hit us while we were setting up.

The next bad news came from above. Whatever the Navy had thought they'd done, to get the Gerin ships out of the way, it hadn't held, and the next thing we knew our guys boosted out of orbit and told us to hold the fort while they fought off the Gerin. Sure. The way things were going, they weren't coming back, and we wouldn't be here if they did. Nobody *said* that, which made it all the clearer that we were all thinking it. During that long day we made radio contact with the survivors at Beta Site. They were about eighty klicks away to our north, trying to move our way through the broken hills and thick scrub. Nobody'd bothered them yet, and they hadn't found any sign of human habitation. Surprise. The major didn't tell them what we'd found, seeing as it wouldn't do them any good. Neither would linking up with us, probably.

The smart thing to do, if anyone had asked me, was for us to boogie on out of there and link with the Beta Site survivors, and see what we could do as a mobile strike force. Nobody asked me, at least nobody up top, where the orders came from. We were supposed to hold the strip, so there we stuck, berries on a branch ready for picking. I know a lot of the guys thought the same way I did, but hardly anyone mentioned it, seeing it would do no good and we'd have a lot more to bitch about later.

Slow as the Gerin were moving, we had time to set up several surprises, fill every available container with water, all that sort of thing. They ignored our flyspy, so we could tell where they were, what they had with them, estimate when they'd arrive. It was spooky… but then they didn't need to bother shooting down our toy; they only outnumbered us maybe a hundred to one. If every one of our ambushes worked, we might cut it down to ninety to one.

Gerin ground troops might be slow to arrive, but once they were there you had no doubt about it. Just out of range of our knuckleknockers, the column paused and set up some tubing that had to be artillery of some sort. Sure enough, we heard a sort of warbling whoosh, and then a vast *whump* as the first shells burst over our heads and spit shards of steel down on us. After a couple or three shots, fairly well separated, they sent up a whole tanker load, and the concussion shuddered the hills themselves.

We watched them advance through the smoke and haze of their initial barrage. They were in easy missile range, but we had to save the missiles for their air support. Everyone's seen the news clips—that strange, undulating way they move. They may be true amphibians, but they're clearly more at home in water or space than walking around on the ground. Not that it's walking, really. Their weapons fire slower on automatic than ours, but they can carry two of them—an advantage of having all those extra appendages. And in close, hand-to-hand combat, their two metal-tipped tentacles are lethal.

They came closer, advancing in little bobbing runs that were similar to our own tactics, but not the same. It's hard to explain, but watching them come I felt how alien they were—they could not have been humans in alien suits, for instance. The very fact that I had trouble picking out the logic of their movements—why they chose to go *this* way up a draw, and not that—emphasized the differences.

Now they were passing the first marker. Rolly tapped me on the shoulder, and I nodded. He hit the switch, and a stormcloud rolled under them, tumbling them in the explosion. Those in the first rank let off a burst, virtually unaimed; the smack of their slugs on the rocks was drowned in the roar and clatter of the explosion, and the dust of it rolled forward to hide them all. Chunks of rock splattered all around; a secondary roar had to mean that the blast had triggered a rockslide, just as we'd hoped. When the dust cleared a little, we couldn't see any of the live ones, only a few wet messes just beyond a mound of broken stone and uprooted brush.

One of the wetears down at the far end of the trench stood up to peer out. Before anyone could yank him back, Gerin slugs took his face and the back of his head, and he toppled over. Then a storm of fire rang along the rocks nearby while we all ducked. Stupid kid should have known they wouldn't all be dead: we'd told them and told them. Our flyspy crew concentrated on their screens; at the moment the critter was reading infrared, and the enemy fire showed clearly. Garrond gave us the coordinates; our return fire got a few more (or so the flyspy showed—we didn't stand up to see).

But that was only the first wave. All too soon we could see the next Gerin working their way past the rockslide toward our positions. And although I'd been listening for it, I hadn't heard an explosion from the other side of the strip. Had they been overrun, or had the Gerin failed to attempt an envelopment?

Suddenly the sky was full of light and noise: the Gerin had launched another barrage. Oddly, the weapons seemed to be intended to cause noise as much as actual damage. And they were noisy: my ears rang painfully and I saw others shaking their heads. Under cover of that noise, Gerin leapt out, hardly ten meters away. Someone to my left screamed; their slugs slammed all around us. We fired back, and saw their protective suits ripple and split, their innards gushing out to stain the ground. But there were too many, and some of them made it to us, stabbing wildly with those metal-tipped tentacles. One of them smashed into Rolly's chest; his eyes bulged, and pink froth erupted from his mouth. I fired point-blank at that one. It collapsed with a gasping wheeze, but it was too late for Rolly.

Even in all the noise, I was aware that the Gerin themselves fought almost silently. I'd heard they had speech, of a sort—audible sounds, that is—but they didn't yell at each other, or cry out when injured. It was almost like fighting machines. And like machines, they kept coming. Even in the dark.

It was sometime in that first night when I heard the row between the captain and the major. I don't know when it started, maybe in private before the Gerin even got to us, but in the noise of combat, they'd both raised their voices. I was going along, checking ammo levels, making sure everyone had water, and passed them just close enough to hear.

"—You can't do that," Major Sewell was saying. "They said, hold the strip."

"Because it's that bastard Ifleta's," said the captain. He'd figured it out too, of course; he didn't turn stupid when he got his promotion. I should have gone on, but instead I hunkered down a little and listened. If he talked the major around, I'd need to know. "So no heavy artillery, no tactical nukes, no damage to his art collection or whatever he thinks it is. And it's crazy… listen, the Gerin are amphibs, they even have swim tanks in their ships—"

"So? Dammit, Carl, it's the middle of a battle, not a lecture room—"

"So they're territorial." I could hear the expletive he didn't say at the end of that… Sewell was a senior officer, however dense. "It's part of that honor stuff: where you are determines your role in the dominance hierarchy. If we move, we're no threat; if we stay in one place they'll attack—"

"They *are* attacking, in case you hadn't noticed, *Captain.* We're dug in here; if we move they can take us easily. Or were you suggesting that we just run for it?" The contempt in Sewell's voice was audible, even through the gunfire.

The captain made one more try. I knew, from our years together, what it took for him to hold his temper at the major's tone; the effort came through in his voice. "Sir, with all due respect, after the massacre on Duquesne, there was a study of Gerin psychology in the *Military Topics Review*— and that study indicated that the Gerin would choose to assault stationary, defended positions over a force in movement. Something about defending certain rock formations in the tidal zone, important for amphibians…"

"Yeah, well, what some egghead scientist thinks the slimes do and what the slimes out here in combat do is two different things. And our orders, Captain, say stand and defend this shuttle strip. It doesn't matter a truckful of chickenshit whether the strip is Ifleta's personal private hideaway or was built by the Gerin: I was told to defend it, and I'm going to defend it. Is that clear?"

"Sir." I heard boots scrape on the broken rock and got myself out of there in a hurry. Another time that I'd heard more than I should have, at least more than it would be comfortable to admit. Not long after, the captain met me as I worked my way back down the line. He leaned over and said in my ear, "I know you heard that, Gunny. Keep it to yourself."

"You got eyes in the dark?" I asked. It meant more than that; we'd used it as a code a long time ago. I didn't think he'd choose that way, but I'd let him decide.

"No," he said. A shell burst nearby, deafening us both for a moment; I could see, in the brief glare, his unshaken determination. "No," he said again after we could hear. "It's too late anyway."

"Ifleta's the owner?" I asked.

"Yeah. Senior counselor—like a president—in Hamny's Consortium, and boss of Sigma Combine. This is his little hideaway—should have been a colony but he got here first. What I figure is this is his price for bringing Hamny's in free: three human-settled worlds, two of 'em industrial. Worth it, that's one way of looking at it. Trade a couple thousand Marines for three allied planets, populations to draft, industrial plants in place, and probably a good chunk of money as well."

I grunted, because there's nothing to say to that kind of argument. Not in words, anyway. Then I asked, "Does the major know?"

The captain shrugged. "You heard me—I told him. I told him yesterday, when they found the house. He doesn't care. Rich man wants the aliens out of his property, that's just fine—treat Marines like mercs, he doesn't give a damn, and *that*, Tinker, is what they call an officer and a gentleman. *His* father's a retired admiral; he's looking for stars of his own." It was a measure of his resentment that he called me by that old nickname... the others that had used it were all dead. I wondered if he resented his own lost patrimony... the rich bottomland farm that would have been his, the wife and many children. He had been a farmer's son, in a long line of farmers, as proud of their heritage as any admiral.

"Best watch him, Captain," I said, certain that I would. "He's likely to use your advice all wrong."

"I know. He backstabbed Tio, got him shipped over to the Second with a bad rep—" He stopped suddenly, and his voice changed. "Well, Gunny, let me know how that number three post is loaded." I took that hint, and went on; we'd talked too long as it was.

So now I knew the whole story—for one thing about Captain Carl Dietz, he never in his life made accusations without the information to back them up. He hadn't accused me when it might have got him a lighter sentence, all those years ago. If he said it was Ifleta's place, if he was sure that our losses bought Ifleta's support, and three planets, then I was sure. I didn't like it, but I believed it.

The pressure was constant. We had no time to think, no time to rest, taking only the briefest catnaps one by one, with the others alert. We knew we were inflicting heavy losses, but the Gerin kept coming. Again and again, singly and in triads and larger groups, they appeared, struggling up the hills, firing steadily until they were cut down to ooze aqua fluid on the scarred slopes. Our losses were less, but irreparable.

It was dawn again—which dawn, how many days since landing, I wasn't at all sure. I glanced at the rising sun, irrationally angry because it hurt my eyes. What I could see of the others looked as bad as I felt: filthy, stinking, their eyes sunken in drawn faces, dirty bandages on too many wounds. The line of motionless mounds behind our position was longer, again. No time for burial, no time to drag the dead farther away: they were here, with us, and they stank in their own way. We had covered their faces; that was all we could do.

Major Sewell crawled along our line, doing his best to be encouraging, but everyone was too tired and too depressed to be cheered. When he got to me, I could tell that he didn't feel much better. One thing about him, he hadn't been taking it easy or hiding out.

"We've got a problem," he said. I just nodded. Speech took too much energy, and besides it was obvious. "There's only one thing to do, and that's hit 'em with a mobile unit. I've been in contact with the Beta Site survivors, but they don't have a flyspy or good linkage to ours—and besides their only officer is a kid just out of OCS. The others died at the drop. They're about four hours away, now. I'm gonna take a squad, find 'em, and go after the Gerin commander."

I still didn't say anything. That might have made sense, before the Gerin arrived. Now it looked to me like more politics—Sewell figured to leave the captain holding an indefensible position, while he took his chance at the Gerin commander. He might get killed, but if he didn't he'd get his medals… and staying here was going to get us all killed. Some of that must have shown in my face, because his darkened.

"Dammit, Gunny—I know what Captain Dietz said made sense, but our *orders* said defend this strip. The last flyspy image gave me a lock on what may be the Gerin commander's module, and that unit from Beta Site may give me the firepower I need. Now you find me—" My mind filled in "a few good men" but he actually asked for a squad of unwounded. We had that many, barely, and I got them back to the cleft between the first and second hills just in time to see that last confrontation with the captain.

If I hadn't known him that long, I'd have thought he didn't care. Sewell had a good excuse, as if he needed one, for leaving the captain behind: Dietz had been hit, though that wound wouldn't kill him. He couldn't have moved fast for long, not without a trip through Med or some stim-tabs. But they both knew that had nothing to do with it. The captain got his orders from Sewell in terse phrases; he merely nodded in reply. Then his eyes met mine.

I'd planned to duck away once we were beyond the Gerin lines—assuming we made it that far, and since the other side of the strip hadn't been so heavily attacked, we probably would. I had better things to do than babysit a major playing politics with the captain's life. But the captain's gaze had the same wide-blue-sky openness it had always had, barring a few times he was whacked out on bootleg whiskey.

"I'm glad you've got Gunny Vargas with you," the captain said. "He's got eyes in the dark."

"If it takes us that long, we're in trouble again," said the major gruffly. I smiled at the captain, and followed Sewell away down the trail, thinking of the years since I'd been in that stuffy little courtroom back on that miserable backwater colony planet. The captain played fair, on the whole; he never asked for more than his due, and usually got less. If he wanted me to babysit the major, I would. It was the least I could do for him.

We lost only three on the way to meet the Beta Site survivors, and I saved the major's life twice. The second time, the Gerin tentacle I stopped shattered my arm just as thoroughly as a bullet. The major thanked me, in the way that officers are taught to do, but the thought behind his narrow forehead was that my heroism didn't do him a bit of good unless he could win something. The medic we had along slapped a field splint on the arm, and shot me up with something that took all the sharp edges off. That worried me, but I knew it would wear off in a few hours. I'd have time enough.

Then we walked on, and on, and damn near ran headlong into our own people. They looked a lot better than we did, not having been shot up by Gerin for several days; in fact, they looked downright smart. The butterbar had an expression somewhere between serious and smug—he figured he'd done a better than decent job with his people, and the glance I got from his senior sergeant said the kid was okay. Sewell took over without explaining much, except that we'd been attacked and were now going to counterattack; I was glad he didn't go further. It could have created a problem for me.

Caedmon's an official record, now. You've seen the tapes, maybe, or the famous shot of the final Gerin assault up the hills above the shuttle strip, the one that survived in someone's personal vicam to be stripped later by Naval Intelligence after we took the hills back, and had time to retrieve personal effects. You know that our cruisers came back, launched fighters that tore the Gerin fighters out of the sky, and then more shuttles, with more troops, enough to finish the job on the surface. You know that the "gallant forces" of the first landing (yeah, I heard that speech too) are credited with *almost* winning against fearful odds, even wiping out the Gerin commander and its staff, thanks to the brilliant tactic of one Marine captain, unfortunately himself a casualty of that last day of battle. You've seen his picture, with those summer-sky-blue eyes and that steadfast expression, a stranger to envy and fear alike.

But I know what happened to Major Sewell, who is listed simply as "killed in action." I know how come the captain got his posthumous medals and promotion, something for his family back home to put up on their wall. I know exactly how the Gerin commander died, and who died of Gerin weapons and who of human steel. And I don't think I have to tell you every little detail, do I? It all comes down to politics, after all. An honest politician, as the saying goes, is the one who stays bought. I was bought a long time ago, with the only coin that buys any gypsy's soul, and with that death (you know which death) I was freed.

AND LADIES OF THE CLUB

"**B**ut you don't tax jockstraps!" Mirabel Stonefist glared.
"No," said the king. "They're a necessity."
"For you, maybe. How do you expect me to fight without my bronze bra?"

"Men can fight without them," the king said. "It's far more economical to hire men, anyway. Do you have any idea what the extra armor for the women in my army costs? I commissioned a military cost-containment study, and my advisors said women's uniforms were always running over budget." The king smirked at the queen, on her throne a few feet away, and she smirked back. "I've always said the costs to society are too high if women leave their family responsibilities—"

"We'll see about this," said Mirabel. She would like to have seen about it then and there, but the king's personal guards—all male this morning, she noticed— looked too alert. No sense getting her nose broken again for nothing. Probably it was the queen's fault anyway. Just because she'd been dumped on her backside at the Harvest Tourney, when she tried to go up against Serena the Savage, expecting that uncompromising warrior to pull her strokes… the queen gave Mirabel a curled lip, and Mirabel imagined giving the queen a fat one. As the elected representative of the Ladies' Aid & Armor Society, she must maintain her dignity, but she didn't have to control her imagination.

"Six silver pence per annum," said the king. "Payable by the Vernal Equinox."

Mirabel growled and stalked out, knocking over several minor barons on the way. In the courtyard, other women in the royal army clustered around her.

"Well?"

"It's true," said Mirabel grimly. "He's taxing bronze bras." A perky blonde with an intolerably cute nose (still unbroken) piped up.

"Just bronze? What about brass? Or iron? Or—"

"Shut *up*, Krystal! Bronze, brass, gold, silver… 'all such metal ornaments as ye

51

female warrioresses are wont to use—' "

"Warrioress!" A vast bosomy shape heaved upward, dark brows lowered. Bertha Broadbelt had strong opinions on the dignity due women warriors.

"Shut *up,* Bertha!" Krystal squeaked, slapping Bertha on the arm with all the effect of a kitten swatting a sabertooth.

"Warrioress is what the law says," Mirabel snapped. "I don't like it either. But there it is."

"What about *leather?*" Krystal asked. "Chain mail? Linen with seashell embroidery?"

"KRYSTAL!" The perky blonde wilted under the combined bellow.

"I was only thinking—"

"No, you weren't," Mirabel said. "You were fantasizing about those things in the *Dark Knights* catalog again. This is serious; I'm calling a meeting of the Ladies' Aid & Armor Society."

"And so," she explained that evening to the women who had gathered in the Ladies' Aid & Armor Society meeting hall, "the king insists that the extra metal we require in our armor is a luxury, to be taxed as such. He expects we'll all go tamely back to our hearths— or make him rich."

"I'll make him sing soprano," muttered Lissa Broadbelt, Bertha's sister. "The nerve of that man—"

"Now, now." A sweet soprano voice sliced through the babble as a sword through new butter. "Ladies, please! Let's have no unseemly threats…." With a creak and jingle, the speaker stood… and stood. Tall as an oak (the songs went), and tougher than bullhide (the songs went), clad in enough armor to outfit most small mercenary companies, Sophora Segundiflora towered over her sister warriors. She had arrived in town only that evening, from a successful contract. "Especially," Sophora said, "threats that impugn sopranos."

"No, ma'am."

"He is, after all, the king."

"Yes, ma'am."

"Although it is a silly sort of tax."

"*Yes,* ma'am." A long pause, during which Sophora smiled lazily at the convocation, and the convocation smiled nervously back. She was so big, for one thing, and she wore so much more armor than everyone else, for another, and then everyone who had been to war with her knew that she smiled all the time. Even when slicing hapless enemies in two or three or whatever number of chunks happened to be her pleasure. Perhaps especially then.

"Uh… do you have any… er… suggestions?' asked Mirabel, in a tone very different from that she'd used to the king.

"I think we should all sit down," Sophora said, and did so with another round of metallic clinkings and leathery creakings. Everyone sat, in one obedient descent. Everyone waited, with varying degrees of patience but absolute determination. One did not interrupt Sophora. One would not have the chance to apologize. Whether she was slow, or merely deliberate, she always had a chance to speak her mind. "What about other kinds of bras?" she asked at last.

Mirabel explained the new decree again. "Metal ornaments, it said, but that included armor. Said so. Called us warrioresses, too." Sophora waved that away.

"He can call us what he likes, as long as we get paid and we don't have to pay this stupid tax. First things first. So if it's not a metal bra, it's not taxed?"

"No—but what good is a bit of cloth against weapons?"

"I told you, leather—" Krystal put in quickly.

Sophora let out a cascade of soprano laughter, like a miniature waterfall. "Ladies, ladies… what about something like my corselet?"

"He was clever there, Sophora. He doesn't want to tax the armor men wear, and of course some men do wear mail shirts or corselets of bronze. But he specified that modifications to the standard designs— marked in diagrams; I saw them—count as ornamentation, and make the whole taxable."

"Idiot!" huffed Sophora. Then she jingled some more as she tried to examine her own mail shirt. "These gussets, I suppose?"

"Yes, exactly. We could, I suppose, wear men's body armor a size larger, and pad it out, but it would be miserably hot in summer, and bulky the rest of the time. There's always breast-binding—"

"I hate binding my breasts," said someone from the back of the room. "You gals with the baby tits can do it easily enough, but some of us are built!" Heads turned to look at her, and sure enough, she was.

"The simple thing is to get rid of our breasts," said Sophora, as if stating the obvious. The resulting gasp filled the room. She looked around "Not like *that*," she said. "I have no intention of cutting mine off. I don't care what anyone says about heroic foremothers, those Amazons were barbarians. But we live in an age of modern marvels. We don't have to rely on old-fashioned surgery. Why, there's a plastic wizard right here in the city."

"Of course!" Mirabel smacked herself on the forehead. "I've seen his advertisements myself. Thought of having a nose job myself, but I've just been too busy."

"That's right," Bertha said. "And he does great temporary bridges and crowns, too: our Desiree had the wedding outdoors, and he did a crystal bridge across the Sinkbat canal, and a pair of crystal crowns for Desiree and the flower girl. Lovely—so romantic— and then it vanished right on time, no sticky residue."

"Temporaries! That's even better. Take 'em or leave 'em, so to speak."

"Let's get down to business," Sophora said. "Figure out what we can pay, and how we can avoid paying it."

"What?"

"Come on in the business office and I'll show you." She led the way into the back room, and began pulling down scrolls and tomes. Mirabel and a couple of others settled down to wait. After peering and muttering through a short candle and part of a tall replacement, Sophora looked up.

"We'll need to kick in two silver pence each to start with."

"Two silver pence! Why?"

"That's the ceiling in our health benefits coverage for noncombat trauma care. It's reimbursable, I'm sure, but we have to pay it first," Sophora said. She had half a dozen scrolls spread on the desk, along with a thick, well-thumbed volume of tax laws. "We might have to split it between a reimbursable medical expense, and a deductible business expense, if they get picky."

"But how?" Mirabel had never understood the medical benefits package anyway. They should've paid to have her nose redone, but the paperpushers had said that because she was a prisoner at the time, it didn't qualify as a combat injury. But since she'd been in uniform, it wasn't noncombat trauma, either.

Sophora smiled and tapped the tax volume. "It's a necessary business expense, required to comply with the new tax code. The chancellor might argue that only the cost related to removing the breasts is a business expense, but the restoration has to count as medical. It's in the law: 'any procedure which restores normal function following loss thereof.' Either it's reimbursable or it's deductible, and of course we aren't paying the tax. With a volume discount, we should be able to get the job done for two silver pence. Bertha says he charged only three for that entire wedding celebration."

Mirabel whistled her admiration. "Very good, dear. You should be a lawyer."

"I will be, when I retire." Sophora smiled placidly. "I've been taking correspondence courses. Part of that G.I.T. Bill the king signed three years ago: Get Into Taxpaying. Now let me get the contract drawn up—" She wrote steadily as that candle burned down; Mirabel lit another. Finally she quit, shook her hand, and said, "See that the wizard signs this contract I've drawn up." She handed over a thick roll. Mirabel glanced down the first part of it.

"It's *heavy*—surely we don't need all this for a simple reversible spell...."

"I added a little boilerplate. And yes, we do need all this. You don't want to wake up with the wrong one, do you?"

"Wrong breast? Ugh—what a thought. Although I expect some of our sisters wouldn't mind, if they could choose which one."

"They can pay extra for full reshaping, if they want. I'm not going to have my children drinking out of someone else's breast, even if it is on my body."

"You want a reversible reduction mammoplasty?" the wizard asked. His eyebrows wavered, unsure whether to rise in shock or lower in disapproval. Mirabel could tell he didn't like her using the correct term for the operation. Wizards liked clients to be humble and ignorant.

"Yeah," Mirabel said. She didn't care if the wizard didn't like smart clients; she wasn't about to let the sisterhood down. "See, there's a new tax on breast-armor. What we need is to lose 'em when we're headed for battle, but of course we want to get 'em back when we're nursing. Or… whatever." Whatever being more to the point, in her case. Two points.

"I… see." The steepled fingers, the professional sigh. Mirabel hated it when wizards pulled all this high and mighty expert jazz. "It could be… expensive…."

"I don't see why," Mirabel said. "It's not like we're asking for permanent changes. Isn't it true that a reversible spell disturbs the Great Balance less? Doesn't cost you that much… of course I can find someone else…."

"Where *do* you people get your idea of magery?" the wizard asked loftily. Mirabel held up the Ladies' Aid & Armor Society's copy of *Our Wizards, Our Spells*. He flushed. "That's a popularization… it's hardly authoritative—"

"I've also read Wishbone and Peebles' *Altering Reality: Temporary vs. Permanent Spellcasting and Its Costs.*"

"You couldn't have understood that!" True, but Mirabel wasn't going to admit it. She merely looked at the wizard's neck, thinking how easily it would come apart with one blow of her sword, until he swallowed twice quickly and flushed. "All right, all right," he said then. "Perhaps you soldiers should get a sort of discount."

"I should hope so. All the women warriors in the kingdom… we could even make it exclusive… ."

"Well. Well, then let's say—how much was the new tax?"

"Irrelevant," said Mirabel, well briefed by Sophora. "We can pay two silver pence apiece per year."

"Per year?" His fingers wiggled a little; she knew he was trying to add it up in his head.

"As many transforms as needed … but we wouldn't want many."

"Uh… how many warriors?"

"Fifty right away, but there might be more later."

"It's very difficult. You see, you have to create an extradimensional storage facility for the… the… tissue, so to speak. Until it's wanted. Otherwise the energy cost of uncreating and creating all that, all the time, would be prohibitive. And the storage facility must have very good—well, it's a rather difficult concept, except that you don't want to mix them up." But what he was really thinking was "a hundred silver pence—enough for that new random-access multidimensional storage device they were showing over in Technolalia last summer."

Still, he was alert enough to read the contract Mirabel handed him. As she'd expected, he threw up his hands and threatened to curse the vixenish excuse for a lawyer who had drawn up such a ridiculous, unspeakable contract. Mirabel repeated her long look at his neck—such a scrawny, weak neck—and he subsided.

"All right, all right. Two silver pence a year for necessary reversible mammoplasties…" He signed on the dotted line, then stamped below with the sigil on the end of his wizard's staff, as Sophora had said he should. Mirabel smiled at him and handed over two silver pence.

"You can do me first," she said. "I'll be in tomorrow morning. We'll need proof that it's reversible."

The operation took hardly any time. The wizard didn't even need to touch the target area. One moment the breasts were there, then they weren't. The reversal took somewhat longer, but it worked smoothly, and then they were again. A slight tingling that faded in moments—that was all the side effects. Mirabel had gone in with her usual off-duty outfit on, and came out moments later with considerably more room in the top of it. The other women in the palace guard, who had come to watch, grinned happily. They would all have theirs done at once, they agreed.

Mirabel thought it felt a bit odd when she stripped for weapons practice, but the look on the king's face was worth it. All the women in the palace now displayed an array of admirably flat—but muscular— chests above regulation bronze loinguards. At first, no one recognized them, not even the sergeants. But gradually, the men they were training with focussed on the obvious—Mirabel's flat nose, Krystal's perky one—and the necessary, like the sword tips that kept getting in their way when they forgot to pay attention to drill.

The king, though… the king didn't catch on until someone told him. "That new draft…" he said to the sergeant. "Shaping well."

"Begging the king's pardon, that ain't no new draft," said the sergeant.

"But—"

"Them's the ladies, Sire," the sergeant said. "Haven't got no thingies anymore." He knew and had already used all the usual terms, but felt that when addressing the king in person, he ought to avoid vulgarisms. "They's fightin' better than ever, your highness, and that's better'n most."

"Women!" The king stared. Mirabel, in the first row, grinned at him. "And no tits!"

"Uh… yes, Sire. No… er… tits." Not for the first time, the sergeant felt that royalty had failed to adhere to standards.

"No tax," Mirabel said cheerfully, as the king's eyes flicked from her face to her chest and back again.

"Oh … dear," said the king, and fled the courtyard. Minutes later, the queen's face appeared at a high window. Mirabel, who had been watching for it, waved gaily. The queen turned her back.

The prince glared at himself in the mirror. The spell was definitely wearing off. The wizard insisted he'd simply grown out of it, but the prince felt that having a handsome throat did not make up for having a... face. He left a blank there, while staring at the mirror. Face it was, in that it had two eyes and a nose and mouth arranged in more or less the right places. Aside from that, he saw a homely boy with close-set eyes under a sloping brow, a great prow of a nose, buck teeth, and a receding chin, all decorated with splotches of midadolescent acne. And even if he had outgrown the spell, it was still wearing thin—last week his throat had been handsome, but this week his Adam's apple looked like a top on a string. This spell should have been renewed a month ago. If only his father weren't such a cheapskate... he had his own spells renewed every three months, and what did he need them for, at his age. Everyone knew the important time of life was now, when you were a young prince desperately trying to find a princess.

She was coming next week. Her parents had visited at Harvest Home; her aunts and uncles had come for Yule. Now, at the Vernal Equinox, she was coming. The beautiful Marilisa—he had seen pictures. She had seen pictures of him, they said: the miniature on ivory done by their own artist. But then the spell had been strong, and so had his chin.

He had to get the spell renewed. His father had said no hurry, but suppose her ship came in early?

"I think we should return to normal for the Equinox," said Bertha. "Think of the dances. The parties. The prince's betrothal ... the wedding, if we're lucky."

"But that's when the tax is due," Mirabel said.

"Only if we're wearing breast-armor," Sophora pointed out. "We can manage not to fight a war for a week or so, I hope. Just wear civilian clothes. Some of you are pulling castle duty then—I suppose you'll have to stay flat, at least for your duty hours but the rest of us can enjoy ourselves again—"

"Yes," said Krystal. "I like that idea..." She wriggled delicately, and Mirabel gave her a disgusted look.

"You would. But... after all... why not?"

They presented themselves at the wizard's hall. "All of you reversed at once?" he asked. "That will take some time—the reverse operation is a bit slower, especially as I now have so many in... er... storage. And I do have other appointments...."

"No," Sophora said. "You have us. Look at your contract." And sure enough, there it was, the paragraph she had buried in the midst of formal boilerplate. She read it aloud, just in case he skipped a phrase. "Because that the Welfare of the Warrior is Necessary to the Welfare of the Land and Sovereign, therefore shalt thou at all times and places be Ready and Willing to proceed with this Operation at the Request of the Warrior and such Request shall supersede all Others, be they common or Royal. And to this Essential shalt thou bind thyself at the peril of thy Life at the hands of the Ladies' Aid & Armor Society."

The wizard gulped. "But you see, ladies, my other clients—the ladies of the court, the chancellor's wife—"

Sophora pointed to *be they common or Royal.* "It is your sworn word, wizard, which any court will uphold, especially this court…."

The wizard was halfway through the restorations when the royal summons came. "I can't right now," he told the messenger curtly. He had just discovered that the newly installed random access multidimensional storage device had a bug in it, and for the fifth time in a row, he'd gotten an error message when he tried to retrieve Bertha Broadbelt's breasts. He was swearing and starting to panic every time he glanced at her dark-browed face.

"But it's the king's command," the messenger said.

"I don't care if it's the king's personal spell against body odor," the wizard said. "I can't do it now, and that's final." He pushed the messenger out the door, slammed it, and tried to calm himself. "Sorry about the interruption," he said to Bertha, who seemed to be calmer than he was. Of course, she had the sword.

"That's all right," she said. "Take your time. Nothing's wrong, is it?"

"Nothing at all," said the wizard. He tried again. No error message in the first part of the spell, at least. He felt the little click in his head that meant the transfer had been made, and glanced at Bertha just as she looked down.

And up. He knew his mouth was hanging open, but he couldn't say a word. She could. "These aren't *my* boobs," she said without any expression at all. "These are Gillian's." He wondered how she could recognize someone else's breasts on her chest just as he realized he was having trouble breathing because she had a vast meaty hand around his throat.

The prince hated being in the throne room with his outgrown spell leaving the most visible parts of himself at their worst. But he'd been summoned to wait for the escort that would take him to the wizard for the spell's renewal, so he'd slouched into the room in a long-sleeved hooded jerkin, the hood pulled well forward and the sleeves down over his awkward hands.

"Stand *up*, boy," his father said.

"Don't wear your hood in the house," his mother said.

"The wizard won't do it," the messenger said, bowing his way up the room.

"Won't do it!" King and queen spoke together, glanced at the prince in unison, and then glared at the messenger. The king waved the queen silent and went on alone. "What do you mean, he won't do it. He's our subject."

"He's busy," the messenger said. "That's what he told me. He said even if your majesty's personal body-odor spell—"

"Silence!" bellowed the king. His face had turned very red and he did not glance at the queen. "Guards!" he called. The prince's escort looked up, with interest. "Go arrest us this pesky wizard and bring him here."

The wizard's shop, when the guards arrived, was open and empty but for the usual magical impedimenta and the mysterious black box with a red light that was humming to itself in the key of E-flat minor. A soldier touched it, and it emitted a shrill squeal and changed to humming in the Lydian mode. "Fatal error," said a voice from the emptiness. The soldiers tumbled out of the shop without touching anything else.

"If you're looking for that there plastic wizard," said a toothless old woman on the street, "one of them there lady warriors took him away."

The soldiers looked at each other. Most of them knew where the Ladies' Aid & Armor Society met. A few of them had been guests at the Occasional Teas. But no man went there uninvited. Especially not when Sophora Segundiflora was leaning on the doorframe, eyeing them with that lazy smile. They had started off to the meeting hall in step, and come around the corner already beginning to straggle... a straggle that became a ragged halt a few yards out of Sophora's reach. They hoped.

"Hi, guys," she said. "Got business with us?"

"Umm," said the sergeant. And then, more coherently, "We heard that plastic wizard might be around here; the king wants him."

"Probably not," Sophora said. "Not now." She glanced suggestively at the door behind her. No sounds leaked through, which was somehow more ominous than shrieks and gurgles would have been.

"Ummm," said the sergeant again. No one had asked his opinion of the new tax code, but he had one. Anything that upset Sophora Segundiflora and Mirabel Stonefist was a bad idea. Still, he didn't want to be the one to tell the king why the wizard wasn't available.

"Anything else?" Sophora asked. She looked entirely too happy for the sergeant's comfort; he had seen her in battle. The sergeant felt his old wounds paining him, all of them, and wished he had retired the year before, when he'd had the chance. Too late now; he'd re-upped for five. That extra hide of land and a cow wouldn't do him much good if Sophora tore him limb from limb. He gulped, and sidled closer, making sure his hands were well away from any of his weapons without being in any of the positions that might signal an unarmed combat assault. There weren't many such positions, and his wrists started aching before he'd gone ten feet.

"Look—can we talk?"

"Sure," said Sophora. "You are, and I am. What else?"

He knew she wasn't stupid. Word had gone around about that correspondence course. She must be practicing her courtroom manner. "It's... kind of sensitive," he said.

"Got an itch?" she inquired. "Down two streets and across, Sign of the Mermaid…"

"Not that," he muttered. "It's *state* business. The prince—"

"That twerp Nigel?"

"It's not his fault he inherited that face," the sergeant said. It would have been disloyal to say more, but everyone had noticed how the prince took after his uncle, the chancellor. "Not a bad kid, once you know him."

"I'll take your word for it," Sophora said. "So what about the prince?"

"He's… that princess is coming this week. For the betrothal, you know."

"I heard."

"He… er… needs his spells renewed. Or it's all off."

"Why'd the king wait so long?" Sophora asked. She didn't sound really interested.

"The gossip is that he felt it would be good for the prince's character. And he thought with enough willpower maybe the prince could hold on until he was full-grown, when they could do the permanent ones, and a crown at the same time."

"I see. But he needs a temporary before the princess arrives. How unfortunate." Without even looking at him, she reached behind her and opened the door. The sergeant peered into the hall, where the wizard could be seen writhing feebly in Bertha's grip. "We have a prior contract, you see, which he has yet to fulfill. And a complication has arisen."

A slender woman jogged up the street, and came to a panting halt at the door. "Got here as soon as I could—what's up?"

"About time, Gillian," Sophora said. "Bertha's got a problem with our wizard and your—" she stopped and gave the sergeant a loving look that made his neck itch. "Go away, sergeant. I have your message; I will pass it along."

The sergeant backed off a spear length or so, but he didn't go away. If he stayed, he might find out what happened to the wizard. Better to return to the palace with a scrap of the dismembered wizard (if that happened) than with no wizard at all. So he and the others were still hanging around when a grim-faced group of women warriors, some flat-chested in armor and others curvaceous in gowns, emerged from the Ladies' Aid & Armor Society hall.

The sergeant pushed himself off the wall he'd been holding up and tried to stop them. "The king wants the wizard," he said.

"So do we," Sophora said. Her smile made the sergeant flinch, then she scowled—a release of tension. "Oh, well, you might as well come along. We're going to see that the wizard corrects his errors, and you can report to the king."

She led the way back to the wizard's house, and the others surrounded the wizard.

Inside, it still looked like a wizard's house, full of things that made no sense to the sergeant.

"Someone touched this," the wizard said, pointing to the black box.

"How can you tell? And who could've touched it?" Sophora asked. But they all turned to look at the hapless soldiers.

"We were just looking for him," the sergeant said. "He wasn't here… we were just looking for evidence…."

"FATAL ERROR," said the voice from the air again. Everyone shivered.

"Can't you shut that up?"

"Not now. Not since some hamfisted boneheaded *guardsman* laid his clumsy hands on it." The wizard looked particularly wizardly, eyebrows bristling, hair standing on end… Mirabel noticed her own hair standing on end, as the wizard reached out his staff and a loud blue SNAP came from the box.

"SYSTEM OVERLOAD," said the voice from the air. "*REALLY* FATAL ERROR THIS TIME."

"Code!" said the wizard.

"A…" the voice said, slowly.

"B!" said the wizard. "B code. B code run." Mirabel wondered what that was about, just as a shower of sparkling symbols fell out of the air into the wizard's outstretched palm.

"NO TRACE," said the voice; the wizard stared at his hand as if it meant something.

"I need a dump," the wizard said. Then he muttered something none of them could understand, nonsense syllables, and a piercing shriek came from the black box.

"NOOOOOOOoooo." Out of the air came a shower of noses, ears, toes, fingers, and a pair of particularly ripe red lips.

"Aha!" said the wizard, and he followed that with a blast of wizardese that made another black object, not quite so boxy, appear shimmering on the desk. Without looking at any of them, the wizard picked it up and spoke into it. "I want technical support," he said. "Now."

The small demon in the black box enjoyed a profitable arrangement with others on various extradimensional planes. Quantum magery being what it was, wizards didn't really understand it, and that kept the demons happy. Nothing's ever really lost, nothing's wasted, and the transformational geometry operated a lot like any free market. It was a lot easier to snatch extra mammaries than to create them from random matter. Demons are particularly good with probabilities, and it had calculated that it need keep no more than a fifth of its deposits on hand, while lending the rest brought in a tidy interest income.

"And I didn't do nothin' wrong, really I didn't," it wailed at the large scaly paw that held it firmly. Far beneath, eyes glowered, flamelit and dangerous.

"Subcontractors!" the universe growled, and the small demon felt nothing more as it vanished in universal disapproval.

"It's under warranty," the wizard insisted.

"Shipping replacement storage device …" the voice said.

"But my data…"

"Recovered," the voice said. "Already loaded. Please stay on the line and give your credit card number—sorry, instruction error. Please maintain connection spell and give your secret name—" The wizard leaned over and said something through cupped hands.

With a flicker, the miscellaneous body parts disappeared, and a black box sat humming in the key of A major; its light was green.

"Me first," said Bertha. "I want Gillian's boobs back on Gillian, and mine on me."

"But the prince—" the sergeant said.

"Can wait," said Bertha.

The royal accountant lagged behind the chancellor, wishing someone else had his job. The chancellor had already given his opinion, and the accountant's boxed ears still rang. It wasn't his fault anyway. A contract was a contract; that's how it was written, and he hadn't written it. But he knew if it came to boxing ears, the king wouldn't clout the chancellor. After all, the chancellor was the queen's brother.

"Well—what is it now?' The king sounded grumpy, too—the worst sort of grumpy.

"Sire—there's a problem with the treasury. There's been an overrun in the military medical services sector."

"An overrun? How? We haven't even had a war!" Very grumpy, the king, and the accountant noticed the big bony fists at the ends of his arms. Why had he ever let his uncle talk him into civil service anyway?

"A considerable increase in claims made to the Royal Provider Organization. For plastic wizardry."

The king leaned over to read the details. "Plastic wizardry? Health care?"

"Sire, in the reign of your renowned father, plastic wizardry to repair duty-related injuries was added to the list of allowable charges, and then a lesser amount was allocated for noncombat trauma—"

The king looked up, clearly puzzled. "What's a reversible reduction mammo-plasty?" The chancellor explained, in the tone of someone who would always prefer to call a breast a bosom.

"Those women again!" The king swelled up and bellowed, "GUARDS!

FETCH ME THOSE WOMEN!" No one, not even the accountant, had to ask which women.

"But your majesty, surely you want the women of your realm able to suckle their own children?" Mirabel Stonefist, serene in the possession of her own mammae, and surprisingly graceful in her holiday attire, smiled at the king.

"Well, of course, but—"

"And you do not want to pay extra for women's armor that will protect those vulnerable fountains of motherly devotion, isn't that right?" She had gotten that rather disgusting phrase from a sermon by the queen's own chaplain, who did not approve of women warriors. Rumor had it that he had chosen his pacific profession after an incident with a woman warrior who had rendered his singing voice an octave higher for a month, and threatened to make the change permanent.

"Well, no, but—"

"Then, Sire, I'm afraid you leave us no alternative but to protect both our womanhood, and your realm, by means of wizardry."

"You could always leave the army," said the queen, in a nasty voice.

Mirabel smiled at her. "Your majesty, if the king will look at his general's reports, instead of his paperpushers' accounts, he'll find that the general considers us vital to the realm's protection." She paused just that necessary moment. "As our customized armor is necessary to our protection."

"But this—but it's too expensive! We shall be bankrupt. Who wrote this contract, anyway?"

"Perhaps I can explain." Sophora Segundiflora strode forward. In her dark three-piece robe with its white bib, she looked almost as impressive as in armor. "As loyal subjects of this realm, we certainly had no intention of causing you any distress, Sire…."

The king glared, but did not interrupt. Perhaps he had noticed the size of the rings necessary to fit over her massive knuckles.

"We only want to do our duty, Sire," she said. "Both for the protection of the realm, and in the gentler duties of maternity. And in fact, had it not been for the tax, we might never have discovered the clear superiority of this method. Even with armor, we had all suffered painful and sometimes dangerous injuries, not to mention the inevitable embarrassment of disrobing in front of male soldiers while on campaign. Now—our precious nurturing ability stays safely hidden away, and we are free to devote our skills to your service, while, when off-duty, we can enjoy our protected attributes without concern for their safety."

"But—how many times do you intend to switch back and forth?"

"Only when necessary." Sophora Segundiflora smiled placidly. "I assure you, we all take our responsibilities seriously, Sire. All of them."

"It was the tax, you say?" the king said. He glanced at the queen. He was remembering her relationship to the chancellor.

"We'd never have thought of it, if you hadn't imposed that tax," Sophora said. "We owe you thanks for that, Sire. Of course, it wouldn't be practical without the military's medical assistance program, but—"

"But it can't go on," the king said. "Didn't you hear me? You're not paying the tax. You're spending all my money on this unnecessary wizardry. You're bankrupting the system. We can't spend it all on you. We have the prince's own plastic wizardry needs, and the expenses of state visits...."

"Well." Sophora looked at Mirabel as if she were uncertain. "I suppose... it's not in the contract or anything, but of course we're very sorry about the prince—"

"Get to the point, woman," said the queen. Sophora gave the queen the benefit of her smile, and Mirabel was glad to see the queen turn pale.

"As long as the tax remains in effect, there's simply nothing else we can do," Sophora said, looking past the king's left ear. She took a deep breath that strained the shoulders of her professional robe. "On the other hand, if the tax were rescinded, it's just possible the ladies would agree to return to the less efficient and fundamentally unsafe practice of wearing armor over their... er... original equipment, as a service to the realm." She smiled even more sweetly, if possible. "But of course, Sire, it's up to you."

"You mean, if I rescind the tax, you'll go back to wearing armor over your own... er..."

"Bosoms," offered the chancellor. The king glared at him, happy to find someone else to glare at.

"I am quite capable of calling a bosom a breast," he said. "And it was on advice from *your* accounting division that I got into this mess." He turned back to Sophora. "If I rescind the tax, you'll quit having these expensive wizardy reversals?"

"Well, we'll have to put it to a vote, but I expect that our proven loyalty to your majesty will prevail."

"Fine, then," the king said. The queen stirred on her throne, and he glared at her. "Don't say a word," he warned. "I'm not about to lose more money because of any parchment-rolling accountants or Milquetoast chaplains. No more tax on women's armor."

"I shall poll the ladies at once, Sire," said Sophora. "But you need not worry."

"About *that*," growled the king. "But there's still an enormous shortfall. We'll have to find the money somewhere. And soon. The prince must have his spells renewed—"

"Ahem." Sophora glanced over her shoulder, and the wizard stepped forward.

"As earnest of our loyalty, Sire, the Ladies' Aid & Armor Society would like to assist with that project." She waved the wizard to the fore.

"Well?" the king asked.

"Sire, my latest researchers have revealed new powers which might be of service. It seems that the laterally reposed interface of the multidimensional—"

"His new black box came with some free spellware," Sophora interrupted before the king's patience shattered.

"Not exactly *free*," said the wizard. "But in essence, yes, new spells. I would be glad to donate the first use to the crown, if it please you."

"Nigel!" the king bellowed. The prince shuffled forward, head hanging. "Here he is, wizard—let's see what you can do."

The small demon in the new black box received the prince's less appetizing morsels with surprising eagerness. In a large multitasking multiplex universe, there's always someone who wants a plague of boils, and a wicked fairy godmother who wants to give some poor infant a receding chin. Available at a reasonable price on the foreign market were a jutting chin, black moustache, and excessive body hair, recently spell-cleared from a princess tormented by just such a wicked fairy. It spit out those requirements, causing a marked change for the better in Prince Nigel's personal appearance. A tidy profit, it thought, and turned its attention to retrieving the final sets of mammary tissue.

The princess in the rose garden was as beautiful as her miniature; Nigel could hardly believe his luck. Her beauty, his handsomeness… he kept wanting to finger his new black moustache and eye himself in any reflecting surface. At the moment, that was her limpid gaze.

"I can hardly believe I never met you until this day," the princess said. "There's something about you that seems so familiar…." She reached out a delicate finger to stroke his moustache, and Nigel thought he would swoon.

Across the rose garden, Sophora Segundiflora smiled at the young lovers and nudged Mirabel, whose attention had wandered to her own new nose job. Mirabel was bored, but Sophora didn't mind chaperoning the young couple. Not with the great gold chain of chancellor across her chest. The previous chancellor had made his last confession the day the wizard tried out his new spells—the other had been a Stretched Scroll, which highlighted certain questionable transactions, such as the withdrawals to the chancellor's personal treasure chest. The fool should have known better. To embezzle all that money, and then choose women warriors as the group to make up the revenues … she hoped the wizard had done something to enhance Nigel's wits. Certainly his mother's side of the family hadn't contributed anything.

Meanwhile, the Ladies' Aid & Armor Society would continue to flourish;

other older warriors had decided to follow Sophora's example and study law. Girls who hitherto had hung around the queen pretending to embroider were now flocking to weapons demonstrations. Even Krystal had been seen cracking something other than a whip.

ACCIDENTS DON'T JUST HAPPEN—THEY'RE CAUSED

The 1330 shuttle from planetside rotated on its longitudinal axis to slip its docking probe into the newly designed collar. Peka, watching from inside the control blister, heard in her ear the pilot's mutter of annoyance.

"Always somebody got to make things harder. Don't know why—"

The status lights flicked through the correct color sequence and came up all green. The station's sensor arrays recognized the umbilical orientation, and flipped open the corresponding inboard covers.

"*I* never had any accidents up here. It was somebody else—"

Peka ignored the complaint. A soothing voice from the station traffic control answered the pilot; she didn't have to. It didn't matter whether this pilot had had an accident; someone had. And someone's accident was reason enough to redesign a docking collar that had allowed a ship to come in sixty degrees offline… because the tuglines that were supposed to correct an offline dock could foul. Had fouled, one coming loose to tangle in another and whack the station end of the umbilical connection, which had then popped its lid and squirted a jet of air and water at the badly docked shuttle, shoving it offline so that the aft stabilizer crumpled one of the com dishes.

In the months since the shuttles had first docked here, the incidence of misalignments had risen steadily. Stationers blamed the pilots' carelessness; pilots blamed the workload, the hours they had to fly without a rest, the crazily shifted schedules that no human metabolism could adjust to.

Peka blamed design, which meant she blamed herself. Even though she had not designed Jacobi Station herself, she had seen the potential problem when she arrived. She had not argued hard enough; she had let the committee override her instincts, her training. Just because it was her first deep-space job, her first *real* job, and she didn't want to be known as a prima donna…

"Looks good to me," Hal said, behind her. Peka jumped; she had not heard him come in, and she hated to be surprised, even by someone she liked.

"This is only one shuttle," she said. The moment it was out of her mouth, she regretted it; Hal looked at her as if he'd bitten into a sour fruit. "Not you," she said, trying to soften the harshness of tone and words. "You and your crew did a fine job of getting that modification built and installed between shuttles. It's just that one shuttle doesn't tell us anything except that it can function right."

"Doesn't prove it can't function wrong," he said, nodding. "I do understand. Even fabrications technologists have read your mother's work, you know."

Peka tried not to move. If she could just freeze in place, perhaps he would never know how that hurt. Her mother, the famous engineer, whose textbooks on quality control and safety were standards in the field… *I should have gone into china painting,* she thought. *Buggy whip-making. Anything but this.*

"I guess it's no accident that you're an engineer," Hal said. "And this kind in particular."

He was going to say it. They all said it.

"After all," he said. "Accidents don't happen… they're caused." He laughed.

It might be funny to someone. It had never been funny to her. "That's right," she said, forcing a smile onto stiff lips. She might as well agree; no one would believe how she had fought off the family destiny. But if you have the talent, her mother had said (and her teachers, from elementary on, and the psychologists she went to, hoping for a way out). If you have the talent—that cluster of talents—and no talents whatever for other things—then it only makes sense to use those talents. Productively—one of her mother's favorite words.

"Was it hard, having such a famous person for a mother?" asked Hal. "I mean, when you were growing up?"

She had no way to answer that didn't sound petulant, selfish, immature, and disloyal. She had been asked that a lot, especially around the time her mother won the second Kaalin award. What people wanted to hear was more about how wonderful her mother had been, and how she had always supported Peka in her own way… and very little else.

Not about the daily frustration of living in a household where the very concept of accident was forbidden. Where every spilled glass of milk, every stain on the carpet, resulted in a formal investigation… down to the simple incident report form her mother devised for a child to fill out. To teach her responsibility, she'd said. Hard? It had been hell, sometimes, and it still was, whenever someone noticed who her mother was. Peka didn't dare say that.

"Sometimes…" she said. "When I was too little to understand about cause and effect, you know."

He chuckled; she must have picked the right tone for an answer. "I'll bet she's proud of you," he said then.

"Reasonably," Peka said. Again an edge had crept into her voice. She hated that edge, and the speculative look that came into Hal's eyes. She wanted to say something to explain it away, but nothing would. She tried anyway. "I—haven't done anything yet. Not really. She's glad I went into this field, of course, but there wasn't much else I could do." That sounded lame; there was always something else, but she had limited her choices to those with good employment opportunities, a reasonable income and chance to travel. She could not have chosen to stay on one planet, could not have tolerated the monotony of a job that stayed the same month after month, year after year.

She looked out the blister, where the cargo lock had mated with the shuttle's cargo bay. In fifteen minutes, the hold would be empty; the pallets would be snaking their way to their designated holds; in another five minutes, the shuttle would be on its way out, and shortly after that the next shuttle would be nosing in.

"Well—guess I'll be going," Hal said. Peka turned. He was looking at her as if he expected some reaction. She felt nothing, but a vague satisfaction that he was going to let her alone.

She was back in her office, reviewing the sensor records of the new collar's performance, when a tap on her door brought her head up. "Yes?" she said, wondering who would be that formal.

Denial, anger—the first stages of grief, her education reminded her—but the woman in the doorway was still there, unscathed by her own emotion. The crisp dark hair, the lively dark eyes, the smooth unweathered skin... the expensive business suit and briefcase.

"Mother," she managed finally.

"Surprised?" her mother asked. "I came in on the *Perrymos* from Baugarten; I'm en route to the Plarsis colonies. Sorry I didn't have a chance to warn you, but they said one of the com channels was out—"

Peka flushed. It was out because the shuttle had knocked the dish awry. Her fault.

"—Some kind of accident, the communications officer said," her mother went on. "I managed not to give him the family lecture." She laughed; Peka couldn't manage even a strangled chuckle.

"We have a two-day layover," her mother said. "I'm sure you're busy now, but I'd love to take you to dinner, or even breakfast, if you can make it."

"Of course," Peka said. She couldn't say anything else.

"Here's my shipboard number," her mother said, holding out a scrap of card. Her own card, no doubt, with the number scribbled on the back of it. Peka got up from her chair, only then realizing she hadn't made any move. Would her mother expect a hug? She couldn't—but her mother held out only the one hand, and when Peka took the card, her mother was already turning away. "Give me a call when you've checked your schedule," her mother said. "I'm free unless someone hires me." She laughed again, over her shoulder, but turned away quickly enough that Peka didn't have to answer.

It was the same card, the familiar name in the same style of lettering. Her mother

didn't need to list her degrees, her honors: ALO ATTENVI, PROCESS QUALITY LTD., CONSULT-
ING and the string of access numbers. Anyone who needed Attenvi's expertise knew
what process quality consulting was, knew that Leisha Attenvi had literally written
the book—several of them. Had won the awards, had (even more important) saved
one company after another from drowning in its own stupidity.

Peka turned the card over and over, and finally stuck it in the minder strip of
her desk. She tried not to look around her office, but she knew too well what it was
like, what her mother had seen in that brief visit. Automatically, her hands moved
across surfaces, straightening everything into perfect alignment. Too late, but she
couldn't help it. Whether her mother said anything or not, she knew what could
have been said. *The professional does not confuse mess with decoration.* Followed
by the accusing finger pointing out this and that bit of disorder.

The headquarters of Process Quality Ltd. were of course decorated, by another
professional, but her mother's office (from which she had regular message cubes
recorded for Peka) had no clutter, no personal touches. The pictures on the walls
had been chosen for their effect on customers; the two photographs were of the
Kaalin awards ceremonies.

"Peka…" That was Einos Skirados, the liaison from Traffic Control assigned
to this project. She didn't bother to flip on the visual; she already knew what he
looked like, and right now she didn't want anyone looking at her. Einos, in particular, would be distracting… something about the shape of his nose and the set
of his eyes seemed to unhinge her logic processor.

"Yes?"

"The values on the second shuttle approach are nominal with the first—it's
looking good. Hal says they'll have another done by the end of the shift, if there
are no modifications."

The second shuttle already? She glanced at the clock, and winced. Lamebrain-
ing wouldn't work. She pulled the figures up onto her screen, and checked. Einos
was good, but it was her responsibility. The computer's own comparison showed
no deviance.

"How much are the pilots complaining?" she asked.

"About what you'd expect," Einos said. "But this was Kiis, who's been in the low
quartile, and if he could get it right—"

"We still haven't had Beckwith," Peka said. She meant it as a joke. Beckwith,
whose shuttle had taken off the com dish, was off the schedule, and complaining
bitterly about that.

"I can hardly wait," Einos said. "I don't know why they hire people like that." He
sounded priggish, but Peka didn't mind. Einos never acted as if she were strange
for being so careful about things, and she felt less guilty about being attracted to
him. Perhaps it wasn't an accident; perhaps it made sense.

"The numbers look good," she told Einos, after rechecking the correspondence.

"I'll tell Hal to go ahead and finish the second."

"Dinner at nineteen thirty?" Einos asked, in the tone that tweaked all her hormonal responses.

"Drat." She'd forgotten completely. She flipped the video on and caught the startled expression on Einos' face. "Einos, I'm so sorry—my mother just turned up—" That sounded lame, and worse than the "drat" before it. She was ready to explain that it didn't matter, that she could still have dinner—her mother would be here for two days—but he interrupted.

"Your *mother? The* Alo Attenvi? Here?" He glanced around as if she might appear miraculously in his office.

The last twinge of guilt disappeared, swamped in anger and envy. Would anyone ever use that tone about her? "Yes, my mother… she came in on the *Perrymos* and she asked me to dinner—and I'm sorry, Einos, but I forgot that this was our night."

"Oh, of course," he said, releasing any claim on the evening. "You have to see her—I don't suppose you'd introduce me… if it's not too much trouble…"

"Maybe later in the visit," Peka said. "Right now I need to call Hal." Right now she needed to get far away from her mother. From everyone who hero-worshipped her mother. From the very concept of mothers. But she called Hal instead.

"Glad to hear it's working well," he said. "Thought it would—good clear design, and not hard to do the modifications."

"Thanks," Peka said.

"Listen—somebody said there's an Attenvi listed as a passenger on that FTL that just docked… relative of yours?"

Station gossip, not just faster than light but faster than reality. "Yes," Peka said, feeling helpless. Everyone would know, and everyone would tell her how she should feel about it. "My mother."

"*The* Attenvi," Hal said. He whistled. "Huh. Must be difficult, after you've been the Attenvi on station."

"She's not staying," Peka said, more sharply than she meant to.

"Just wants to check up on her little girl," Hal said, making it almost a question.

"On her way somewhere else," Peka said. "And I have to get going—we're having dinner." She hadn't told her mother yet, but the way the gossip net worked, her mother would probably be waiting at the right table at the right time even without a formal invitation.

Jacobi Station had been designed to handle outsystem transport, offering more docking and storage space than Janus, the first-built primary station. Peka had arrived before any direct docking of FTL ships was possible. She'd had to travel from starship to station in a little twelve-person hopper, sweating in her p-suit and entirely too aware of the accident rate of near-station traffic in overcrowded situations.

Someday these wide corridors would bustle with traffic; the blank spaces on either side would be filled with shops, hotels, restaurants. Only one was out here now, a pioneer branch of Higg's, the universal fast-food chain. The concentric blue, green, and purple circles promised that its limited bill of fare would be the same as—or at least reminiscent of—that in every other Higg's. A bosonburger... an FTL float... Dirac dip... the names were so familiar they didn't sound silly anymore, and only third graders got a kick out of realizing that they meant something else.

Ahead, a green arch confirmed that the *Perrymos* was docked safely, its access available. Beyond that arch, the waiting area with its array of padded chairs in muted colors, and a TranStar employee at a desk, a young man whose shaved skull had been tattooed with the TranStar logo. Peka blinked; she hadn't realized anyone was that much of a brownnose.

"May I help you?"

"I'm here to meet—" *My mother* tangled with the name, and Peka felt herself flushing, but she got out the more formal "Alo Attenvi."

"Oh yes. Are you her daughter? She said her daughter was here... you're lucky to have a mother like her... she doesn't look old enough...." Peka refrained from violence and waited until the torrent ceased. The man finally quit talking and picked up the shipcom to ask for her mother.

"You're early," her mother said, stepping out the access hatch. "Would you like to come aboard and see my cabin?"

"No thanks." Be trapped in a small space—no doubt immaculate—with her mother?

"Lead on, then," her mother said cheerfully, and started toward the corridor herself. Peka had to scurry to keep up. Lead on, indeed. She stretched her legs— she *was* as tall as her mother—and caught up. This was her station, and she would lead the way.

"Do you like it out here?" her mother asked at dinner. They were seated in one of the little alcoves of Fred's Place, at present the only independent eating place on the station. Since it was two decades to payday, they had the place to themselves except for another pair of passengers from the *Perrymos*.

Peka nodded, and hurried to swallow her mouthful of fried rice. "It's... stimulating," she said. That seemed the safest adjective. Her mother looked up at her.

"Is that all? What about men... are you meeting anyone interesting?"

"They're fine, Mother, really." She hadn't talked to her mother about boys— men—since her sixteenth birthday, when her mother had taken her in for her first implant. *I won't pry,* her mother had said, and she hadn't. It was too late to start now.

"Well... have you heard from your father lately?"

"What brought that up?" she asked, before she could censor it. No question that her mother would notice the hostility.

"Sorry if it's a touchy point," her mother said, brows raised. "I only wondered… at one time, I recall, you said you didn't want to hear from him again."

"I don't." Peka tried not to let the anger out, but it was stuck in her throat, choking her. "I haven't heard—since graduation, I think." A graduation her mother had not attended because she was consulting somewhere, in another system, and couldn't come back for just that day. She had understood even then, but it still rankled.

"I wish you'd tell me what upset you so," her mother said. Of course her mother didn't understand; her mother had had a wonderful father, a father who was there. She could not tell her mother what her father had said, those damning words that had put an end to the last of her childhood innocence, her trust. "Please," her mother said quietly. "It's been several years, you say. It's still bothering you. You need to get it out."

She had never been able to resist that voice when it was quiet and reasonable. She would have to say, but she didn't have to say it the way he had said it. "He said it was—that I was—just an accident."

Her mother's face paled to the color of the tablecloth. "He said *what?*"

Anger surged out of control. "He said I was an accident!" Peka yelled. "An *accident.* The great engineer who doesn't believe in accidents had… an… accident!" From the corner of her eye she saw heads turn, the other two diners glancing quickly toward her and away, and leaning to each other. A waiter paused in midstride, then dodged through the kitchen door.

"No. You were not an accident." Her mother had flushed now, unbecoming patches of red on her spacer-pale skin.

"Right." With that great blast, all her strength left her; Peka wanted to sink through the chair into the deck and disappear. She could not look across the table.

"I… loved him," her mother said, in the same even, reasonable tone. "Louse though he was, in many ways, I did love him. He was everything I wasn't. Irresponsible, spontaneous, gregarious… just being around him was like an endless party. And he liked me. Loved me, within the limits of his ability…"

"Love *is* responsibility," Peka said, quoting. She ran her finger around and around the plate. "Love is acts, not feelings or words."

Her mother sighed. "I taught you very well. Too well, maybe. Yes, that's the kind of love parents must have, to be parents together… and any parent to a child, to be a good parent. Anything less won't survive, won't sustain the child. But there's a… a chaotic quality, an incalculable dimension. I fell in love with him, and he with me, and together we engendered you—"

"By accident," Peka insisted.

"No. Not on my part." A long pause. "It's—it's difficult to explain, and harder now because those feelings are so far back. But—I wanted a child. Wanted *his* child, his genes mixed with mine, to temper my own rock-ribbed values. He said he wanted a child too, but—as it turned out, he didn't."

"He has others—" Peka remembered their pictures, a row of pretty children standing in front of a wide white door.

"Yes. And a compliant, sweet wife who brought them up while he voyaged from system to system."

"You know her?"

"I met her, of course. Court-ordered family therapy, to determine whether you should be removed from my custody and given to him. Luckily—or I thought it was luckily—his wife was pregnant with twins and didn't want you. You couldn't possibly remember, but you were a very imperious three. You explained to the judge that it was rude to drink in front of others without offering them anything. You explained to the therapist when she tried to give you a developmental test that you didn't make guesses… you either knew the answer or not, and it was foolish to pretend otherwise. She said you were too rigid, and Tarah said she couldn't possibly handle you and the twins she knew she was carrying."

Peka thought she did remember the therapist, but not Tarah. She didn't pursue it. "But if he says I was an accident, why was he trying to get custody?" Peka asked. She had no clear idea of how family law worked, but surely the parent suing for custody had to want the child.

"I don't like to say," her mother said, lips tight. Peka knew that look; it was hopeless. But years of training and practice in following chains of logic led her there as if by a map.

"Gramps Tassiday's estate," she said. Her mother looked guilty, which confirmed it. "He was after my *money?*"

"I don't know that for a fact," her mother said quickly. She had never allowed herself an expression of bitterness; she had never allowed Peka to express anger or resentment of her absent father. Consider all sides, she had said. Everyone has reasons, she had said. "But it did seem odd that he hadn't wanted you until after my father died, and the will became available to the public."

Peka could think of nothing more to say. Her mother went on with her meal; Peka tried to do the same but the food stuck in her throat. She glanced around the restaurant. The couple they'd startled had left; she could imagine the story they'd tell. As her gaze shifted past the entrance again, she saw Einos coming in. She ducked her head, hoping he wouldn't see her.

"Peka!" Too late. She had to look up, had to see the alert interest on her mother's face, had to greet him—but he was rushing on, not giving her time. "Peka, there's a problem with the second collar installation—I hate to interrupt, but—"

She could feel her face going hot; bad enough to have lost her poise with her mother, but to have her mother aware that her work had failed… she managed to smile at her mother. "Excuse me—"

"Of course," her mother said. "I hope I'll get to talk to you some more—perhaps if this doesn't take too long…?"

"Have to see," Peka said, struggling with a napkin that seemed determined to stick to her lap. She felt like a preschooler again, clumsy and incapable. Einos wasn't watching her; he was giving her mother the wide-eyed look of admiration he usually gave Peka.

"I'm sorry to interrupt your dinner, ma'am, but I'm glad to have the chance to meet you." He reached out a hand, which her mother took. "I'm Einos Skirados, in traffic control—we're really fortunate to have you on the station—your daughter's been a great help, but there's this problem—"

Rage flooded Peka as she peeled the napkin off and threw it on the table. The scum-sucking rat was going to ask her mother to solve the problem because he thought she had messed up! And her mother would step in, all cool competence, and show everyone why she was famous, and why Peka would always be Alo Attenvi's daughter, not someone with a name and career of her own.

Her mother's voice, ice-edged, stopped her. "Excuse me," she said to Einos. "Are you offering me a contract?"

Einos turned red himself. "Well—not me—I mean, ma'am, I don't have the authority myself, but—but I just thought since you were here, and it was your daughter, you could sort of help her out."

Peka had not seen her mother really angry for years; even now, she was glad when she realized the famous temper was turned on someone else. "Young man, let me make this quite clear. In the first place, I do not take on consulting jobs without a contract. In the second place, I doubt you can afford me— since, as you say, you don't have authorization from your employer. In the third place, you have a perfectly competent engineer—not only one in whose training I have complete confidence, but a member of my family. Even if you were offering me a contract, I wouldn't take it—you have insulted my daughter. If she had asked me first, I might advise her—but in the present circumstances, I think the only advice she needs is to have nothing whatever to do with you."

"But I—" Einos began. Peka's mother ignored him, and looked at Peka.

"I do hope we'll have time to chat after you deal with your problem," her mother said. "You have my number—"

Peka found her voice and her intent at the same moment. "Why don't you come along to my office— perhaps this will only take a few minutes."

"Thank you," her mother said. "Just let me take care of dinner—"

On the way to Peka's office, her mother said nothing. Peka walked along feeling the edges of what had happened like someone exploring the hole where a tooth had fallen out… something had changed, something important, but she wasn't sure yet what it meant. Was it just a hole, or would something grow out of it?

In the office, Peka called up the design stats on one screen, and then called Hal. He looked a little surprised, and not much concerned.

"I thought Einos said you were having dinner with your mother… I told him not to bother you."

"He said it was urgent—some problem with the second collar installation."

"Yeah, but it could've waited an hour or so. But since you're here—" Hal plunged into a description. As often happened during construction, the electrical and other connections in the area had been installed a little differently than the specifications ordered. "It wasn't a bad idea, really, because someone moved the whole thing five or six meters to allow for the bulk cargo handler's turn radius, after they decided to make this the bulk cargo shuttle dock, instead of the one they'd first planned. It makes sense, because this one's in a direct line to service the FTL traffic when we get it. But you weren't here when they rerouted the plumbing, and they didn't document it in the main specs, so you didn't know. Here's the modification—" Hal fed in the local scanner's analysis, and it came up on Peka's screen.

She glanced at her mother, who was studiously ignoring the screen and looking at the framed diplomas on the wall. She could read nothing of her mother's expression. She looked back at the screen.

"What I'd like to do," Hal went on, "is run the connections like so—" New lines, highlighted in the standard red, green, blue, yellow, orange of the necessary components, overlaid the black and white of the original. "My question is whether there's any reason to worry about the interaction of the control power supply with the main lines here—" An arrow showed, along with the measured clearance.

"Let me check," Peka said. She wasn't going to answer off the top of her head, with her mother standing there behind her. She didn't work that way anyway. On another screen, she called up the relevant references, and considered the influence of incoming shuttle avionics as well. Close, but reasonable—but was there a better solution? She peered at the displays, thinking. Something tickled the side of her head that she thought of as the seat of new ideas. "That's reasonably safe," she said to Hal, "but I'd like to come take a look. There's still a possibility, especially if someone's onboard systems were running hot for some reason…"

"That's why I asked," Hal said cheerfully. "Coming down now?"

"I suppose so. Yes." She turned to her mother. "I have to go out to the docking bay—you could wait here, or come along—"

"If you don't mind, I'd love to come," her mother said.

Did she mind? She wasn't sure which she would mind more, leaving her mother here to rummage in her office, or taking her along. Five hours before, either would have been intolerable, but now…. "Come on," she said. "We'll have to get p-suits somewhere. It's aired up, but—" Then she remembered whom she was talking to, and shut up. One chapter in her mother's textbook dealt with safety procedures necessary in chambers at different pressures.

Hal greeted her mother courteously but with none of the covetous glee Einos had expressed. He turned at once to Peka. "Here's the challenge," he said, and then stood quietly to let her get a good look at it. She saw at once that Hal's solution had the virtues of simplicity and directness, which made it hard to put his solution out of her mind to think of her own. She walked back around to the cargo lock side of the docking bay. The bulk handler took up most of the space… it would turn like so… it would have to have service access here and here. She squinted, her mind tickling persistently. Then she saw it.

"Hal, come see this." He looked where she pointed. "If the bulk handler's out of service, they'll push it around here to work on it, and its back panel can bump into this—" she meant the control nexus for the docking collar modification. "Over time, those bumps could shift it enough to allow interference." She looked around the whole compartment. "First, we'll need a safety stop on this bulkhead anyway—we don't want something the mass of that thing bumping it. In fact, we need a double stop, one on the deck and one on the bulkhead." Hal nodded, and made a note.

"We're still going to need to reroute things, but I think it should be the other lines. That's not as bad as it looks—here—" She had sketched it out for him. He took the pad and frowned a moment, then nodded.

"Yes. I see. It takes a bit longer, but it avoids the problem entirely. It's not a patch but a redesign. Good. Thanks, Peka."

"You're welcome," Peka said. "It's my job…"

"If you wouldn't mind—could you come back and give us a go-ahead when we've got the rerouting done and the stops in? Just in case?"

"Of course—got an estimate?"

"Couple of hours, I think. If that's too late—"

"No… you're already working over shift. Just give me a call; I'll have my beeper this time."

Peka led the way out; she signed her mother off the site, and they turned in their p-suits at the section storehouse. Now she was hungry—the dinner she hadn't eaten left an empty hole in her midsection.

"I don't know about you," her mother said, "but I'm still hungry. Is there any place where we can get dessert?"

"Fred's is the only thing, other than the company mess hall. And they'll be through serving dinner by now."

"Ah. Fred's, then—if you don't want to come, don't worry about me. I can find my own way."

"No… I'll come too, but I need to go by the office first and log the changes we're making."

"Who was that very officious young man who interrupted us?" her mother finally asked, as Peka entered notes into her workstation.

"Einos." Peka considered her options and made a clean breast of it. "I've been going out with him—to the limited extent that's possible on this station."

"Oh." Her mother chewed that over in silence.

"It's not… um… serious," Peka said. It might have been, but at the moment she wanted to wring his neck.

"Good," her mother said. "I mean, it's your own business, but—backstabbers don't reform."

"Then how did you fall for my father?" Peka said, shocking herself. Her mother gave her a look she could not read. "Or was that an accident?"

Her mother laughed. "I thought so, at the time. Not my fault, I told myself. Could happen to anyone, bolt from the blue, I told myself. You weren't an accident, but he was, I told myself."

"And now?"

Her mother sighed. "I had years, Peka, to argue that out with myself after you were born, after he left. What is an accident? The effect of a cause you didn't recognize, you didn't anticipate. That's what I was taught, and that's what I had to face. Why did I fall in love with a bright-eyed, laughing, charming young prince with honey-colored curls and blue eyes?"

"Hormones," said Peka drily, amazed at her own temerity. Her mother's laugh this time was almost a bark.

"Excuses," she said. "Not hormones—that would explain falling in lust, maybe, but not what I felt, for that man. Animals have reasonable ways to choose mates, or the species dies. It was no accident… it was the direct result of my family and my beliefs. Because deep down, I let myself think it was no accident, but that other form of causation, destiny."

"Destiny?"

"Fate. Luck. Or, in my grandmother's vernacular, the will of God. Her God, at least, was wont to impose his will pretty firmly—or so she said when imposing it on me. I wanted to believe that there was some supernatural intervention which could get me out of the logical trap I'd built for myself… which could rescue me—"

Peka saw it all, in one flash of insight. "And so you blamed me," she breathed. "For proving it wasn't that at all, and you had after all done it to yourself…"

"Good grief, no!" That with enough force, enough stunned surprise and horror, to convince. "I never blamed you. You were the one good thing that came out of it."

"But you always said—"

"I didn't want you to make my mistakes, of course. That's all. I had my family's mistakes to avoid: women who had married obvious losers out of duty to some social scheme, women who had buried their brains in the waste recycler. A family—a culture really—which believed that accidents not only happen, it's almost impious to prevent them. After all, how can you work up a good case of blame-

and-guilt if there are no accidents?"

Peka had never heard this. She wondered if she were being cozened; her mother had always been smarter. But her mother went on.

"You asked one time why we never visited my relatives that much—I know you thought I disapproved of them."

"Yes…" Peka said cautiously.

"I was scared of them," her mother said. "I can't—even now—talk about my grandmother's beliefs, her influence on me, without getting a cold sweat."

Her mother? Her famous, much-honored, much-published mother? Still that twitchy about people from her past? That didn't bode well for Peka's own middle and old age. She didn't say that.

"It was all reaction," her mother said. "And it always is, generation after generation, and you don't know it before you've gone and had children and started another daisy chain of complication. Accidents have causes. Actions have consequences. I reacted to my family, and—by no accident, but the logic of human development—fell in love with your father. Wanted his child—you cannot know how much, or how dearly, until you want a child of your own. Brought you up to avoid my mistakes, and presented you with the opportunity to make your own, equally grave ones."

"Like what?" Peka asked, her mouth dry.

Her mother looked at her, that appraising dark eye that had been scanning the inside of her head forever. "So far, my dear, you haven't… but I can't assume you won't. The thing is, you aren't an accident: neither in your conception, nor in your birth, nor in your upbringing, nor in your self as you are now. You are the result, the consequence, of causes and actions which, if you know them, may allow you more leeway than most. At least you understand—*really* understand—how causation works."

"You've made me," Peka said.

"I gave you half your genetic material and all your early training," her mother corrected. "But you began making yourself from the joining of egg and sperm— and you withstood a good bit of my influence even as a small child." She grinned, the most relaxed look yet. Peka had always known that grin meant the storm was nearly over; her mother's good humor, once aroused, lasted far longer than her tempers. "And the further you go, the more you will be your own creation."

"Another safety expert," Peka said, not quite as a question.

"Not like me," her mother said. "I didn't hover, while you were in college, but they kept telling me— and I've looked at your work here. You don't solve the same problems the same way I do. You have a… a quirk, a twist, to your work that I find startling— but very elegant, once I understand it."

"You do?" Peka couldn't keep her voice from squeaking. She choked back the *Really? Really?* that wanted to beg for more.

"Yes," her mother said. She wasn't looking at Peka now; she was looking at the plots on the wall. "Look at this—this collar redesign. I'd have changed it from the annular orifice to a linear slot, perhaps with one end square—something different from the other end. That would have meant redesigning the shuttle docking probe *and* the collar, classic lock-and-key design. Your solution would never have occurred to me."

"But it—" She didn't want to say "but this was obvious" to her mother, her sainted and brilliant mother for whom it had not been obvious.

"You're not me; I'm not you." That platitude came out with all the force of divine decree. Peka wondered if her mother's head still echoed with her grandmother's religious fervor. "Your work is elegant, my dear— not only right, but right with a flair all your own. That's not an accident either—I suspect your father's genetics did exactly what I'd hoped, and gave you some abilities I don't have." Her mother smiled at her, a smile without an edge. Then she yawned, and blinked. "On the other hand, I'm thirty years older than you, and I'm running out of steam. If I want morning to feel like good fortune, I'd better skip dessert and go back to my berth."

Peka came back to the shuttle docking bay three hours later, when Hal called. She had walked out to the ship with her mother, then stopped on the way back for a bosonburger at Higg's. Now, as she nodded over the changes Hal and his crew had made, and entered them all in the main stats file, she felt better than she had all day.

Not an accident. Ladders of causation fell from the windows of the burning tenement, step after step leading to safety... her mind might be going up in smoke, but she could still escape. Acts have consequences. Accidents don't just happen.

When Einos Skirados showed up in her office the next day, with a box of her favorite candy and a bouquet of apologies, her first reaction was the old familiar one that had made her so happy to go out with him.

She looked at the bright brown eyes, the sleek dark hair, the composed face; her mind brought up his resume. Here was her accident, if she lied to herself; she had the hormones, and plenty of them.

"Not only accidents have causes," her mother had pointed out as she left. "So do the best plans ever laid, the ones that come to good ends."

She smiled at Einos Skirados with no more than professional courtesy. "No, thank you," she said. "I already have plans for this evening."

And so she did. Somewhere in her future loomed the fortunate accident she wanted... and she had better start causing it.

NEW WORLD SYMPHONY

It was his first world. On the way out, resting in the half-doze of transfer, he imagined many things. A fire world, all volcanic and rough, showers of sparks against a night sky, clouds of steam and ash, firelit. Or a water world like Pella, with all the endless quivering shades of color, the blues and silvers, purples and strange greens. It might have mountains like Lelare, a purple sky, six moons or none, rings like golden Saturn's, rainbowed arcs... he saw against the screen of his mind these and other worlds, some seen once in pictures, others created from his mind's store of images.

All he knew for certain was that no one yet had set foot on it. Only two probes had been there: the robot survey, which had noted it as a possible, and the manned scout, which had given it a 6.7, a marginal rating, out of 10. He didn't know why the rating was 6.7; he knew he might not have understood it even if they'd told him. It had been approved, and then assigned, and he—just out of the Academy, just past his thesis—he had been given that assignment

He half-heard something in his chamber, felt a pressure on his arm, hands touching his face. He struggled to open his eyes, and heard the quiet voice he had heard so far ago.

"Please, sir, wait a moment. It's all right; you're rousing now. Take a deep breath first... good. Another. Move your right hand, please..."

He felt his fingers shift, stiffly at first, then more easily. More than anything else, the reported stiffening had frightened him: his hands were his life. But they'd explained, insisted that it was no more than missing a single week of practice, not the three years of the voyage. He moved his left hand, then tried again with his eyelids. This time they opened, and he had no trouble focussing on the medical attendant. Gray hair, brown eyes, the same quiet face that had put him in his couch back at the station.

He wanted to ask if they had arrived, and felt childish in that desire. The attendant smiled, helped him sit and swing his legs over the edge of the couch. "Your first meal, sir; it's important that you eat before standing." He pushed over a sliding table with a tray of food. "Do you recall your name, sir?"

Until he was asked, he hadn't thought of it. For a moment the concept of his name eluded him. Then he remembered, clearly and completely. "Of course," he said. "Georges Mantenon. Musician-graduate."

"Yes, sir." The attendant fastened a strap around his left arm while he ate with his right. "I must check this, just a moment."

Mantenon paid no attention to the attendant; he knew the man wouldn't answer medical questions, and even if he did it would tell him nothing. He had an appetite; the Class Three food tasted the same as always. His hands felt better every moment. He held his left arm still until the medical attendant was through with it, and went on eating.

When he'd finished, the other man showed him to a suite of rooms: bath, workroom, sitting room. Along one wall of the workroom was the keyboard/pedal complex of a Meirinhoff, the same model he'd used for his thesis. He made himself shower and change before climbing into it. He adjusted the seat, the angle of keyboard and pedal banks, the length of cord from the headpiece to output generator. Then he touched the keys, lightly, and felt/heard/saw the Meirinhoff awake.

His fingers danced along the keyboard, touching section controls as well as pitch/resonance indicators. Woodwinds, brass—he felt festive, suddenly aware that he'd been afraid, even during the transfer dreams. He toed a percussion pedal, tipped it off. Wrong blend, wrong tempo. For a long moment he struggled with the pedals, then remembered what was wrong. He'd put on exactly what the attendant laid out, which meant he had on slippers.

Slippers! He scraped them off with his toes, and kicked them out of the way. His toes, surgically freed at the metatarsal, and held for walking by special pads in his shoes (not that he walked much), spread wide. Years of practice had given him amazing reach. He tried again for the percussion he wanted, toed cymbal on delay, pitched the snares down a tone, added the bright dash of the triangle. He played with balance, shifting fingers and toes minutely until the sound in the phones matched that in his head. Then he paused, hands and feet still.

His head dipped, so that the subvoc microphone touched the angle of his larynx. His hands lifted briefly, his toes curled up. Then he reached out, curling his tongue up in his mouth to let the clean sound come free, and put the Meirinhoff on full audio/record. He could feel, through his fingers, his feet, his seat, the wave of sound, the wave he designed, drove, controlled, shaped, and finally, after two glorious minutes of play, subdued. He lay back in his seat, fully relaxed, and tapped the system off audio.

"Sir?" The voice brought him upright, the short cord of the headset dragging at his ears.

"Klarge!" It was the worst oath he knew, and he meant it. No one, *no one,* not even a full professor, would walk in on someone who had just composed. And for someone who had had no outlet for years—! He pulled off the headset and glared at the person standing in the doorway. Not the medical attendant; that blue uniform meant ship's crew, and the decorative braid all over the front probably meant some rank. He forced a smile to his face. "Sorry," he said, achieving an icy tone. "It is not usual to interrupt a composition."

"I didn't," the person pointed out. He realized she was a woman. "You had finished, I believe; I did not speak until you had turned off the audio."

Mantenon frowned. "Nonetheless—"

"The captain wishes to speak with you," said the woman. "About projecting all that without warning."

"Projecting—?" He was confused. "All I did was compose—that's my job."

"You had that thing on external audio," she said, "and you nearly blasted our ears out with it. You're not supposed to be hooked up to the ship's speakers without permission."'

"Was I?" He remembered, now he came to think of it, something the attendant had said about the bank of switches near the console. He had been so glad to see the Meirinhoff, he hadn't paid much attention. He gave a quick glance at the recording timer: two minutes fifteen seconds—quite a long time, actually, if they didn't know it was coming or how to interrupt it.

"You were." Her mouth quirked; he realized she was trying not to laugh at him. "Your suite has an override for anything but emergency; that's so we could hear if anything was wrong." She nodded at the Meirinhoff. "That was more than we bargained on."

"I'm sorry. I—it had just been so long, and I didn't know the hookup was on…" He hadn't felt so stupid since his second year in the conservatory. He knew his ears were red; he could feel them burning.

"All right. I understand it wasn't intentional. I'd thought maybe you were going to insist that we listen to every note you played—"

"Klarge, no! Of course not. But the captain—?"

She grinned at him. "I'm the captain, Mr. Mantenon. Captain Plessan. You probably don't recall meeting me before; you were sedated when they brought you aboard."

"Oh." He couldn't think of anything to say, polite or otherwise. "I'm sorry about the speakers—"

"Just remember the switch, please. And when you've recovered fully, I'd be glad to see you in the crew lounge."

"I'm—I'm fine now, really—" He started clambering free of the Meirinhoff, flipping controls off, resetting the recorders, fumbling for his slippers. He'd like to have stayed, listened to his composition, refined it, but everything he'd been told about shipboard etiquette urged him to go at once. He'd already insulted the captain enough as it was.

He had hoped the lounge viewscreens would be on, but blue drapes with the Exploration Service insignia covered them. The captain waved her hand at them. "You were probably hoping to see your world, Mr. Mantenon, but regulations forbid me to allow you a view until your initial briefing is complete. You must then sign your acceptance of the contract, and acknowledge all the warnings. Only then can I allow you to see the world."

"And how long will that be?"

"Not long. Only a few hours, I expect." A chime rang out, mellow, with overtones he recognized at once. Several others came into the lounge, and the captain introduced them. Senior crew: officers, the Security team, medical, heads of departments. These would see to his needs, as well as the ship's needs, in the coming months. He tried to pay attention to them, and then to the final briefing the captain gave, but all he could think of was the new world, the unknown world, that hung in space outside the ship. He signed the papers quickly, glancing through them only enough to be sure that the Musician's Union had put its authorization on each page. What would that world be like? Would he be able to express its unique beauty in music, as his contract specified, or would he fail?

At last the formalities were over. The other crewmembers left, and the captain touched controls that eased the curtains back over the viewscreens and switched video to the lounge.

His first thought was simply *NO*. No, I don't like this world. No, I can't do this world. No, someone's made a mistake, and it's impossible, and it wouldn't take a musician to express this world in sound. A large crunching noise would do the job. His trained mind showed him the score for the crunching noise, for both Meirinhoff and live orchestra, and elaborated a bit. He ignored it and stared at the captain. "That?" he asked.

"That," she said. "It's going to be a mining world."

That was obvious. Whatever it was good for, anything that disgusting shade of orange streaked with fungus-blue wasn't a pleasure world, or an agriculture world. That left mining. He forced himself to look at the screens again. Orange, shading from almost sulfur yellow to an unhealthy orange-brown. The blue couldn't be water, not that shade... he thought of bread mold again. Something vaguely greenish blue, and a sort of purplish patch toward the bottom... if that was the bottom.

"Does it have any moons or anything?" he asked.

"All that information is in the cube I gave you, but yes, it has three of them. Let me change the mags, here, and you'll see..." She punched a few buttons and the planet seemed to recede. Now he saw two moons, one small and pale yellow, the other one glistening white. "I'll leave you now," she said. "Please don't use the ship speakers for your composition without letting me know, and if you need anything just ask." And without another word she turned and left him.

Monster, he thought, and wasn't sure if he meant the planet or the captain. Ugly bastard—that was the planet. Someone must have made a mistake. He'd been told—he'd been *assured*—that Psych service had made assignments based on his personality profile and the planet's characteristics. The planet was supposed to represent something central to his creativity, and draw on the main vectors of his genius. Or something like that; he couldn't quite remember the exact words. But if he hated it from the beginning, something was wrong. He'd expected to have to court a reaction, the way he'd had to do with so many projects: the Karnery vase, the square of blue wool carpet, the single fan-shaped shell. Each of those had become an acceptable composition only after days of living with each object, experiencing it and its space, and the delicate shifts his mind made in response.

But he saw nothing delicate in that planet. And nothing delicate in his response. It hung gross and ugly in the sky, an abomination, like a rotting gourd; he imagined he could smell it. He could not—he *would* not—commit that atrocity to music.

In spite of himself, a melodic line crawled across his brain, trailing harmonies and notations for woodwinds. He felt his fingers flex, felt himself yearning for the Meirinhoff. No. It was ridiculous. Anything he might compose in this disgust would be itself disgusting. His study was beauty; his business was beauty. He glanced at the viewscreen again. The white moon had waned to a nail paring; the yellow one was hardly more than half-full. He wondered how fast they moved, how fast the ship moved. How could they be in orbit around the planet, and yet outside its moons' orbits? He wished he'd paid more attention to his briefings on astro-science. He remembered the cube in his hand, and sighed. Maybe that would tell him more, would explain how this world could possibly be considered a match for him.

But after the cube, he was just as confused. It gave information: diameter, mass, characteristics of the star the planet circled, characteristics of atmosphere (unbreathable), native life forms (none noted by surveys), chemical analysis, and so on and so on. Nothing else; nothing that gave him any idea why the psychs would pick that planet for him.

Restless, he moved over to the Meirinhoff. He couldn't tell the captain no, not after signing the contract. He had to compose something. He checked to make sure he was not hooked into the speaker system and climbed back into his instrument. At least he could refine that *crunch* of dismay… it might make an accent in something else, sometime.

With his eyes closed, he stroked the keys, the buttons, the pedals, bringing first one section then another into prominence, extrapolating from what he heard in the earphones to the whole sound, once freed. The crunch, once he had it to his satisfaction, became the sound a large gourd makes landing on stone... he remembered that from his boyhood. And after, the liquid splatter, the sound of seeds striking... in his mind a seed flew up, hung, whirling in the air like a tiny satellite, a pale yellow moon, waxing and waning as his mind held the image. He noted that on subvoc, recorded that section again.

The melody that had first come to him, the one he'd suppressed, came again, demanding this time its accompaniment of woodwinds. He called up bassoon, then the Sulesean variant, even deeper of pitch, and hardly playable by a human. Above it, the oboe and teroe. He needed another, split the oboe part quickly and transposed pedals to woodwinds, his toes and fingers racing while the thought lasted. He wasn't sure it had anything to do with the planet, but he liked it. He paused, then, and called the recordings back into the earphones.

The crunch: massive, final, definitive. A long pause... he counted measures this time, amazed at the length of it before the splattering sounds, the flute and cello that defined the seed/satellite. He stopped the playback, and thought a moment, lips pursed. It was a conceit, that seed, and maybe too easy... but for now, he'd leave it in. He sent the replay on. The melody was all right—in fact, it was good—but it had no relation to the preceding music. He'd have to move it somewhere, but he'd save it. He marked the section for relabelling, and lay back, breathing a little heavily and wondering what time it was.

The clock, when he noticed it on the opposite wall, revealed that he'd spent over three hours in the Meirinhoff. No wonder he was tired and hungry. He felt a little smug about it, how hard he'd worked on his first day out of transfer, as he levered himself out of the instrument and headed for the shower.

In the next days, he found himself working just as hard. An hour or so in the lounge alone, watching the planet in the viewscreen, changing magnification from time to time. Disgust waned to distaste, and then to indifference. It was not responsible, after all, for how it looked to him. The planet could not know his struggles to appreciate it, to turn its mineral wealth, its ugly lifeless surface, into a work of art.

And when he could look at it no longer, when he found himself picking up what little reading material the ship's crew left lying about, he returned to his instrument, to the Meirinhoff, and fastened himself into that embrace of mingled struggle and pleasure. His mind wandered to the Academy, to the lectures on esthetic theory, on music law, all those things he'd found so dull at the time. He called up and reread the section in General Statutes about colonization and exploitation of new worlds, until he could recite it word for word, and the rhythm worked itself into his composition.

"It is essential that each new world be incorporated into the species ethic and emotional milieu…" Actually it didn't make much sense. If it hadn't been for whoever wrote that, though, most musicians wouldn't have a job. The decision to send musicians and artists to each newly discovered, rated world, before anyone actually landed on it, and to include artists and musicians on each exploration landing team had provided thousands of places for those with talent. Out of that effort had come some superb music and art—Keller's "Morning on Moondog," and the ballet *Gia's Web* by Annette Polacek—and plenty of popular stuff. Miners, colonists, explorers—they all seemed to want music and art created for "their" world, whatever it was. Mantenon had heard the facile and shallow waltzes Tully Conover wrote for an obscure cluster of mining worlds: everyone knew "Mineral Waltz," "Left by Lead," and the others. And in art, the thousands of undistinguished visuals of space views: ringed planets hanging over moons of every color and shape, twinned planets circling one another… but it sold, and supported the system, and that was what counted.

Georges Mantenon had hoped—had believed—he could do better. If nothing as great as *Gia's Web,* he could compose at least as well as Metzger, whose *Symphony Purple* was presented in the Academy as an example of what they were to do. Mantenon had been honored with a recording slot for two of his student compositions. One of them had even been optioned by an off-planet recording company. The Academy would get the royalties, if any, of course. Students weren't allowed to earn money from their music. Still, he had been aware that his teachers considered him especially gifted. But with a miserable, disgusting orange ball streaked with blue fungus—how could he do anything particularly worthy? The square of blue carpet had been easy compared to this.

He tried one arrangement after another of the melody and variations he'd already composed, shifting parts from one instrument to another, changing keys, moving the melody itself from an entrance to a climax to a conclusion. Nothing worked. Outside, in the screens, he saw the same ugly world; if his early disgust softened into indifference, it never warmed into anything better. He could not, however calmly he looked, see anything beautiful about it. The moons were better—slightly—and the third, when it finally appeared around the planet's limb, was a striking lavender. He liked that, found his mind responding with a graceful flourish of strings. But it was not enough. It fit nowhere with the rest of the composition—if it could be called a composition—and by itself it could not support his contract.

He had hardly noticed, in those early days, that he rarely saw any of the crew, and when he did, they never asked about his work. He would have been shocked if they had asked: he was, after all, a licensed creative artist, whose work was carried out in as much isolation as Security granted any of the Union's citizens. Yet when he came into the crew lounge, after struggling several hours with his arrangement for the lavender moon, and found it empty as usual, he was restless and dissatisfied. He couldn't, he thought grumpily, do it *all* himself. He lay back on the long couch under the viewport and waited. Someone would have to come in eventually, and he'd insist, this time, that they talk to him.

The first to appear was a stocky woman in a plain uniform—no braid at all. She nodded at him, and went to the dispenser for a mug of something that steamed. Then she sat down, facing slightly away from him, inserted a plug in her ear, and thumbed the control of a cubescreen before he could get his mouth shaped to speak to her. He sat there, staring, aware that his mouth was still slightly open, and fumed. She could at least have said hello. He turned away politely, shutting his mouth again, and folded his arms. Next time he'd be quicker.

But the next person to come in ignored him completely, walked straight to the other woman and leaned over her, whispering something he could not hear. It was a man Mantenon had never seen before, with a single strip of blue braid on his collar. The woman turned, flipped off the cubescreen, and removed her earplug. The man sat beside her, and they talked in low voices; Mantenon could hear the hum, but none of the words. After a few minutes, the two of them left, with a casual glance at Mantenon that made him feel like a crumpled food tray someone had left on the floor. He could feel the pulse beating in his throat, anger's metronome, and a quick snarl of brass and percussion rang in his head. It wasn't bad, actually... he let himself work up the scoring for it.

When he opened his eyes again, one of the med techs stood beside him, looking worried.

"Are you all right, sir?"

"Of course," said Mantenon, a bit sharper than he meant. "I was just thinking of something." He sat up straighter. "I'm fine."

"Have you been overworking?"

He opened his mouth to say no, and then stopped. Maybe he had been.

"Are you feeling paranoid, sir?" asked the med tech.

"Paranoid?"

"Does it seem that everyone is watching you, or talking about you, or refusing to help you?"

"Well..." If his bad mood was a medical problem, maybe they would give him a pill or shot, and he'd be able to compose something better. He nodded, finally, and as he had hoped, the med tech handed him a foil packet.

"Take this, sir, with a cup of something hot—and you really ought to eat your meals with the crew for a day or so."

Med could override his artist's privileges, he remembered suddenly—if they thought he was sick, or going crazy, they would tell Security, and he'd be put on full monitor, like everyone else.

He made himself smile. "You may be right," he said. "I guess I started working, and just forgot about meals and things."

The med tech was smiling now, and even brought him a hot drink from the dispenser. "Here. You'll feel better soon. Shall I tell the captain you'll be eating with crew today?"

He nodded, gulping down the green pill in the packet with a bitter cup of Estrain tea.

He showered and changed for the next meal, unsure which it would be, and walked into the crew mess to find himself confronted with piles of sweet ration squares and fruit mush. He forced himself to smile again. He had hoped for midmeal or latemeal, when the ration squares were flavored like stew of various kinds. Sweets made his head ache. But the med tech, halfway around the ring, waved to him, and Mantenon edged past others to his side.

The yellow ones aren't sweet," the med tech said. He handed over a yellow square and a bowl of mush. "You'll like it better than the brown ones."

Mantenon found the yellow squares similar to the ones he had had delivered to his suite: those were orange, but the taste was the same, or nearly so. He ate two yellow squares while listening to the others talk. None of it made sense to him. It was all gossip about crewmembers—who was sleeping with whom, or having trouble with a supervisor—or tech talk, full of numbers and strange words. Finally someone across the ring spoke to him, in a tone which seemed to carry humor.

"Well, Mr. Mantenon—how's your music coming?"

He choked on his bite of ration, swallowed carefully, and folded his hands politely to answer.

"It's… well, it's coming. It's still unsettled."

"Unsettled?" The questioner, Mantenon now realized, was the same stocky woman he'd seen earlier in the lounge.

"Yes, it—" His hands began to wave as he talked, mimicking their movements on the Meirinhoff. "It's got some good themes, now, but the overall structure isn't settled yet."

"Don't you plan the structure first?" asked someone else, a tall person with two green braids on his collar. "I would think rational planning would be necessary…"

Mantenon smiled. "Sir, your pardon, but it is not the way creative artists work. We are taught to respond to a stimulus freely, with no preconceptions of what form might be best. When we have all the responses, then we shape those into whatever structure the music itself will bear."

"But how do you know…?"

"That's what our training is for." He dipped a bite of fruit mush, swallowed it, and went on. "Once we have the responses, then our training shows us what structure is best for it."

The tall man frowned. "I would have thought the stimulus would determine the correct structure… surely anything as large as a planet would call for a serious, major work—"

"Oh no, Kiry!" That was a young woman who hadn't spoken before. "Don't you remember *Asa's Dream*? It's just that short, poignant dance, and yet the planet was that big pair of gas giants over in Harker's Domain. I've seen a cube of them: it's perfect."

"Or the truly *sinister* first movement of Manoken's 5th Symphony," said Mantenon, regaining control of his audience. "That was not even a planet… he wrote that it was inspired by the reflections of light on the inside of his sleepcase." They all chuckled, some more brightly than others, and Mantenon finished his breakfast. The med tech seemed to be watching him, but he expected that.

That day he incorporated the bits he'd scored in the crew lounge—the "anger movement" as he thought of it—into his main piece. It was the planet's response to the insult of his initial crunch; for a moment he wondered about himself, imputing emotions to planets, but decided that it was normal for an artist. He wouldn't tell Med about it. And at latemeal, several crew chose to sit near him, including him casually in their chatter with questions about well-known pieces of music and performers. He felt much better.

Still, when he decided, several days later, that his composition was complete and adequate, he had his doubts. The planet was ugly. Had he really made something beautiful out of it—and if he had, was he rendering (as he was sworn to do) its essential nature? Would someone else, seeing that planet after hearing his music, feel that it fit? Or would that future hearer laugh?

That doubt kept him doodling at the console another few days, making minute changes in the scoring, and then changing them back. He spent one whole working shift rooting through the music references he'd brought along, checking his work as if he were analyzing someone else's. But that told him only what he already knew: it had a somewhat unconventional structure (but not wildly so), it was playable by any standard orchestra (as defined by the Musicians Union), it could be adapted for student or limited orchestras (for which he would earn a bonus), none of the instruments were required to play near their limits. It would classify as moderately difficult to play, and difficult to conduct, and it contained all the recommended sections for a qualification work (another bonus): changes in tempo, changes from simple to complex harmonics, direct and indirect key changes.

He played it back, into the headphones, with full orchestration, and shook his head. It was what it was, and either it would do, or it wouldn't. And this time he could not depend on a panel of professors to check his work and screen out anything unworthy. This time, if he judged it wrongly, the whole CUG system would know. He frowned, but finally reached for one of the unused memory cubes and slid it into place. And punched the controls for "Final Record: Seal/No Recall." It was done.

With the cube in hand, and the backup cubes in his personal lockbin, he made his way to the lounge area once more. The curtains were drawn; the captain sat on one of the couches. He opened his mouth, and realized that she already knew he'd finished. Security must keep a closer watch on musicians than he'd thought. He wondered if they'd listened to his music as well... he'd been told that no one did, without permission of the artist, but Security was everywhere.

The captain smiled. "Well—and so you've finished, Mr. Mantenon. And we've not heard it yet..."

"Do—do you want to?" He felt himself blushing again, and hated it. Yet he wanted her to hear the music, wanted her to be swept away by it, to see and feel what he had seen and felt about that planet.

"It would be an honor," she said. He watched the flicker of her eyelid. Was it amusement? Weariness? Or genuine interest? He couldn't tell. He wavered, but finally his eagerness overcame him, and he handed her the cube.

"Here," he said. "It runs about twenty-nine, Standard."

"So much work for this," she said, with no irony, holding the cube carefully above the slot. "Twenty-nine minutes of music from—how many weeks of work?"

He couldn't remember, and didn't care. Now that she held it, he wanted her to go on and play the thing. He had to see her reaction, good or bad, had to know whether he'd truly finished. "Go on," he said, and then remembered that she was the captain. "If you want to." She smiled again.

Played on the lounge sound system, it was different, changed by the room's acoustics and the less agile speakers which were not meant to have the precision of the Meirinhoff's wave generators. Even so, and even with the volume held down, Mantenon thought it was good. And so, evidently, did the captain; he had been taught to notice the reactions of the audience to both live and replayed performances. Smiles could be faked, but not the minute changes in posture, in breathing, even pulse rate that powerful music evoked. In the final version, his original reaction framed the whole composition, the *crunch* split, literally, in mid-dissonance, and the interstice filled with the reaction, counterreaction, interplay of themes and melodies. Then the crunch again, cutting off all discussion, and the final splatter of the seeds—the moons. As the cube ended, Mantenon waited tensely for the captain's reaction.

It came, along with a clatter of applause from the speakers—she had switched the lounge sound system to transmission, and the crew evidently liked it as well as she did.

Mantenon felt his ears burning again, this time with pleasure. They were used to hauling musicians; they must have heard many new pieces... and he... he had pleased them.

The captain handed his cube back to him. "Remarkable, Mr. Mantenon. It always amazes me, the responses you artists and musicians give..."

"Thank you. Is it possible—excuse me, Captain, but I don't know the procedure—is it possible to transmit this for registry?"

Her expression changed: wariness, tension, something else he couldn't read, swiftly overlaid by a soothing smile. "Mr. Mantenon, it is registered. You mean you weren't aware that immediate... transmission... for registry was part of the Musicians Union contract with this vessel?"

"No. I thought... well, I didn't really think about it." He was still puzzled. He remembered—he was sure he remembered—that the licensed musician had to personally initiate transmission and registration of a composition. But Music Law had always been his least favorite subject. Maybe it was different the first time out.

"You should have read your contract more carefully." She leaned back in her seat, considering him. "Whenever you're employed to do the initial creative survey, you're on CUG Naval vessels, right?"

"Well... yes."

"It's different for landing parties, though not much. But here, all communication with the outside must be controlled by CUG Security, in order to certify your location, among other things. In compensation for this, we offer immediate registration, datemarked local time. You *did* know there was a bonus for completion within a certain time?"

"Yes, I did. But—does this mean we aren't going back soon?"

"Not to Central Five, no. Not until the survey's complete."

"Survey?" Mantenon stared at her, stunned.

"Yes—you really didn't read your contract, did you?"

"Well, I—"

"Mr. Mantenon, this was just the *first* of your assignments. Surely you don't think CUG would send a ship to each separate planet just for artistic cataloging, do you? There are seven more planets in this system, and twelve in the next, before we start back."

"I... don't believe it!" He would have shouted, but shock had taken all his breath. Nineteen *more* planets? When the first one had taken... he tried to think, and still wasn't sure... however many weeks it had been. The captain's smile was thinner. She held out a fac of his contract.

"Look again, Mr. Mantenon." He took it, and sat, hardly realizing that the captain had settled again in her seat to watch him.

The first paragraph was familiar: his name, his array of numbers for citizenship, licensure, Union membership, the name of the ship (CSN *Congarsin*, he noted), references to standard calendars and standard clocks. The second paragraph... he slowed, reading it word for word. "...to compose such work as suitably expresses, to the artist, the essential truth of the said celestial body in such manner..." was a standard phrase. There was specification of bonuses for instrumentation, vocal range, difficulty, and time... but where Mantenon expected to find "... on completion of this single work..." he read instead, with growing alarm, "... on completion of the works enumerated in the appendix, the musician shall be transported to his point of origin or to some registered port equidistant from the ship's then location as shall be acceptable to him, providing that the necessary duties of the CUG vessel involved allow. In lieu of such transportation, the musician agrees to accept..." But he stopped there, and turned quickly to the appendix. There, just as the captain had said, was a complete listing of the "celestial bodies to be surveyed musically." Eight of eleven planets in the CGSx1764 system, and twelve of fifteen planets in the CGSx1766 system. It even gave an estimated elapsed time for travel and "setup," whatever that was... cumulative as... Mantenon choked.

"Twenty-four *years!*"

"With that many planets in each system, Mr. Mantenon, we'll be traveling almost all the time on in-system drive."

"But—but that means by the time we finish, I'll be—" he tried to calculate it, but the captain was faster.

"By the time we return to Central Five, if we do, you'll be near sixty, Mr. Mantenon... and a very famous composer, if your first work is any indication of your ability."

"But I thought I'd—I planned to conduct its premier..." He had imagined himself back at the Academy, rehearsing its orchestra on their first run through his own music. If not his first contract composition, then a later one. "It's not fair!" he burst out. "It's... they told us that Psych picked our first contracts, to help us, and they gave me that disgusting *mess* out there, and then this!"

"To help you, or best suited to you?" The captain's lips quirked, and he stared at her, fascinated. Before he could answer, she went on. "Best suited, I believe, is what you were told... just as you were told to read your contract before signing it."

"Well, but I—I assumed they'd screened them..."

"And you were eager to go off-world. You requested primary music survey, that's in your file. You asked for this—"

And with a rush of despair he remembered that he had, indeed, asked for this, in a way he hoped the captain did not know—but he feared she did. He had been too exceptional... he had challenged his professors, the resident composers, he had been entirely too adventurous to be comfortable. When he looked at the captain, she was smiling in a way that made her knowledge clear.

"The Union has a way of handling misfits, Mr. Mantenon, while making use of their talents. Adventure, pioneering, is held in high esteem—because, as a wise reformer on old Earth once said, it keeps the adventurers far away from home." And with a polite nod, she left him sitting there.

He knew there was nothing he could do. He was a musician, not a rebel; a musician, not a pioneer; a musician, not a fighter. Without the special shoes to counteract the surgery on his feet, he couldn't even walk down the hall. Besides, he didn't want to cause trouble: he wanted to compose his music, and have it played, and—he had to admit—he wanted to be known.

And this they had taken away. They would use his music for their own ends, but he would never hear it played. He would never stand before the live orchestra—that anachronism which nonetheless made the best music even more exciting—he would never stand there, alight with the power that baton gave him, and bring his music out of all those bits of wood and metal and leather and bone, all those other minds. By the time he returned—if they ever let him return—he would be long out of practice in conducting, and long past his prime of composing. He would know none of the players anymore: only the youngest would still be active, and they would be dispersed among a hundred worlds. That was the worst, perhaps—that they had exiled him from his fellow musicians.

He came to himself, after a long reverie, sitting with clenched hands in an empty room. Well. He could do nothing, musician that he was, but make music. If he refused, he would be punishing himself as much as he punished the government or the Union. So… Georges Mantenon rose stiffly, and made his way back to his quarters. So he would compose. They thought he was too good to stay near the centers of power? They would find out how good he was. Anger trembled, cymbals lightly clashed, a sullen mutter of drums. Outrage chose a thin wedge honed by woodwinds, sharpened on strings. They would refuse power? He would create power, become power, bind with music what they had forbidden him to hold.

His mind stirred, and he felt as much as heard what music was in him. He had not imagined *that* kind of power before. Hardly thinking, he slipped into the Meirinhoff's embrace, thumbed it onto the private circuit only he could hear, and began. He had plenty of time.

When he spoke to the captain again, his voice was smooth, easy. He would not repeat, he said, his earlier mistake of isolation and overwork… he requested permission to mingle with the crew, perhaps even—if it was permitted—play incomplete sequences to those interested. The captain approved, and recommended regular Psych checks, since the mission would last so long. Mantenon bowed, and acquiesced.

He began cautiously, having no experience in deceit. He asked the crew what they'd thought of Opus Four, and what they thought he should call it. He chatted with them about their favorite musicians and music. He told anecdotes of the musicians he'd known. And he composed.

He made a point of having something to play for them every few days… a fragment of melody, a variation on something they already knew. One or two played an instrument as a hobby. Gradually they warmed to him, came to ask his advice, even his help. A would-be poet wanted his verses set to music to celebrate a friend's nameday. The lio player wondered why no one had written a concerto for lio (someone had, Mantenon told him, but the lio was simply not a good solo instrument for large spaces).

In the weeks between the first planet and the next in that system, Mantenon did nothing but this. He made acquaintances out of strangers, and tried to see who might, in the years to come, be a friend. He knew he was being watched for a reaction, knew they knew he was angry and upset, but—as he told the most clinging of his following with a shrug—what could he do? He had signed the contract, he was only a composer (he made a face at that, consciously seconding the practical person's opinion of composers), and he had no way to protest.

"I could scream at the captain, I suppose," he said. "Until she called Med to have me sedated. I could write letters to the Union—but if in fact the Union wants me out here, what good would that do?"

"But doesn't it make you *angry?*" the girl asked. He was sure it was a Security plant. He pursed his lips, then shook his head.

"I was angry, yes—and I wish I could go back, and hear my music played. It doesn't seem fair. But I can't *do* anything, and I might as well do what I'm good at. I have a good composing console—that's a full-bank Meirinhoff they gave me—and plenty of subjects and plenty of time. What else could I do?"

She probed longer, and again from time to time, but finally drifted away, back into the mass of crew, and he decided that Security was satisfied—for a time. By then they were circling the second planet he was to survey.

This one, luckily for his slow-maturing plans, was one of those rare worlds whose basic nature was obvious to everyone. Habitable, beautiful, it was the real reason that the system was being opened; the other worlds—like the marginal mining planet he had begun to call "Grand Crunch"— were merely a bonus. It had three moons, glinting white, pale yellow, and rosy. Its music had to be joyous, celebratory: Mantenon thought first of a waltz, with those three moons, but then changed his mind. Three light beats and a fourth strong, with a shift here to represent that huge fan of shallow sea, its shadings of blue and green visible even from orbit. It wrote itself, and he knew as he wrote it that it would be immensely popular, the sort of thing that the eventual colonial office would pick up and use in advertising.

So lighthearted a work, so dashing a composition, could hardly come from someone sulking and plotting vengeance. Mantenon enjoyed the crew's delighted response, and noted the captain's satisfaction and Security's relaxation. He was being a good boy; they could quit worrying. For a while.

One solid piece of work, one definite hit—he wished he could see his credit balance. It hadn't occurred to him to ask earlier, and he was afraid that if he asked now, he'd arouse their suspicions again. But—assuming they were registering these as they were supposed to, he would end up as a *rich* old man.

The next worlds were each many weeks apart. Mantenon wrote an adequate but undistinguished concerto for one of them; a quartet for woodwinds for another; a brass quintet for the crazy wobbling dance of a double world. Week after week of travel; week after week of observing, composing, revising. Even with his music, with the Meirinhoff, it was monotonous; he had been accustomed to the lively interaction of other musicians, people who understood what he was doing, and appreciated it. He had enjoyed afternoons spent lazing in the courtyards or gardens, listening to others struggling in rehearsal halls.

Without the music he knew he would have gone mad. CUG ships used a seven-day week and four-week month; since there was no reason to worry about a planetary year (and no way to stay in phase with any particular planet), months were simply accumulated until mission's end, when the total was refigured, if desired, into local years. Mantenon felt adrift, at first, in this endless chain of days… he missed the seasonal markers of a planet's life, the special days of recurrent cycles. Surely by now it was his birthday again. He asked one of the med techs about it during one of his checkups… surely they had to keep track of how old people were?

"Yes, it's simple really. The computer figures it—ship time, background time, factors for deepsleep. Most people like to choose an interval about as long as their home planet's year, and flag it as a birthday."

"But it's not their *real* birthday… I mean, if they were back home, would it be the same day?"

"Oh no. That's too complicated. I mean, the computer could do it, but it's not really important. The point is to feel that they have their own special day coming up. Look— why don't you try it? What day of the week do you like your birthday to come on?"

"Well… Taan, I suppose." The best birthday he'd ever had fell on Taan, the year he was eight, and his acceptance to the Academy was rolled in a silver-wrapped tube at one end of the feast table.

"Taan… right. Look here." The tech pointed out columns of figures on the computer. "Your true elapsed age is just under thirty." Mantenon had to force himself to stay silent. Thirty already? He had lost that many years, in just these seven planets? The tech noticed nothing, and went on. "Today's Liki... what about next Taan? That gives you three days to get ready. Is that enough?"

There was nothing to do to get ready. Mantenon nodded, surprised to feel a little excitement even as he knew how artificial this was. A birthday was a *birthday;* you couldn't make one by saying so. But then there were the birthdays he had already lost—that had gone unnoticed. The tech flicked several keys and one number in one column darkened.

"Now that's marked as your shipday—your special day. The interval will be about what it was on Union Five, because that's given as your base, and next time you'll be given notice four weeks in advance. Oh—you get an automatic day off on your shipday... I guess it won't mean much to you, you don't have crew duties. But you get special ration tabs, any flavor you like, if it's on board, and a captain's pass for messages. You can send a message to anyone—your family, anywhere—and for no charge."

Mantenon's shipday party enlivened the long passage between worlds, and he ended the lateshift in someone else's cabin. He had dreaded that, having to admit that he was a virgin, but, on the whole, things went well.

The last world of that system was a gas giant with all the dazzling display of jewelry such worlds could offer: moons both large and small, rings both light and dark, strange swirling patterns on its surface in brilliant color. Mantenon found himself fascinated by it, and spent hours watching out the ports, more hours watching projections of cubes about this satellite or that. Finally the captain came to see what was wrong.

"Nothing," he said, smiling. "It's simply too big to hurry with. Surely you realize that an artist can't always create instantly?"

"Well, but—"

"I'm starting," he assured her. "Right away." And he was, having decided that he was not about to wait the whole long sentence out. They couldn't be planning to stay in deep space for that long without resupply, with the same crew growing older along with him. They must be planning to get supplies and replacements while he was in deepsleep, while he thought they were using the deepspace drive. And he intended to be free of this contract at the first stop.

He had written a song for the poet: three, in fact. He had taken a folksong one of the lifesystems techs sang at his shipday party, and used it in a fugue. He listened to their tales of home, their gossip, their arguments and their jokes, saying little but absorbing what he needed to know. Gradually the crew was responding to him, to his music; he heard snatches of this work or that being hummed or whistled, rhythmic nuances reflected in tapping fingers or the way they knocked on doors. Everything he wrote carried his deepest convictions, carried them secretly, hidden, buried in the nerve's response to rhythm, to timbre and pitch and phrase. And gradually the crew had come to depend on his music, gradually they played their cubes of other composers less. But he knew his music could do more. And now it would.

Mantenon sat curled into the Meirinhoff's embrace, thinking, remembering. He called up his first reaction to his contract, refined it, stored it. Then he began with his childhood. Note by note, phrase by phrase, in the language of keychange, harmonics, the voice of wood and metal and leather and bone, of strings and hollow tubes, vibrations of solids and gases and liquids, he told the story of his life. The skinny boy for whom music was more necessary than food, who had startled his father's distinguished guest by insisting that a tuning fork was wrong (it was), who had taught himself to read music by listening to Barker's *Scherzo To Saint Joan* and following the score (stolen from that same guest of his father's, the conductor Amanchi). The youth at the Academy, engulfed for the first time in a Meirinhoff, able for the first time to give his imagination a voice.

He stopped, dissatisfied. It wasn't only *his* dilemma. He had to make them understand that it was theirs. He couldn't take the ship; they had to give it to him; they had to want him to go where he wanted to go. Either they would have to understand his need for music, or he would have to offer something they wanted for themselves.

He let himself think of the different homeworlds he'd heard of. The famous worlds, the ones in the stories or songs. Forest worlds, dim under the sheltering leaves. Water worlds. Worlds with skies hardly speckled with stars, and worlds where the night sky was embroidered thick with colored light. And in his mind the music grew, rising in fountains, in massive buttresses, in cliffs and shadowed canyons of trembling air, shaping itself in blocks of sound that reformed the listening mind. Here it was quick, darting, active, prodding at the ears; there it lay in repose, enforcing sleep.

In the second week, the captain came once to complain about the fragments he'd played in the crew lounge.

"It's unsettling," she said, herself unsettled.

He nodded toward the outside. "That's unsettling. Those fountains…"

"Sulfur volcanoes," she said.

"Well, they look like fountains to me. But clearly dangerous as well as beautiful."

"No more, though, to the crew. Check with me, first, or with Psych."

He nodded, hiding his amusement. He knew already that wouldn't work. And he kept on. The music grew, acquired complex interrelationships with other pieces… the minor concerto, the brass quintet, the simple song. Humans far from home, on a ship between worlds, with a calendar that accumulated months and gave no seasons, what did they want, what did they need? The rhythmic pattern gave it, withheld it again, offered it, tempting the listener, frustrating the ear. Yet… it *could* satisfy. It wanted to satisfy. Mantenon found himself working until his arms and legs cramped. To hold that power back, to hold those resolving discords in suspension, took all his strength, physical as well as mental.

He knew, by this time, that Security had a tap in his Meirinhoff. They monitored every note he brought out, every nuance of every piece. He did what he could: kept the fragments apart, except in his head, and devised a tricky control program, highly counterintuitive, to link them together when he was ready. It disgusted him to think of someone listening as he worked; it went against all he'd been taught— though he now suspected that Security had taps in the Academy as well. If they wanted to, they could make him look ridiculous all over CUG, by sending out the preliminary drafts under his name. But they wouldn't do that. They wanted his music. So they had to monitor everything. Someone was having to listen to it, all of it; someone whose psych profile Mantenon was determined to subvert.

First he had had to learn more about it. The Central Union boasted hundreds of worlds, each with its own culture… and in many cases, multiple cultures. The same music that would stir a Cympadian would leave a Kovashi unmoved. For mere entertainment, any of the common modes would do well enough, but Mantenon needed to go much deeper than that. He needed one theme, one particular section, that would unlock what he himself believed to be a universal desire.

It was the poet who gave him the clue he needed. At latemeal, he hurried to sit beside Mantenon, and handed over four new poems.

"For Kata," he said. "She's agreed to marry me when we—" He stopped short, giving Mantenon a startled look.

"When you get permission, Arki?" asked Mantenon. He thought to himself that the poet had meant to say "… when we get back to port." He wondered which port they were near, but knew he dared not ask.

"Yes… that is… it has to clear Security, both of us being Navy."

"Mmm." Mantenon concentrated on his rations; Arki always talked if someone looked away.

"It's Crinnan, of course," Arki muttered. "He'll approve, I'm sure—I mean, he's from Kovashi Two, just as we are."

"You're from Kovashi?" asked Mantenon, affecting surprise.

"I thought I'd told you. That's why I write in seren-form: it's traditional. I suppose that's why I like your music, too… all those interlocked cycles."

Mantenon shrugged. "Music is universal," he said. "We're taught modes that give pleasure to most."

"I don't know…" Arki stuffed in a whole ration square and nearly choked, then got it down. "Thing is, Georges, I'd like to have these set to music… if you have time…"

"I've got to finish this composition," Mantenon said. "Maybe before I go into deepsleep for the outsystem transfer… how about that?" He saw the flicker in Arki's eye: so they really were close to a port.

"Well…" Arki said, evading his glance. "I really did want it soon…"

"Klarge." Mantenon said it softly, on an outbreath, which made it milder. "The second movement has problems anyway—maybe it'll clear if I work on your stuff briefly. But I can't promise, Arki—the contract has to come first."

"I understand," said Arki. "Thanks, and—oh, there's Kata." He bounced out of his chair to greet the woman who'd just come in.

Mantenon hugged the double gift to himself. Now he knew the home system of the senior Security officer aboard, and, thanks to the poet, had an excellent excuse for composing highly emotional music designed to affect someone from that system. If Arki was telling the truth: if that whole conversation were not another interlocking scheme of Security. Mantenon glowered at the Meirinhoff's main keyboard, now dull with his handling. It would be like Security, and like any Kovashi, to build an interlocking scheme. But—he thought of the power hidden in his composition—it was also a Kovashi saying that a knifeblade unties all knots.

As if Arki's poems were a literal key for a literal lock, he studied them word by word, feeling how each phrase shaped itself to fit into a socket of the reading mind. And note by note, phrase by phrase, he constructed what he hoped would be the corresponding key of music, something that fit the words so well it could not have been meant for anything else, but which acted independently, unlocking another lock, opening a deeper hidden place in the listener's will. Briefly, he thought of himself as a lover of sorts: like Arki's penetration of Kata, opening secret passages and discovering (as the Kovashi still called it) the hidden treasures of love, his penetration of Crinnan's mind searched secret byways and sought a hidden treasure… of freedom. The songs—asked for by crew, and therefore surely less suspect—could be played openly, without Psych review, and he hoped by them to stun Crinnan and the captain into musical lethargy long enough to play the whole song of power that would free him.

It was hard—very hard—to stay steady and calm, with that hope flooding his veins. Against it he held up the grim uncertainty of success, the likely consequence of failure. He could be killed, imprisoned, taken to a mining planet and forced into slavery. He might live long and never hear music again, save in his own ears… and they might twist his mind, he thought bleakly, and ruin even that. Surely others had tried what he was trying. In all the years the artists and musicians had gone out, surely some of them had tried to use their art to free themselves. If Crinnan were chuckling to himself now, listening to his work through a tap, he was doomed.

But he wanted out. He had to keep going. And shortly after that he had finished the work. The knife, a mere three minutes of Arki's lyrics set to music, lay at hand: the heavy weaponry was loaded, ready to play on his signal. Mantenon called Arki on the intercom.

"Want to hear it?" he asked.

"It's ready? That's good, Georges; we don't have much— I mean, I've got a few minutes before the end of shift. Can you send it along?"

"Certainly." His finger trembled over the button. He could *see* the music, poised like a literal knife, heavy with his intent. He pushed the button, positioned his hand over the next control, the one that would send the main composition over the main speakers. And thumbed with his other hand the intercom to Security. Crinnan would be listening— had to be listening—and if asked *while* he was listening...

Crinnan's voice was abstracted, distant. Mantenon reported that the planetary composition was finished at last. He requested permission to play it, as he had all the others, on the main speakers. Crinnan hesitated. Mantenon visualized the speaker tag in his other ear, could see the flutter of his eyelid as the song slipped through the accumulated tangle of CUG regulations and Security plots, straight for the hidden center of his life, the rhythm woven in it by his homeworld and its peoples. "I suppose..." he said, a little uncertainly. "You've always done that, haven't you?"

Mantenon answered respectfully, soberly. Now the song would be at *this* phrase; Crinnan should be nearly immobile. He heard in his ear a long indrawn breath, taken just as he'd designed. For a moment the sense of power overwhelmed him, then he heard Crinnan grant his request. More: "Go on—I'd like to hear it," said Crinnan.

The interval between song and main composition was crucial. Those who heard both must feel the pause as an accent, precisely timed for the composition on either side of the interval. Those who were not in the circuit for the song must have no warning. But for someone whose fingers and toes controlled whole orchestras, this was nothing: Mantenon switched his output to full ship, and pressed the sequence for the linking program.

Even though he'd written it—even though he knew it intimately, as a man might know a wife of thirty years, sick, healthy, dirty, clean, sweet, sour, fat or lean—even so, its power moved him. For twenty bars, thirty, he lay passive in the Meirinhoff, head motionless, toes and fingers twitching slightly, as the music built, with astonishing quickness, a vision of delight. Then he forced himself up. He, alone, should be proof against this: he could give it a formula, dissociate from its emotional power. And he had things to do.

Their farewells were touching, but Mantenon could hardly wait to be free of them. His new world seemed huge and small at once: a slightly darker sky than Central Five's, a cooler world of stormy oceans and great forested islands. A single continent fringed with forest, its inner uplands crowned with glacial ice, and a broad band of scrubby low growth—for which he had no name, never having seen or studied such things—between. He had seen it on approach, for an hour or so, and then been landed in a windowless shuttle. At the port, green-eyed dark men and women in dark lumpy garments had scurried about, complaining to the shuttle's crew in a sharp, angular language as they hauled the Meirinhoff across to the blocky shelter of the single port building. He himself shivered in the chill wind, sniffing eagerly the scent of his new prison: strange smells that brought back no memories, mixed with the familiar reek of overheated plastics, fuel, and ship's clothing. He wondered—not for the first time— if he'd done right. But at least he would have the Meirinhoff. Or the planet would. He didn't yet know what his status would be, after all the turmoil on the ship. He'd had no chance to play the cube the captain had given him.

"Ser Mantenon?" It was a narrow-faced, dour man whose CUG insignia had tarnished to a dull gray. His accent was atrocious; Mantenon could just follow his words. "It is our pleasure to welcome such an artist as yourself to the colony. If you will follow…"

He followed, down a passage whose walls were faced with rounded dark cobbles. Around a turn, left at a junction, and the walls were hung with brilliant tapestries, all roses, pinks, reds, glowing greens. Into a room where a cluster of people, all in dull colors, waited around a polished table. He was offered a chair: richly upholstered, comfortable. His escort found a chair at the head of the table.

"So you are a rebel, Ser Mantenon?" the man asked.

Mantenon pondered his reply. "I am a musician," he said. "I want to make music."

"You suborned an official vessel of the CUG Navy," the man said. "This is not the act of a musician."

"How he did so…" interrupted a woman near Mantenon. He looked at her. Her eyes were the same green as the others, her dark hair streaked with silver.

"How he did so is not the issue, Sera. *Why* he did so matters to me. What he will do in the years ahead matters to me. Will he bring trouble on us?"

"No," said Mantenon firmly. "I will not. I am not a rebel that way—stirring up trouble. I only want to make music: write music, play music, conduct—"

"Your music makes trouble." That was a balding man halfway around the table. "Your music made them bring you… it might make us go. If you have that power, you must have plans to use it."

"To give pleasure," said Mantenon. Suddenly the room felt stuffy. He'd been so sure anyone living on a planet would understand why he *had* to get off that ship. "I don't want to control people with it. I only did it because it was the only way."

"Hmmm." Eyes shifted sideways, meeting each other, avoiding his gaze.

"Pleasure," said the woman who'd spoken. "That's a good thought, Ser Mantenon. Do you like this world?"

"I hardly know it yet, but it seems… well, it's better than the ship."

She chuckled. "I see. And you want to give *us* pleasure— the colonists?"

"Yes. I want to make music you will enjoy."

"And not to send us to war with Central Union?"

"Oh, no." This time, after his answer, he felt an odd combined response: relaxation and amusement both rippled around the table.

"And you are willing to work?"

"At music, certainly. I can teach a number of instruments, music theory, conduct, if there's an orchestral group with no conductor, as well as compose. But I have had surgical modifications that make some kinds of work impossible."

"Of course. Well." She looked sideways; heads nodded fractionally. "Well, then, we are pleased to welcome you. We think you will find a place, though it will not be what you're used to."

And from there he was led to a ground vehicle of some kind (he noticed that the shuttle had already been canted into its takeoff position), and was driven along a broad hard-surfaced road toward a block of forest. Within the forest were clearings and buildings. Before he had time to wonder what they all were, he found himself installed in a small apartment, with clean bedding stacked on the end of a metal bunk, and the blank ends of electrical connections hanging out of the walls. His original escort yelled something down the passage, and two men appeared with utility connections: cube player, speakers, intercom.

"We have not installed your machine… your composing machine… because we do not yet know if you will stay here, or prefer to live somewhere else."

"That's fine," said Mantenon absently, watching the men work.

"The group kitchen is on the ground floor, two down," the man said. "If you think you will wish to cook here, we can install—"

"Oh, no," said Mantenon. "I don't know how to cook." The man's eyebrows rose, but Mantenon didn't ask why. He was suddenly very tired, and longed for sleep. The workers left, without a word, and the escort twitched his mouth into a smile.

"You are tired, I'm sure," he said. "I will leave you to rest, but I will come by before the next meal, if that is all right"

"Thank you." Mantenon didn't know whether to wave or not; the man suddenly stepped forward and grasped his hand, then bowed. Then he turned away and went out the door, shutting it behind him.

Mantenon spread a blanket over the bunk and lay down. Something jabbed him in the ribs, something angular. The captain's message cube. He sighed, grunted, and finally rolled off the bunk to stick the cube in the player.

It was a holvid cube, and the captain's miniature image appeared between his hands. He stepped back, slouched on the bunk.

"Mr. Mantenon," she began, then paused. Her hair was backlit by the worklight on her desk, her face the same cool, detached face he'd known for these years of travel. "You are an intelligent man, and so I think you will appreciate an explanation. Part of one. You resented being tricked, as all young artists do. You were smart enough to avoid violence, and obvious rebellion. I suspect you even knew we had experienced attempts to use art against us before. And I know you suspected that I knew what you were doing. If you are as smart as I think you are, you're wondering now if you're in prison or free, if you've won what you thought you were winning. And the answer is yes, and the answer is no.

"You are not the first to try what you tried. You are not the first to succeed. Most do not. Most are not good enough. Your music, Mr. Mantenon, is worth saving… at the cost of risking your effect on this colony. Although you will never be allowed to leave that planet, for you I think it will be freedom, or enough to keep you alive and well. Students to teach, music to play… you can conduct a live orchestra, when you've taught one. You were not ambitious, Mr. Mantenon, and so you will not miss the power you might have held at the Academy. You can curse me, as the representative of the government that tricked you, and go on with your life. But there's one other thing you should know." Again she paused, this time turning her head as if to ease a stiff neck.

"You can think of it as plot within plot, as your music wove theme within theme. The government removes the dangerous, those who can wield such power as you, and protects itself… and yet has a way to deal with those who are too powerful for that isolation. But the truth is, Mr. Mantenon, that you *did* overpower my ship. You are free; we must return, or be listed as outlaws, and if we return, our failure will cost all of us. You hoped we would rebel, and follow you into freedom. You did not know that our ship is our freedom… that I had worked years for this command, and you have destroyed it. You see the government as an enemy—most artists do—but to me it is all that keeps the worlds together, providing things for each other that none can provide alone. Like the Academy, where you may send a student someday. Like my ship, in which we traveled freely. I don't expect you to believe this, not now. But we were honored to have you aboard, from the first: truly honored. And we were honored by the power of your music. And you destroyed us, and we honor you for that. A worthy enemy; a worthy loss. If you ever believe that, and understand, write us another song, and send *that*."

And nothing lay between his hands but empty air. After a long moment he breathed again. In the silence, he heard the beginnings of that song, the first he would write on his new world, the last gift to the old.

NO PAIN, NO GAIN

Meryl the shepherdess woke from nightmares in which she waded through glue on grotesquely swollen legs. She opened her eyes to the smoky rafters of her mother's little hut, and stretched luxuriously. Bad dreams make good days, Gran always said. Flinging back the covers, she rolled out of bed and burst into screams. There they were, attached to her own wiry body—the plump soft legs of her dream, and when she took a step, it felt as if she were wading through glue. She didn't stop screaming until her mother slapped her smartly across the mouth. Gran said it was the Evil Eye, and probably the fault of Jamis the cowherd's second wife, no better than she should be, jealous because *her* girl had a mole on her nose, for which she had blamed everyone but herself. Everyone knew that the Evil Eye didn't cause moles on the nose: those came from poking and prying.

Meryl's new flabby legs ached abominably for days, but eventually she was able to keep up with her flock without too much trouble. Gran had a quiet word with The Kind One, and the cowherd's stepdaughter broke out in disgusting pustules very like cowpox next market-day. Meryl figured it was all over, but she still wished for her own legs back.

Dorcas Doublejoints, justly famed dancer at The Scarlet Veil, could do things with her abdominal musculature which fascinated the most discerning clients, and resulted in a steady growth in her bank account. She had trained since childhood, when her Aunt Semele had noticed the anatomical marks of potential greatness. So now, in the lovely space between her ribs and her pubic bone, all was perfectly harmonious, muscle and a delicately calculated amount of "smoothing," and unblemished skin with one artfully placed mole—the only plastic wizardry in which Dorcas had ever had to indulge, since by nature she had no marks there at all.

She woke near noon, after an unpleasant dream she attributed to that new shipment of wine… until she rolled on her side and felt… different. Where her slender supple belly had been, capable of all those enticing ripples hither and yon, she now had… She prodded the soft, bulging mass and essayed a ripple. Nothing happened. Dorcas thought of her burgeoning bank balance—not nearly as much as she wanted to retire on—and groaned.

Then she wrapped herself in an uncharacteristic garment—opaque and voluminous—and sought the advice of her plastic wizard.

Mirabel Stonefist had done her best to avoid it, but she'd been snagged by the Finance Committee of the Ladies' Aid & Armor Society. Instead of a pleasant morning in her sister-in-law's garden, watching the younglings at play, she was spending her off-duty day at the Ladies' Hall, peering at the unpromising figures on a parchment roll.

"And just after we ordered the new steps the court ladies wanted, they all quit coming," Blanche-the-Blade said. "I haven't seen hide nor hair of them for weeks—"

"They'll be back," Krystal said, buffing her fingernails on her fringed doeskin vest. "They still want to look good, and without our help, they'll soon return to the shapes they had before."

The court ladies, in the fitness craze that followed the repeal of the tax on bronze bras, had asked the women of the King's Guard how they stayed so trim. In anticipation of a profitable side-line, the Ladies' Aid & Armor Society had fitted up a couple of rooms at the Hall for exercise classes. But unlike the younger girls, who seemed to like all the bouncing around, the married women complained that sweating was unseemly.

"What annoys me," Blanche said, "is the way they moan and groan as if it's our fault that they're not in shape. I personally don't care if every court lady is shaped like a sofa pillow and about as firm—I never made fun of them—" She gave Mirabel a hard look. Mirabel, a few years before, had been caught with pillows stuffed under her gown, mimicking the Most Noble Gracious Lady Vermania, wife of the then Chancellor, in her attempt to line-dance at the Harvest Ball. That story, when it got back to the Most Noble Gracious Lady and her husband, had done nothing for the reputation of the Ladies' Aid & Armor Society as a serious organization.

"I was only nineteen at the time," Mirabel said. "And I've already done all the apologizing I'm going to do." She unrolled another parchment. "Besides, that's not the point. The point is—our fitness program is losing money. We're not going to have enough for the annual Iron Jill retreat sacrifice unless we get some customers. And we're stuck with all those flower-painted step-stools and those beastly mirrors which have to be polished…"

"Recruits' work," Blanche said.

"Yes, but not exactly military training. As for the ladies themselves—they looked pretty good at the dance two days ago." Mirabel had been on what the Guard called "drunk duty" that night, and had attributed certain ladies' newly slender limbs to her sisters' efforts in the Ladies' Aid & Armor Society Shape-up Classes.

"Who looked good?" asked Krystal. No one would trust Krystal for drunk duty at a royal ball; she was entirely too likely to disappear down dark corridors with one of the drunks she was supposed to sober up. She claimed her methods worked as well as the time-honored bucket of water from the stable-yard well, but the sergeants didn't agree. Mirabel, like most of the guards, thoroughly enjoyed sousing the high-born with a bucket of cold water.

"Well—the queen, for one, and the Capitola girls. You know how thick their ankles were, and how they complained about exercising…" The Capitola girls had taken their complaint to the queen, who hated the women soldiers.

"Yes…?"

"They were wearing those new gowns slit up to here, that float out on the fast turns, and their legs were incredible."

"I can imagine," Krystal sniffed. "People with thighs like oxen shouldn't wear that style—"

"No—I mean long, slender, graceful. Even their ankles. I wondered what the Shape-Up Classes had been doing."

"But—" Blanche frowned. "The last time they were in our classes, they had taken perhaps a tailor's tuck off those thighs, but their ankles were still thick."

"They must've found someone who knows more about exercise than we do," Mirabel said. "And that's why they're not coming to our classes anymore."

"Nobody knows more about exercise than soldiers," Blanche said. "There's no way to change flab to muscle that our sergeants haven't put us through."

"There must be something," Mirabel said, "and we had better find it."

They were interrupted by the doorward, who ushered in a handsome woman muffled in a cloak far too warm for the day. Mirabel perked up; anything was better than staring at those figures another moment. She had the feeling that staring at them would never change red ink to black.

"Ladies," the woman said, in a voice meant to carry only from pillow to pillow, not across a drillfield. "I understand that you have a… an exercise program?"

"Why yes," Blanche said, before Mirabel could speak. "We specialize in promoting fitness for women…"

"I have a problem," the woman said, and put back the hood of her cloak. Mirabel gaped. She knew Dorcas by sight, of course, because she had often been the official escort for visiting dignitaries when they went out on the town. She had watched the more public parts of Dorcas's performance, and had thought to herself that if the dancer were instead a fighter, she would already be in condition.

"You?" got out before Mirabel could repress it.

"Someone stole my belly," the woman said. She stood up, and unwrapped the cloak. Under it she wore a sheer, loose, nightshift… and under the nightshift was a soft, billowy expanse of crepey skin. "My plastic wizard," Dorcas went on, "tells me that this belly belongs to someone else, but he cannot tell whose it is—only that it's very likely she—whoever she is—has mine. He can't get mine back, until he knows where it is, and whether this was a simple exchange or something more complicated. Even then he's not sure… he says he's never seen a case like this before." She glared at her belly, and then at them. "This one must be over forty years old—just look at this skin!—and it has all the muscle tone of mud. How am I supposed to earn a living with this? I can't even do my usual warm-up exercises. Do you have something—*anything*—which will tone me up?"

Mirabel felt a twinge of sympathy. This was no spoiled court lady, but a hard-working woman. "I'm sure we can help," she said. "But I don't know about the age part…"

"I don't expect miracles," Dorcas said. "I just want something to work with, so I don't lose money while I'm hunting for the trollop who did this to me."

"You have no idea?"

"No… I thought of that redheaded slut down at the Brass Bottom Cafe… you know, the one who thinks she can dance…" Mirabel nodded; she didn't feel it was the time to mention that the lissome redhead was reputed to perform the famous Gypsy dance "In Your Hat" even better than Dorcas. "But," Dorcas went on, with an air of someone being fairer than necessary, "she's in better shape than this." She patted the offending belly. "If anything, she's too thin. No, I'll be looking for someone whose skirts are too loose." She sighed. "So—when's class? And is there any possibility of getting private lessons. I hate to advertise my problem…"

"Private lessons?—" Mirabel was about to explain that since their classes had disappeared, all lessons were private, when Blanche interrupted.

"There's a ten percent surcharge for private lessons, Dorcas…"

"That's all right," Dorcas said.

"But I was going to say, since you're a working woman, like us, we'll waive that fee. It's mostly for the rich ladies who are looking for a way out of the work. And we could schedule you—" She made a pretense of going through the scrolls. "Well, as a matter of fact, I could just fit you in now, if that's convenient. Or two hours after first bell tomorrow, if not."

"Thanks, ladies," Dorcas said. "Soon begun, soon done."

At the end of the table, Krystal stirred. "Mirabel, you don't suppose—?"

"Those court ladies!" Mirabel said, slamming her fist on the table. "That would be just like them!" Lazy, hated sweating and grunting for it, but wanted svelte bodies anyway. They would think of stealing, and if they had found a black plastic wizard....

"I wonder if it's happened to anyone else," Krystal said. "There aren't enough exotic dancers to supply flat tummies and perky breasts and slender thighs and smooth haunches and..."

"All *right*, Krystal. I get the point." Mirabel closed her eyes, trying to think how many court ladies she'd seen at the dance with markedly better figures. Had any of the other dancers been robbed? "I'm going to check on some things," she said. "You stay here and let Blanche know what we came up with."

Out on the street, she headed for the Brass Bottom Cafe, and stopped short outside. For the past half-year, a poster advertising the red-haired Eulalia's charms had been displayed... but it wasn't here anymore.

"Painting a new poster?" she asked, as she came through the door.

"She's not here," said the landlady. "But we've got Gerynis and Mythlia and..."

"When did she leave?" Mirabel asked.

"Are you on official business?" asked the landlady. "Or just snooping?"

"Official as in King's Guard, no. Official as in Ladies' Aid & Armor Society, yes."

The landlady sniffed. "So what does the Ladies' Aid & Armor Society have to do with exotic dancers? Going to learn to be graceful in armor? Or sleep your way to promotions?"

Mirabel remembered why she never came here. The landlady cooed over male soldiers, and had a rough tongue for the women. "Ma'am," she said, trying to sound both pleasant and businesslike, "information from another exotic dancer suggests that all of them may be at risk. If so, the LA&AS wants to offer protection—"

"And make a tidy profit, no doubt." The landlady glared. "Well, you're too late for Eulalia, I can tell you that. What's been done to her is nothing short of blasphemy, and now you come along with your story about protection. It wouldn't surprise me a bit if you didn't have something to do with her troubles, just trying to scare all the girls into buying into your protections—" She advanced from behind the counter, and Mirabel saw that she held an iron skillet almost as broad as her hips. Mirabel beat a hasty retreat. So much for that... but if she could find Eulalia, the redhead might have more sense.

Back at the Hall, Eulalia was slumped at the table with a bright-eyed Krystal. Eulalia's midsection had gone the way of Dorcas's, although the replacement wasn't quite as big. Krystal had already signed her up for classes.

Eulalia knew of two other dancers so afflicted. "And my cousin, who just came to the city last week, told me about a plague among shepherd girls out in the Stormy Hills. Only with them it's not bellies—it's legs. Those girls do have gorgeous legs, from all that running and climbing."

Mirabel looked at the map on the wall. "Umm." She remembered that the court ladies had made a Progress into the Stormy Hills a few weeks before. Or so they'd said. She had thought at the time it was an odd place to go for a Progress in late winter—or at any time, really. There was nothing up in the Stormy Hills but bad weather and sheep... and of course the herding families that tended them.

They had insisted on being escorted by male soldiers, too. At the time, Mirabel had thought that was just another of their ladyish attitudes, of which they had many. Most likely, they were still in a snit about the exercise classes, and thought that the women soldiers would make them walk too fast. They had refused to go on hill walks as part of their fitness program.

"Something is definitely going on here," Mirabel said. "We'd better have a word with our favorite plastic wizard." He was still on retainer for the Society. And much as she sympathized with the dancers, if even half of them suddenly needed fitness classes, it would help make up the deficit from the court ladies' defection. They might come up with enough for the Iron Jill retreat sacrifice after all.

The first break in the case came from one of the girls who was in the pre-recruit class. She arrived full of giggles, and Blanche had to speak quite sharply to her.

"Sorry, ma'am," she said, her shoulders still shaking. "It's the older ladies—my Aunt Sapphire and her bunch. You know they didn't like coming down here to your fitness classes—"

"I know," Blanche said.

"Well, they've got a dancing master now, calls himself Gilfort the Great, who claims that the female body is especially suited to fitness by dancing. They wear these little silk tunics—some of them even wear just a bandeau on top—and carry long scarves and ribbons and things, and while the court string quartet plays in the corner, they hop about—but never enough to sweat."

"But surely they're... er... losing condition?" Blanche asked.

"Terribly, at first," the girl said. "Then—overnight, almost—the dance began to work, and they were gorgeous. If I didn't want to learn swordplay, I'd go there myself." She caught the look on Blanche's face and stepped back. "Not really, of course, ma'am, but—it is kind of pretty. In its own way."

"But what were you laughing at, then?"

"Well... on my way here, I passed behind the potted palms, and the dancing master was telling them all they had the bellies of belly dancers, and the legs of shepherdesses, and the arms of apple-pickers. And I just couldn't help think-ing, 'and the brains of boiled cabbages'..." Her voice trailed off, with the quick mood change of adolescence. "I don't know why I thought it was so funny, really, just—most of the time they'd be horrified if anyone called them dancers or shepherdesses, and they were lapping it up, giving him these soppy grins."

"Apple-pickers," Blanche said. "I never thought of apple-pickers."

"If they're wearing those two-piece outfits, we can certainly recognize our bellies," Dorcas said. Eulalia nodded. "But we don't want them to see *us*."

"That's what potted palms are for," Mirabel said. "Those giggling girls are always hiding behind the potted palms; you can wrap up to look like chaperones."

She herself looked like nothing but what she was, one of the Royal Guard. She took up her stance at the door of the third-best ballroom, sent Dorcas and Eulalia behind the potted palms, and waited.

The queen glared at her when the ladies arrived. "Where's Justin? He's our regular guard!"

"Justin's sick this morning, your majesty," Mirabel said. Justin knew when it was healthier to be sick; he'd said he was tired of watching them fancy ladies misbehave in front of a foreigner anyway.

"Well... I certainly hope he gets well soon."

The queen's body looked, Mirabel had to admit, about half the age it had at Prince Nigel's wedding. Trim waist, slender taut legs. Too bad nothing had improved her sour face. The other ladies twittered and cooed as the dancing master appeared, leading the musicians.

He was a handsome fellow, in his way. He had broad manly shoulders, a deep chest, a light step, and white teeth in a flashing smile. In fact, if not for his thick gray hair, he would have seemed the picture of handsome, rugged, young manhood.

Gray hair? She looked again. Smooth-skinned, no wrinkles; hands of a man no more than thirty, if that. Some people grayed early, but their hair usually came in white, and his was the plain gray of stone. Wasn't there something about gray hair on a young face, some jingle? She was trying to remember it when she noticed that the fronds of one potted palm were shaking as if in a windstorm, and strolled casually over.

"Be still," she said as softly as possible. With the wailing of the dance music, she didn't think they'd hear.

"That—!" Whatever Dorcas had been about to say, Eulalia smothered successfully with a scarf.

"Get her out of here," Mirabel said. "We'll sort this out later."

What Dorcas had seen, it transpired, was her belly—unmistakable not only for its singular beauty and talents, but for its mole.

"But she's letting it go," Dorcas wailed. "It's been two weeks, and I can tell she hasn't done a full set of ab crunches yet."

"I saw mine, too," Eulalia said. "And that woman must eat eight meals a day. The hipbones are already covered."

"You *could* use a little more contouring, dear," Dorcas said to her, too sweetly.

"*You* could use a little *less*," Eulalia said, not sweetly at all. They looked like two cats hissing; Mirabel slapped the table between them.

"Ladies. This is more important. Can you identify your bellies well enough for a court?"

"I'm sure," Dorcas said, eyes narrowed.

"And I," Eulalia agreed.

The judge, however, insisted that they had no proof. "A belly," he said firmly, "is just a belly. There is no evidence that it can be moved from one person to another."

"But that's *my* belly!" Dorcas said.

"Prove it," the judge said.

"That mole—"

"According to expert testimony, that mole was so placed by plastic wizardry, and Lady Cholerine has a receipt from a plastic wizard to show that she paid to have it put there. You, madam, do not have a mole... or a receipt."

"Of course *this* belly doesn't have a mole," Dorcas said. "It's not mine. *You* should know—"

"Keep her quiet," the judge said icily, "Or I'll have her in contempt!"

Dorcas glared at the judge, but said no more.

Afterwards she exploded to Mirabel. "He knows perfectly well that's my belly—he's had his tongue on that mole, when it was where it should be, on me. He just doesn't want everyone to know it."

Feristax, the LA&AS wizard, smiled when Mirabel told him about that fiasco. "If we can get them into court again, I think I may have something."

"What?" asked Mirabel crossly. She was not about to humiliate herself again in court.

"It's a new concept." She had heard that before. "After that problem with the random access storage device—"

"When you got our tits mixed up," Mirabel said. "I remember perfectly. Go on."

"Well... there's always been exchange, you know. Someone with red hair wants yellow hair; they get the red hair spelled off, and yellow hair spelled on. That puts red hair into the universe, and removes yellow hair. So if someone else wants red hair, there it is— it's an exchange, not a creation. But it's not a theft or anything."

"Like money," Mirabel said.

"Exactly." The wizard beamed at her. He had found the right level to communicate. "But, as with money, there are thieves. If there's no red hair—just for an example—"

"YES!" said Mirabel, stroking the haft of her knife; the wizard blenched and went on hurriedly.

"If there's no red hair, then they'll do a universal search for an individual with red hair. And contact a local practitioner—sometimes not even a licensed wizard!— to spell-steal it away, where it becomes available to the person who wanted red hair."

"What color hair does the victim get?" Mirabel asked. "Or do they just snatch them baldheaded?"

"Gray, usually," the wizard said. "Very few people ask for gray, except of course wizards." He patted his own storm-colored hair, so incongruous with his youthful unlined face.

"Aha!" That was the thing about gray hair. *Gray hair on young visage, might be a wizard.* "He had gray hair, that dancing master. And he was young."

"Did he have a badge of license?" asked Feristax, touching his.

"Not that I saw," Mirabel said.

"Then, if he *is* a wizard, I'll bet he's a renegade. Do you know his name?"

"Gilfort the Great," Mirabel said.

"Sounds like somebody's apprentice pretending," Feristax said.

"Dorcas's belly isn't pretending," Mirabel pointed out. "So—what is this new technique that might get everyone's legs and bellies back where they belong?"

"Ah. That. Well, the incidence of what we call 'prosthetic theft' has been rising in Technolalia, and they've developed a way to trace the origin of exchanges through something known as a virtual watermark."

"Watermark? Like on silk?"

The wizard laughed deprecatingly, but with a nervous look at the dagger in Mirabel's hand. "In the… er… flesh. Another possibility is a transunion connectivity spell, which allows the individual who originally inhabited the body part to control it while under the spell."

"Huh?"

"You mean," Dorcas said slowly, "that if we used this spell, and I wanted to, I could make my belly dance on someone else's body?"

"Precisely," the wizard said.

"I like it," Dorcas said, with a dangerous smile.

Half a dozen shepherd girls and apple-pickers, plus Dorcas and Eulalia, stood in a row on one side of the courtyard, and the court ladies they accused stood on the other.

"You can't make us undress in public!" the queen's first lady-in-waiting said, her cheeks mottled red.

"That isn't necessary at all," Sophora Segundiflora said. "All you have to do is stand there and watch." She had been invaluable in getting the court ladies there; they were no more inclined to disobey the new chancellor than the women soldiers had been when she was the senior member of the LA&AS.

"Watch what?"

Sophora said nothing, but waved to the musicians.

At the wailing of the pipes minor and the nose-flutes, Dorcas and Eulalie began to dance "In Your Hat," their limbs describing fluid arcs and volutes, though their still-reluctant substitute bellies came nowhere near the movements required.

"This is disgusting," the queen said. "In *our* court—!"

"Well, it's not up to standard," the king said, without taking his eyes off the dancers, "but worth watching nonetheless…" The queen glared.

The observers gasped suddenly. Two of the court ladies were jerking spasmodically, clutching at themselves with both arms.

"What's wrong with them?" the king asked. "Are they sick?"

"They're trying to dance," Dorcas said, without missing a beat of the dance. "That's my belly—"

"No, that one's mine," Eulalia said. "It's got that little extra spiralling wiggle…"

Some of the guards had begun to make enthusiastic noises, and now they burst into cheers: "Eulalia! Eulalia!" and "Dorcas! Dorcas!" as they pointed at their candidates for those respective abs among the court ladies twitching and writhing.

Sophora held up one massive hand, and the courtyard fell silent.

"It's clear," she said, "that terrible things have been done to your people, your majesty, but I don't believe that these ladies had evil intent."

"Ha!" muttered Mirabel.

"I believe they were deluded by the enchantments of a black plastic wizard—" A gasp of horror swept the yard. "—who posed as a dancing master." She pointed.

The dancing master attempted a fast reverse shuffle, but found himself up against the bronze breastplates of a half-dozen Royal Guard, several of them women.

"See his gray hair!" Sophora thundered. Several small bits of masonry fell from the castle walls and shattered on the pavement. "That is no natural hair—that is a wizard's choice." She waved, and Feristax came forward. "You all know this wizard, long a respected practitioner in our fair city. Let him now examine this imposter."

"He's not even a licensed wizard," Feristax said confidently. A night's work on the informational plane of the multiverse had located the man's own identity codes. "He's a supplier of magical components for *real* wizards… In fact, he is the fellow who shipped me that very imperfect random access storage device which caused so much trouble last year. I've been told that he lost his franchise with several reputable manufacturers recently, that he has been suspected of tampering with network traces and virtual watermarks."

"It's all a stupid conspiracy!" the man—dancing master or black plastic wizard—yelled. "It's just a way to keep down the talented and let lazy fools like you—" He stopped, a dagger at his throat.

"Gilfort, he calls himself," Feristax said. "If it pleases your majesty, I can reverse his iniquitous and illegal spells."

"Perhaps in a more private place," Sophora murmured in the king's other ear. "These ladies have been foolish and gullible, but you would not want to humiliate them…"

"Oh… no…" the king looked bewildered, his habitual expression. The queen glared at Sophora, who smiled back.

"For your own benefit, your majesty," Sophora said.

At the end of the speedy trial—the judge, with Sophora leaning over his shoulder, did not delay proceedings in any way—all body parts were restored to their original owners, except for one: a shepherd girl in the Stormy Hills, slowed by Lady Alicia's flabby legs, had not outrun a wolf. Alicia got to keep the girl's legs, but had to send twenty gold crowns in compensation… or choose to spend the summer herding sheep for the girl's family. She sent the money.

Because the Ladies' Aid & Armor Society had incurred unreasonable expense in acquiring exercise equipment for the court ladies to use, the ladies had to agree to three classes a week for the next year, by which time the step-stools, mirrors, and showers would be paid off.

And, as a special reward for their discovery and solution of the problem, the Ladies' Aid & Armor Society received a unique contribution to their annual Iron Jill retreat.

Thirty sulky ladies in silk tunics stepped smartly up and down the flower-painted stools to the rhythm of mallet on shield, and the brusque commands of the LA&AS top instructors.

"Aaaall right, ladies… and FIVE and FOUR and THREE and TWO and ONE… now the other foot and EIGHT and SEVEN and SIX and FIVE…"

"Let's see those smiles, ladies! A proper court lady always smiles!"

"More GLOW, ladies! Let's see some GLOW!"

Gilfort the Great, Dancing Master to the Royal Court and (privy) black plastic wizard, sat on the rock in the middle of the clearing, hands bound to the ring thereon, and wished he had never left Technolalia. Twenty-seven of the women of the Ladies' Aid & Armor Society had shown up for the annual Iron Jill retreat, at which (so he had heard) terrible rituals were performed. No male had seen them and lived to tell about it.

The corresponding male-bonding ceremonies he knew about, having been taken to the fire-circle to drum and dance by his father and uncles. He had been forced to down raw fish and even a luckless mouse; he had run naked through the meadows and woods screaming the worst words he knew.

But this? Around the rock, the women swirled, seeming to ignore him, as they stripped off armor, kicked off heavy boots, and unpacked provisions for the first night's dinner.

"Hunting tomorrow," said the tall muscly one who had prodded him in the back most of the way here. "Tonight's the last night for this boughten stuff."

"Yeah…" breathed the others, and then they did look at him, and he wished they hadn't.

"By the time we find and kill, we'll be ravenous," a perky blonde said, growling a little. "If the Mother sent us off as usual, we won't really have much of a supper tonight…"

He could see that they didn't. Bread, cheese—not much of it—some pickles. To his surprise, they brought him a pot of stew, and urged him to eat his fill.

"It's all right for *you*," they said. He wasn't hungry, but the menace of their swords suggested he had better obey, and he forced the stew into a reluctant belly. Later, he hardly slept—it was amazingly difficult to sleep on a hard rock, with his hands tied, and the knowledge that twenty-seven hungry women had plans for him the next day.

Just as the first gray light seeped into the clearing, the women began to wake. First one then another stopped snoring, rolled to her feet, spat, and let out a loud yell. Birds took off, wings clapping, in all directions. Twenty-seven yells, in everything from lyric soprano (with a fine vibrato) to tenor, and afterwards they all looked at him again.

"Now didn't that feel *good*?" asked the brown-haired brawny one. "Let's do it again, and this time let *all* the tension out. Iron… JILLLL!"

Twenty-seven women yelling Iron Jill at the tops of their lungs sent all remaining birds thrashing out of the trees at high speed, and in the echoing silence afterwards he could hear distant hoofbeats becoming ever more distant.

"Ahhh," said the brawny one, stretching. "Usually we can't do that right away, not if we want any breakfast, because it scares the game, but this time…" She smiled. Gilfort the Great fainted.

When he woke up, he was being slapped gently enough by several of the women.

"Oh goodie! He's awake," said the perky blonde.

"Now, what you have to do," said another, "is this: we point you away from the castle and city, and then you run. And then we chase you."

"Such fun," said the blonde one. "You've had more food and a good night's sleep." He tried to protest, but his mouth was dry. "We give you a flagon of water and some sandwiches; we have nothing. You might well outrun us; we might have to subsist on nuts and berries. Even beetle grubs." She giggled.

They sounded so cheerful. They sounded so confident.

"It's just—" Strong fingers clamped his cheeks; bold eyes stared into his. "Don't come back this way, Gilfort. I shouldn't warn you, not really, but—the rules are, if you come back this way, we can do it all. Tear you. Slowly. Limb. From. Limb. We like it, but you probably wouldn't. So best to run *that* way, Gilfort. We do it quickly, when it's a running prey."

"Like a deer," one of the others said. "Prey, not sacrifice."

"Attaboy," said the brawny one, and they hauled him to his feet, attached the water flagon to his belt with care, tucked a packet of sandwiches in his pack, and unbound his hands. "That way," the brawny one said again. "We give you ten Iron Jills head start."

Gilfort staggered away, the stagger quickening to a run as his body found a use for all that adrenaline. Behind him, the first roar of the women: "Iron… JILL!" He leapt over a fallen log, raced down a little slope, splashed through the creek. "Iron JILL!" Up the slope on the far side, slipping in drifts of leaves, fingers desperate for a grip on branches, rocks, anything… on up, and up, a long gentle slope that offered his burning lungs no rest. "Iron JILL!" Down again at last, gasping, sweat burning his eyes, to another creek too wide to jump. He plunged into icy water, slipped on a rock and fell headlong. "Iron JILL!" came faintly from behind.

Hours later, sore, panting, blistered, stung, scraped, scratched, and very aware of his great good fortune, he emerged on the Hacksaw Pass road back to Technolalia. He had heard the strident call over and over, in those desperate hours, sometimes nearer, sometimes farther away, as the crazed pack of starving warrior women sought their lawful prey. But now he was at the road, and once over the pass he would be safe. Forever safe, because he certainly wasn't ever coming back.

The crazed pack of starving warrior women, sprawled at ease on the soft spring turf of the clearing, burped in varying tones. A couple of hours after they'd sent Gilfort off, the supply cart arrived, complete with the festive foods appropriate to an Iron Jill retreat, including the molded chocolate statue of the Mother of All Women Warriors. It had taken the last coin in the treasury, but without the sacrificial chocolate, it just wasn't an Iron Jill retreat.

They were full now, overfull, and hardly able to sing along when Dorcas and

Eulalie (honorary inductees to the rites this year) struck up the traditional Hymn to Iron Jill:

> "Women must cook, so women can eat
> Is mostly the rule,
> But *not* on retreat…
> Too much fat, and too much sweet
> Should be avoided
> But *not* on retreat…
> An iron woman's no fun at all
> So eat your fill and have a ball.
> Food in the belly
> Love in the night
> Chocolate today
> Will make all right."

When night fell, the flames leaped high, and when the vision for which they had come, Iron Jill herself, walked among them… they rolled over and ate another piece of chocolate. Iron Jill smiled at her daughters, and her daughters smiled back.

HAND TO HAND

Ereza stood in the shadows at the back of the concert hall. She had promised to be silent, to be motionless; interrupting the final rehearsal would, she had been told, cause untold damage. Damage. She had survived the bombing of her barracks; she had survived being buried in the rubble for two days, the amputation of an arm, the loss of friends and all her gear, and they thought interrupting a rehearsal caused *damage?* Had it not been her twin on-stage, she might have said something. But for Arlashi's sake she would ignore such narrow-minded silliness and do as she was told.

She had seen concerts, of course; she had even attended the first one in which Arlashi soloed. This was somewhat different. From the clear central dome the muted light of a rainy day lay over the rows of seats, dulling the rich colors of the upholstery. The stage, by contrast, looked almost garish under its warm-toned lights. Musicians out of uniform wore all sorts of odd clothes; it looked as if someone had collected rabble from a street fair and handed them instruments. Ereza had expected them to wear the kinds of things Arlashi wore, casual but elegant; here, Arlashi looked almost too formal in purple jersey and gray slacks. Instead of attentive silence before the music, she could hear scuffing feet, coughs and cleared throats, vague mutters. The conductor leaned down, pointing out something to Arlashi in the score; she pointed back; their heads finally moved in unison.

The conductor moved back to his podium and tapped it with his baton. "From measure sixty," he said. Pages rustled, though most of the musicians seemed to be on the right one. Silence, then a last throat clearing, then silence again. Ereza shifted her weight to the other leg. Her stump ached savagely for a moment, then eased. Arla, she could see, was poised, her eyes on the conductor.

His hand moved; music began. Ereza listened for the bits she knew, from having heard Arla practice them at home. Arla had tried to explain, but it made no sense, not like real things. Music was either pretty or not; it either made her feel like laughing, or crying, or jumping around. You couldn't say, as with artillery, what would work and what wouldn't. This wasn't one she knew without a program. It sounded pretty enough, serene as a spring evening in the garden. Arla's right arm moved back and forth, the fingers of her left hand shifting up and down. Ereza watched her, relaxing into the sweetness of the music. This was the new cello, one of only four wooden cellos on the planet, made of wood from Scavel, part of the reparations payment imposed after the Third Insurrection. Cravor's World, rich in military capacity, had far too few trees to waste one on a musical instrument. Ereza couldn't hear the difference between it and the others Arla had played, but she knew Arla thought it important.

Her reverie shattered as something went drastically wrong with the music. She couldn't tell what, but Arla's red face and the conductor's posture suggested who had caused the problem. Other instruments had straggled to a halt gracelessly, leaving silence for the conductor's comment.

"Miss Fennaris!" Ereza was glad he wasn't her commanding officer; she'd heard that tone, and felt a pang of sympathy for Arla. Somehow she'd thought musicians were more lenient than soldiers.

"So sorry," Arla said. Her voice wavered; Ereza could tell she was fighting back tears. Poor dear; she hadn't ever learned toughness. Behind her twin, two other musicians leaned together, murmuring. Across the stage, someone standing behind a group of drums leaned forward and fiddled with something on the side of one of them.

"From measure eighty-two," said the conductor, this time not looking at Arla. Arla had the stubborn, withdrawn expression that Ereza knew well; she wasn't going to admit anything was wrong, or share what was bothering her. Well, musicians were different, like all artists. It would go into her art, that's what everyone said.

Ereza had no idea what measure eighty-two was, but she did recognize the honeyed sweetness of the opening phrase. Quickly, it became less sweet, brooding, as summer afternoons could thicken into menacing storms. She felt breathless, and did not know why. Arla's face gave no clue, her expression almost sullen. Her fingers flickered up and down the neck of the cello and reminded Ereza of the last time she'd played the game Flight-test with her twin, last leave. Before the reopening of hostilities, before some long-buried agent put a bomb in the barracks and cost her her arm. Arla had won, she remembered, those quick fingers as nimble on the controls as on her instrument.

Suddenly the impending storm broke; the orchestra was off at full speed and volume, Arla's cello nearly drowned in a tumult of sound. Ereza watched, wondering why it didn't sound pretty anymore. Surely you could make something stormy that was also good to listen to. Besides, she wanted to hear Arla, not all these other people. Arla was leaning into her bowing; Ereza knew what that would mean at home. But the cello couldn't dominate this group, not by sheer volume.

The chaos grew and grew, very much like a summer storm, and exploded in a series of crashes; the man with the drums was banging away on them.

The music changed again, leaving chaos behind. Arla, she noted, had a moment to rest, and wiped her sweaty face. She had a softer expression now and gazed at the other string players, across from her. Ereza wondered what she thought at times like this. Was she thinking ahead to her own next move? Listening to the music itself? What?

Brasses blared, a wall of sound that seemed to sweep the lighter strings off the stage. Ereza liked horns as a rule, but these seemed pushy and arrogant, not merely jubilant. She saw Arla's arm move, and the cello answered the horns like a reproving voice. The brasses stuttered and fell silent while the cello sang on. Now Arla's face matched the music, serenity and grace. Other sections returned, but the cello this time rose over them, collecting them into a seamless web of harmony.

When the conductor cut off the final chord, Ereza realized she'd been holding her breath and let it out with a whoof. She would be able to tell Arla how much it meant to listen to her and mean it. She was no musical expert, and knew it, but she could see why her sister was considered an important cultural resource. Not for the first time, she breathed a silent prayer of thanks that it had been her own less-talented right arm she'd lost to trauma. When her new prosthesis came in, she'd be able to retrain for combat; even without it, there were many things she could do in the military. But the thought of Arla without an arm was obscene.

The rehearsal continued to a length that bored Ereza and numbed her ears. She could hear no difference between the first and fifth repetition of something, even though the conductor, furious with first the woodwinds and then the violas, threw a tantrum about it and explained in detail what he wanted. Arla caused no more trouble—in fact, the conductor threw her a joke once, at which half the cello section burst out laughing. Ereza didn't catch it. At the end, he dismissed the orchestra and told Arla to stay. She nodded, and carried her cello over to its case; the conductor made notes on his papers and shuffled through them. While the others straggled offstage, she wiped the cello with a cloth and put the bow neatly into its slot, then closed the case and latched it.

Ereza wondered if she should leave now, but she had no idea where Arla would go next, and she wanted to talk to her. She waited, watching the conductor's back, the other musicians, Arla's care with her instrument. Finally all the others had gone, and the conductor turned to Arla.

"Miss Fennaris, I know this is a difficult time for you—" In just such a tone had Ereza's first flight officer reamed her out for failing to check one of the electronic subsystems in her ship. Her own difficult time had been a messy love affair; she wondered why Arla wasn't past that. Arla wisely said nothing. "You are the soloist, and that's quite a responsibility under the circumstances—" Arla nodded while Ereza wondered again *what* circumstances. "We have to know you will be able to perform; this is not a trivial performance."

"I will," Arla said. She had been looking at the floor, but now she raised her eyes to the conductor's face—and past them, to Ereza, standing in the shadows. She turned white, as if she'd lost all her blood, and staggered.

"What—?" The conductor swung around then and saw that single figure in the gloom at the back of the hall. "Who's there? Come down here, damn you!"

Ereza shrugged to herself as she came toward the lighted stage. She did not quite limp, though the knee still argued about downward slopes. She watched her footing, with glances to Arla who now stood panting like someone who had run a race. What ailed the child—did she think her sister was a ghost? Surely they'd told her things were coming along. The conductor, glaring and huffing, she ignored. She'd had permission, from the mousy little person at the front door, and she had not made one sound during rehearsal.

"*Who* told you you could barge in here—!" the conductor began. Ereza gave him her best smile, as she saw recognition hit. She and Arla weren't identical, but the family resemblance was strong enough.

"I'm Ereza Fennaris, Arla's sister. I asked out front, and they said she was in rehearsal, but if I didn't interrupt—"

"You just did." He was still angry but adjusting to what he already knew. Wounded veteran, another daughter of a powerful family, his soloist's twin sister... there were limits to what he could do. To her, at least; she hoped he wouldn't use this as an excuse to bully Arla.

She smiled up at her sister. "Hello again, Arlashi! You didn't come to see me, so I came to see you."

"Is *she* why—did you see her back there when you—?" The conductor had turned away from Ereza to her sister.

"No." Arla drew a long breath. "I did not see her until she came nearer. I haven't seen her since—"

"Sacred Name of God! Artists!" The conductor threw his baton to the floor and glared from one to the other. "A concert tomorrow night, and you had to come now!" That for Ereza. "Your own sister wounded, and you haven't seen her?" That for Arla. He picked up his baton and pointed it at her. "You thought it would go away, maybe? You thought you could put it directly into the music, poof, without seeing her?"

"I thought—if I could get through the concert—"

"Well, you can't. You showed us that, by God." He whirled and pointed his finger at Ereza. "You—get up here! I can't be talking in two directions."

Ereza stifled an impulse to giggle. He acted as if he had real authority; she could just see him trying that tone on a platoon commander and finding out that he didn't. She picked her way to a set of small steps up from the floor of the hall and made her way across the stage, past the empty chairs. Arla stared at her, still breathing too fast. She would faint if she kept that up, silly twit.

"What a mess!" the conductor was saying. "And what an ugly thing *that* is—is that the best our technology can do for you?" He was staring at her temporary prosthesis, with its metal rods and clips.

"Tactful, aren't you?" She wasn't exactly angry, not yet, but she was moving into a mood where anger would be easy. He would have to realize that while he could bully Arlashi, he couldn't bully her. If being blown apart, buried for days, and reassembled with bits missing hadn't crushed her, no mere musician could.

"This is not about tact," the conductor said. "Not that I'd expect you to be aware of that…. Arriving on the eve of this concert to upset my soloist, for instance, is hardly an expression of great tact."

Ereza resisted an urge to argue. "This is a temporary prosthesis," she said, holding it up. "Right now, as you can imagine, they're short-staffed; it's going to take longer than it would have once to get the permanent one. However, it gives me some practice in using one."

"I should imagine." He glared at her. "Now sit down and be quiet. I have something to say to your sister."

"If you're planning to scold her, don't bother. She's about to faint—"

"I am *not*," Arla said. She had gone from pale to a dull red that clashed with her purple tunic.

"You have no rights here," said the conductor to Ereza. "You're just upsetting her—and I'll have to see her later. But for now—" He made a movement with his hands, tossing her the problem, and walked offstage. From that distance, he got the last word in. "Miss Fennaris—the *cellist* Miss Fennaris— see me in my office this afternoon at fourteen-twenty."

"You want lights?" asked a distant voice from somewhere overhead.

"No," said Arla, still not looking at Ereza. "Cut 'em." The brilliant stage light-ing disappeared; Arla's dark clothes melted into the gloom onstage, leaving her face—older, sadder—to float above it. "Damn you, Ereza—why did you have to come now?"

Ereza couldn't think of anything to say. That was not what she'd imagined Arla saying. Anger and disappointment struggled; what finally came out was, "Why didn't you come to see me? I kept expecting you…. Was it just this concert?" She could—almost—understand that preparing for a major appearance might keep her too busy to visit the hospital.

"No. Not… exactly." Arla looked past her. "It was—I couldn't practice without thinking about it. Your hand. My hand. If I'd seen you, I couldn't have gone on making music. I should have—after I beat you at Flight-test I should have enlisted. If I'd been there—"

"You'd have been asleep, like the rest of us. It wasn't slow reflexes that did it,

Arlashi, it was a bomb. While we slept. Surely they told you that." But Arla's face had that stubborn expression again. Ereza tried again. "Look— what you're feeling—I do understand that. When I woke up and found Reia'd been killed, and Aristide, I hated myself for living. You wish I hadn't been hurt, and because you're not a soldier—"

"Don't start that!" Arla shifted, and a music stand went over with a clatter. "Dammit!" She crouched and gathered the music in shaking hands, then stabbed the stand upright. "If I get this out of order, Kiel will—"

Ereza felt a trickle of anger. "It's only sheets of paper—surely this Kiel can put it back in order. It's not like... what do you mean 'Don't start that'?"

"That *you're not a soldier* rigmarole. I know perfectly well I'm not, and you are. Everyone in the family is, except me, and I know how you all feel about it."

"Nonsense." They had had this out before; Ereza thought she'd finally got through, but apparently Arla still worried. Typical of the civilian mind, she thought, to fret about what couldn't be helped. "No one blames you; we're *proud* of you. Do you think we need another soldier? We've told you—"

"Yes. You've told me." Ereza waited, but Arla said nothing more, just stood there, staring at the lighter gloom over the midhall, where the skylight was.

"Well, then. You don't want to be a soldier; you never did. And no need, with a talent like yours. It's what we fight for, anyway—"

"Don't say that!"

"Why not? It's true. Gods be praised, Arlashi, we're not like the Metiz, quarreling for the pure fun of it, happy to dwell in a wasteland if only it's a battlefield. Or the Gennar Republic, which cares only for profit. Our people have always valued culture: music, art, literature. It's to make a society in which culture can flourish—where people like you can flourish—that we go to war at all."

"So it's my fault." That in a quiet voice. "You would lay the blame for this war—for that bomb—on me?"

"Of course not, ninny! How could it be your fault, when a Gavalan terrorist planted that bomb?" Musicians, Ereza thought, were incapable of understanding issues. If poor Arla had thought the bombing was her fault, no wonder she came apart—and how useless someone so fragile would be in combat, for all her hand-eye coordination and dexterity. "You aren't to blame for the misbegotten fool who did it, or the pigheaded political leadership that sent him."

"But you said—"

"Arlashi, listen. Your new cello—you know where the wood came from?"

"Yes." That sounded sullen, even angry. "Reparations from Scavel; the Military Court granted the Music Council first choice for instruments."

"That's what I mean. We go to war to protect our people—physical and economic protection. Do you think a poor, helpless society could afford wood for instruments? A concert hall to play in? The stability in which the arts flourish?"

Arla stirred, but Ereza went on quickly before she could interrupt. "I didn't intend to lose a hand—no one does—but I would have done it gladly to give you your music—"

"I didn't ask you for that! You didn't have to lose anything to give me music. I could give *myself* music!"

"Not that cello," Ereza said, fighting to keep a reasonable tone. She could just imagine Arla out in the stony waste, trying to string dry grass across twigs and make music. Surely even musicians realized how much they needed the whole social structure, which depended on the military's capacity to protect both the physical planet and its trade networks. "Besides—war has to be something more than killing, more than death against death. We aren't barbarians. It has to be *for* something."

"It doesn't have to be for me."

"Yes, you. I can't do it. You could fight—" She didn't believe that, but saying it might get Arla's full attention. "Anyone can fight, who has courage, and you have that. But I can't make music. If I had spent the hours at practice you have, I still couldn't make your music. If I die, there are others as skilled as I am who could fight our wars. But if you die, there will be no music. In all the generations since Landing, our family has given one soldier after another. You—you're something different—"

"But I didn't ask for it."

Ereza shrugged, annoyed. "No one asks for their talent, or lack of it."

"That's not what I mean." Arla struggled visibly, then shrugged. "Look— we can't talk here; it's like acting, being on this stage. Come to my rehearsal room."

"Now? But I thought we'd go somewhere for lunch. I have to leave soon."

"Now. I have to put my precious war-won wood cello away." Arla led the way to her instrument, then offstage and down a white-painted corridor. Ereza ignored the sarcastic tone of that remark and followed her. Doors opened on either side; from behind some of them music leaked out, frail ghosts of melody.

Arla's room had two chairs, a desk-mounted computer, and a digital music stand. Arla waved her to one of the chairs; Ereza sat down and looked over at the music stand's display.

"Why don't you have this kind onstage? Why that paper you spilled?"

Her attempt to divert Arla's attention won a wry grin. "Maestro Bogdan won't allow it. Because the tempo control's usually operated by foot, he's convinced the whole orchestra would be tapping its toes. Even if we were, it'd be less intrusive than reaching out and turning pages, but he doesn't see it that way. Traditionally, even good musicians turn pages, but only bad musicians tap their feet. And we live for tradition—like my cello." Arla had opened the case again, and then she tapped her cello with one finger. It made a soft *tock* that sounded almost alive.

With a faint sigh she turned away and touched her computer. The music stand display came up, with a line of music and the measure numbers above it. She turned it to give Ereza a better view.

"Do you know what that is?"

Ereza squinted and read aloud. "Artruud's Opus 27, measure seventy-nine?"

"Do you know what *that* is?"

Ereza shook her head. "No—should I? I might if you hummed it."

Arla gave a short, ugly laugh. "I doubt that. We just played it, the whole thing. This—" She pointed at the display, which showed ten measures at a time. "This is where I blew up. Eighty-two to eighty-six."

"Yes, but I don't read music."

"I know." Arla turned and looked directly at her. "Did you ever think about that? The fact that I can play Flight-test as well as you, that my scores in Tac-Sim—the tests you had me take as a joke—were enough to qualify me for officers' training if I'd wanted it... but not one of you in the family can read music well enough to pick out a tune on the piano?"

"It's not our talent. And you, surrounded by a military family—of course you'd pick up something—"

"Is war so easy?" That in a quiet voice, washed clean of emotion. Ereza stared at her, shocked.

"Easy! Of course it's not easy." She still did not want to think about her first tour, the near disaster of that patrol on Sardon, when a training mission had gone sour. It was nothing she could discuss with Arla. Her stump throbbed, reminding her of more recent pain. How could Arla ask that question? She started to ask that, but Arla had already spoken.

"But you think I picked it up, casually, with no training?"

"Well... our family... and besides, what you did was only tests, not real combat."

"Yes. And do you think that if you'd been born into a musical family, you'd have picked up music so casually? Would you be able to play the musical equivalent of Flight-test?"

"I'd have to know more, wouldn't I?" Ereza wondered where this conversation was going. Clearly Arla was upset about something, something to do with her own wound. *It's my arm that's missing*, she thought. *I'm the one who has a right to be upset or not upset.* "I'd still have no talent for it, but I would probably know more music when I heard it."

"Yet I played music in the same house, Eri, four to six hours a day when we were children. You had ears; you could have heard. We slept in the same room; you could have asked questions. You told me if you liked something, or if you were tired of hearing it; you never once asked me a *musical* question. You heard as much music as many musicians' children. The truth is that you didn't care.

None of our family cared."

Ereza knew the shock she felt showed on her face; Arla nodded at her and went on talking. "Dari can tell you how his preschool training team pretended to assault the block fortress, and you listen to him. You listen carefully, you admire his cleverness or point out where he's left himself open for a counterattack. But me—I could play Hohlander's first cello concerto backward, and you'd never notice. It's not important to you—it's beneath your notice."

"That's not true." Ereza clenched the fingers of her left hand on the arm of the chair. "Of course we care; of course we notice. We know you're good; that's why you had the best teachers. It's just that it's not our field—we're not *supposed* to be experts."

"But you are about everything else." Arla, bracing herself on the desk, looked almost exultant. Ereza could hardly believe what she was hearing. The girl must have had this festering inside for years, to bring it out now, to someone wounded in her defense. "You talk politics as if it were your field— why this war is necessary, why that legislation is stupid. You talk about manufacturing, weapons design, the civilian economy—all *that* seems to be your area of expertise. If music and art and poetry are so important—if they're the reason you fight—then why don't you know anything about them? Why don't you bother to learn even the basics, the sort of stuff you expect Dari to pick up by the time he's five or six?"

"But—we can't do it all," Ereza said, appalled at the thought of all the children, talented or untalented, forced to sit through lessons in music. Every child had to know something about drill and survival techniques; Cravor's World, even in peacetime, could be dangerous. But music? You couldn't save yourself in a sandstorm or grass fire by knowing who wrote which pretty tune, or how to read musical notation. "We found you teachers who did—"

"Whom you treated like idiots," Arla said. "Remember the time Professor Rizvi came over, and talked to Grandmother after my lesson? No—of course you wouldn't; you were in survival training right then, climbing up cliffs or something like that. But it was just about the time the second Gavalan rebellion was heating up, and he told Grandmother the sanctions against the colonists just made things worse. She got that tone in her voice—you know what I mean—and silenced him. After that he wouldn't come to the house; I went into the city for my lessons. She told the story to Father, and they laughed together about the silly, ineffectual musician who wouldn't stand a chance against real power—with me standing there—and then they said, 'But you're a gifted child, Arlashi, and we love it.'"

"They're right." Ereza leaned forward. "What would a composer and musician know about war? And it doesn't take much of a weapon to smash that cello you're so fond of." She knew that much, whatever she didn't know about music. To her surprise, Arla gave a harsh laugh.

"Of *course* it doesn't take much weaponry to smash a cello. It doesn't take a weapon at all. I could trip going down the stairs and fall on it; I could leave it flat on the floor and step on it. You don't need to be a skilled soldier to destroy beauty: any clumsy fool can manage that."

"But—"

Arla interrupted her. "That's my point. You take pride in your skill, in your special, wonderful knowledge. And all you can accomplish with it is what carelessness or stupidity or even the normal path of entropy will do by itself. If you want a cello smashed, you don't need an army: just turn it over to a preschool class without a teacher present. If you want to ruin a fine garden, you don't have to march an expensive army through it—just let it alone. If you want someone to die, you don't have to kill them: just *wait!* We'll all die, Ereza. We don't need your help."

"It's not about that!" But Ereza felt a cold chill. If Arla could think that... "It's not about killing. It's protecting—"

"You keep saying that, but—did you ever consider asking me? Asking any artist, any writer, any musician? Did you ever consider learning enough of our arts to guess how we might feel?"

Ereza stared at her, puzzled. "But we did protect you. We let you study music from the beginning; we've never pushed you into the military. What more do you want, Arlashi?"

"To be myself, to be a musician just because I *am,* not because you needed someone to prove that you weren't all killers."

That was ridiculous. Ereza stared at her twin, wondering if someone had mindwiped her. Would one of the political fringe groups have thought to embarrass the Fennaris family, with its rich military history, by recruiting its one musician? "I don't understand," she said, aware of the stiffness in her voice. She would have to tell Grandmother as soon as she got out of here, and find out if anyone else had noticed how strange Arla had become.

Arla leaned forward. "Ereza, you cannot have me as a tame conscience... someone to feel noble about. I am not a simple musician, all full of sweet melody, to soothe your melancholy hours after battle." She plucked a sequence of notes, pleasant to the ear.

"Not that I mind your being soldiers," Arla went on, now looking past Ereza's head into some distance that didn't belong in that small room. Ereza had seen that look on soldiers; it shocked her on Arla's face. "It's not that I'm a pacifist, you see. It's more complicated than that. I want you to be honest soldiers. If you like war, admit it. If you like killing, admit that. Don't make me the bearer of your nobility, and steal my own dark initiative. I am a person—a whole person—with my own kind of violence."

"Of course you're a whole person—everyone is—"

"No. You aren't. You aren't because you know nothing about something you claim is important to you."

"What do you want me to do?" Ereza asked. She felt grumpy. Her stump hurt now, and she wanted to be back with people who didn't make ridiculous emotional arguments or confuse her.

"Quit thinking of me as sweet little Arlashi, your pet twin, harmless and fragile and impractical. Learn a little music, so you'll know what discipline really is. Or admit you don't really care, and quit condescending to me."

"Of course I care." She cared that her sister had gone crazy, at least. Then a thought occurred to her. "Tell me—do the other musicians feel as you do?"

Arla cocked her head and gave her an unreadable look. "Come to the concert tomorrow, Eri."

"I don't know if I can—" She didn't know if she wanted to. A long journey into the city, hours crammed into a seat with others, listening to music that didn't (if she was honest) interest her that much. She'd already heard it, parts of it over and over. "How about tomorrow's rehearsal?"

"No. The concert. I can get you in. If you want to know how musicians think, and why… then come."

"Are the others—?"

"I don't know. Grandmother usually comes to my performances, but the others less often. I wish you would, Eri."

Ereza sat in the back row of the concert hall, surrounded by people in formal clothes and dress uniforms. Onstage the orchestra waited, in formal black and white, for the soloist and conductor. She saw a stir at the edge of the stage. Arla, in her long swirling dress, with the cello. The conductor—she looked quickly at her program for his name. Mikailos Bogdan.

Applause, which settled quickly as the house lights went down. Now the clear dome showed a dark night sky with a thick wedge of stars, the edge of the Cursai Cluster. The conductor lifted his arms. Ereza watched; the musicians did not stir. His arms came down.

Noise burst from speakers around the hall. As if conducting music, Bogdan's arms moved, but the noise had nothing to do with his direction. Grinding, squealing, exploding—all the noises that Ereza finally recognized as belonging to an armored ground unit in battle. Rattle and clank of treads, grinding roar of engines, tiny voices yelling, screaming, the heavy thump of artillery and lighter crackling of small arms. Around her the others stirred, looked at one another in amazement, then horror.

Onstage, no one moved. The musicians stared ahead, oblivious to the noise; Ereza, having heard the rehearsal, wondered how they could stand it. And *why?* Why work so for perfection in rehearsal if they never meant to play? Toward the front, someone stood—someone in uniform—and yelled. Ereza could not hear it over the shattering roar that came from the speakers, then— low-level aircraft strafing, she thought. She remembered that sound. Another two or three people stood up; the first to stand began to push his way out of his row. One of the others was hauled back down by those sitting near him.

The sound changed, this time to the repetitive *crump-crump-crump-crump* of bombardment. Vague, near-human sounds, too… Ereza shivered, knowing before it came clear what that would be. Screams, moans, sobs… it went on far too long. She wanted to get up and leave, but she had no strength.

Silence, when it finally came, was welcome. Ereza could hear, as her ears regained their balance, the ragged breathing of the audience. Silence continued, the conductor still moving his arms as if the orchestra were responding. Finally, he brought the unnerving performance to a close, turned and bowed to them. A few people clapped, uncertainly; no one else joined them and the sound died away.

"Disgracefully bad taste," said someone to Ereza's right. "I don't know what they think they're doing."

"Getting us ready to be ravished by Fennaris, no doubt. Have you heard her before?"

"Only on recordings. I've been looking forward to this for decads."

"She's worth it. I heard her first in a chamber group two years ago, and—" The conductor beckoned, and Arla stood; the gossipers quieted. Intent curiosity crackled around the hall, silent but alive.

"Ladies and gentlemen," Arla said. She had an untrained voice, but even so it carried to the back of the hall. "You may be wondering what happened to the Goldieri Concerto. We chose to make another statement about music."

The conductor bowed to her, and signaled the orchestra. Each musician held an instrument at arm's length; at the flick of his baton they all dropped to the floor, the light rattling cases of violins, the softer boom of violas, the clatter and thud and tinkle of woodwinds, brasses, percussion. A tiny round drum rolled along the floor until it ran into someone's leg and fell over with a final loud tap. Louder than that was the indrawn breath of the audience.

"I'm Arla," she said, standing alone, facing a crowd whose confusion was slowly turning to hostility. Ereza felt her skin tingling. "Most of you know me as Arla Fennaris, but tonight I'm changing my name. I want you to know why."

She turned and picked up her cello, which she had left leaning against her chair. *No*, Ereza thought, *don't do it. Not that one. Please.*

"You think of me as a cellist," Arla said, and plucked three notes with one hand. "A cellist is a musician, and a musician—I have this from my own sister, a wounded veteran, as many of you know—a musician is to most of you an impractical child. A fool." She ran her hand down the strings, and the sound echoed in Ereza's bones. She shivered, and so did the people sitting next to her. "She tells me, my sister, that the reason we're at war right now—the reason she lost her arm—is that I am a mere musician, and need protection. I can't protect myself; I send others out to die, to keep me and my music alive." Another sweeping move across the strings, and a sound that went through Ereza like a jagged blade. All she could think was *No, no, don't… no…* but she recognized the look on Arla's face, the tone of her voice. Here was someone committed beyond reason to whatever she was doing.

But Arla had turned, and found her chair again. She was sitting as she would for any performance, the cello nestled in the hollow of her skirt, the bow in her right hand. "It is easy to make noise," Arla said. With a move Ereza did not understand, she made an ugly noise explode from the cello. "It takes skill to make music." Arla played a short phrase as sweet as spring sunshine. "It is easy to destroy—" She held the cello up, as if to throw it, and again Ereza heard the indrawn breath as the audience waited. Then she put it down. "It takes skill to make—in this case, millennia of instrument designers, and Barrahesh, here on Cravor's World, with a passion for the re-creation of classic instruments. I have no right to destroy his work—but it would be easy." She tapped the cello's side, and the resonant sound expressed fragility. "As with my cello, with everything. It is easy to kill; it takes skill to nurture life." Again she played a short phrase, this one a familiar child's song about planting flower seeds in the desert.

"My sister," Arla said, and her eyes found Ereza's, and locked onto them. "My sister is a soldier, a brave soldier, who was wounded… she would say protecting me. Protection I never asked for, and did not need. Her arm the price of this one—" She held up her right arm. "It is difficult to make music when you are using your sister's arm. An arm taught to make war, not music. An arm that does not respect music."

She lowered her arm. "I can make music only with my own arm, because it's my arm that learned it. And to play with my arm means throwing away my sister's sacrifice. Denying it. Repudiating it." *No,* Ereza thought at her again. *Don't do this. I will understand; I will change. Please.* But she knew it was too late, as it had been too late to change things when she woke after surgery and found her own arm gone. "If my sister wants music, she must learn to make it. If you want music, you must learn to make it. We will teach you; we will play with you—but we will not play *for* you. Good evening."

Again the conductor signaled; the musicians picked up their instruments from the floor, stood, and walked out. For a moment, the shuffling of their feet onstage was the only sound as shock held the audience motionless. Ereza felt the same confusion, the same hurt, the same realization that they would get no music. Then the catcalls began, the hissing, the programs balled up angrily and thrown; some hit the stage and a few hit the musicians. But none of them hurried, none of them looked back. Arla and the conductor waited, side by side, as the orchestra cleared the stage. Ereza sat frozen, unable to move even as people pushed past her, clambered over her legs. She wanted to go and talk to Arla; she knew it would do no good. She did not speak Arla's language. She never had. Now she knew what Arla meant: she had never respected her sister before. Now she did. *Too late, too late,* cried her mind, struggling to remember something, anything, of the music.

TRADITION

July 31, 1914. Durazzo, Albania

Rear Admiral Sir Christopher George Francis Maurice Cradock strode briskly along the deck of his flagship, H.M.S. *Defence,* walking off the effects of last night's dinner with the officers of the S.M.S. *Breslau.* Despite the political tension of the past few weeks, it had been a pleasant evening of good food and good talk, punctuated by the clink of silver on china and the gurgle of wine into glasses as the mess stewards kept them filled.

Only once had Commander Kettner revealed any hint of that German confidence which so nearly approached arrogance. "You English—" he had said, his voice rising. Then he had chuckled affably. "You have so much invested in tradition," he had continued, more relaxed. "We Germans have a tradition to make. It is always so for vigorous youth, is it not?" The clear implication that the Royal Navy was superannuated had rankled, but Cradock had passed it off graciously. Time enough to compare traditions when the young eagle actually flew and dared its talons against Britannia's experience. He had no doubt that rashness would be well reproved.

Cradock took a deep breath and eyed the steep tile roofs, bright in morning sunlight, that stepped down to the harbor, its still water perfectly reflecting both ships and buildings. Behind them rose the mountains in which—in happier years—he had hunted boar. No foxhunting here, but a sportsman could find some game anywhere.

He glanced over at *Breslau,* admitting to himself that the Germans had certainly reached a high standard of seamanship. Every detail he had seen the day before had been correct. Several of the officers had read his books; they had asked him to expand on some of the points he'd made. Only courtesy, of course, but he could not help being pleased.

A thicker ooze of smoke from *Breslau*'s funnels stained the morning air. Cradock slowed. On her decks a subdued flurry of movement he recognized at once. Astern, the smooth reflection of the mountains shattered like a dropped mirror as her screws churned. He turned to his flag lieutenant.

"What do we know of Admiral Souchon and the *Goeben?*" Cradock asked.

"At last report, sir, the *Goeben* had made port in Trieste, then gone to sea for gunnery practice."

A cold chill ran down Cradock's back. Gunnery practice? If the Germans were intending to declare war first, only they would know when. The Japanese had given no warning to the Russians at Port Arthur in 1904.

"When *Breslau* weighs anchor, send word to Admiral Milne," Cradock said. "And inform Captain Wray that we will be returning to Corfu immediately."

"Sir."

In short order, the German light cruiser was moving out of the anchorage, a demure curl of white at her bow that would, Cradock was sure, lengthen to a streak when she was out of sight.

August 6, 1914. Early morning off Corfu

Admiral Cradock considered, as he took several rashers of bacon onto his plate, at what point his duty to His Majesty might require disobedience to his superior, Admiral Sir Berkeley Milne. It was not a dilemma in which he had ever expected to find himself.

When he raised his flag in H.M.S. *Defence,* a British admiral in command of a cruiser squadron in the Mediterranean could expect a constant round of visits to attractive ports, dinners with dignitaries who all wanted some concession, meetings with other naval officials, all conducted with the utmost ceremony. Here were the smartest ships in the Royal Navy, and the most favored officers.

Now he commanded a squadron at war, a situation calling for very different talents than the ability to dance with a prime minister's daughter or make polite conversation with French magistrates and Turkish pashas. And—more to the point—a situation in which mistakes would imperil not merely an officer's reputation and future career, but the very survival of the Empire.

Cradock knew himself to be an old-fashioned sailor. Seamanship was his passion, correct and accurate handling of ships in all weathers, placing them where they could best effect strategy. Seamanship required comprehensive knowledge of exact details: how to organize coaling, how to coil ropes, how to turn a ship in formation precisely where she should turn. Most important, it required naval discipline, on which both naval tradition and the whole towering edifice of empire depended. Lack of discipline led to slovenly seamanship, and that, in the end, to disaster.

His responsibility, therefore, was to do what his commander told him. Therein lay the rub.

Admiral Sir Berkeley Milne, Commander in Chief of the Mediterranean Fleet, had in the past few days revealed himself no Nelson. For three days, Milne had thrashed around the Mediterranean in vain pursuit of the German ships, shifting Cradock's own squadron about in useless dashes, a waste of coal and energy. Now, on the second full day of war, when the German ships were in Messina and could have been bottled up by placing adequate force at either end of the Strait of Messina, Milne had instead taken his battle cruisers off to coal in Bizerte—all the way to North Africa. He had ordered Cradock to stay at the mouth of the Adriatic, and placed only little *Gloucester* to watch the exit to the eastern Mediterranean, because he was sure the Germans would try to go west.

Cradock was not so sure of that. What he knew, with absolute certainty, was that the *Goeben* would cause the Royal Navy immense trouble if she were not sunk, and that the Admiralty wanted her sunk. And he could not sink her from here, sitting idly off Corfu waiting for Milne to give sensible orders. That fox Souchon had plans of his own.

As a technical problem of naval tactics, it came down to speed and guns. The German ships were faster, especially the turbine-powered *Goeben,* and *Goeben* had bigger guns that outranged his by several nautical miles. Thus the *Goeben* could, in theory, stand off at a distance where her great shells could pound the cruisers, and their shots would all fall short.

He could think of ways to trap such a ship, ways to neutralize her superior speed and gunpower. What he could not imagine was any way to do it within the confines of his duty as a subordinate to Admiral Sir Berkeley Milne. This latter problem, one more of strategy than tactics, had occupied his mind the day before, disturbed his sleep, and—this hot August morning—it affected his appetite.

He stroked his beard. He could understand why Milne had not followed the German ships into the Strait of Messina. England had gone to war because the Germans violated Belgian neutrality; she could hardly, in such circumstances, violate neutral Italy's territorial waters. In terms of strategy, as well, Italy's unexpected neutrality was a precious gift, freeing the British and French fleets from the threat they had most feared.

But to leave the strait unguarded, except by ships too small to engage the Germans—that was folly indeed. Should he, even in the face of Milne's contrary orders, move his squadron to back up Kelly in *Gloucester?* No, because all that dashing about had left his destroyers short of coal, and in a fight with *Goeben* he would need their help. Coaling had to come first.

He finished his breakfast without really noticing the taste and smell, mechanically downing bite after bite, and put his mind to the easier problem.

He would need every ship under his command, cruisers and destroyers alike. If he could have ordered the weather, a storm at night would have been ideal, but this was the season of burning blue days, one after another, and bright moonlight made night attack in the open sea as dangerous as in daylight. Not in the open sea, then. Wherever the Germans went, after Messina, they would have to run to earth eventually. For all her speed, the *Goeben* devoured coal; that meant coming into harbors. Close to the intricate coastline of Greece or Albania, her speed and her range would be of less use, and he could—if he guessed where she was headed— be in position to intercept her, appear at his range, not hers.

But only if he was free to do so. The solution of one problem doubled back to the insoluble greater one: Milne's refusal to let him act as he thought best. Cradock felt like a horse reined in by a timid rider, unable to run freely down to his fences. And he knew he would be blamed for any failure, as a horse is blamed for a fall by the very rider who caused the problem.

He pushed that thought aside—it did no good—and in order to place himself ahead of Souchon considered where in the Mediterranean he might go. West to harry the French, or escape via Gibraltar into the Atlantic? Not with three battle cruisers that outgunned the *Goeben,* not to mention the French fleet, awaiting her there. North to the Austrians at Pola, their allies? No, because the Adriatic was a trap, and Souchon too smart a fox to run to an earth with only one door. Southeast to harry Port Said and the Suez, or Alexandria? Possibly, but where would he resupply? Or northeast, to Constantinople, with exits to both the Black Sea and the Mediterranean, exits easily mined and guarded by forts on land?

If Souchon had reason to believe that the Turks would let him in, that they were thinking of allying with the Germans... that is where he would go. Of course the Turks should do no such thing—they had declared themselves neutral. But... *were* they?

That was the question. Cradock spread marmalade on his toast and considered. Turks were Orientals, with who knew what logical processes. The British had been advising their navy, but the Admiralty had just seized two Turkish dreadnoughts under construction in British yards. The British had helped defend the Turks against the Russians, but they had also helped Greece gain her independence from the Turks. Which, at this juncture, would sway those devious pashas?

A tap heralded the arrival of his captains for the morning conference. It began with a situation report from his flag lieutenant that located each ship in the Mediterranean, so far as was known. Cradock suppressed the comment he wanted to make. Milne was only just around the northwest corner of Sicily, and proceeding with measured pace back toward the Strait of Messina.

"Where's *Indomitable*?" one of the others asked.

"Back in Bizerte, coaling," Fawcett Wray, his flag captain said. "There was some problem with requisitions..."

Cradock said nothing. He had done his small best to improve the coaling efficiency of his squadron, but Milne's insistence on personally approving every detail made it almost impossible. He seemed to think initiative more dangerous than any enemy.

"Requisitions!" That was Coode, captain of destroyers. Cradock had heard him on other occasions; now he cocked an eyebrow at the young man, who subsided like a kettle moved off the fire, steam almost visibly puffing from his ears.

"Gentlemen, the German ships will have to emerge today, or face internship." That got their attention. "Let me explain what I expect them to do." Quickly he retraced his reasoning on the possible courses of action open to the Germans.

"The Turks would not dare harbor them," Wray said. "They must know it would turn us against them. We are their naval advisors; they asked for an alliance with us only last year—"

"Which was refused," Cradock pointed out. "The government did not want to inflame the Russians or the Germans with a formal alliance there... but I daresay the Turks took it differently. In addition, on our most recent visit to Turkey, I heard from the locals that Admiral Souchon was a great man. When I asked why, they told me about his having sent the crew of the *Goeben* to help fight a fire in a Turkish barracks in Constantinople, back in May. Several of the Germans died; the Turks—you know how emotional they are—got up a celebration of some kind."

"But... the Turks are neutrals. Even if they admire Souchon—"

"They're Turks. Intrigue is their nature, along with theft and pillage. They have as well that touchy Oriental vanity, which a trifling matter like assistance in a barracks fire would flatter. For Orientals, this is enough. It does not occur to them that any British captain would have done the same."

"But you don't seriously believe they would come into the war as German allies? Not after all we've done for them—"

"I doubt very much they would ally with Germany... but I can imagine them giving sanctuary to the *Goeben* and then finding Souchon more than a match for them. With those guns leveled at the city, can you imagine the pashas refusing his demands?"

"Well, sir," Coode said, "if this is what you think the Germans are going to do, then why aren't we blockading the southern end of the Strait of Messina, instead of sitting over here watching for Austrians?"

"Admiral Milne's orders," Cradock said. "I intend to ask Admiral Milne for permission to position the squadron where we can engage the *Goeben* under more favorable terms. We will need to move south to do so. Therefore, we must attend to coaling the destroyers at once."

Cradock took a turn on the deck, observing every detail of his squadron, the sea, the signs of weather in the sky, trying to avert his mind from the signs of weather— heavy weather—ahead in his relationship with his commander. Across the blue water, Corfu rose in terraces of gold and green; the mingled scents of lemon groves, thyme, and roses on the breeze competed with the nearer whiff of coal, oil, metal polish, and the freshly holystoned deck. Westward, beyond the blue morning shadows, sunlight burned on the lapis sea, and in the distant haze Italy's heel formed a vague smudge on the horizon. In this second day of war, peace lingered here, where nothing but his own ships seemed warlike.

When Milne finally answered his signal, it was to refuse permission to reinforce *Gloucester* at the western exit of the Strait of Messina.

Cradock did not tell Milne he had sent the destroyers to coal at Ithaca. Half-formed in his mind, a plan grew, like a stormcloud on a summer's day, hidden in wreaths of haze. If the *Goeben* broke free and ran east, as he expected, where and how could he catch her, given that his ships were slower? Not by a stern chase—she had outpaced even the big battle cruisers. Not by an interception—she could spot his smoke as far away as he could spot hers, and with her speed easily avoid him. No—he had to decide where she was going to be, and surprise her.

Which he could not do if he waited to ask Milne's permission. Like a thunder-cloud suddenly revealed, his dilemma stood clear. Was he seriously considering ignoring his orders to guard the Adriatic, making an independent decision to anticipate Souchon's movements and engage the enemy ships? Without inform-ing Milne, in direct contravention of custom and naval law?

The very thought made him wince. He had had it drummed into him, and he had drummed it into others: commanders command, and juniors obey. To act on his thoughts risked not only his ships and his men, but the very foundations of naval discipline. Even if he was right, even if he caught and sank the *Goeben*, he might well be court-martialed; he would certainly not be given another com-mand. Milne would never forgive the insult; Beattie, Jellicoe... he winced again, imagining the astonishment and anger of men he respected, whose respect he desired. He was appalled himself. It was like a member of the field intervening in place of the M.F.H. and giving orders to the huntsmen.

Yet—he remembered the cold day when he'd first seen the bumptious red-headed young officer of hussars who was now First Lord of the Admiralty. For a moment he warmed himself in the glow of that infectious grin, that intensity so akin to his own. Stirrup to stirrup they had faced stone walls, sunken lanes, hedges that in memory seemed as much larger as last year's salmon. Bold, free-going, young Churchill's mistakes would be those of confidence and high courage; he might fall, but he would never shirk a fence. *He* would approve.

Yet again—Churchill was a civilian now, and had never been in the Navy. He had never been the model of an obedient young officer, even in a service as le-nient as the cavalry. Moreover, he had a reputation as a weathercock, changing parties for profit. Cradock dared not trust that memory.

His mind strayed to the First Sea Lord, Prince Louis Battenberg. An able man, who had earned his rank and position, but—would he understand the dilemma in which Cradock found himself? If only Jacky Fisher were still First Sea Lord! There was a fire eater who would approve anything, were the *Goeben* destroyed.

He took a long breath of Corfu's aromatic air, and reminded himself that, after all, he might be wrong. Souchon might run for the Adriatic. Or even Gibraltar. He might not have to make that choice.

Cradock ate a lunch that had no more flavor, in his distraction, than his breakfast. His destroyers had had to search all the way into the Gulf of Corinth for their collier, whose foreign captain had somehow gone to the wrong Port Vathi. Now they were coaling. Milne had finally reached the western exit of the Strait of Messina, with battle cruisers who could surely defeat *Goeben* if Souchon were stupid enough to go that way. His own rebellious thoughts spurred him toward bigger obstacles.

He could not wait until a crisis to decide what his priorities were, just as a fox-hunter could not wait until the last few strides before a fence to decide whether to jump. That way lay shies and refusals. No, the bold rider sent his horse at every fence resolved to clear it. His officers and men needed his direction, his resolution.

Nelson had been blind to a stupid order at Copenhagen— could he not be deaf to a stupid order in Greece?

Who was he, to compare himself to Nelson?

Should not every English admiral compare himself to Nelson, and strive to match his stature? Would Nelson be more afraid of displeasing a senior, or letting an enemy escape?

But Nelson had not had a wireless to pass on every whim of commanders far away. How would a Nelson have dealt with that distraction? Again he thought of Copenhagen, of Nelson putting the telescope to his blind eye.

He had one advantage surely more valuable than speed or guns: a depth of knowledge of the Mediterranean which neither Milne nor Souchon could match. He knew it in all seasons, all weathers, in more detail than Souchon could possibly have acquired in only ten months. His mind held not only chart data, but mental images of bays and inlets and passages apt for coaling, for unseen passage from one island to another. Shingle beaches, sand beaches, steep cliffs dropping straight into deep water, sea caves… like familiar fields long hunted over, whose every hedge and fence and gate is known to members of the hunt, he could bring it all to mind.

August 6, 2030 hours.

On the broad breast of the sea, the moonlight shone, as it had for thousands of years, lighting sailors home. Now it lit dark billows of coal smoke against a sea like hammered pewter. Two long, lean shapes slid through the quiet sea, menacing even as they fled. Behind them, a third, much smaller: H.M.S. *Gloucester* trailing the German ships *Goeben* and *Breslau*, and by her own smoke they knew she was shadowing them. To port, the coast of Italy, opening northward into the Gulf of Otranto; far ahead, on this course, the boot heel of Taranto, aimed in a backward kick at the narrow strait that led into the Adriatic.

On *Defence*, south of Corfu, Cradock stared at the charts and finally shook his head. *Gloucester* had reported the German ships leaving the Strait of Messina just after 1700 GMT, 1800 local time. Now, over two hours later, the German ships were still steaming ENE, as if aiming for the Adriatic. If that was where they were going, it was time to move the squadron north to intercept them. Cradock did not believe it.

"He must turn, and turn soon," he said.

"If they go north…" Captain Wray glanced at him. The other cruiser captains said nothing; they would let the flag captain do the talking, for now. "Our orders said keep them out of the Adriatic."

"He is a fox; he will not run into that trap." He felt a prickle of annoyance; he had explained this before. He sensed in Wray less enthusiasm for the chase than he would have wished in his flag captain. Weeks before, during a discussion of the German ship, Wray had kept harping on the German battle cruiser's strength, the range of its guns. Now he repeated himself.

"But… even if you're right, sir… the *Goeben* is far too powerful for us to engage without at least one of the battle cruisers to assist."

Cradock smiled at Wray, trying to hearten him. "She has bigger guns, certainly. And more armor. And more speed. But she is only one—no—" He put up his hand to forestall the younger man's correction. "I know, she has *Breslau*. But we easily overmatch *Breslau*. At night, along the coast of Greece… the *Goeben*'s advantages lessen markedly."

"Ah." Wray's face lightened. "You intend a night engagement in navigation waters? With the destroyers…"

"Yes. Pity it's so clear. But if we position ourselves where I am convinced she is likely to go, we can pick our best location, where the *Goeben*'s speed and range cannot help her. Then our numbers must count. I expect she will pick up her pace after her turn—she is only luring *Gloucester* on, loafing along at eighteen knots or so, hoping her lookouts will slack off."

"Not Captain Kelly's lookouts," Wray said, grinning.

"Quite so. So when she turns, I expect her to pick up speed, to twenty-four knots or more, and be off the southern capes of Greece before dawn. Now—this is what I propose—" He spread the chart out and explained in more detail.

2130 hours.

Cradock was dozing in his cabin, taking what rest he could, when Captain Wray called him. "Signal's just in from *Gloucester*, Admiral," he said. "The Germans have turned, just as you thought. They were trying to jam the signal, but *Gloucester* kept sending. I took the liberty of informing Admiral Milne, but have received no reply yet."

Milne, Cradock thought, would be sure it was a trick. Luckily Milne would still be at dinner, and unlikely to give a return signal until he had finished. Cradock didn't want to talk to Milne about what he planned, and be told not to do it. "What's her speed?" he asked.

"Nineteen knots," Wray said.

"Odd," Cradock said. "I expected a spurt. Souchon must want to evade *Gloucester;* that would have been the ideal time to do so."

"She just turned."

"Mm. Ask *Gloucester* to inform us instantly of any change in her course or speed. And set the squadron's course to take us south to Sapienza behind Cephalonia and Zante." If the German ships kept that speed, his ships could easily arrive at Sapienza well before them, and choose their best place to engage.

Within minutes, he felt the cruiser thrust into the gentle swell with more urgency. Far below, sweating stokers would be shoveling coal into the furnaces… coal he would have to replenish. His mind ranged ahead, to the location of colliers.

It was near midnight when Captain Wray tapped at his door. Cradock woke instantly, the quick response of the seaman.

"Another report from *Gloucester,* sir. The German ships have separated; Captain Kelly's following the *Goeben,* and she is on the same course, at seventeen knots. *Dublin's* trying to find them; she has two destroyers with her, *Bulldog* and *Beagle.*"

"Seventeen knots." Cradock ran a hand through his hair. Why was such an admiral, with such a ship, crawling across the Mediterranean at a mere seventeen knots when he could have outpaced the *Gloucester* and been free of her surveillance? "He has some problem," Cradock said. "He didn't get coal—no, we know he got some coal. He didn't get enough to go where he wants to go—he's moving at his most economical speed to conserve it until he meets a collier somewhere. Or… he has boiler trouble."

"You can't know that, sir."

He didn't know it. He knew only that no man with a ship fast enough to shake a shadower would fail to do so unless something had gone wrong. And *Goeben* had been snugged away at the Austrian naval base of Pola for weeks before the war started. She could have been undergoing repairs… and those repairs could have been interrupted by the outbreak of war, just as his own ships' repairs had been.

"And our position?"

"About eight miles off Santa Maura, sir, here…" Wray pointed out their position on the chart. "We'll be entering the channel between Santa Maura and Cephalonia in the next hour. Oh—and Admiral Milne wants to know your dispositions."

"I'm sure he does," Cradock said, stretching. "So do the Germans. Signal Admiral Milne that we are patrolling. I'm going up on deck for a while." Wray looked as he himself might have looked, had his admiral ever told him to send a false signal. But they were, he thought, following the orders Milne would have given—that the Admiralty wanted him to give—if Milne had but the wits to give them. *They don't pay me to think,* Milne had said once… but they might pay a high price because Milne didn't.

The moon swung high overhead. To either side, the other cruisers knifed through the water, pewter ships on a pewter sea, blackening the starry sky with smoke. Behind them, sea-fire flared and coiled from their passage. Ahead, he could see the signal cones of the destroyers, and the white churn of their wakes, the phosphorescence spreading to either side. To port, Santa Maura, Leucas to most Greeks, rose from the sea in a tumble of jet and silver, the moon picking out white stone like a searchlight. Southward, the complicated shapes of Cephalonia and Ithaca, with the narrow straight passage between them.

"Have the squadron fall into line astern," he told Wray. The signal passed from ship to ship; the cruisers dropped smartly into line at four cables… his drills had accomplished that much. He hoped the gunnery drills had done as well. He noticed that the cones were all correctly hung. "Reduce speed if necessary, but not below fifteen knots."

He thought of little *Dublin,* with her two destroyers, desperately trying to find the Germans by their smoke. She might be lucky, but she surely could not sneak up on *Goeben* in this clear moonlit night. The Germans could not fail to see her any more than he could fail to see the ships of his squadron. Perhaps he should send her to guard the Adriatic gate which he had left wide open. That made sense, but so did another plan. Let her go to Crete, where the Germans might have another collier standing by. At dawn, when he hoped to spring his trap on the Germans near the Peloponnese, the smoke of *Dublin* and her destroyers might make the Germans swing closer to the Greek capes.

He gave these instructions, and eventually—atmospherics, the radioman explained—*Dublin* acknowledged them.

August 7, 0230.

He had dozed again, his body registering every slight change of course, every variation in speed, while the squadron passed Santa Maura, Ithaca, the rugged heights of southern Cephalonia, the northern part of Zante. The tap at his door roused him instantly. It was Wray.

"Sir… I have to say I don't like it."

"What?" Cradock yawned as he checked the time. Two-thirty.

"At the speed *Goeben* is making, sir, she will not be at the Greek coast until late morning. We cannot bring her to battle in daylight; you said so yourself." Wray stood there like someone who expected a vice admiral to have the sun at his command. Cradock yawned again and shook his head to clear it.

"Where is she now?"

Wray moved to the table and pointed out *Gloucester*'s most recent position on the chart. Cradock smoothed his beard, thinking. "It's inconvenient," he murmured.

"It's impossible," Wray said.

Cradock looked at him. Surely he could not mean what that sounded like. "Explain, Captain."

"It's what I said before, sir. She's too fast, and her guns outrange ours. She can circle outside our range, picking off the cruisers one by one before they can get a shot." Cradock frowned; was Wray seriously suggesting they abandon the attempt?

"And you propose?"

"To preserve the squadron for action in which it can have an effect," Wray said. "We cannot possibly sink the Germans…"

"I think you're missing something," Cradock said, smiling.

"Sir?"

"If the Germans do not appear until late morning—as it now appears—then we have time to entrap them where their greater speed will do them no good."

"But sir—she will see us if we're in the Messinian Gulf. She can stand off Sapienza far enough—in fact it would be prudent to do so. We cannot fight her there."

"That is not the only place, not with the lead we seem to have. But it will require a new plan. Signal the squadron and the destroyers: we will heave to while I decide what to do."

"Yes, sir." Wray left for the bridge; Cradock leaned over the charts.

"Is it cleverness, or some difficulty?" Cradock said to himself. Souchon had the reputation of a bold man. He had thrust all the way to Bone and Phillipeville, and made it safely back to Messina. Clever of him to leave Messina in daylight, clever to attempt that feint to the north. If he anticipated trouble in navigation waters, it was clever of him to slow, to arrive when he had the best visibility, when he could see a waiting collier, or British warships.

He felt *Defence* shiver successively, like a horse shaking a fly from its skin, as the revolutions slowed and her speed dropped. Deliberately, he did not go on deck to see how the following cruisers obeyed the signals. *Defence* shuddered through her secondary period of vibration and steadied again.

How many hours ahead were they? If they pressed on as quickly as possible and *Goeben* did not speed up, they would be a clear eight hours ahead… she could not possibly spot them. What then? His fingers traced the familiar contours of the Morean coast. If *Goeben* held on the shortest course for the east, she would pass between Cythera and Elafonisi. But that provided the obvious place for a trap, and if she chose to go south of Cythera—or worse, south of Cerigotto—his ships could not catch her. He must not head his fox; he trusted that *Gloucester's* pressure would keep Souchon running a straight course.

Behind the rocky coast of the Peloponnese, the rosy-fingered dawn broadened in classical design over a wine-dark sea. Westward, day's arch ran to a distant horizon unblemished by German smoke. They had passed Navarino, where almost ninety years before the British had—with grudging help from their French and Russian allies—scotched a Turkish fleet. Under the cliffs to the east, little villages hugged narrow beaches. Spears of sunlight probed between the rough summits, alive with swallows' wings.

As they cleared the point of Sapienza, the squadron came out of the shadows of the heights, and into a sea spangled with early sun. To port, the Gulf of Messenia opened, long golden beaches between rocky headlands; the old Venetian fort at Korona pushed into the water like a beached ship. Ahead, the longer finger of Cape Matapan reached even farther south. Water more green than blue planed aside from the bows; Cradock felt his heart lift to the change in the air, the light, the old magic of the Aegean reaching even this far west.

He glanced aloft at the lookout searching for the smoke of German ships. One of the destroyers had already peeled off to investigate the gulf for a German collier in concealment; another had gone ahead to investigate the Gulf of Kolokythia. Here he could have ambushed *Goeben* in the dark, but in daylight these gulfs were traps for slower ships.

"You must signal Admiral Milne," Wray said.

"And let the *Goeben* hear how close we are? I think not," Cradock said. "Admiral Milne is… cruising somewhere around Sicily. He will follow when he thinks it convenient, when he feels certain of events." Cradock smiled, that wry smile which had won other captains' loyalties. "We are the events. We will sink *Goeben*—or, failing that, we will turn her back toward him, and the 12-inch guns of the battle cruisers."

"But if we don't—" Wray was clearly prepared to argue the whole thing again.

"I had a hunter once," Cradock said, meditatively. He gazed at the cliffs rising out of the sea as if he had no interest in anything but his story. "A decent enough horse, plenty of scope. But—he didn't like big fences. Every time out, the same thing… you know the feeling, I suppose, the way a reluctant hunter backs off before a jump."

"I don't hunt," Wray said, repressively.

"Ah. I thought perhaps you didn't." Cradock smiled to himself. "Well, there was only one thing to do, you see, if I didn't want to spend all day searching for gaps and gates."

"And what was that, sir?" asked Wray, in the tone of one clearly humoring a superior.

Cradock turned and looked at him full face. "Put the spurs to him," he said. "Convince him he had more to fear from me than any fence." Wray reddened. "I thought you'd understand," Cradock said, and turned away. He hoped that would be enough.

By 0730, they were clearing Cape Matapan; Cythera lay clear on the starboard bow. Cradock peered up at the cliffs of the Mani, at the narrow white stone towers like fangs... still full of brigands and fleas, he supposed. Some of the brigands might even be spying for the Germans. They would do anything for gold, except, possibly, spy for the Turks.

The German ships were likely to pass Matapan fairly close, if they wanted to take the passage north of Cythera... plenty of places along that coast to hide his cruisers. But none of them were close enough, especially if the Germans went south. He dared not enter those gulfs, to be trapped by the longer reach of the German guns.

No. The simplest plan was the best, and he had time for it. Ahead now was the meeting of the Aegean, the white sea with its wind-whipped waters, and the deeper blue Ionian. This early on a fair summer's day, the passage went smoothly; the treacherous currents hardly affected the warships on their steady progress past Elafonisi's beaches, the fishing village of Neapolis, and the steep coast of Cythera, that the Venetians had called Cerigo.

Around the tip of Cape Malea, he found the first proof that Souchon intended to use that northern passage. Off the port bow, a smallish steamer rocked uneasily in the Aegean chop.

"Greek flag, sir," the lookout reported. "The *Polymytis*."

"If I were Souchon," Cradock said, "this is where I would want to find a collier. I would want one very badly."

"But it's Greek."

"Souchon flew a Russian flag at Phillipeville," Cradock said. "And our destroyers could use more coal." He sipped his tea. "I think we will have a word with this collier. An honest Greek collier—if that is not a contradiction in terms—should be willing to sell the Royal Navy coal, in consideration of all the English did to free Greece..." He peered at the ship. Something tickled his memory... something about the way her derrick was rigged, her lines. The German ship *General* had appeared in Messina tarted up like a Rotterdam-Lloyd mail steamer, though she belonged to the German East Africa Line.

"From where, and where bound?" he asked; Wray passed on his questions.

The dark-haired man answered in some foreign gibberish that sounded vaguely Turkish or Arabic, not Greek.

"He says he doesn't understand," he heard bawled up from below.

"He understands," Cradock said quietly. His eye roved over the steamer again. Ignore the paint (too new for such a ship), the unseamanlike jumble of gear on the deck, the derrick… and she looked very much like a ship he had seen less than a year before putting out from Alexandria, when she had flown the German ensign. He even thought he could put a name to her.

"We'll have a look at her," he said to Wray.

Wray swallowed. "Yes, sir, but—if I may—she is flying a neutral flag."

"She's a German Levant Line ship—imagine her in the right colors. She's no more neutral than *Goeben*. She is most likely old *Bogadir* with her face made up. If, as I suspect, she's carrying coal, then—one of our problems is solved. Possibly two."

Under the guns of the secondary battery, *Polymytis*'s captain submitted to a search.

"She's not a very *good* collier," the sublieutenant remarked when he came back aboard, much smudged. "Her bunkers are even harder to get at than ours… but she's bung full of coal, and her engineering crew is German, I'd swear. White men, anyway."

"Take her crew into custody, and put a prize crew aboard." Collecting the collier might be enough. But it might not. The *Goeben* still might have enough coal to reach the Dardanelles, and she would surely be able to call on other colliers. Even a lame fox could kill chickens. He would have to bring her to battle.

The sea was near calm, but that wouldn't last, not here at the meeting of the two seas. Already he could see the glitter off the water that meant the Aegean was about to live up to its name. The Etesian wind off Asia Minor crisped little waves toward him… and at day's end it would blow stronger.

Unfortunately, it would blow his smoke to the south; if he stayed here, off Cape Malea, that black banner across the channel would reveal his presence to the Germans. How could he make them come *this* way, the only place where he could be sure his guns would reach them?

They must see nothing to alarm them. He would position three cruisers south of the passage, behind the crook of Cythera's northeast corner, where the smoke would blow away behind that tall island, invisible. The other, with the destroyers, would wait well around the tip of Cape Malea, far enough north that their smoke would be dispersed up its steep slopes. He would put parties ashore who could signal when the Germans were well into the channel.

The signal flashed, and flashed again. Cradock smiled at the charts, and then at his flag captain. Souchon was as bold and resolute as his reputation. He had chosen the direct route, after shaking off *Gloucester* back at Matapan. Cradock had fretted over the signals from above that told of the exchange of shots between *Gloucester* and *Breslau;* the minutes when the *Goeben* turned back to support *Breslau*—when he feared she might turn away from the northern passage altogether—had racked his nerves, the more so as he could not see for himself what was going on. .

But the Germans had gone straight on when *Gloucester* turned away, and now—now they were well into the passage.

Defence grumbled beneath him, power held in check like a horse before the start of a run. Below, stokers shoveled more coal into the maws of the furnaces; boilers hissed as the pressure rose. Thicker smoke oozed from the funnels, whirled away in dark tendrils by the wind. Cradock could almost see the engineering officers and engine crew, alert for every overheated bearing, every doubtful boiler tube. Gun crews were at their stations, the first rounds already loaded and primed, awaiting only the gunlayers' signals.

But ships could not reach racing speed as fast as horses; he had to guess, from the positions signalled to him, the moment to begin the run-up. He wanted the cruisers to be moving fast when they cleared the island. So much depended on things he could not know—how fast the *Goeben* was, how fast she could still go, how Souchon would react to the sudden appearance of hostile ships in front of him.

Signals flashed down, translated quickly into *Goeben*'s position on the chart in front of him. She was not racing through; she was up to nineteen knots now, but keeping a steady course, well out from either side of the channel, *Breslau* trailing her. When… when…? He felt it, more than saw it in the figures on the chart. *Now.*

Defence surged forward, behind *Black Prince,* and ahead of *Warrior.* Cradock squinted up at the lookout. The Germans would be watching carefully; they had the sun over their shoulders, perfect viewing. But surprise should still gain *Black Prince* the first shot. She had won her vanguard position on the basis of an extra knot of speed and her gunnery record. He put into his ears the little glass plugs the Admiralty provided.

Across the passage, fourteen sea miles, he saw dark smoke gush from the funnels of the *Duke of Edinburgh* and the destroyers. In minutes, it would drift out across the passage, but by then they would be visible anyway.

For an instant, the beauty of the scene caught him: on a fair summer afternoon, the trim ships steaming in order under the rugged cliffs. Then his vision exploded in fire and smoke, as *Black Prince* fired her port 9.2-inch guns; the smoke blew down upon *Defence* coming along behind, and obscured his vision for an instant. Then *Defence* was clear of the point, and at that moment he saw the raw fire of *Goeben*'s forward turrets, just as *Defense* rocked to the recoil of her own. White spouts of water near *Goeben* showed that *Black Prince*'s gunners had almost found her range.

Too late now for fear or anxiety; his heart lifted to the raw savagery of the guns, shaking every fiber, the heart-stopping stink of cordite smoke, chocolate in the afternoon sun, blowing over him. *Black Prince*'s port guns fired again, and behind, he heard the bellow of *Warrior*'s, as she too cleared the point. The shells screamed on their way like harpies out of Greek legend.

The *Goeben*'s first shots rocked the sea nearby, sending up spouts of white. Had she picked out the *Defence?* She would surely try to sink the flagship, but he trusted his captains to carry on. His orders had been clear enough: "Our objective is to sink the *Goeben*, first, and the *Breslau* second."

The German ship's guns belched again; she could bring six of her ten 11-inch guns to bear on any of the three ships on her starboard bow. Cradock hoped her gun crews were not as good as he had been told.

White flashes of water, and then an explosion that was surely on the *Goeben* herself. She steamed on, but another hit exploded along her starboard side, even as her guns belched flame. Then a curtain of water stood between him and the German ships, and *Defence* rocked on her side, screws shuddering.

"Very close, sir," Wray said. He looked pinched and angry. Cradock looked away.

"Yes, excellent shooting." But his own crews were doing well, maintaining a steady round per minute per gun. Where were the destroyers in all this? They were supposed to have raced around the tip of Malea, laying smoke that would blow into the battle area and confuse the *Goeben*—he hoped. He looked ahead, to find dark coils of smoke already rolling over the afternoon sea, and the flash of *Duke of Edinburgh*'s guns… she was finally out from behind Malea, moving more slowly than his own ships. They had not wanted Souchon to see all that smoke until he was well into the trap.

Defence bucked a little as the sea erupted behind her, another near miss that dumped a fountain over *Warrior*'s bows. The guns rocked the ship again. Cradock looked at the chart, and his stopwatch. *Black Prince* should be near the point at which she was to start her turn, bringing her end on to the *Goeben*. He had worried over that point, on which so much depended. For three of his ships, it reduced by one the 9.2-inch guns that could bear on the *Goeben*… but it reduced the range more quickly, and that would, he hoped, be sufficient advantage.

Black Prince's stern yawed starboard as her bow swung into the turn. Cradock felt *Defence* heel to the same evolution. Then, just as he glanced aft to look at *Warrior,* he saw the aft 9.2 turret erupt in flame, like a column of fire. *Defence* bucked and slewed, like a horse losing its grip on slick ground. Black smoke poured from the turret. If they had not turned—he was sure that salvo would have hit *Defence* amidships.

Even as he watched, *Warrior's* forward turret exploded in a gout of flame—seconds later, the starboard turret blew, and then the next... as if some demon artificer had laid a fuze from one to the other. In his mind's eye, he saw what had happened, the flash along the passages. Another vast explosion that showered *Defence* and the sea around with debris, and the *Warrior* disappeared forever beneath the restless sea.

"I told you," Wray was saying, fists clenched, when he could hear again. They watched as shell after shell struck the *Goeben* without apparent effect. "We don't have the weight of guns to damage her even this close; she'll sink one after another... the whole squadron lost to no purpose."

"He's slowing," Cradock said, peering through the curls and streamers of smoke. The only possible reply to what Wray had said would disrupt his command. He concentrated instead on the battle. If he had been Souchon, in that ship, and if she could still make twenty-seven knots, he would have tried to run the gauntlet. Was Souchon, instead, turning to run away westward? Or had he suffered damage? No ship, however armored, could withstand a steady barrage of 380-pound shells forever. One of them would have to hit something vital. Enough of them, and she must, eventually, go under.

Minute by minute, the ships converged through a hell of smoke and fire and spouting water, battered and battering with every gun that might possibly bear. Despite the blown turret, *Defence's* boilers and engines drove her forward at twenty knots, a nautical mile every three minutes, and the interception became a matter of interlocking curves, the *Goeben* weaving to bring her undamaged guns to bear, the British responding as they could. From fourteen thousand yards to twelve, to ten, to eight. Destroyers darted in and out, zigging wildly from *Goeben's* secondary batteries. Three were gone already, blown from the water by shells too small to hole the cruisers.

Cradock, eyes burning with smoke and sweat, struggled to keep his gaze on the *Goeben*, to distinguish her smoke from the rest. A stronger gust of wind lifted the smoke, and there she was. One funnel blown askew, and the smoke from its opening unhealthily pallid with escaping steam, most of her secondary guns on this side dismounted... but the big guns still swung on their mounts to aim directly at *Defence*. His mouth dried. Below him, *Defence* fired, and he saw the flare from *Goeben's* guns just as someone jerked him off his feet and flung him down. The bridge exploded around him; he felt as if he had been thrown from a horse at high speed into timber, and then nothing.

He could not catch his breath; his sight had gone dark.

Voices overhead... a weight lifted off him, and someone said, "Here's the admiral!" How much time had gone by? What had happened? He struggled to open his eyes, and someone said, "Easy, sir…" More weight came off; he could breathe but the first breath stabbed him. Ribs, no doubt. Wetness on his face, stinging fiercely, then he got his eyes open to see a confusion of bundles he knew for bodies, blood, steel twisted like paper.

"*Goeben,*" he managed to say.

They didn't answer, struggling with something that still pinned his legs. He couldn't feel it, really, but he could see a mass of metal. Shouts in the distance, something about boats away. His mind put that together. Was the ship sinking?

"Is—?" he started to ask, but a sudden explosive roar drowned out his words. He felt the tilt of the deck beneath him. No need to ask. "You'd better go," he said instead, to the faces that hovered around him.

"No, sir," said one, in the filthy rags of what had been a Royal Marine uniform. "We're not leaving you, Admiral."

He didn't have the strength to argue. He couldn't focus on what they were saying, what they were doing; his vision darkened again. Then he felt himself lifted, carried, and eased into a boat that rocked in the choppy water. He could see *Defence*'s stern lifting into the sky.

"*Goeben?*" he asked again. The men in his boat looked at each other.

"She's still making for the Aegean, sir. Slow, but so far she's not sunk."

"Captain Wray?" he asked.

"Got off in another boat, sir."

For the first time in years, the motion of the sea made him feel sick. He asked one of the men to hold his head up, and over the gunwale saw the *Goeben* in the distance, battered, listing a little, but still whole, limping eastward almost to the tip of Cape Malea. Behind her, hanging on like bulldogs, were two destroyers. Somewhere, big guns still roared; he saw one shell explode on the cliff face, spouts of water.

He could not see the torpedo that, after so many misses, exploded under the *Goeben*'s stern and jammed one of her rudders. But he saw the sag of her bow toward the Cape, and he knew what that meant.

"Dear God," he said softly. "She's going to hit the rocks."

"Admiral?" The face bent over his looked worried; Cradock tried to point and managed only a weak flap of his hand. But they looked… as the *Goeben* yawed in the current, her bow swinging more and more to port, into the rocks that had claimed, over thousands of years, that many ships and more.

Another half-mile and she would have been well beyond Cape Malea, with sea room to recover from steering problems. Instead, her remaining steam and the current dragged her abraded hull along the rocks, and the destroyers fired their last torpedoes into her. With a vast exhalation of steam, like the last breath of a dying whale, the *Goeben* settled uneasily, rolling onto her side.

August 8, aboard H.M.S. *Black Prince*

Cradock lay sweating in his bandages in the captain's cabin, more than a little amazed that he was alive. Too many were not. *Warrior* gone with all hands. *Defence* sunk, and only 117 of her crew recovered. Six of eight destroyers… *Scorpion* and *Racoon* were still afloat, but of the others only a very few hands had survived. Only eighty-three of the Germans, Admiral Souchon not among them. *Black Prince* and *Duke of Edinburgh* were both in need of major repairs, unable to do more than limp back to Malta. Admiral Milne had already expressed his displeasure with the loss of so many ships and men, and, as he had put it, "reckless disregard of his duty to his superior." He foresaw that Milne would take credit for the success, and condemn the method by which it had been achieved. Like Codrington at Navarino, he would be censured for having exceeded his orders, while the Admiralty shed no tears over the vanquished enemy. Well, they would have retired a one-legged admiral anyway.

A tap at his door introduced yet another problem.

"Sir." Wray stood before him like a small boy before a headmaster.

"Captain Wray," Cradock said mildly.

"I was… wrong, sir."

"It happens to all of us," Cradock said. "I've been wrong many times."

"But—"

But he wanted to know what Cradock would say about him, in his official reports.

"Captain Wray, I never finished telling you the story of that hunter," he said. A long pause; Wray looked haggard, a *What now?* expression. "I sold him," Cradock said. "To a man who wanted a good hack." Wray seemed to shrink within his uniform. "Have some tea," Cradock offered, seeing that the message had been received.

"Nothing can change the nature born in its blood," he said, quoting a Greek poet, most apt for this ocean. "Neither cunning fox, nor loud lion." Nor coward, though he would not say that. He could take no pleasure in Wray's humiliation, but in the Navy there were no excuses. That was the great tradition.

FOOL'S GOLD

"It's been done to death," Mirabel Stonefist said.

"It's traditional." Her sister Monica sat primly upright, embroidering tiny poppies on a pillowcase. All Monica's pillowcases had poppies on them, just as all the curtains on the morning side of the house had morning glories.

"Traditional is another word for 'done to death,'" Mirabel said. Her own pillowcases had a stamped sigil and the words PROPERTY OF THE ROYAL BARRACKS DO NOT REMOVE.

"It's unlucky to break with tradition."

"It's unlucky to have anything to do with dragons," Mirabel said, rubbing the burn scar on her left leg.

Cavernous Dire had never intended to be a dragon. He had intended to be a miser, living a long and peaceful life of solitary selfishness near the Tanglefoot Mountains, but he had, all unwitting, consumed a seed of dragonsfoot which had been—entirely by accident—baked into a gooseberry tart. That wouldn't have changed him, if his neighbor hadn't made an innocent mistake and handed him dragonstongue, instead of dragonsbane, to ease a sore tongue. The two plants do look much alike, and usually it makes no difference whether you nibble a leaf of *D. abscondus* or *D. lingula*, since both will ease a cold-blister, but in those rare instances when someone has an undigested seed of dragonsfoot in his gut, and then adds to it the potent essence of *D. lingula*... well.

Of course it was all a mistake, and an accident, and the fact that when Cavernous went back to the village to dig his miser's hoard out from under the hearthstone it was already gone meant nothing. Probably. And most likely the jar of smelly ointment that broke on his scaly head—fixing him in his draconic form until an exceedingly unlikely conjunction of events—was an accident too, though Goody Chernoff's cackle wasn't.

So Cavernous Dire sloped off to the Tanglefoots in a draconish temper, scorching fenceposts along the way. He found a proper cave, and would have amassed a hoard from the passing travelers, if there'd been any. But his cave was a long way from any pass over the mountains, and he was far too prudent to tangle with the rich and powerful dragons whose caves lay on more lucrative trade routes.

He was forced to prey on the locals.

At first, sad to say, this gave him wicked satisfaction. They'd robbed him. They'd turned him into a dragon and robbed him, and—like a true miser—he minded the latter much more than the former. He ate their sheep, and then their cattle (having grown large enough), and once inhaled an entire flock of geese— a mistake, he discovered, as burning feathers stank abominably. He could not quite bring himself to eat their children, though his draconish nature found them appetizing, because he knew too well how dirty they really were, and how disgusting the amulets their mothers tied round their filthy necks. But he did kill a few of the adults, when they marched out with torches to test the strength of his fire. He couldn't stomach their stringy, bitter flesh.

Finally they moved away, cursing each other for fools, and Cavernous reigned over a ruined district. He pried up every hearthstone, and rooted in every well, but few were the coins or baubles which the villagers left behind.

Although the ignorant assert that the man-drake has powers greater than the dragonborn, this is but wishful thinking. Dragons born from the egg inherit all the ancient wisdom and power of dragonkind. Man-drakes are but feeble imitations, capable of matching true dragons only in their lust for gold. So poor Cavernous Dire, though fearsome to men, had not a chance of surviving in any contest with real dragons—and real dragons find few things so amusing as tormenting mandrakes.

'Tis said that every man has some woman who loves him—at least until she dies of his misuse—and so it was with Cavernous. Though most of the children born into his very dysfunctional birth-family had died of abuse or neglect, he had a sister, Bilious Dire, who had not died, but lived—and lived, moreover, with the twisted memory that Cavernous had once saved her life. (In fact, he had merely pushed her out of his way on one of the many occasions when his mother Savage came after him with a hot ladle.) But Bilious built her life, as do we all, on the foundation of her beliefs about reality, and in her reality Cavernous was a noble being.

She had been long away, Bilious, enriching the man who owned her, but at last she grew too wrinkled and stiff, and he cast her out. So she returned to the foothills village of her childhood, to find it ruined and empty, with dragon tracks in the street.

"That horrible dragon," she wailed at the weeping sky. "It's stolen my poor innocent brother. I must find help—"

"So you see, it's the traditional quest to rescue the innocent victim of a dragon,"

Mirabel's sister said. "Our sewing circle has taken on the rehabilitation of the faded blossoms of vice—" Mirabel mimed gagging, and her sister glared at her. "Don't laugh! It's not funny—the poor things—"

"Isn't there Madam Aspersia's Residence for them?"

"Madam Aspersia only has room for twenty, and besides she gives preference to women of a Certain Kind." Mirabel rolled her eyes; her sister combined the desire to talk about Such Things with the inability to *name* the Things she wanted to talk about.

"Well, but surely there are other resources—"

"In this city perhaps, but in the provinces—" Before Mirabel could ask why the provinces should concern the goodwives of Weeping Willow Street, her sister took a deep breath and plunged on. "So when poor Bilious—obviously past any chance of earning a living That Way— begged us to find help for her poor virgin brother taken by a dragon, of course I thought of you."

"Of course."

"Surely your organization does *something* to help women—that is its name, after all, Ladies' Aid & Armor Society...."

Mirabel had tried to explain, on previous occasions, what the LA&AS had been founded for, and why it would not help with a campaign to provide each orphaned girl with hand-embroidered underclothes for her trousseau, or stand shoulder to shoulder with the Weeping Willow Sewing Society's members when they marched on taverns that sold liquor to single women. (Didn't her sister realize that all the women in the King's Guard hung out in taverns? Or was that the point?)

Now, through clenched teeth, Mirabel tried once more. "Monica—we do help women—each other. We were founded as a mutual-aid society for all women soldiers, though we do what we can—" The LA&AS charity ball, for instance, supported the education of the orphaned daughters of soldiers.

"Helping each other is just like helping yourself, and helping yourself is selfish. Here's this poor woman, with no hope of getting her brother free if you don't do something—"

Mirabel felt her resistance crumbling, as it usually did if her sister talked long enough.

"I don't see how he can be a virgin, if he's older than his sister," she said. A weak argument, and she knew it. So did Monica.

"You can at least investigate, can't you? It can't hurt..."

It could get her killed, but that was a remote danger. Her sister was right here and now. "No promises," Mirabel said.

"I *knew* you'd come through," said Monica.

As Mirabel Stonefist trudged glumly across a lumpy wet moor, she thought she should have chosen "stonehead" for her fighting surname instead of "stonefist." She'd broken fingers often enough to disprove the truth of her chosen epithet, and over a moderately long career more than one person had commented on her personality in granitic terms. Stonehead, bonehead, too stubborn to quit and too dumb to figure a way out…

She had passed three abandoned, ruined villages already, the thatched roofs long since rotted, a few tumbled stone walls blacked by fire. She'd found hearth-stones standing on end like grave markers, and not one coin of any metal.

And she'd found dragon tracks. Not, to someone who had been in the unfortunate expedition to kill the Grand Dragon Karshnak of Kreshnivok, very big dragon tracks, but big enough to trip over and fall splat in. It had been raining for days, as usual in autumn, and the dragon tracks were all full of very cold water.

Her biggest mistake, she thought, had been birth order. If she'd been born after Gervais, she'd have been the cute little baby sister, and no one would ever have called on her to solve problems for the family. But as the oldest—the big sister to them all—she'd been cast as family protector and family servant from the beginning.

And her next biggest mistake, at least in the present instance, had been telling the Ladies' Aid & Armor Society that she was just going to check on things. With that excuse, no one else could find the time to come with her, so here she was, trudging across a cold, wet slope by herself, in dragon country.

They must really hate her. They must be slapping each other on the back, back home, and bragging on how they'd gotten rid of her. They must—

"Dammit, 'Bel, wait up!" The wind had dropped from its usual mournful moan, and she heard the thin scream from behind. She whirled. There—a long way back and below—an arm waved vigorously. She blinked. As if a dragon-laid spell of misery had been lifted, her mood rose. Heads bobbed among the wet heather. Two— three? She wasn't sure, but she wasn't alone anymore, and she felt almost as warm as if she were leaning on a wall in the palace courtyard in the sun.

They were, of course, grumbling when they came within earshot. "Should've called yourself Mirabel Longlegs—" Siobhan Bladehawk said. "Don't you ever sleep at night? We were beginning to think we'd never catch up."

"And why'd you go off in that snit?" asked Krystal, flipping the beaded fringe on her vest. "See this? I lost three strings, two of them with real lapis beads, trying to track you through that white-thorn thicket. You could just as easily have gone around it, rather than making me get my knees all scratched—"

"Shut up, Krystal," Siobhan said. "Though she has a point, 'Bel. What got into you, anyway?"

Mirabel sniffed, and hated herself for it. "Bella said if I was just investigating, I could go alone—nobody should bother—"

"Bella's having hot flashes," Siobhan said. "Not herself these days, our Bella, and worried about having to retire. We unelected her right after you left, and then we came after you. If you had just waited a day, stead of storming out like that—"

"But you're so impetuous," Krystal said, pouting. She pulled the end of her silver-gilt braid around, frowned at it, and nipped off a split end with her small, white, even teeth.

The third member of the party appeared, along with a shaggy pack pony, its harness hung with a startling number of brightly polished horse brasses.

"I needed a holiday," Sophora said, her massive frame dwarfing everything but the mountains. "And a chance for some healthy open-air exercise." The Chancellor of the Exchequer grinned. "Besides, I think that idiot Balon of Torm is trying to rob the realm, and this will give him a chance, he thinks. The fool."

Mirabel's mood now suited a sunny May morning. Not even the next squall off the mountain could make her miserable. Krystal, though, turned her back to the blowing rain and pouted again.

"This is *ruining* my fringes."

"Shut up, Krystal," said everyone casually. The world was back to normal.

Cavernous Dire had subsisted on rockrats, rock squirrels, rock grouse, and the occasional rock (mild serpentine, with streaks of copper sulfate, eased his draconic fire-vats, he'd found). In midwinter, he might be lucky enough to flame a mountain goat before it got away, or even a murk ox (once widespread, now confined to a few foggy mountain valleys). But autumn meant hunger, unless he traveled far into the plains, where he could be hunted by man and dragon alike.

Now, as he lay on the cold stone floor of his cave, stirring the meager pile of his treasure, he scented something new, something approaching from the high, cold peaks of the Tanglefoots. He sniffed. Not a mountain goat. Not a murk ox (and besides, it wasn't foggy enough for the murk ox to be abroad). A sharp, hot smell, rather like the smell of his own fire on rock.

Like many basically unattractive men, Cavernous Dire had been convinced of his own good looks, back when he was a young lad who coated his hair with woolfat, and had remained convinced that he had turned his back on considerable female attention when he chose to become a miser. So, when he realized that the unfamiliar aroma wafting down the cold wet wind was another dragon, his first thought was, "Of course." A she-dragon had been attracted by his elegance, and hoped to make up to him.

Quickly, he shoved his treasure to the back of the cave, and piled rocks on it. No thieving, lustful she-dragon was going to get his treasure, though he had to admit it was pleasant to find that the girls still pursued him. He edged to the front of his cave and looked upwind, into the swirls of rain. There—was she there? Or—over there?

The women of the expedition set up camp with the swift, capable movements of those experienced in such things. The tent blew over only once, and proved large enough for them all, plus Dumpling the pony, over whose steaming coat Siobhan labored until she was as wet as it had been, and so were half their blankets. Then she polished the horse brasses on Dumpling's harness; she had insisted that any horse under her care would be properly adorned and she knew the others wouldn't bother. Meanwhile, the others built a fire and cooked their usual hearty fare, under cover of the front flap.

They were all sitting relaxed around the fire, full of mutton stew and trail bread, sipping the contents of the stoneware jug Sophora had brought, when they heard a shriek. It sounded like someone falling off a very high cliff, and unhappy about it.

Scientific experimentation has shown that it is impossible to put on breast-plate, gorget, helm, greaves, armlets, and gauntlets in less than one minute, and thus some magical power must have aided the warrior women, for they were all outside the tent, properly armored, armed, and ready for inspection when the dragon fell out of the sky and squashed the tent flat.

"Dumpling!" cried Siobhan, and lunged for the tent as the pony squealed and a series of thumps suggested that hind hooves were in use.

"No, wait—" Mirabel grabbed her. Siobhan, doughty warrior that she was, had one weakness: an intemperate concern for the welfare of horseflesh. "You can hear he's alive."

"Ssss…." A warm glow, as of live coals being revived, appeared in the gloom where the tent had been. Dumpling squealed again. Something ripped, and hoofbeats receded into the distance. "Ahhh… sss…"

"A dragon fell on our tent," Mirabel said, with the supernatural calm of the truly sloshed. "And it's alive. And we're out here in the dark—"

Light flared out of the sky; when she looked up, there was a huge shape, like a dragon made all of fire. It was about the color of a live scorpion, she thought wildly, as it grew larger and larger….

"That one's bigger," Sophora said, in her sweet soprano. "At least it's not dark anymore."

Mirabel had never noticed that dragons could direct their fire, in much the way that the watch commander could direct the light of his candle lantern. Silver threads of falling rain… a widening cone of light… and in the middle of it, their flattened tent held down by a lumpish dragon the color of drying slime along the edge of a pond. Its eyes—pale, oyster-colored eyes—opened, and its gray-lipped mouth gaped. Steam curled into the air.

"Is it a baby?" asked Siobhan. Then she, like the others, looked again at the expression in those eyes. "No," she said, answering her own question. Even Siobhan, whose belief that animals were never vicious until humans made them so had survived two years in the King's Cavalry, knew nastiness when she saw it.

"It's hovering," Sophora said, pointing upward. Sure enough, the bigger dragon, now only a bowshot above, had stopped its descent and was balancing on the wind. Its gaping mouth, still pointed downward, gave fiery light to the scene, but its body no longer glowed. Sophora waved her sword at the big dragon. "This one's ours," she shouted. "Go away, or—"

The dragon laughed. The blast of hot air that rolled over them smelt of furnaces and smiths' shops and deserts—but it did not fry them. It laughed, they knew it laughed; that was enough for the moment, and the great creature rose into the dark night, removing its light and leaving them once more in darkness.

With a live and uncooperative dragon on their flattened tent.

"We haven't seen the last of that one," Sophora said.

"My best jerkin is probably getting squashed into the mud," said Krystal.

"Shut up, Krystal," they all said. All but the dragon.

Cavernous Dire had never seen a dragon before he became one, and thus had only the vaguest idea what they were supposed to look like. Big, of course, and scaly, and breathing fire from a long, toothy mouth. Long tail with spikes on it. Legs, naturally, or dragons would be just fire-breathing snakes. If he'd known that dragons have wings, he'd forgotten it after he became a dragon, and his own wings were, like those of all man-drakes, pitiful little stubs on the shoulders, hardly more than ruffles of dry itchy skin.

So when the real dragon swooped down the valley, he was amazed. She—he still thought, at this point, that the dragon was female—was an awe-inspiring sight, with the wide wings spanning the valley from side to side. She was so much bigger than he was. Crumbs of information about insects in which the male was much smaller than the female tried to coalesce and tell him something important, but he couldn't quite think, in the presence of this great beast. Dragons have this effect on all humans, but it's much stronger with man-drakes, and it amuses them to reduce their toys to mindlessness right before they reduce them to their constituent nutrient molecules.

The dragon flew past, and out of sight. Cavernous thrust his own long scaly neck out of his cave, trying to see where she'd gone. Nothing but wet rock, nothing but wet wind, nothing but curtains of fine rain stirred by her passage. She must be shy...

Strong talons seized his neck and plucked him from his cave as a robin plucks out a worm from the ground. The wings boomed on either side of him, and boomed again, and he was rising upward so fast that he felt the blood rushing to his dependent tail.

It is not for Men to know, or Bards to tell, what true dragons do to mandrakes in the high halls of the air, but it took several hours, during which time Cavernous realized how little he knew about dragon anatomy, his own or that of others, and how little he liked what he was learning now. Night had fallen by then, and soon he had fallen—was falling—and the glowing beast beside him rumbled warm laughter all the way down to the base of the clouds, then let him fall away into the wet night.

He didn't remember hitting the ground, but waking up was terrible. Darkness, cold, rain pelting his hide, and more pain than he had ever imagined inside him. His fire-vats had slopped over, burning other internal parts he hadn't known he possessed. Since it is the nature of dragons of all kinds to heal with unnatural speed, his broken bones were already knitting, but they hurt as they knit. Something was hitting him repeatedly, hard punches to the nasal arch, and squealing in his lower ear. He tried to draw in a breath, which hurt, and finally whatever it was quit hitting him and ran away. It was a long moment before he realized it had been a horse.

Light stabbed through his third eyelid, and he smelt the big dragon hovering above him. If he could have thought, he would have begged for mercy. Then darkness returned, and he closed his eye again, hoping that he'd wake up in his own cave and find it had all been a bad dream.

Experienced campaigners can light a fire in a howling wet gale, if sober and industrious. Those whose tents have been flattened by dragons, and whose last prior calories were derived from potent brew may have more problems.

Siobhan was off somewhere in the distance, calling Dumpling. It wouldn't do any good to call her back; as long as she was fretting over the pony her brain wouldn't work anyway. Krystal muttered on about her ruined wardrobe, but Mirabel heard Sophora give a gusty sigh.

"I suppose I'll have to do something about that dragon," she said. "And that means making a light—"

Experienced campaigners always have a few dry fire-starters in their packs, but the packs were inside the tent, underneath the dragon. Mirabel felt in her pockets and discovered nothing but a squashed sugared plum, left over from the Iron Jill Retreat some months back. Sophora had her Chancellor's Seal, with the crystal which could double as a lens to start a fire from sunlight… but not in the middle of the night. Glumly, they huddled against the dragon and sank into a state of numb endurance familiar from past campaigns.

Morning arrived with a smear of light somewhere behind the Tanglefoot Mountains. Eventually the sodden expedition could make out the shape of the fallen dragon, still lying on their tent.

Compared to the Grand Dragon Karshnak, it was a small specimen, not much larger than the tent it had flattened. Its color in this cold gray light reminded Mirabel most of a mud turtle, a dull brownish green. It lay as it had fallen, in an untidy heap.

But it wasn't dead. Even if thin curls of steam hadn't been coming from its nostrils and partially open mouth, the slow undulation of its sides would have indicated life within. Siobhan, returning with the mud-streaked Dumpling, eyed the dragon suspiciously.

Dumpling whinnied. At that, the dragon opened one gelid eye. Its mouth gaped wider, and more steam poured out. It stirred, black talons scraping as its feet contracted.

"We ought to kill it now," Siobhan said, soothing the jittery pony. "While we can."

"No," Krystal said. "If we kill it now, it'll bleed on the tent, and there go all our clothes."

"If we don't kill it now, and it wakes up and kills us, what use will our clothes be?"

Recovery from the dragon-change induced by eating a dragonsfoot seed, and then a leaf of dragonstongue, and then being slathered with Goody Chernoff's anti-wrinkle ointment (guaranteed to hold your present form until a certain conjunction of events) requires three unlikely things to happen within one day, as foretold in the Prophecies of Slart.

> "Whanne thatte murke-ox be founde,
> in sunlight lying on the grounde,
> in autumn's chill to gather heate,
> and when the blonde beautie sweete,
> her lippes pressed to colde flesh,
> and also dragons' song be herde,
> then shalle the olde Man spring afresh,
> and hearken to commandinge werde."

If the warrior women had known that Cavernous Dire *was* the dragon, be-spelled into that form, and if they had known of the Prophecies of Slart—but they didn't. The Prophecies of Slart were only then being penned three kingdoms away by a young woman disguised as a young man, who had not been able to make a living as a songwriter.

Toying with the man-drake had been fun, but now the big dragon wanted meat.

He could always go back and eat the man-drake—but if he did that, he'd be tempted to play with his food awhile longer, and his body wanted food *now.* He sniffed, a long indrawn sniff that dragged the prevailing winds from their courses.

Somewhere… ah, yes, murk ox. He sniffed again, long and low. It had been a long time—centuries, at least—since he'd eaten the last murk ox near his own lair. And he did like murk ox. Huge as he was, even one murk ox made a pleasant snack and a herd of them was a good solid meat, food for the recreation he rather thought he'd enjoy later.

The trick with murk ox was extracting them from the murk. They lived in narrow, steep-sided valleys too narrow for his great wings, where the fog lingered most of the day. The great dragon had learned, when much smaller, that flying into murk ox terrain, into the fog, led to bruised wings or worse. There were better ways— entertaining ways—to hunt murk ox.

The great dragon drew in another long, long breath and then *blew.*

For days a chill wet wind had blown down from the mountains. Now, in the space of a few minutes, it had shifted to the southwest, and then gone back to the northeast, then back to the southwest again. Back and forth, as if the sky itself were huffing in and out, unsure whether to take in air or let it out.

Then, with startling suddenness, the clouds began rolling up from the southwest, toward the mountains, the bottoms lifting higher and higher until the sun struck under them, guttering and sparkling on the drenched moorland. Higher still the clouds rose, blowing away eastward, and leaving a clear blue sky behind.

Mirabel squinted in the sudden bright gold light, but as far as she could see the land lay clear—wet but drying—in the sun, which struck warmer with every passing minute.

"It's certainly a break from Court procedure," Sophora said. "There every day's much the same, but this—"

"What's that?" asked Siobhan, pointing to a cleft in the mountains a few leagues distant. Little dark dots were moving quickly from what must be the entrance to a narrow mountain valley, out onto the moorland.

Sophora held up her Chancellor's Seal, centered with crystal, and put it to her eye. "I had our guild wizard apply a scrying spell," she told the others. "Good heavens—I do believe—it's a kapootle of murk ox."

"Murk ox! But they never come out in the open. Certainly not the whole kapootle."

"Not unless they're chased," Sophora said. "Look." She pointed.

Mirabel recognized the flying shape without having to be told what it was. The big dragon, now gliding very slowly down the mountainside and aiming a stream of fire into the valley where the murk ox had been concealed until the clouds lifted.

Soon the last murk oxen had left the valley, but the great dragon seemed in no haste to snatch them. Instead, it floated low overhead, herding them closer and closer to the women and the smaller dragon. Then it dipped its head from the glide—not even swooping lower, they noticed, and snatched one murk ox from the herd. They could see it writhe… and then the lump sliding down the dragon's long throat, just like an egg down a snake.

Another jet of flame, and the murk ox kapootle picked up speed, lumbering nearer—those splayed hooves now shaking the boggy heath.

"That dragon," Mirabel said. "It's herding them at *us*."

"Oh, good," Sophora said. "I was hoping for some fresh meat on this trip, and hunting's been poor…"

"Not that much fresh meat," Mirabel said. The heaving backs of many murk oxen could now be seen quite clearly, though the curious twisted horns could not be distinguished from the muck they were kicking up.

Although it is well known—or at least believed—that a herd of horses or cattle will divide around a group of standing humans rather than trample them, the murk ox kapootle has quite another reputation, which explains why it has not been hunted to extinction by men. No one knows what the murk ox thinks as it galumphs along, but avoiding obstacles smaller than hills isn't part of its cognitive processes. A kapootle of murk ox will trample all but the stoutest trees, and the mere human form goes down like straw before the reaper.

With the quick decision that characterizes the combat-experienced soldier, the warrior women bolted for the only cover available, that of the still-recumbent dragon on their collapsed tent. Siobhan dragged Dumpling along behind.

In moments, the lead murk ox overran their campsite. Emitting the strident squeaks of a murk ox in mortal fear, the lead ox galloped right over the dragon, digging him painfully in the snout and eye on the way up to his shoulder, and then staggering badly on the slippery scaled ribs, before running on down the declining tail. Only a few of his followers attempted the same feat, and all but one slid off the dragon's ribs, there to be trampled by their fellows. That one, unable to match its leader's surefooted leap down to the tail, launched itself right over the heads of the cowering warrior women, tripped on landing, and broke its neck.

"That was lucky!" shouted Mirabel over the piercing squeaks of the kapootle, now thundering past on either side.

"Yes," Sophora agreed. "Quite plump—a nice dinner for us." She started toward the twitching carcass, but a shadow loomed suddenly. They looked up. The great dragon lowered one foot and plucked the murk ox off the ground, meanwhile watching them with an expression which mingled challenge and amusement.

"You are a wicked beast," Sophora said, undaunted. Mirabel remembered that

Sophora had been undaunted even by the Grand Dragon Karshnak, at least until she'd been knocked unconscious by a wing blow.

The dragon winked, and popped the murk ox into its mouth. Flames licked around it; they could smell the reek of burning hair, and then the luscious smell of roasting meat. Then, with a boom and a whirl of air, the dragon was up and away, chasing laggard murk oxen on with a lick of flame, and crooning something that might have been meant for music.

"Well," said Krystal, flicking dabs of muck off her vest. "Now *that's* over, maybe we can do something about getting this mess off our tent, so I can find out what's happened to my clothes."

Cavernous Dire had slept uneasily, with cold rain trickling down his ribs and under his tail, but each time he'd roused, he'd managed to force himself back to sleep. It hurt less that way. When sunlight struck his eyes in the morning, he clenched his outer lids tight to block it out and hoped for the best. He could feel that his broken bones were mostly mended, and the internal burns were nearly healed as well. But he did not feel like coping with the real world.

He had, however, sneaked peeks at the humans in his immediate vicinity. Four women in bronze and leather, with swords and short hunting spears. Cavernous Dire had not enjoyed human meat when he tried it before, and three of the four warrior women looked unappetizing in any form. The fourth, though, he might have fancied in other situations. She had silvery blonde hair, peach-blossom cheeks, a perky nose, teeth like pearls, and a ripely pouting mouth. Years of solitude as a dragon, with a meager and uninteresting hoard to guard, had given him time to fantasize about women, and this woman met all his qualifications except that she was carrying a very sharp sword.

If he just lay there and pretended to sleep, maybe the women would go away. His draconic scales dulled his tactile awareness enough that he didn't realize he was lying on their tent, and before he listened to enough of their conversation, he became aware of something else.

The ground was shivering. Then shuddering. Cavernous opened one eye just in time to see a dark hairy shape hurtling toward him, and snapped his eye shut. Sharp hard things hit the same tender parts of his snout which the horse had kicked in the dark, and then dented his scales on their way up his head, his shoulder, and along his ribs, where they tickled. And he could sense, with that infallible sense given to man-drakes, that somewhere in the sky the large dragon who had hurt him so badly was lurking, waiting for him to show life so he could be tormented again.

Better the tickle of murk ox hooves than the talons of a dragon. Cavernous hunkered down, feigning unconsciousness as best he could, as the kapootle squeaked and thundered past, though the moment when he sensed the great dragon close above him was almost impossible to bear. Then it was gone, and he dared open his outer eyelids again, just a tiny bit, to see what was going on.

"—And I say we butcher it now!" That was his diminutive blonde, she of the perky nose and accouterments.

"You were the one who said it'd bleed on our gear," the tallest one said. "Besides, Krystal, you really should be grateful to it. It saved our lives."

"And if you say 'What's life without my embroidered nightshirt with the suede fringe?' I will personally roll you through that squashed murk ox," said the one with the crooked nose.

"I am grateful," Krystal said, sounding very cross. "What do you want me to do, Mirabel, kiss it and make it well?"

"Don't be silly," said the one petting the very dirty pony, whose harness was adorned with gleaming gold shapes. For a moment all Cavernous could think of was the treasure wasted on that stupid pony. "We all know you wouldn't kiss anything that ugly, no matter what it did for you."

"You—you—"

"Like when Rusty the Armorer fixed that helm for you, and all you did was wave at him—"

"Well… he's *old*. And he has only three teeth."

The one named Mirabel grinned suddenly. "Come on, Krystal—I dare you. Kiss a dragon. Maybe it *will* cure it."

"Eeeeuw!"

"Scaredy-cat."

"Am not!"

"Just think, Krystal, how your… mmm… special friends will be impressed… if you do dare the dragon's breath, that is. If you don't—are they going to respect you, even if you do have that fancy mask?"

Krystal glared at them, shrugged, and twitched the twitchable parts of her anatomy. Then, with a pout the dragon was finding increasingly adorable, she shrugged. "All right. But only because I know you'll make up some horrid story about me if I don't. And not—*not* on the lips."

She sauntered toward the dragon's mouth. Cavernous had to roll his big man-drake eye down to watch her. She leaned over his snout, lips pursed.

From the man-drake's point of view, the kiss was an explosion of sensation unlike anything he'd ever felt, and the strange feelings went on and on. No one had told him he could turn back into a man, so he hadn't bothered trying to imagine what it would feel like. His eyes opened very wide, but all he could see were whirling colors.

From Mirabel's point of view, Krystal put her lips to the dragon's snout, and the dragon collapsed like a bagpipe's bag, with a sort of warm whooshing noise, and almost simultaneously, the moor burst into spring flower. Where the dragon had been, a scruffy-looking naked man hunched against the cool air. Although Mirabel knew nothing about physics, she had just observed that the energy released when a large form condensed to a small one could generate enough heat to activate seeds and accelerate their growth.

Krystal, who had had her eyes shut, stepped back and opened them. When she saw that the tent was no longer covered by a dragon, and that lumps within the wrinkled canvas suggested the remains of their gear, she made straight for the collapsed entrance. A dirty old man didn't interest her at all.

Mirabel had gone on guard instinctively, as had Sophora, and the appearance of Cavernous Dire did not reassure them. Decades of life as a man-drake had left him no handsomer than when he had chosen misering over marriage. Now his greasy hair was stringy gray instead of black, and his lanky form even more stooped. A dirty-looking gray beard straggled past his chest no farther than necessary… in fact, not quite far enough. He looked like the sort of man who would lurk in dark alleys to accost the sick or feeble.

"Who are you?" Sophora asked, in her Chancellor voice.

"Cavernous Dire," the man said. His voice squeaked, like an unoiled hinge.

"You're Cavernous Dire?" Mirabel asked. Her mind boggled, then recalled the shape and expression of Bilious Dire, made a quick comparison, and knew it must be true.

"You were a dragon…" Sophora said.

"They tricked me," the man said. "Just because I was getting rich and they wanted my money…" He sounded peevish, like someone whose neighbors would trick him every chance they got.

At that moment the big dragon returned. They had not heard it gliding nearer, but they heard the long hiss as its shadow passed over them.

"Noooo!" wailed Cavernous. "Don't let it get me!"

"He's Cavernous Dire?" Krystal said, crawling out from under the tent. "He's the one we were supposed to rescue? Eeeeuw!" Nonetheless, she struck an attitude, peering up at the big dragon with conscious grace.

Mirabel and Sophora both had swords in hand, but Mirabel knew that they hadn't anywhere near the force necessary to tangle with a dragon this size. But they also had nowhere safe to run. The dragon smiled, and let its long, thin, red tongue hang out a little, steaming in the morning air.

What might have happened next, she never knew, but Cavernous Dire suddenly snatched her belt knife, and lunged toward Siobhan and the pony Dumpling.

"Here's treasure!" he screamed, hacking at the horse brasses on Dumpling's harness.

"Hey—stop that!" Siobhan tried to grab his arm, but Dumpling interfered. The pony backed and spun, fighting Siobhan's hold and cow-kicking at Cavernous. The dragon seemed to be amused, and let another yard or so of tongue slide out. Cavernous quit hacking at the brasses individually, and slid Mirabel's knife up under the harness, which parted like butter. Two more slices, and he'd cut it free, all the while dodging Siobhan's angry swats and Dumpling's kicks. He snatched it from the ground, dropping Mirabel's knife, and turned back to the dragon, holding the harness at arm's length.

Treasure! Gold! Take it! Go away!"

"Yesss...." The long tongue lapped out, and gathered it in—but Cavernous did not let go, and the tongue wrapped round him too, snatching him back into the dragon's toothy maw as a lizard might snatch a fly.

A gulp, and the bulge that had been Cavernous Dire disappeared into the dragon's innards. A flick of the wings, and another, and the dragon was gone, sailing low over the heather, back toward the distant kapootle of murk ox.

Dumpling squealed and bucked, landing on Mirabel's knife, which shattered.

"My best knife—!" Mirabel said.

"I hope he hasn't cut his hoof," Siobhan said.

"My best shirt, ruined!" Krystal held up a nightshirt with a wet stain down one side.

"Shut up, Krystal," they all said.

On the way back to the city, they agreed that Bilious Dire need not know the whole story, only that at the end Cavernous had sacrificed himself for others, and been eaten.

Mirabel's sister had things to say about the outcome, which left a coolness of glacial dimensions between them for more than a year. At Monica's instigation, the Weeping Willow Sewing Society paid for a plaque commemorating the Dauntless Courage of Cavernous Dire, in saving the life of four of the King's Guardswomen from a dragon. Every May-morn, they lay a wreath beneath it. Mirabel Stonefist won't walk by that corner at all anymore. Siobhan Bladehawk narrowly escaped punishment for defacing the plaque as she tried to correct "Four of the King's Guardswomen" to "Three of the King's Guardswomen and One of the King's Cavalrywomen."

In the belly of the dragon, Cavernous Dire remains undigested, a situation acceptable to neither him nor the dragon. Neither of them knows that it is Cavernous's miserly grasp of the pony Dumplings horse-brass which maintains this uneasy stasis.

Meanwhile, the Chancellor of the Exchequer had a very satisfactory chat with Balon of Torm, whose arms, dyed orange to the elbow, proved he had been dipping into the treasury. Sophora Segundiflora may be the only person satisfied by the expedition.

JUDGMENT

"That's odd," Ker said, picking up the egg-shaped rock. "I never saw a rock shaped like an egg before." It was heavy, like any rock, cool in his hand. Smoother than any rock he'd ever seen.

"You find rocks like that in the hills west of here, lad," Tam said. He sounded as if he'd seen many such rocks before. "Someone dropped it," he said, looking around as if he expected to see that someone. "Gnome. Dwarf. Rockfolk would have something like that. And what'd they be doing here, I wonder? Never saw them this near the village; they need rocky hills to live in."

"They wouldn't drop it, not they." Ker turned the rock, rubbing it with his thumb. Stories said the rockfolk had grasping hands that never let go what they held. "It's smoother than most rocks anyway. Like someone'd polished it."

"Carried in a pocket with a hole in it. A sack—"

"I reckon as it belongs to someone, then," Ker said, putting the rock back on the path. "Best leave it be."

"For someone to stub a toe on in the dark?" Tam picked it up, hefted it, ran a calloused thumb over the smooth surface. "You're right, lad, it is smooth." He put it down just off the path, near a brambleberry tangle. "Now no one'll kick it in the dark and call a curse on us for leaving a tripstone, but it's easy enough to find, if whoever dropped it recalls what way they came."

Ker nodded and walked on, down past the brambleberry tangle, taking the steps made by its roots and those of the yellowwood thicket, steps worn into hollows by the feet of those who went daily from the creek up to the cow meadows and back. Under his bare feet the warm earth turned cool, and then chill and damp as he neared the stream.

Tam followed; Ker could hear Tam's slower, more careful footfalls, the slight grunt as he came down the slope. Caution was in Tam's movements, in his words, as was proper for an older man, an Elder in the vill. Ker would not have worried about someone tripping on a rock in the path at night, though now Tam mentioned it, he knew he should worry. Others than humans used

171

that path; the first humans here had found it bitten deep into the land, so that now the bushes and thickets towered over it, and here near the creek he walked between walls of fern and flowers. The people of light used it, and the people of shadow, singers and unsingers, and the people of earth, those of the law and those of the forge. A curse from any of these might bring desolation to humans within its reach, and the curses of the Elders reached a long way.

Just beyond the old way marker, put there by no human hands in ancient times, he saw another of the odd egg-shaped rocks in the path. He made the sign to avert a curse. The rock remained. He stopped.

"Go on," said Tam from behind him, touching his shoulder.

"It's another one," Ker said.

"Another one what? Oh." Tam edged past Ker. "It's not the same color."

Ker had not noticed that; he had seen the shape only. Now he could not remember just what color the other one was. Stone colored, or he'd have noticed, but what color was stone? His mind threw up images of gray stone and brown, black stone and reddish yellow. This one was pale gray, speckled with dark.

"What if it is eggs?" he asked. "What if something lays stone eggs?"

Tam laughed, a harsh barking laugh. "What—you think maybe dwarfwives lay eggs?"

"I didn't say that." Ker stepped carefully around the rock. He wasn't going to pick it up this time. He'd averted a curse, or tried to, but handling things that might be cursed was a good way to catch bad luck anyway. He wished he hadn't touched the first one. "I only said—we found two. If they are eggs, what laid them?"

"They're not eggs. They're rocks." Tam bent down, picked up the rock, and shifted it from hand to hand. "This one's a little grayer. Heavier, not by much. Could be it has pretties inside. Some of them egg-shaped rocks over to Blackbone Hill has pretties inside. Gems, or near as need be."

Ker shivered. Blackbone Hill had a bad reputation, for all that some claimed to bring burning stone and valuable gemstones out of it. Stories were told about what lay under Blackbone Hill, what bones those were. A dragon, some said, had been killed there for his gold, and others said the dragon had died of old age, and still others argued that the dragon had choked on magegold. Tam had always said the stories were fool's gold, that only rock lay under the grass.

"Was there as a youngling," Tam went on. Ker knew that; everyone in the vill had heard Tam's stories of his travels. "A long ways off, and not much worth the trouble, but for his pretties." He hefted the rock in his hand. "I've half a mind to crack this open and see if it's that kind. Had to trade all the pretties I found at Blackbone for food by the time I'd come home."

Ker shook his head. "What if it is something's egg? Bad luck, then, for sure."

"It's not an egg. Nothing lays stone eggs."

Nothing Tam knew of. Ker knew that he himself knew less than Tam, but surely even Tam did not know everything.

"We should ask somebody," he said, seeing Tam about to crack the rock egg against the old way marker that stood at the foot of the cut. The way marker came from the Elder People; it might be bad luck to break anything on it.

"Ask who?" Tam said.

That was the stopper. Tam knew more than anyone else Ker could think of; he was an Elder, but...

"Somebody," he said. "The singers, maybe?"

"Finders, keepers," Tam said, and his arm came down. The egg-shaped rock hit just on the edge of the way marker, and it broke open to show a serried rank of purple and white crystals.

"Pretties," Tam said with satisfaction. "Just as I thought. Here, Ker—you can have one." He probed with thick fingers and broke off a single crystal spike, about the length of his finger from knuckle to nail. He held it out.

Ker felt cold sweat break out on his face and neck. He could not refuse a gift from his future father-in-law, not without risking a quarrel, but he didn't want to touch that thing, whatever it was. He whipped off his neck cloth, and took the crystal in that. "I don't want to risk breaking it," he said. It was partly true, but the partial lie made a bad taste in his mouth. For courtesy, he looked closely at the crystal. Cloudy purple, the eight facets glinting in the light, the point narrowing abruptly at the tip... it looked sharp, and he did not test it with his finger. Carefully he folded the cloth around it and tucked it into his shirt, snugging his belt so it wouldn't fall out.

Tam took off his own neck cloth. "Good idea," he said. "Best not break the pretties. They're worth more unbroken." He wrapped the fragments of the rock, and put them in his shirt. Then he started off, leading the way this time. Ker did not see the next egg-shaped rock until Tam bent over, halfway across the gravelly ford of the creek, and picked it up. He showed it to Ker—this one was greenish-gray, streaked with darker green—before tucking it into his shirt with a grin. "If this'n has pretties too, I'm set for a long time. It's easy to trade pretties for 'most anything at the Graywood Fair. I'll pick up the other one tomorrow or the next day."

No more worries about who might've dropped it, Ker noticed. He followed Tam into the village, turning aside to his mother's house as Tam went straight on to his own. He lifted the hearthstone that guarded their treasures, and laid the pretty beside the armlet of bronze, the bronze pendant with a flower design, the string of glass beads he would give Tam's daughter the day they were wed, and eight silver bits that would, at his mother's death, be his inheritance and pay his cottage fee.

Then he went to sit in the village square, holding the staff of his approaching marriage, and endured until nightfall the taunts and teasing of those who tested a bridegroom's will and temper. It was hard not to respond when Dran's daughter kissed him full on the lips, or Roder's son told everyone about the time he had eaten a woods pear so fast he'd bitten a grub in two without noticing it, then thrown up. But this was the way of it. Lin had spent her time sitting in the square and now it was his turn; as he had sat on the judicar's bench and watched her, so now she sat on the same bench and watched him for any sign of impatience, bad temper, or unfaithfulness.

When full dark had come, and no one more bothered him, he went home and slept as usual until—in the darkest hours of night—he woke with a start, staring about him, bathed in cold sweat. Fragments of a dream swirled through his mind and vanished. Lin's face. Flame. Darkness. A great roaring that was almost music.

His ears hummed with the noise, as if someone had smacked him in the head with a rock. He tried to lie quietly, breathe slowly, return to sleep, but the humming itched at his ears and quieted only slowly. At last he slept.

In the morning he remembered waking, but nothing of the dream except that it was unpleasant. Today he would again spend the hours until homefaring with Tam, and then sit in the village square in the evening. He rose, fanned the embers of the fire into flame, then fetched water to boil. Lin's mother, Ila, a guest in this house these five days, opened an eye and watched him, as his mother had guested with Tam for the days of Lin's testing and watched Lin. Ker measured grain into the pot, adding a pinch of salt from the salt-crock, then he left while the others rose. Tam was just coming out of his house.

"Guardians bless your rising," Ker said.

Tam grunted. "Guardians should bless my sleep instead. The water boils?"

"It boils," Ker said.

"Good. I'm hungry." Tam walked to Ker's mother's house, twitching his shoulders as if they hurt. Ker stood beside the door of Tam's house and waited, stomach growling, until Lin's little sister brought him a bowl of gruel and a small round of bread, lumpy and hard, the girl's own baking. Lin's would be better than this, he knew.

He ate it standing by the door, and the girl came to take away his bowl. He walked over to his mother's house, and waited until Tam came out, belching, his face red from the heat of the fire.

"Well, now, to work," Tam said. Today they would join the other men ditching a field near the creek, draining it. All morning Ker hacked at the soggy soil with a blackwood spade, careful not to strain it to the breaking point. Old Ganner, who'd died before Midwinter, had carved the black-wood spade years back, and traded it to Ker's father for a tanned sheepskin. Ker knew himself lucky to have it. Tam and the other men watched him as much as they worked themselves. No one liked ditching; it was hot, hard, heavy work that drew the back into tight knots, but the blackwood spade cut through the roots better than one of oak or ash.

Shortly after the noon break, Tam beckoned to Ker. Ker scraped the muck off the spade with the side of his foot and went to Tam's side. "Stay here, lad, and keep working. I'm going to check the cow pastures for us both," Tam said.

Ker's head throbbed. He knew what Tam would do. He would try to find that other egg-shaped stone, and break it open for more pretties. His heart sank, stonelike, and he found no words.

"You have the shoulders for digging," Tam said. "It's young man's work." He grinned and clapped Ker on the shoulder, then turned away.

Ker stabbed the ditch with the spade, more in worry than anger, and the spade groaned. Sorry, he thought to the wood, and stroked the handle. He looked closely at the shaft, but the grain had not split. Blackwood, best wood, supple and strong… blackwood made good bows as well as digging tools. Tam came back in late afternoon, his hands empty and his face drawn into a knot like Ker's shoulders.

"You didn't sleep much last night," he said to Ker.

How had he known? "I had a bad dream," Ker said.

"You followed a dream out through the dark?" Tam asked.

Ker shook his head, confused. "I didn't go out," he said.

"It was gone," Tam said, not naming it. Ker knew what he meant.

"I did not take it," Ker said.

Tam shrugged. "Someone did. Rocks don't walk by themselves."

"Maybe the one who dropped it," Ker said.

"Maybe. No matter. I have the other for pretties." His sideways glance at Ker accused, though he said nothing more.

They went back to the village then, and Ker spent another evening in the square, with Lin on the bench watching him and the young people standing around making jokes. Old Keth, Bari's mother, came and reminded everyone of the time he had spoiled a pot she was making, bumping her at her work. Lin's little sister reported that he had slurped his gruel that very morning, gobbling like a wild pig of the forest. He bore it patiently, as Lin had borne it when his mother told that Lin had made a tangle in the weaving.

That night he dreamed again: fire, smoke, Lin's face, noise. Again he woke struggling against that fear, and again his ears hummed for a time before he could sleep again. In the morning he knew he had had the same dream again, but still remembered nothing of it. That frightened him: To repeat a dream meant something, but he could not interpret a dream he could not remember.

That day he finished the ditch before it was time to sit in the square, and decided to cool off in the creek. Tam was talking to the older men in the shade of the trees. Ker waved, mimed splashing, and walked off to the creek. Upstream from the ford the creek had scooped out a bowl waist deep at this time of year.

Under the trees the sun no longer bit his shoulders, but the air lay still and hot. His feet followed the path as his mind cast itself ahead into the cool water. The scent of damp and fresh growth filled his nose, promising comfort. He came to the ford, where the water scarcely wet the top of his foot, and turned aside to the pool, stripping off his shirt and trews to hang them on the bushes to one side.

He eased into the water, murmuring the thanks appropriate to the merin of the creek, and splashed it over his head and shoulders. Something tickled his heart foot, then the other. Slowly he sank down in the water, crouching, until only his head was out. He had always loved the way the water's skin looked, seen from just above it like this. Its surface would have looked flat from above, but now, in the wavering reflection of the trees overhead, he could see its true shape, the grain of its flow. On his back, the current's gentle push, and between his legs the water flowing away downstream, past the village lands, beyond into lands unknown.

He let his eyes close and listened. No sound of breeze in the trees, no leaf rustle. Something moved on a tree trunk; he heard the scritch of claws on bark.

He had known Tam all his life. Cautious Tam, careful Tam, thoughtful Tam, perhaps not as wise as Granna Sofi, but then she was older, deeper in wisdom. Now he wondered if he knew Tam at all. And if he knew too little of Tam, what of his daughter Lin? If Tam could turn grasping, so late in life, would Lin draw back her hand from life-giving? Would she be a fist and not an open hand after all?

He wished his father had lived. He could not talk to his mother about this, not now. She had asked the ritual questions back before Lin sat in the square, and he had said yes, he was sure the Lady's blessing lay on Lin and on their union. He had been sure.

He was not sure now. He knew only that he woke each night in the darkest hours, after foul dreams, with strange music humming in his head.

He squeezed his eyes shut and sank below the surface. Cool water lifted the strands of his hair, washing away the sweat and grime. Cool water supported him everywhere. If he were a fish, he could live in this cool cleanliness always, in this silence. He opened his eyes underwater and watched tiny silver bubbles from his nose rise past his eyes. Air seeking air, its own kind. He was not waterkind or airkind, neither fish nor bird.

His lungs ached. He lifted slightly, rolling his head back to catch a breath, and blinked the water out of his eyes. Even as he heard a startled hiss, he saw them.

Two squat shapes, half the height of the men but not boys, stood in the shallows staring at him. One muttered at the other, no tongue he knew. Of course not: They were Elders, rockfolk Elders. He knew that from the tales, every detail of which came back to him in that instant. Squat, broad, long-haired, bearded, teeth like stone pegs, hands and feet overlarge for their height. Clothed in leather and metal. Armed with metal weapons. And angry. In the tales, the rockfolk were always angry, usually with a human who invaded their fastnesses or stole something from them.

He was aware of a chill from more than the water, and aware too of his own nakedness. His clothes... one of the rockfolk had them now, stretching and poking at his shirt with a finger he knew would tear it... yes. He heard it rip. That one sniffed at the shirt, and wrinkled a broad nose; it gave a harsh sound that might've been a laugh. The other answered in its language.

Then came the sound of someone else brushing through the bushes, crackling leaves underfoot, nearer and nearer. The two rockfolk looked at each other and vanished. His shirt fell to the water's surface, where the current took and folded it, then slid it downstream, slowly, rumpling over the shallows. Ker lurched forward out of the pool, back to the shallows, and made a grab for it. The wet mass resisted, and he yanked it up just as Tam broke through the bushes and stood on the bank scowling at him.

"Looking for another?" Tam asked.

"No, I was hot," Ker said. "I was in the pool..."

"You're not in the pool now. What have you got in that shirt?" Tam sounded almost as angry as the rockfolk had looked.

"Nothing," Ker said. He held it up, wrung out the water, and spread it. The rent was a hand long, a three-cornered tear.

"Something made that—" Tam came into the ford, looking around as if he expected to find another of the odd rocks, as if one might have fallen through that hole in Ker's shirt.

"It was the dwarf," Ker said. "Two rockfolk were on the ford when I came up from the water. One of them had my shirt. Then I heard someone coming, and they were gone. My shirt fell into the water—"

Tam's eyebrows rose. "Gone? Where?" he asked. "I don't see any rockfolk." He looked around, then back at Ker.

"I don't know," Ker said. "They just... weren't there. Maybe it was magic."

"Maybe there weren't any rockfolk," Tam said, his voice hard. "Maybe that's why I didn't see them."

"I saw them," Ker said. "I came up from the water and they were there, in the ford, with my shirt—one of them poked a hole in it—"

"And you didn't say anything?"

"No. I couldn't think—"

"Mmm." Tam didn't say more, but Ker suspected he hadn't believed a word of it. He didn't know what to say, how to convince Tam that he had seen dwarves, and they had disappeared. "I think I need a soak too, lad," Tam said. "Best you get back to the village, now, and sit your time."

Ker nodded and fetched the rest of his clothes from the bush he'd laid them on. He put on the trews and draped his wet shirt on his head. He would have to put it on to enter the village, but it might be drier by the time he'd made it to the clearing. And he'd have to explain that rent to his mother. Would she believe him about the dwarves or would she be like Tam? Perhaps he could tell her simply that the shirt had gotten torn, and nothing more.

His mother turned the shirt in her hands, examining the ripped cloth, seeming to half-listen to his explanation. "I will fix it this evening," she said. "Don't worry about it." Ker felt guilty. Though he was almost sure that not telling everything was not the same as telling something untrue, that *almost* pricked him like a thorn.

He thought so hard about that, sitting in the square that evening, that he scarcely noticed what anyone said or did. The Elders said that lies ripped the fabric of the community, destroyed the trust between people on which community rested. Between him and his mother stood the not-telling about the rockfolk. Between him and Lin's family stood the lies Tam had told and Tam's grasping at what was not his. Like father like daughter, like mother like son. Did he want to be married forever to the daughter of someone like Tam... the daughter of Tam himself?

He stumbled home in the dark finally, more miserable than he had been since his father died, and lay down sure he would not sleep. At least he would not dream if he did not sleep.

Despite himself, he dozed off after a time, and woke to voices whispering in the dark, just out of clear hearing. His heart pounded; he lay still, trying to breathe quietly so that he could hear what they said. Dry voices, evoking the rustle of winter leaves crisped by frost and blown by wind, or the little streaked birds of open grassland in midsummer. The blurred edges of speech sharpened slowly; he could hear more and more... but he could not understand. He shook his head, blinked against the dark, but the voices still spoke words he did not know. Then he heard his own name, clear within the bird-sounds of the voices. Once, and then again, "Ker." And "Lin" and "Tam" as well.

Blood rushed in his ears; he lost the voices in its rhythmic noise. He shivered, suddenly drenched in sweat and cold. Voices that knew his name when he did not know their speech. That must be the Elders, but which race? The people of light were the Singer's children; they had singing voices. The people of darkness, once also of the Singer's tribe, had fallen away but retained their beauty, it was said. The rockfolk spoke loud and deep; the people of the law with almost mincing precision. None of these fit the sound he heard.

He sat up and peered through the dark at the hearthstone. It must be the pretty Tam had given him; that must be what caused this. He must get rid of it. He thought of throwing it in the creek, burying it in the woods.

"Fool!" came the voice, now in his own tongue. "Put it back."

Back? He tried to remember just where on the path Tam had picked it up—just this side of the waystone, yes—and the voice crackled like a fire as it said "No! Fool! Restore, restore…"

Restore what? How?

Above the hearthstone now, a blue flame danced where no fire had been laid. Behind it, the banked embers of last night's fire sighed and collapsed with a soft puff of ash; the air chilled again, and the blue flame brightened. Ker could not take his eyes from it. Within it, a tiny shape he could not quite see clearly twisted and turned.

"Put it back together. Every piece. Make whole, make well. Else—" A blast of fear shook him, shattering his concentration, implying every disaster that could come to him and his family, his whole village.

Then it vanished, leaving only a blurry afterimage against the dark, and Ker lay back on his pallet, sweating and shivering, until the first dawnlight crept through the windows. He put the water on and started the porridge as usual. He would have to talk to Tam about this, and he had no idea how to say what he must say.

Tam came out looking even grumpier than the day before. "Guardians bless your rising," Ker said.

"Guardians should bless my sleep," Tam said, as he had before. That was not the ritual greeting. Was he also having bad dreams?

"Honored one," Ker began, then stopped as Tam rounded on him.

"Don't you start!" he said. "You're not my son-in-law yet." He strode off to Ker's mother's house before Ker could say anything more.

When Lin's little sister came out with his bowl of lumpy gruel and piece of bread, she shook her head at him. "Da's angry with you," she said. "What did you do wrong?"

"I don't know," Ker said. Did Tam still think he had taken that other rock from the brambleberry patch? The only wrong he knew of was keeping the pretty, but Tam had given it to him.

"Yes, you do," Lin's sister said, staring at him wide-eyed. "You have a liar's look. I'll tell Linnie."

That was all he needed now, for Lin to believe him untrue. If she didn't already, if her father had not convinced her.

"I do not know why your father is angry with me," he said. "That is the truth."

She shifted from foot to foot, staring at him. "It sounds true, but something is wrong. Da isn't sleeping well—we're all tossing and turning and when I asked him what was wrong, he said it was you. You are a thief, he said."

"A thief! Me?" That accusation bit like an ax blade. "I am no thief. I have taken nothing—" He almost said: It was your father, but stopped himself in time.

"That sounds true," she said. Now her face changed, crumpling into misery. "But Da—my Dad—he tells the truth."

Sometimes, Ker thought. Not always. He would not tell the child, though; a child's trust in a parent was too precious to risk.

"You must have done something wrong," the child persisted. "Or he wouldn't be angry with you."

"I will ask him," Ker said. "I will find out and make it right."

"Truly?"

"Truly. You will see."

"Lin is crying," the child said, then ducked back inside.

Ker took a long breath of morning air flavored with cooking smells, and struggled to finish his gruel and bread. It would be discourteous, an insult to Lin's entire family, if he did not finish the food. It lay in his belly like a stone. When he was done, he walked back to his own house and waited for Tam to emerge.

"We have to talk," Tam said when he came out. His eyes looked red as well as his face. His hard hand on Ker's arm felt hot as a cooking pot.

"Yes," Ker said. "We do." He didn't resist as Tam pushed him away from the house, toward the woods and then into them. Before Tam could say anything, Ker spoke. "It's wrong."

"What?"

"That… thing. That rock. With the pretties. It's wrong. You have to put it back together, fix it, put it back."

Tam snorted. "So you can just happen to find it and take it for yourself? Not likely, my lad. That's just the sort of sneaky lie I'd expect from someone like you."

"I had a dream," Ker said, ignoring the insult. "Three nights in a row, and last night I woke and heard voices, and saw a flame on the hearthstone…"

"You didn't bank the fire right, and it burned through. You're lazy as well as a liar, Ker. I've done my best by you, but you needed a father years ago to teach you right from wrong…"

The unfairness of this stopped Ker's tongue in his mouth. Tam went on. "It has to stop, Ker. I didn't say anything because I thought, it's not his fault, he's just a boy, he'll learn. But after that day on the trail… you sneaking back to find more…"

"I wasn't," Ker said. He could hear the tension in his own voice.

"Lying to me about your shirt… did you think I couldn't tell you were lying? Rockfolk tore it, you said, when there were no rockfolk to be seen. You had something in that shirt, something heavy, and when you heard me coming you threw it into deep water. I say it was the other rock. You found something, saw something…" Tam's voice carried complete conviction; he had convinced himself that it was all Ker's fault.

"I was hot," Ker said. He thought, but didn't say, that he'd been working a lot harder than Tam out in the sun. "I went to cool off in the creek. I saw the rockfolk and then they were gone. That's all." Even to himself that sounded sullen and secretive; he saw again in his mind the rockfolk in their leather, their great axes, their sudden disappearance.

"Last year I might've believed that, Ker. This year… this year I think you want my daughter and my pretties as well. Maybe my life."

"Your—Tam, what are you talking about?"

"Sitting outside my house putting a curse on my sleep, and then claiming you have bad dreams—"

"I didn't—"

"Whispering mean things, putting ugly pictures in my head. That's not what I want in a son-in-law, a witchy man, an ill-wisher, a doomsayer. I'm taking back my daughter's troth, and I want that pretty I gave you before I knew about you."

"But I didn't do what you think," Ker said. "It's the pretties—they send the bad dreams, I'm sure of it. That's why we need to put it back together, so it will stop doing that, so the village will be safe. That's what it told me."

"Pretty rocks don't give bad dreams," Tam said. "They don't talk in the night, or make a man see his children flayed and burning… bad things. Ill-wishers do that. You can't fool me, Ker, trying to blame all that on a rock. My Ila woke in the night and saw you sitting up by the window—easy enough for you to slide in and out, with your pallet right there." He made a chopping motion with his hand. "No daughter of mine will marry a man who sends evil dreams. Now—for the last time—give me that pretty I gave you, and understand the troth is broken. You have today to make your peace with your mother, for this evening I will tell the Elders why the troth is broken. It would be best for you if you were gone by then."

"Gone—?" Ker stared.

"Wake up, boy. Whatever dream of power you had is over. We will not tolerate an ill-wisher in this vill, not while I'm an Elder. If I were not a kind man, forbearing, I would kill you where you stand."

"But I didn't—"

"Enough. Come now, and return to me that which is mine." Tam's hot, hard hand closed again on Ker's arm, and dragged him back toward the village and his house. Ker stumbled along, his mind in a whirl of confusion.

The other men had gone out to the fields already, but two children and their mother stared as Tam strode along. Ker kept up now, but Tam still held his arm as if he might try to escape. At Ker's mother's house, he heard his mother inside chanting the baking rhyme.

"I can't go in now," Ker muttered. Men did not intrude when women were singing the dough up from the trough. Tam must know that. Tam merely grunted, glaring into the distance, and kept his hold on Ker's arm. Ker sneaked a glance at him. Tam's face, his ears, his neck, were all as red as if he'd worked all day in the hot sun. Was he fevered, was that the source of his wrong thinking?

When Ker's mother finished the chant, Tam cleared his throat loudly and called to her. "We men must enter."

"Come, then," she said. Tam gave Ker a shove, pushing him through the doorway first.

"What is it?" she asked. She covered the dough with a cloth, and wiped her hands.

"Get the pretty," Tam said to Ker, then turned to his mother. "I have broken the troth, Rahel," he said. "My daughter shall not marry your son."

"Why—what is it? What's wrong? Ker—?"

"It gives me pain to say this," Tam said, putting his fist over his heart. "Your son is an ill-wisher."

"No!" His mother gave him one frantic look, then turned back to Tam, her hands twisting in her skirt. "No, you're wrong. Not Ker. He's always been a sweet boy—"

"He lies," Tam said loudly. "He lied to me. He tried to steal. And he sneaks out at night to lay a curse on my sleep and give me bad dreams."

"I don't believe it," she said. "Not Ker."

"Three nights I've had of broken sleep, and voices whispering, and in the morning he is there to wish me well, with a look on his face that would curdle milk."

"Ker…?" Again she looked at Ker, her face pale in the dimness.

"Get the pretty, damn you!" Tam roared. He seemed to fill the room.

Ker scrabbled at the stone and pried it up. The pretty looked smaller, dusty, in the room's dimmer light. He picked it up in bare fingers, and nearly dropped it again—it was so heavy and so very cold. He held it to the light for a moment; in the cloudy center he could almost see something, some tiny writhing shape. Did it really move, or did he imagine it?

"Give it to me," Tam said. Before Ker could comply, Tam grabbed his hand and forced the fingers open. Tam's breath whooshed in, and back out on "Ah-hhhh..." He took it and put it in his pocket.

"What is that?" asked his mother. "That thing—a rock?"

"Some rocks have pretties inside," Tam said. "They bring a good price at the fair, pretties do. I found such a rock when your son was with me. I broke it open, and gave him one of the pretties inside, because he was to be my son-in-law, and in token of the care I had for him. That was before I knew about him."

"I can't believe what you say," his mother said.

"It doesn't matter what you believe," Tam said. "I will tell the Elders tonight why the troth is broken. I told him, make peace with your family and then leave before that meeting. For I will not have an ill-wisher in this vill."

"But—surely Ker may tell his story..."

"If he is that foolish, he may. But who would believe a liar and a thief, someone who has put a curse on the sleep of my household? The Elders respect me."

"Ker, did you lie to Tam? About anything? At any time?" The look in her eyes expected *no* but though he had lied to Tam he could not lie to his mother.

"When he gave me the pretty, I did not want to touch it," Ker said. "I was afraid of bad luck. So that is one reason I wrapped it in my neck cloth, and I did not tell him that reason."

"That's not what I mean and you know it," Tam said. "I found you in the creek ford, hunting for more—"

"I was not," Ker said.

"Spinning that yarn about rockfolk," Tam said. "As if I couldn't see with my own eyes that you were alone, scrabbling in the rocks of the ford. No rockfolk upcreek or down, uptrail or down. Did they fly up into the air like birds?"

Ker's mother looked at him as if he should have the answer. "I don't know," he said to her; he knew Tam would not believe him. "They just—weren't there, after I heard Tam coming."

"Not a skilled liar," Tam said. "If you think to make your way as a storyteller, Ker, you must do better than that. But never mind—a self-confessed liar, a thief, an ill-wisher— I am going now, and you may tell your mother whatever ice-stories you wish before nightfall. They will melt by day, as all such do." He strode out of the house, and the heat of the day went with him.

"Ker, I don't understand," his mother said. In her face he saw lines he had never noticed before. "You know that lies are wrong..."

He could not bear it that she would think he was what Tam had said. "Please," he said. "I did not lie. Let me tell you about it."

She did not quite shrug, leaning on her work table. Ker told her all about that day—only a few days ago, it was. Finding the first stone, and the second and third, Tam's actions and his own feeling of dread, his unwillingness to touch the pretty. His nightmares, his awareness of Tam's unfounded suspicions, and finally—last night—his realization that someone—something—demanded that the broken rock be fitted together again, mended, and then restored to its former location. Tam's anger this morning, and his accusations, his refusal to believe the rock and its pretties were dangerous.

"It is like a tale out of legend," she said when he had fallen silent. "Strange rocks and frightening dreams and dwarves that say nothing but disappear when someone else comes. Tam is respected, as he said, a father and Elder, a man with knowledge beyond our fields. You are scarce old enough to wed, and you have admitted lying to him about your reason for not touching the pretty."

"It wasn't a lie," Ker said. "I just didn't tell him all. And I didn't steal anything, or curse his sleep. The rock did that."

"It was a kind of lie," his mother said. "Not telling the whole truth, and now see what comes of it. He can say truly that you were not always true. As for the rest, I believe you." She sighed, wiped her hands on her apron, and shook her head. "But will anyone else?"

His heart sank. "Surely they will. They have known me from my birth. They know I tell the truth. They know you. And even if they do not believe me—must I really go? Leave the village?"

"I think you must, Ker. Tam will not give you—nor any of us—peace until you're gone." She seemed calmly sure of this.

"They know me," Ker said again. It seemed impossible that this might make no difference. "Why do you think they will think I'm lying?"

"They know Tam better, or think they do." His mother picked up a hand-broom and swept the hearth where the ashes had spilled out onto it.

"I have to talk to them myself. It isn't fair…"

"Fairness is for the gods, Ker. We are not gods, to know for certain what is and is not fair."

"But if Tam doesn't put the rock back together, something bad will happen. Not just to him, to Lin and maybe the whole village. They should be warned." He was sure of it now, sure that his dream was right, that Tam was wrong about more than his own conduct.

His mother sighed. "It's you should be warned, Ker. You have never seen a shunning; you don't know… if you talk to them and they side with Tam we will both be shunned away."

"And if I don't, and the village burns or the rockfolk come in anger? Will that not be my fault if I have not warned them?"

She sighed again, shaking her head. "It is the cleft stick, and we are fairly in the trap. For you are my son; what they judge you to be, they will judge I have made you. I tell you, Ker, it is never easy for a vill to choose a young man's story over that of a wise Elder. And it is a hard thing to be thrust out into the world alone at my age."

As he watched, she began to set in piles all their belongings, and Ker realized she meant to leave… for the smaller pile would fit in the packbasket his father had used to carry fleeces to market or in the basket she herself used to carry sticks or berries or nuts home from the wood.

Slowly at first he moved to help her, thinking ahead to what they would need if they were cast out. Food, clothes, cooking things, tools. Everything he touched brought memories of the one who had made it, and stabbed his heart with the possibility of loss. It must not happen. He must find the words to say, words to convince the others that he was right about the danger. He tried not to let himself think about Lin, about never seeing her again.

When the men came in from work that evening, Ker stood outside his house with his mother. Tam glared at him, even redder of face than in the morning. "I told you—" he began, but Ker interrupted.

"I ask the village Elders to meet," Ker said, as loudly as Tam. "Tam has a grievance against me, and I have my own words to say, a warning to give."

The other men looked at each other. For the first time Ker wondered if Tam had said anything to them during the day's work. How had he explained Ker's absence?

"After you sit your time?" Beryan asked, glancing at Tam. He was senior of the men in that group.

"No," Ker and Tam said together.

"I am not sitting my time," Ker said. "I abide the meeting."

"Not for long," Tam said, and strode away to his own house. The other men looked at Ker. He felt the force of their stares, but said nothing.

"At starshine, then," Beryan said. "Lady's grace on you, until." He turned away and the others followed.

Ker's mother set out a supper that Ker saw included most of the perishables in the larder. He tried to eat, but the food sat uneasily in his stomach. Outside the day waned, and he knew word of something unusual would have spread. He and his mother came out into the dusk and looked up, waiting until the first star appeared.

The oldest men and women in the village had gathered around the well, holding candles; others, he knew from murmurs and shufflings in the dark, hung back in the houses or between them. No one spoke to him. As Ker and his mother walked toward them, the Elders drew back into two wings on either side of the well.

"Guardians bless the hour," Granna Keth said. Her voice quavered.

"Guardians bless the air that gives breath," Granna Sofi said.

"Guardians bless the earth that gives grain," Othrin said. He was eldest of the men.

"Guardians bless the water that gives life," Ker's mother said.

"Guardians bless the fire that gives light," Ker said.

"Lady's grace," they all said together.

Then Othrin said, "Tam says he has a grievance against you, Ker, and you have acknowledged such a grievance. As he is elder, he will speak first."

Tam began at once in a voice thick with anger. His version of events now included a long-festering suspicion that Ker had asked permission to court Lin only because he sought to rob her father... that Ker had always intended to go back and steal the special rocks, that Ker had learned sorcery while wandering in the woods and used it to harm anyone he disliked. A fatherless boy, Tam said, despite the care he and every other man had given him... such boys might easily find a way to learn evil things.

Ker could feel, as if it were a chill wind, the suspicion of the others as Tam blamed him for one mishap after another. Yes, he had been in the field that spring when Malo stepped on a rake, but no one then had blamed him. Malo had left his own rake tines-up and forgotten where he laid it. Yes, he had been at the well when two scuffling boys slipped and one cut his chin on the well-curbing, but their mother had scolded them, not Ker. Now she eyed Ker askance.

By the time his turn came to speak, he felt smothered under the weight of their dislike, their anger. Had they always disliked him? He was no longer sure.

He did his best to tell his own story, straight from first seeing the stones to the uneasy dreams, and his conviction that it was wrong to keep the stones, that they must be returned to their real owner.

"Wrong! Yes, wrong to have an ill-wisher—" Tam burst out. Othrin put out a hand.

"Let the lad say his say," he said.

Ker said it again, trying to make them understand, but Tam's obvious anger and certainty drew their attention.

"Liar!" Tam said finally. "I was there. I saw no rockfolk at the ford. The first rock I found was gone, and only you knew where it was."

"They were there," Ker said. "Two of them, this high." His hands sketched their size. "They had my shirt; one of them sniffed at it and poked it and it tore. It is all true, what I told you then. I do not know how they disappeared—how would I know the ways of rockfolk?—but they did. You must believe me—you must put the rocks back, all the pieces together, or something bad will happen."

"Bad things will happen to a vill with a liar and an ill-wisher in it," Tam said. "A man who lies about one thing lies about all." Ker saw heads nodding. "A rock is a rock— look—" He showed the unbroken rock to the elders, who leaned closer; several touched it. A drop of hot wax fell on the rock, and Ker flinched. Tam went on. "It is easy for him to say that bad dreams woke him, but I tell you that he did not sleep because he was putting bad dreams into my sleep. Ill-wishing. There is the bad thing."

A low mutter of agreement, heads moving from side to side. At the back of the group several women turned their backs on his mother. His heart went cold.

"I did not…" he began, but Othrin held up his hand.

"It is not right that a young man not yet wed should tell the Elders what to do," he said. "You make threats as if you were a forest lord or city king, but you are a boy we knew from birth. Even if the rockfolk come here, I have no doubt Tam will restore to them their property, if indeed it is their property. They would have no complaint against us. As for the rock, it looks like a rock to me. It is shaped like an egg, but what of that? You all but accuse Tam of stealing and lying, when he is your elder and would have taken you into his family. It is not right." He looked around the circle of Elders, and they all nodded.

"Go out, Ker, and do not return. You are not of us any longer." He glanced again at the others, who nodded again. "And your mother as well. Like mother, like son; like son, like mother. Take her with you, liar and ill-wisher." He turned his back. The others turned their backs, until Ker faced a dark wall of backs. Only Tam still faced him, his red face almost glowing in the dark.

"Drive them out now!" Tam said. "They will ill-wish us all—"

"Not by night," Othrin said without turning around. "We are not people who would turn a widow and orphan out to face the perils of night, no matter what they did. But be gone by the time the sun's light strikes the well-cover, Ker. After that, it shall be as Tam wishes."

Ker and his mother walked back to their house in silence and darkness; the others had all gone inside and barred doors against them.

"Well," said his mother when they were inside, with their own door barred. She did not light a candle; Ker remembered that their few candles were in the packs already. "We must sleep, and rise early." Her voice was calm, empty of all emotion.

"Mother—" he began.

She put up her hand. "No. I do not want to talk. I want to remember my life here, before it ends forever."

That night Ker had no frightening dreams, but woke in the dark before dawn to hear his mother sobbing softly. "I'm sorry," he said into the darkness.

"It is not your fault," she said. "Not entirely. I could wish you had not lied even in so small a thing as leaving out one reason for an action. But if you are awake, let us go. I have heard the first bird in the woods, and I want to be long gone by daybreak."

They rose and felt their way to the bundles packed the day before, unbarred the door, and came out into the fresh smells of a summer night. Overhead the stars still burned, but less bright than in deep night. Ker could see the dark bulks of the other houses, the looming darkness of the wood, and the pale thread of path leading toward the fields. The dust was dew-damp under his feet.

He could not believe he was seeing his home for the last time, but even as he hesitated he heard a cry from Tam's house up the lane. Light blossomed behind the windows, around the door, and Tam's angry voice grew louder. Ker took a step back onto the path.

"Come," his mother said. "Come now."

Still he hesitated. And then Tam flung open the door of his house—outlined against the light inside—and yelled into the night. "Damned ill-wisher—he's still here, he's putting his evil on the village even now—burn him out! Burn him out, I say!"

Up and down the lane Ker saw light appear in windows and doors as men and women snatched up brands from their fires and waved them into bright flames.

"Come on," his mother said, tugging at his arm. Ker turned and stumbled after her as fast as he could under the load he carried. Behind, he could hear angry voices. As they reached the turn into the first field, he glanced back and saw that the twinkling brands were together in a mass near their house.

"We must go to the hills," his mother said. They had crossed the ford, stumbling on rocks that seemed to have grown all points in the darkness and now stood among the bushes that edged one of the grazing areas. "My mother's mother's people came that way; I will have kin-sibs somewhere in that direction."

"But it's the wrong way," Ker said. "That's the path the stones were on, that the rockfolk were on. We should stay far away from it and the curse they bore."

"If we see any stones, we won't touch them," his mother said. "And we have none, so the rockfolk—if they were seeking the stones—should not bother us."

He was not so sure, but they had to go somewhere: They could not just stand here arguing. The smoke from their burning house trailed after them like an evil spirit. He could hear the villagers yelling in the distance; they might pursue. His mother started off and Ker followed, bending under the load as they climbed away from the creek and back onto the trail.

By afternoon they were beyond the vill's farthest cow pastures; taller hills loomed ahead. The well-trodden path had thinned to a track scarcely wide enough for one. When they came to a little dell with trees arching over a spring, Ker's mother left the trail and went down to it. She sat down in the shade with a sigh. Her face sagged with weariness. "We will sleep here," she said. "It has been too long since I walked the day away. Go and find us some firefuel, Ker, while I sing the water."

Ker shrugged out of the packbasket's straps and leaned it against a tree. He paused to take a drink from one of the waterskins they had filled the day before, then left everything with his mother and climbed back to the trail and looked around. Back down the trail, a narrow fringe of trees and shrubs they had passed a handspan of sun before. Far in the distance he could just see a smudge of smoke where the village lay. Ahead the woods in the dell widened up the slope to meet the trail ahead. That was closer, and he'd be coming downhill with the load.

He walked up the trail, light-footed now without the load on his back, and turned aside where the scrub met the trail. He found a rocky watercourse, now dry, though the trees overhead indicated water somewhere underground. Tiny ferns decorated cracks in the gray rock. One delicate-petaled pink flower hugged the ground just below that ledge. All the rocks were rough, gray, blocky; none were egg-shaped. Lodged against one of the rocks was a tangle of sticks, all sizes and all dry. He pulled a thong from his pocket and bound them together. Working his way down the dry creek-bed, he found here a branch that he could break over his knee, and there another flood-tangle.

As he neared the dell he heard his mother moving about, but no more singing.

"I'm coming," he called, just in case.

"Come, then," she said.

He worked his way slowly toward her, the bulky bundle catching on vines and undergrowth. Just above the spring a rock ledge jutted from the watercourse, flood-worn to smoothness. Here was another tangle of sticks—a quick flood, he thought, must have dropped it before the water could push it over the edge. It looked almost like a house of sticks. Perhaps some animal—? He bent over awkwardly and picked them up. Blackwood, yellowwood, blood oak, silver ash. Odd. He hadn't seen any blackwood or silver ash uphill. But they burned well; he carried them in one hand as he found a way down and around the ledge into the dell.

After a meager supper of bread wrapped on sticks and cooked over the fire, Ker sat watching the coals as the fire died down. No need to bank the fire; they would be moving on at dawn in the morning. His mother, tired out by the day's walk, had already fallen asleep, warded from the night's chill by their blanket. He was tired too, drained by all that had happened. His head dropped forward on his chest, and he dozed.

Pain shocked him awake, stinging blows to his face; he heard his mother cry out and struggled up from sleep to find himself facing a blazing fire and four rockfolk as angry as any in the tales. Two held his mother, and two more confronted him. His cheeks burned with the slaps that had wakened him.

"Where are they?" asked one. His voice could have been rocks grinding together.

Ker blinked sleep out of his eyes. "What?" he asked. Another slap.

"You stink of them," the dwarf said. "Do not lie. You have held what we seek: Where are they?"

He realized what they meant. "I don't have them," he said.

"Who does, then? Where are they?"

He hesitated, and the other one slapped him again. Again his mother cried out. "Don't hurt her!" Ker said, suddenly as much angry as scared. "She's my mother—"

"She is not hurt," the first one said. "She is scared."

"Ker..." came his mother's voice.

"Don't hurt her," he said again, surprised to hear his own voice deep and firm. "It's not right."

"It was not right of you to steal what was not yours," the dwarf said.

"I didn't," Ker said. *It was Tam* hovered behind his lips, but he stopped himself. Tam had been unjust to him, but he would not help that ill seed grow.

"But you know what we seek. How do you know, if it was not you who took them?"

Ker glanced at his mother. The whites of her eyes glinted; he could not read her expression as the light of leaping flames came and went across it. Which was worse, to betray Tam to the rockfolk, or see his mother frightened... hurt... dead?

Another slap rocked his head, more bruise than sting. "Who?" the dwarf demanded.

"What will you do to that one?" Ker asked. His mouth hurt; he tasted the salt that meant his mouth was bleeding. "It is not for me to bring someone else into trouble."

"Ha!" The dwarf facing him straightened. Standing upright he was taller than Ker sitting down, but not by much. Firelight glinted on the metal in his harness; he looked strong as a tree. "You invade our lands, steal our patterans for firewood, despoil our spring, and you worry about getting someone else in trouble? You have enough trouble of your own."

"But the trail is open to all... I thought," Ker said. "And what is a patteran?"

The dwarf grunted. "The trail, yes. So the treaties ran, from the days the first men came here: The trail is for all, folk of the air and folk of the forest and folk of the rocks. This is not the trail. The trail is there—" a thick finger pointed up-slope. "This is not the trail. You took our patterans—our trail markers—for firewood—"

Ker remembered the curious shape of the "flood drift" he'd found on the rock ledge; his face must have shown that memory because the dwarf nodded sharply. "Yes. Leaving aside the other, that is a thief's action. And you have polluted this spring—"

"We did not," Ker said. "My mother sang the blessing."

The dwarf cocked his head. "Did she now? And does human woman not know that such a blessing sung by a woman must not be heard by a man, and sung by a man must not be heard by a woman?" He looked across at Ker's mother, now sitting slumped between the other two rockfolk. She said nothing.

"I left so she could sing it—to gather firewood," Ker said. "I did not hear it."

"And you took our patteran."

"I didn't know it was a marker—a patteran," Ker said.

"What matters that? You took it. If not for your fire, and your snores, which made you easy to find, we might have gone astray from the path our comrades left for us. But we found you, and you have knowledge we seek. So, human, let us come back to that; if indeed you did not take our treasure, why do you bear its smell? Who took it? Where can this person be found? For if we find it not, and quickly, great peril falls on all this land."

Ker believed that. Between his dreams and the rockfolk, he believed absolutely in the certainty of some dire fate.

"I will tell you," he said. "But you must not hurt my mother."

"That is our business, not yours. Yet I say that it is not our habit to harm human women. Or human men, if they do us no harm."

With a last glance at his mother, Ker told the story yet again. "I was coming back from the cow pasture with an older man, the father of my betrothed," Ker said. "I saw a strange rock in the path…" He told about the egg-shaped rocks, about Tam's reaction to the second and third rock. "He said it was like rocks from Blackbone Hill."

"Blackbone Hill! Your people travel so far?"

"Most do not, but he had, he said, when he was young. And he had found round rocks with pretty crystals inside, he said, and he wondered if this might be such a one. So he—he broke it on the waystone. It had pretty things inside; he gave me one."

The dwarf growled something Ker could not understand. Then: "Fool! Idiot! Stupid child of dirt and water! On the *way marker!* Tell me, is this person accounted a simpleton, one with scant mind?"

"No… he is an Elder."

The dwarf stared, busy brows raised high. "This man is what you call wise?" Then he scowled. "I do not believe it! No one who has been to Blackbone Hill could fail to know the dangers of such things."

"He said they fetched a good price at the fair." Curiosity finally got past fear. "What are they, those rocks?"

"Rocks." The dwarf turned away and tipped out the packbasket. Pots clattered onto the ground. "Is it in here?"

"No! I gave it back to him," Ker said. "I told you—" The dwarf paid no attention, pawing through the pile... skeins of wool twisted on wooden knitting needles, his mother's spare skirt, two aprons, his spare shirt and trews, his winter shoes, last year's straw rosette from above the fireplace, the jar of bread starter, the jar of lard, the waterskins, the sack of beans. Those hard, stubby fingers probed through the pile, found the bracelet and tossed it aside, found the silver bits and paused.

"Where came these? Did you sell that piece of rock for them?"

"My father," Ker said. "He had many sheep and sold their fleece; over years, he saved that much."

"Where is he?"

"Dead," Ker said. The dwarf grunted.

"Tell me more. This person gave you a piece of the... the broken stone. And you did what with it?"

Ker told the rest, while the dwarf stared at him out of shiny black eyes.

"You put it under the hearthstone? Near a fire?" From the tone, that had been the worst place to put the pretty. Ker nodded.

"And then?"

"I had dreams. Bad dreams." The dwarf nodded.

"Yes, yes. It is dangerous to put such near fire."

"But you said it was just a rock," Ker said. The dwarf grunted again; Ker saw his boots shift a little on the ground. "I don't understand," Ker said. "I mean, I understand that if it belongs to you—to the rockfolk—then you must have it back. But why is it dangerous to put it under a hearthstone?"

"You ask too much," the dwarf said. He looked at the others, and began talking in a language Ker had never heard before. Soon they were arguing—or so it sounded—waving their arms and stamping their feet. Ker wondered if he and his mother might escape unnoticed and glanced across at her, but she was sitting slumped, her head in her hands. The argument died down finally, and the dwarf who had been talking to him turned to him again.

"You have a problem," the dwarf said. "It is that you have the scent of... of what we seek about you. And you travel on the Way. And you have *nedross* words."

"*Nedross?*"

"Rock is *dross* or *nedross*. *Dross* does not crumble; it is rock to trust, grain pure throughout. *Nedross* rock cannot be trusted, even if it looks solid and pure in grain: It fails. It is—" he paused, searching, "not truth."

Ker felt this as another blow. "I am not lying," he said.

"The words you speak are not whole," the dwarf said. "You know more you do not say."

His mother shifted slightly; the dwarf holding her said something that sounded like rocks grinding and the one facing Ker nodded. Then he spoke again to Ker.

"This is who to you?"

"My mother," Ker said. Did the rockfolk have mothers? Would he understand at all what mothers were to humans?

"Mother is one who birthed you?"

"Yes." Much more than that, but that was the beginning.

The dwarf left Ker abruptly to the hold of the others and went to his mother. Ker started to move, but the ones holding him tightened their grip. It was like being held by rock.

"No smell of dragonspawn," the dwarf said, facing Ker's mother. His hands were clasped behind his back, near the handle of the dagger thrust through his belt. His voice was slightly softer, speaking to her. "You never touched this thing... but you know something. What do you know?"

"I don't know what you speak of," Ker's mother said. "I saw a pretty piece of crystal that Tam said he had given Ker, and he wanted it back."

"Tam. Tam is this one who picked up the stone and broke it? Tam is where?"

"In the vill—the village you call it. Ravenfield, we say," Ker's mother said. Her face, across the fire, was patched with moving light and shadow. Ker could not read her expression. Her voice sounded tense, even angry. "He is an important man in the village, is Tam Gerisson. And he drove us out— drove us out for nothing. For nothing, I say!"

"Your son did not say that." The dwarf looked back at Ker, scowling. "I said you were not telling all you knew." Then again, to his mother, "Whose words are *nedross*, your words or those of your son?"

"Ker is a good boy," she said. "It is not for the young to condemn their elders or to bear tales of them."

The dwarf's clasped hands shifted, the fingers of one spreading and then folding again around the other. He spoke in his language, and a dwarf Ker had not noticed before moved into the firelight carrying wood, and put it on the fire. The fire leapt higher, giving more light. He turned back to Ker's mother.

"So this is why he told us not more of this person Tam? Because in your folk the young must respect the old?"

Ker's mother nodded. "The young are hasty; the young do not understand everything. So they could make trouble, not understanding, and they must not spread tales of wrongdoing, especially not to strangers. The Lady commands peace."

"But you?"

"I am a widow, a mother, and of the same age as Tam Gerisson. I can judge the rightness of my own words, and I can bear the load of shame or sorrow if I misspeak."

"And you say—" the dwarf prompted.

"I say that Tam planted falsely from the beginning. I say he tricked us, lured my son into plighting troth with his daughter, gave false gifts, lied and plotted to fashion an excuse to send me away."

Ker felt his jaw drop in shock. He had never imagined his mother saying anything like this. "No!" he said. His mother ignored him and went on.

"Ker does not know this, but years ago I turned aside Tam's offer of marriage. He was a lightfaring man, I thought, and I married Ker's father instead, for he had been steady in his affection since we were children. Tam must have held anger against me, though he pretended friendship…"

In the brighter light of the fire her face looked intent, determined.

"Was he selfish, this Tam?" the dwarf asked. "Hungry for power among your people?"

"Not in seeming. We do not esteem selfish men," his mother said.

Ker stirred. The dwarf whipped around as if he had seen that slight movement.

"What is it?"

"Granna Sofi said Tam became an Elder younger than others. He had the knowledge from his travels…" Ker said.

"So he did," Ker's mother said. "I had forgotten. His oldest children were scarce hip-high. It seemed reasonable, though, because he did know so much. He had often advised the Elders."

"And your husband?"

"He tended the sheep of our people," she said. "He died out on the hills in a storm. He fell and hit his head on a rock."

"Tam had just become an Elder," Ker said. If his mother was telling all about Tam, he had no reason not to tell what he remembered. "He came to tell us the news, and he offered friendship. He said I would be like a son to him, and he a father to me."

"He said he would not hold against me that earlier refusal," Ker's mother said. "He said he would care for me as for a sister. After that, he taught Ker as his own son in the lore of field and woods."

"Not sheep?" the dwarf asked.

"He was not good with animals," Ker's mother said. "He did not like them, nor they him. Barin Torisson took over the village sheep herd, and Ker learned the arts of planting and harvest. I gave his father's shepherd's crook to Barin for an extra share of wool."

"And for this Tam gave what?"

"We shared the village harvest. Tam never failed to bring our full measure of grain." Ker saw the sparkle of tears in his mother's eyes, and her head dropped suddenly. "He must have held that anger close, so long... I was afraid, at first, but then all seemed well, until Ker and Tam's daughter saw each other."

"Saw—?"

"As man and woman, not child and child, sister and brother," his mother explained. Ker had not thought about Lin for hours in the shock of leaving. Now he let his mind wander back to those first hours in which he had seen her truly, not as one of the gaggle of village girls, not as Tam's daughter, but as herself. An individual. A person someone might desire and marry and live with. Suddenly she had seemed wreathed in light, set apart from the others. And on that same day she had looked at him, recognized him as himself. While he still stood, staring, amazed at what was happening, she had spoken his name, *Ker,* and it had reverberated through his whole body.

Everyone knew marriage meant joining a family, a lineage, an inheritance of body and mind and soul. But beyond that was the delight of a pairing that worked—fit neatly in all respects as in body. Mere liking was never enough—for as the Elders said, in the spring of youth all maids liked all men and all men liked all maids—but desired in addition to the other criteria.

"The flower of love is the children thereof, but the fruit is peace, harmony, contentment in the whole village," his mother said to the dwarf, as she had told him often. A good marriage enriched everyone; a bad marriage impoverished everyone with the tensions it brought.

"Dwarflove is not like that." The dwarf grinned suddenly, showing those square yellowish pegs. "It is that we find grain match, and of gems those most desired. Dwarflove is blending of the rock, as when fire mountains melt rock into liquid fire."

Ker could not imagine that. The blending he understood was root into soil, or water into root: the growth of green things, flower and fruit.

"But no matter," the dwarf said. It was as if he had never grinned. "It is not the time to speak of love, but of judgment and justice. It is our saying that you go to this man, this Tam Gerisson, and bring back those things of which we spoke, with or without his consent. Bring him also if you can."

Ker felt a cold gripe in his belly. "I can't," he said. "We were banished. If I return, they will kill me. What good will that do?"

"If you do not return and fulfill this task," the dwarf said. "*We* will kill you." He fingered the ax handle in his belt.

"It is your rock," Ker said. "Why can you not get it for yourself now that you know where it is?"

The dwarf glowered, then shook his head. "You humans! You know nothing of the matter, and yet you will give orders. The Singers say we are hasty, and men say we are greedy, but in all the world none are so hasty and greedy as humans."

"I didn't say—"

"Be quiet." The dwarf's expression stopped the words in Ker's throat. He sat as still as he could, stone-still, and waited. Finally the dwarf heaved a gusty sigh, and shook his head. "It is not good for the Elders to mingle with humankind, so our wisest say. For where there is no mingling of blood in families, there comes mingling of blood in battle, and we would not begin a war without cause. For this reason, we ask humans to deal with humans, when needs must."

"But why? What is the need? And why didn't those other dwarves just come into the village and talk to Tam? Why did they vanish when he came near?"

"Were you not listening? Have you stones in your ears? You had seen them already: one human already, and I misdoubt they knew you were there until you rose from the water. We are not suited to seeing in water, we rockfolk. So one had seen, but there was no need for two to see. And you had the scent of dragonspawn on you—"

"Dragonspawn... you said that before, but you said rocks—"

The dwarf muttered what must have been a curse from the tone. "The scent of what we seek, I mean. Have you no words that mean different things—is there not a food you call dragoncake?

"Yes..." Ker remembered the village dragoncake, centerpiece of Midwinter Feast. "But—I was in the water. Water washes off scent—"

"Not this scent, not to our noses. Touch it but once, and you bear that scent to the end of your days. Faint, yes, if it is but once, and yet it marks the one who touches it forever."

Ker shuddered. The dwarf nodded.

"You see, now, why this matters. It is worse than that, for the one who handles such carelessly for long, and someone who desires many... they are ill luck for those who do not know how to master them."

"I thought at first," Ker said, "that it was some kind of egg. That it might hatch—" Even now he wouldn't mention Tam's comment about dwarfwives laying eggs.

"Men!" The dwarf spat into the fire and a green flame shot up. "Can you do nothing but think of that which should not be spoken and bellow it aloud? Be quiet, now."

Again Ker sat silently while the dwarf paced back and forth between him and the fire.

"It is ill, very ill, to speak of some things outside the fortresses of stone," the dwarf said finally. His voice was softer, still gruff but almost pleading. "It will be worse for you and your mother and every one of us, if the wrong ears hear certain things, or the wind carries the tale to certain lands I will not name. You must trust me in this. In time, perhaps, you will know of what I dare not speak. Now—now you must retrieve those stones, to the last splinter, and bring them to us, before… before trouble comes."

"They *were* eggs, weren't they?" Ker said, hardly above a breath in loudness.

The dwarf threw up his hands. "O powers of earth! Save me from this insanity!" He leaned close to Ker then, his strong-smelling breath hot on Ker's face, and murmured into his ear. "Yes, fool, they are eggs. Dragon's eggs. And full of dragonspawn, as your dreams tried to convey. Every crystal splinter holds one, and every unbroken splinter can transform into a dragon if nothing stops it. A hundred, two hundred, a thousand dragons from one egg, do you understand? Those eggs were a thousand and three years old, given into the care of my great-great-uncle straight from the mouth of the dragon himself—"

"Males lay eggs?" Ker asked in a normal voice, forgetting in his curiosity the need for quiet. Quick as a snake's tongue, the dwarf clouted him across the head. He had his dagger in his other hand; he had moved so quickly Ker had not seen him draw it.

"Fool! Idiot! Be quiet before you get us all killed." He sat back on his heels, then twisted to look at Ker's mother. "Madam, speak to your son! If you have any of the proper powers of a mother make him be silent—"

"Ker, please," his mother said. "Please just listen."

Ker nodded, and the dwarf heaved another sigh before going on. "We must be more careful," he said. In his own tongue he spoke to the others, and three of the dwarves trotted away from the fire, up toward the trail. Then he turned back to Ker. "Man, if you try to run I will kill you myself with great gladness and your mother's heart will be reft in twain."

"I will not run," Ker said. "I would not leave her."

"Thanks be for that," the dwarf said. The dwarves holding Ker let go his arms and walked away; he could not hear their footsteps, and once they passed beyond the bright firelight, they disappeared into the darkness. The remaining dwarf watched Ker, and ran his thumb along the side of his dagger with an unmistakable intent. For a time there was no sound but the crackle and hiss of the fire as it burnt lower, and then the dwarf spoke in a low voice.

"It is a trust, a trust between the firefolk of the mountains and my folk of the rocks. No land could sustain all the firefolk that might be born if they all came hatchlings from the egg, and nothing now in the world can prey upon the great ones, do you understand?"

Ker nodded without speaking. He did not understand what the dwarf meant by all this, but he did understand that the dwarf's patience had worn to nothing, and the dagger blade, naked in the dwarf's hand, glinted in the light that ran blood-red along it.

"For ages of ages, we rockfolk have had this trust, and for ages of ages the firefolk have not numbered more than the land could sustain. Some say of us—the Treesingers would say of us—that we and the firefolk are one in powerlust and greed, but this is not so. The hatchlings, aye: the young of every race are hasty and quick to grab and snatch. Human younglings, I have no doubt, run about and take more than they can use." He turned back to Ker's mother. "Is it not so, mother of a man?"

"It is so," she said.

"Age brings long sight and steady thought," the dwarf said. "The firefolk live long—even longer than we rockfolk, as long as the windfolk perhaps—and the firefolk in their age hold mountains in their care, mountains and valleys and the lands around. They have no wish to despoil what they love."

Ker opened his mouth to say what he knew of dragonkind, but the look on the dwarf's face stopped him. He wanted to say: But they are wicked, greedy, vicious; they are misers who heap up stolen treasure; they prey on travelers. Like dwarves. He did not say it.

"Long ago they made pacts with us rockfolk, for we know the ways of stone as they know the ways of fire, and between us great magics wrought protection for both their younglings and the world. Stone only can stand against such fire; only rockfolk can withstand the pressure of their desire to be free. They enter the bodies of those who touch them, bringing the fire of their ancestors but no wisdom, for they are young and full of foolish ambition. They grow, feeding on their host's body and spirit, until the host is consumed and all but dragonet itself: greedy for power and wealth, proud and lustful."

"I had dreams," Ker said. "Something trapped in the crystal. When I woke up I saw a blue flame, a shape, dancing, and then the banked coals went cold."

"And you touched it with bare hands—"

"It felt cold."

"It found no host in you. Perhaps in truth you are *drossin,* as the rockfolk are, for the spawn cannot take a *drossin* host without its consent. Yet from what you say, one or more found a host in this Tam. You say his face was red, and his touch hot: This is indeed the way humankind reacts when filled with dragonspawn."

"So it's… eating him?" Ker's gut twisted as he thought of it. Would it be like maggots that sometimes infested the sheep?

"Not exactly. Changing him. When it's grown as far as that host permits, it moves to another. To another of the same household, often. This man has many children?"

"It would go into *children?*"

"Indeed. For it takes time and more time to mature to its next stage."

Lin. Whatever was in Tam would get into Lin, would consume her, change her. Ker forgot his earlier concern, that she had inherited her father's clenched fist. It was not Tam; it was the dragonspawn inside him, and Lin—he could think only of Lin, his Lin, corrupted and consumed by dragonspawn.

"I have to go," he said abruptly, and stood. The dwarf swung a massive fist and knocked him down with a blow to the chest.

"Stay. I am not finished."

"You want me to go. I want to go." Ker could feel his heart pounding. "I have to save her—"

"Save who?"

"Lin. My—Tam's daughter—the girl I was to marry—"

"Ker, no!" That was his mother, across the fire. "She may already—"

"It doesn't matter. I have to—"

"You have to find and return the stones and fragments," the dwarf said. "That is what you must do. Anyone already harboring a dragonspawn is beyond your power. Only a dragon can deal with such a one."

"But if she isn't—" Ker could hear his voice rising like a girl's.

"Take her away, if you can. But I do not think you can." The dwarf shook his head.

"If they do not kill me first, I will," Ker said.

"If you rush in to save a girl, they will kill you," the dwarf said. His voice now held amusement. "By Sertig's hammer, I find myself where you were but an hour agone. You cannot go without being killed—not in this mood—so you must not go until you see sense."

"I won't rush in," Ker said. "I'll be careful."

"And why do you now think being careful will work, while before you did not?"

Ker could not answer that, but an idea came to him. "If you would show me how to do that—what the others did— to not be seen, then I could get in and out and no one would know."

"It is not something for humans to learn," the dwarf said. "It is born in us. But perhaps we can help without that." He pulled from his pocket a gray cloth about the size his mother draped over the dough trough. "This is not a way to be unseen, but a way to be unnoticed, if someone moves quietly and quickly. I do not know if it will work on you, but we shall see."

He draped it on Ker's head; for an instant the fire seemed to blur, then his vision cleared. The dwarf leaned close. "Get up and walk around the fire, very quietly, until you are near your mother. Say nothing. When you are beside her, speak to her."

Ker stood; he was stiff from sitting so long, but he moved as quietly as possible. When he looked at his mother, she was looking where he had been, not at him. He spoke, then, and her head turned sharply. "Ker! I didn't see you move! Are you leaving, then?"

"Yes—very soon, now." He looked back at the dwarf.

"It is only deception, and not as strong on you as on us; I could see you easily. But then, I knew about it. Stay close to hedges and thickets, cast no shadows into someone's eyes, and you may pass unseen." Or may not, the dwarf's expression said. "Rest a little," the dwarf said. "You will need your rest." That, as if he and his fellows had not broken Ker's sleep in the first place. But under that commanding gaze, Ker lay down. When the dwarf shook him awake, dawn was gray to the east. "You had better go now," the dwarf said. "Take this—" He handed Ker a flattened lump. "It is food, and will give you strength. And whatever you do, do not trust one who might have the dragonspawn already, no matter who it is."

The journey back went swiftly, for it was mostly downhill and Ker had no burden to carry. The dwarf's food brought him fully awake with the first bite and lent speed to his feet.

He moved cautiously as he came into the vill's pasturelands.

No one watched the cattle grazing in the upper pasture; Ker knew where the herdsmen rested, and no herdsmen lay there. No one watched the sheep in their meadow; half had strayed into the hedge where the rustvine grew, which no shepherd would allow, for the thorns that tangled the fleece. Ker wondered at that, for it meant the shepherd had been away for hours. He took the sheep's path to the stream, to the shelving bank where the sheep drank. Here the water swirled in, clean and clear, but there was no ford and no path on the far side.

The water cooled his feet, and he waded upstream to the women's bathing pool, alert for voices, half-hoping he would find Lin bathing alone and could speak to her. No voices. He came out into a little glade, the grass dry underfoot, and followed the women's path back to the village. He saw no one, heard no one, until he was very close, close enough to see through the fringe of vines at the wood's edge. The blackened ruin of his mother's house, burnt to ash and scorched stone hearth, lay between him and the rest of the village. It still stank of the burning.

Now he could hear voices, many voices and one angry voice louder than them all. He could see Tam in the middle of the square, yelling, and the other adults talking. The men should have been in the fields at this time of day, and the women in houses and gardens, or at the well, but all the people seemed to be there milling about. Ker watched, trying to hear what they said, but he could not. He wondered what had happened.

"You have to!" Tam yelled louder than before. "I know more! I have power!" He raised a fist.

Ker edged around one house and then another, working his way toward Tam's. If they were all in the meeting arguing, perhaps he could get in and out with the eggs before someone saw him. At the corner of Granna Sofi's garden, he looked across at Tam's house. Its only door faced the square, but two windows looked out on this side. He had only to cross the garden with its clusters of pie plant and redroot, and climb in through the window. If no one was inside.

He dared not look to see if Tam's family were all in the square; he was too close. Even with the dwarf's cloth, someone might notice him. He could see safely out of Granna Sofi's windows though, and she had a back door. He eased through it, blinking as his eyes adjusted to the darker room, pulled off the cloth, and took two steps toward the front of the house before he realized that Granna Sofi was there staring at him, her mouth open. She lay on a narrow bed, propped on pillows.

"You…" she breathed in her quavery old woman's voice.

"Please," Ker said, not even sure what he was asking. Don't raise an alarm. Don't be afraid. Don't turn your back on me.

"You came back," she said. Her voice rasped.

"Yes. I have to do something."

"You said something was wrong with Tam," she said. He looked more closely at her, with the way she lay, with the shape of her legs and the color of her skin.

"Granna Sofi, what is it?"

"You were right," she said. "He has changed. He has become something else."

"I know. I have to stop it—"

"You cannot stop it. He will kill you. He killed me because I spoke against him."

"But—" But you're alive, he thought, even as her eyes sagged shut and her last breath rattled free of her ribs. He saw then that her legs were broken, that great bruises marred her arms. Ker made the signs to send her spirit away in peace, and looked around for the necessary herbs. There they were, wrapped in a twist of sourgrass, as if the old woman had known she was going to die that day. Perhaps she had. He shivered, and laid the herbs on her eyes and mouth, at her head and feet.

When he looked out her front window, he could see Tam clearly, the red sun-burnt face and arms, the fierce expression on his face. He could feel the waves of heat that came off the square. Tam's wife, Ila, stood beside him, and she too looked ruddy under the sun, her yellow hair blazing with light. Around them at a little distance stood the others of the town, children at the back, peering between the adults.

It must be now. He hurried out Granna Sofi's back door, and quickly stepped across the first row of plants, then the second, and then he was flattened against the wall of Tam's house. He listened a long moment, hearing nothing from within. Tam continued to harangue the villagers from the square. Ker tried not to listen, as he would have tried not to swallow filth, but some words leaked through his ears anyway.

He must do it. He must enter the house as a thief, and as a thief he must steal away Tam's treasure, both the dragon's eggs and the daughter. He turned and climbed in through the low window. As before, his eyes took a moment to adjust to the dimness. He reached for the cloth to take it off, and realized he'd left it in Granna Sofi's house. He moved aside from the window and stumbled against a bench, and then in an instant he was wrapped in someone's arms and a hot mouth pressed against his, and the voice he had long dreamed of said, "Oh… you came back…"

Lin. He freed his mouth and said, "Lin. I have to do something."

"Yes—you have to kiss me. Oh, Ker, I've been so unhappy—" She clung to him and he could feel every sweet curve of her body. They had never been this close; he had dreamed of being this close. "Take me away, Ker; take me away with you! I want you, I want you forever."

He had never imagined that she would choose him over her father's will. He had expected to have to argue with her, persuade her.

"I will," he said. "But first I have to do something. Help me, and then we'll go—"

"No, let's go now," she said, dragging him toward the window.

"No, Lin, it's important—" He pulled back far enough to see her clearly. Lin with her yellow hair inherited from her mother, her clear eyes, her creamy skin… now flushed with passion, with love for him.

"What, then?" she said, clearly impatient. "If Da finds you here, he'll kill you—maybe both of us. We have to go—"

"In a moment. Lin, where does he keep the rock eggs, the ones with the pretties—"

"You're going to steal his pretties?" Her voice rose, then hushed quickly, and she grinned at him. "What a sweet vengeance, Ker. I hardly dared think you could think of that—"

"Under the hearthstone?" he asked, turning toward it. The dragon had told him he would feel the pull of the dragonspawn, but all he felt now was Lin's nearness and his own body's response.

"Some of them," she said. "But not all—" And with a gesture very unlike the girl he'd known, she pulled open her bodice to show him the purplish crystal spike hung from a thong around her neck, nestling between her breasts. His heart faltered, then raced.

"Lin, no! Take it off! It will hurt you!"

"Take it off? I will not! Da gave it to me, to make up for sending you away. It's the one you had; I'll never take it off."

"But Lin, they're dangerous!"

"Ker, don't be silly. It's a rock, a pretty rock. How can it be dangerous? The only dangerous thing here is Da, if he finds us. Here—I'll show you the others—" And she lifted the massive hearthstone as easily as Ker would have lifted a hoe, and scooped up two whole egg-shaped rocks, and a handful of shards. "This should be enough."

"We have to get them all," Ker said, and his own voice sounded strange to him. Where had Tam found another egg? He looked around and took a cloth from a hook near the fireplace. "Here—put them in this. We shouldn't touch them."

"They don't burn," Lin said, but she gave him what she held, then reached down for the other shards. As she did, the banked fire went out with a last hiss, and Ker saw the glow of her skin against the dark hole, and all at once her hand seemed clawlike, the nails talons. When she looked up at him, his stomach clenched at the expression on her face... exultant, hungry, eager...

"Is that all?" Ker asked. "Are you sure?"

"My father was right," Lin said with a giggle that froze his heart. "You are a greedy thief, aren't you?"

He could say nothing. He was robbing her father, though it was not greed, and he had no way to explain it. Not to the girl whose skin shone in the dim room. He wanted to tell her everything, but the dwarf's final warning stopped his tongue. That and his fear.

"Come now," Lin said, moving to the window. "I don't mind if you're greedy. I'm used to that in a man. I know you'll provide for me—"

"Lin—" What could he say? What he had most feared had happened already; he could not prevent it; he had come too late. He could not go with her, wherever she was going; he could not stay here.

"Come *on*, Ker," she said, reaching back to grasp his arm and tug at him. "We need to leave now. We can find a place later, and—"

He moved, hardly aware of moving, following her out through the window, across the garden again, behind Granna Sofi's house toward the next garden, the next house. Behind them the crowd in the square gave a concerted gasp. Lin did not look around, but Ker did.

Above the square hung a shadow of light, light condensed into form, form overwhelming light. The shape writhed, growing until it filled the air above the square, brightening more and more. Ker paused, terrified but fascinated.

What could it be? What was Tam doing? Beneath that light, Tam looked up, and the other villagers edged away, pushing at the children behind them.

"Ker!" Lin's voice, from the edge of the village, near the ashes of what had been his house. "Come quickly! Before Da sees us!"

Light squirmed in the air; shifting colors flowed over the crowd, then faded. Tam's face paled; his mouth opened; his hands spread as if to push the light away. Heat pressed down, heavy, inexorable. Something crackled; Ker looked across the crowd and saw a ribbon of flame leap up the thatch of Othrin's house and spread. Those nearest turned, opened their mouths to start a warning. With a roar two other houses burst into flame, then a third. People screamed; Ker could see their mouths open, but only the roar of the fires sounded in his ears.

Pain stung his hands. He looked down and saw the cloth wrapping of his burden browning like toast over coals.

He ran. He ran without thought, without plan, away from the heat, away from the light, straight into the woods on no path at all, blundering into trees and stumbling over briars until he fell headlong into the stream. Steam hissed away from his burden; the blackened cloth fell to pieces. His hands opened; water flowed between his fingers, cooling, soothing. Under the water he could see the stones: two whole, one broken, a heap of shards.

Behind him in the village fire raged; he could hear the roar, the crackling; he could hear screams. Acrid smoke spread through the trees. Overhead, thunder boomed in the cloudless sky; lighter light departed. Shaking, Ker got to his feet in the shallow water, took off his shirt, and wrapped his scorched hands, then fished the stones and pieces out of the slow current and waded downstream to look for a place to climb out.

When he came around a turn of the stream, Lin stood on the ford waiting for him. She looked flushed and lovely, her hair curling around her shoulders, her body the shape of every man's dream. She smiled at him.

"We don't have to worry about Da now," she said. "We can go back. You can be an Elder—"

"No," Ker said.

"Well, then, we can go somewhere else. With Da's pretties we'll have enough to start a new place—" A little breeze blew a lock of shining hair across her face; she tossed it back, the gesture he remembered from their childhood.

"No," Ker said.

"You're not running away," she said. The smile changed, reshaped into a mask of anger. "Don't think you can take what's mine and run away from me, leave me again!" Her hand reached for the crystal she wore, and he could see in her all that he had seen in her father. "Give them back then, thief!"

The words echoed, throbbing in air that once again thickened into light incarnate. He had a momentary image of Lin consumed in light, rising into its maw.

She was gone. The strange light was gone. On the ford stood a man dressed in such finery as Ker had never seen or imagined: brilliant colors, glossy fabrics, feathers and lace... he did not even have the words to say what he saw. The man stood in a shaft of brilliant sunlight that pierced the overarching trees, and the smoke filtering through the trees flowed around him.

"I believe," the man said, "you have something of mine."

Ker tightened his grip on his bundle. "It belongs to the rockfolk," Ker said. "I do not know you."

"To the rockfolk." A dry chuckle, thornbush scraping on stone. "I suppose that is one way of saying it. Are you then returning it, or are you the thief she called you?"

"I am not a thief," Ker said. "I am taking it back to them."

The man stared at him until Ker coughed on the smoke blowing through the trees, and then the man shrugged and blew away, as if he had been smoke himself. Ker struggled out of the water, and made his way up the trail, coughing now and then as the smoke eddied past him.

Over the first rise, the same man stood by the path, leaning on a tree. "You might fare better if you had a horse," he said.

"I have never had a horse," Ker said.

"A walking stick, then," the man said, and held out a trimmed length of wood with the bark still on. "You have a long way to go."

"It is ill luck to take gifts of strangers," Ker said.

"It is ill luck to refuse gifts of dragons," the man said, and as before he blew away... but this time into the thickening of light, which condensed into a shape the size of a hill. Green as the man's coat on the back, and yellow as the man's shirt underneath, clothed in shining scales that shimmered from one color to another. Ker gulped, swallowed, and stood still.

"Mortals," said the dragon. The dragon was not looking at Ker, but up into the air as if talking to it.

Ker took a step forward up the trail, and the dragon's great eye rolled toward him. He stopped.

"You interest me," the dragon said. A long flame-colored tongue flicked out of its mouth and touched Ker on the forehead; he felt it as a bee sting, hot and then sore. "I taste my children on you, but not in you. I taste dwarf on you. Perhaps you tell the truth?"

"I—I am," Ker said. Sweat rolled down his face; heat came off the dragon as off a rock wall on which the sun has lain all day. "They sent me to bring these back—" He shifted the burden in his hands.

"It is... difficult," the dragon said. "They do belong... there." The dragon sighed, and the grass before it withered and turned brown at the edges. For a moment the dragon's eye looked down its snout, then it lifted its head. "Lowland life is so fragile," it said, as if to itself. Then to Ker: "Approach me."

With the dragon's eye on him, he could not disobey. He took one step after another, until the heat beat against his face and body.

"What do your people say of dragons?" the dragon asked.

It was impossible to lie. "My people say dragons are wise," Ker said. "And greedy, treacherous, and cruel."

"My people say humans are stupid," the dragon said. "And greedy, treacherous, and cruel. Which is better if one must be cruel: stupid and cruel, or wise and cruel?"

In the worst of the nightmares, Ker had never dreamt of holding a conversation with a dragon. "Wisdom is good," he said, trying for caution.

"Wisdom alone is useless," the dragon said. "Wisdom without power is wind without air… it can do nothing of itself." Ker said nothing; he could think of nothing to say. The dragon twitched his head. "And power without wisdom is fatal. Power without wisdom is a mad bull running through the house." The dragon focused both eyes on Ker. "A fool should have no power, lest he bring ruin with him, but a wise man must have power, lest his wisdom die without issue. So which are you, mortal: fool or wise man?"

Something more than his own life hung on his answer, Ker knew, but not what it was. "I try to be good," he said.

The dragon vented flame from its nostrils, over its head. "Good! Evil! Words for children to use. Can fools ever bring good, or true wisdom do evil? No, no, little man. You must choose: Are you fool or wise man?"

"Anyone would choose to be wise, but it is not possible to choose," Ker said. "Some are born unable to become wise."

Something rattled off to his right; Ker glanced that way and saw the tip of the dragon's tail slithering across its vast hind leg.

"You interest me again," the dragon said. "So you would choose to be wise if you could be wise?"

"Of course," Ker said.

"And of what does wisdom consist?" the dragon asked.

Ker could think of no answer for that. He knew he was not wise; how then could he know what wisdom was? Finally he said, "Only the wise know."

"Does beauty know what beauty is?" the dragon asked. "Does water know wetness, or stone hardness?" Its head tilted so that one great eye was higher than the other, and both looked cross-eyed down its snout at Ker. His mouth went even dryer than before. Scaled eyelids slid up over the dragon's eyes for a moment and dropped back down, leaving that penetrating gaze even clearer than before. Ker's stomach twisted; eyelids should not move like that. "Surely not," the dragon said, hissing slightly. "Nor the blue of the sky know its blueness, nor the green of grass its greenness."

A throbbing silence followed; Ker could find nothing to say. He glanced around, trying to think of something, anything, that would free him from the dragon's gaze, and saw that its tail now lay between him and the trail back, a narrow but steep ridge. He was trapped in the dragon's circle.

"I will tell you," the dragon said finally, "what wisdom is, if you will promise to become wise."

"How can I promise that?" Ker blurted in a panic. Sweat ran down his ribs, and dried in the heat of the dragon's breath.

"Small beings can have small wisdom," the dragon said. "And small wise beings are better than small fools. Listen: Wisdom is caring for afterwards."

"Caring for afterwards...?" Ker repeated this without understanding.

"After action, afterwards," the dragon said. "Choose the afterwards first, then the action. Fools choose action first."

Ker opened his mouth to say that only fortune-tellers could know what would happen, but fear stopped him: Would he really argue with a dragon while trapped in its circle?"

The dragon's snout edged closer, nudged him. He staggered back: A dragon's nudge was like a blow from a strong man. Or a dwarf.

"You see," the dragon murmured. "You do know."

He didn't know. He didn't know anything except that he was surrounded by large lumps and ridges of dragon and too afraid to shake or fall down. He closed his eyes, expecting searing flame or rending teeth, and tried to think of the village as it had been, before Tam found those terrible eggs... of Lin before she had been invaded... of his mother, who now waited out on the hills in a hollow with a spring and a handful of rockfolk.

Cool air swirled around him, rose to a gale of dust and leaves, then stilled. He opened his eyes. No dragon. No strange light in the air. He blinked. A streak of dead grass, scorched, where the dragon had breathed that tongue of fire... and new grass, growing quick as a flame, brilliant green against the charred ground. At his feet lay the walking stick he had refused before, now sprouting incongruous flowers and leaves.

Ker looked up and around and saw nothing of the dragon, but he had seen nothing of the dragon before. Cautiously, he picked up the stick in his free hand. At once, strength flowed back into his limbs. He felt rested, strong, as if he had just come from a full night's sleep and a full meal. The scent of those flowers filled his nose. He took a step and stared as the land blurred around him, reappearing when he put that foot down. A league, two leagues, had fled behind him. Already he could see the hill where his mother waited with the rockfolk.

One more step and he was there, standing above the dell and looking down into it with eyes that saw through leaves and wood to where his mother sat knitting, while the rockfolk snored. The ones who should have been watching the trail slumped near it, also snoring. The little camp looked orderly and peaceful; someone had put their scattered belongings back into the packs. Probably his mother; he could not imagine the dwarves being so helpful. Somewhere a bird called, and another answered. Ker looked at the walking stick. Flowers and leaves had disappeared, leaving it bark-covered once more.

Ker came carefully down the slope into camp; his mother looked up and her face brightened but she said nothing.

"I'm back," he said.

"What happened?"

He did not know how to tell her; he was not sure exactly what had happened.

"Why are they sleeping?" he asked instead. His mother shrugged.

"I know not. Only that at noon the light changed and they all fell into sleep. I would have slept, but their snores were too loud and I was worried... did you bring Lin?"

"No." Ker leaned the walking stick against a tree; the tree's foliage thickened. His mother stared at him.

"What happened? What is that? How did you come so soon?"

"I don't understand," Ker said. "It was a dragon—" He could say no more; exhaustion fell on him like a sack of wet grain, and he slumped to the ground. In a moment, his mother was at his side. A long drink of water, a hunk of bread smeared with jam, and he struggled up again to sit with his back against a tree. She handed him his spare shirt, and he put it on. He tried to tell her everything, but how could he say what he did not understand?

The rockfolk roused suddenly, their snores cut off in an instant. Their eyes opened; they sat up and stared at him.

"Why are you here?" asked the leader. "Why did you come back before you had finished?"

"I brought you what you asked for," Ker said. He nudged the wrapped bundle with his foot.

"You could not have gone so far so fast—" the dwarf broke off, staring now at the bundle. He muttered in his own language, and two of the others approached, one drawing a thick leather bag from his pack and opening its mouth. The first unwrapped the bundle gingerly, and revealed the same egg-shaped rocks, the same shards. He reached out, touched them, turned them over. Then he glared at Ker. "How did you do this?"

"Do what?"

"They're dead. They're all dead. What did you do to them?"

"I did nothing," Ker said. He couldn't see any difference in the rocks and shards, but the dwarves clearly did.

"These can't be the same... you could not have traveled so fast..."

"It was the dragon," Ker said. They all stared at him now. "It—gave me a walking stick. It helped me."

Now they stared at the walking stick, and the thick growth of new leaves on the tree overhead.

"You talked to a dragon and it *helped* you? It brought you eggs to carry?"

"No." His head ached now, sudden as if someone had hit him again. "Let me tell you—"

"Go ahead."

He told it as well as he could and they listened without interruption, though some of them muttered softly in their own tongue. When he finished, with "And then you woke up," the questions began. What was the dragon's name, and how big, and what color, and what had it done with Tam and the villagers and Lin? Ker said "I don't know" over and over.

"You cannot know so little," the dwarf said. "You were there! You say you saw these things, and yet—"

"Don't bully him," his mother said. "You're as bad as Tam, you lot." She glowered at them, and to Ker's surprise they gave way. "What would he know of dragons? Do you think they give their names away to anyone?"

"Rarely," drawled a new voice. Ker twisted around to see the same elegant man lounging on the slope above, a stalk of sweetgrass in his mouth. The dwarves drew into a huddle, eyes wide. The man lifted one shapely eyebrow. "Frightened, stonebrethren? Lost something? It would have been wise, would it not, to have told me before I heard it from others? Before I had to reveal myself, to undo the harm that came from that loss?"

One of the dwarves burst into speech in their tongue, but the man held up a hand. "Be courteous; these human folk have not your language nor mine. Speak as they can hear."

"We weren't sure," the dwarf said. "Not at first. We thought—"

"You hoped you could retrieve what you lost before I learned of it, is that not true?"

"Yes." The dwarf scuffed one boot against another.

"So this human—this idiot, this fool, I believe you called him—has proved more wise than you, has he not? He, not you, retrieved the lost. You sent him to do it, knowing it was perilous—"

"It was his fault in the first place," muttered one of the dwarves.

"You accuse him of thievery?" the man said. "You think he slit the carrybag and filched the eggs in the first place?"

"Well... no. Probably not." The dwarf looked down, hunching his shoulders.

"You know they seek life," the man said. "My kind always do. Whoever carried them grew careless, I have no doubt: drank deep and slept, as you slept today, or set the carrybag on sharp rock, and so they fell free, to be found by something or someone they could use." He sighed. "I should remember that ages are long for you, stonebrethren, and a trust passed from generation to generation can be a trust weakened."

"We didn't mean—" began the first dwarf, but his voice trailed away as the man looked at him.

"Intentions…" the man said slowly. Then he looked at Ker's mother. "Madam, what does a mother say about intentions?"

"Meaning to never mended a wall," Ker's mother said. "Not meaning to drop it never patched a pitcher."

"So wise a lady," the man said. "This must be your son." Now he looked at Ker, and it seemed that behind his mild brown eyes red flames danced.

"He's a good boy," she said.

"He's an interesting man," the man said, in a tone of mild correction. "He may become wise one day. We shall see." Now he looked at Ker. "What of you? What do you see in all this?"

Ker's throat tightened, but he forced words past the tightness. "You are not a man," he said.

That elegant figure laughed. "True and true: what then, am I?"

"A dragon."

"Perhaps. Perhaps merely the shape a dragon sends to talk to those who cannot bear the sight of dragons. For if the shape be the thing, then this shape of man cannot be a dragon, nor—" The man was gone; words hung in the air as the light condensed once more and a very visible dragon sprawled on the trail above, its head lying aslant on the slope to the dell. "Nor can this be a man's shape. But if some essence, not the shape, be the thing, then either the man's shape or some other could be dragon."

"Lord dragon," one of the dwarves said, coming forward past Ker. Ker noticed that he was paler than usual. "If you permit us—"

"I do not," said the dragon. "Be still, rockbrethren; we will talk hereafter." There was in that a chill threat. Ker and the dwarf both shivered, but the dragon was looking at Ker. "You remember we talked of wisdom… what would a wise being say of these who lost somewhat of value held in trust and did not warn the owner that it was lost?"

"You ask me to judge them?" Ker said. He glanced at the dwarves, now standing motionless as if the command to be still had turned them to stone.

"I ask your opinion only," the dragon said. "I am capable of judgment; it is my gift."

"I do not know the ways of rockfolk," Ker began. The dragon's eye kindled, and he went on hastily. "But these had cause to hate and distrust us—me and my mother—and instead they listened and did not harm us."

"You bear their bruises on your face," the dragon commented.

Ker shrugged. "I bear them no malice for it," he said. "They were frightened; they thought I might have stolen those things they sought, and that danger would come of it."

"They sent you into danger," the dragon said.

"Yes, but—" The dwarves' reasons now seemed like excuses, as he'd first thought. Even so he wanted no part of vengeance. "They did not force me; when I thought of Lin I wanted to go."

"To save a friend."

More than a friend, but he did not think the dragon would care for a correction. "Yes. And these dwarves were trying to make right what had gone wrong. They wanted to restore what was lost. I think they are honest, but too frightened—of you, I suppose—"

"Oh, yes, I am frightening…" The dragon rolled its head and inspected its own length. A cloud of steam gushed from its mouth, warm and moist, smelling of baked apples. "And so fear is their excuse, is that what you would say? But you… you were not frightened enough to give me what you were not sure was mine. Are you then braver than the rockbrethren?"

"No," Ker said instantly. "I'm—I was scared. I am scared. But I had to do it anyway."

"Hmmmm." That vibrated in the rocks beneath their feet; the trees trembled. "So, you make no judgment against them for the harm they did to you, by loosing such dangers on you and your people, and then by striking you, and then by sending you into danger?"

"I am not the judge," Ker said. The dragon's eyelids flipped up and back down again, and again Ker felt sick at his stomach.

"You are more clever than you seemed at first. Remember what wisdom is?"

"Care for afterwards," Ker recited promptly.

"Yes… and have you a care for afterwards here? What about *their* afterwards?"

Ker looked at the dwarves. They all looked at him with an expression of resigned defeat.

"If I were the judge," Ker said, "I would do no more than has already happened. They have been afraid to the marrow of their bones; they have suffered enough."

"Would you trust them again?" the dragon asked, cocking its head to peer closely at Ker out of one eye.

"I would," Ker said. His back felt cold; he glanced around to see that the fire had died down to glowing embers.

"Why?"

Ker shrugged. "I don't know. They feel honest to me."

"So in *their* afterwards they prosper as the result of their carelessness… will this make them less careless?" The dragon had propped its chin on one vast front claw.

"I do not know," Ker said. "You asked what I thought."

"So." The dragon's head lifted a little, and the warmth of its breath touched Ker. "Hear my judgment, rockbrethren. For your carelessness in a sworn trust, you shall lose the gems in these—" A lance of flame, accurate as a pointing finger, touched the rocks and shards; Ker hardly felt warmth as it struck past him. When he turned to look, the rocks and shards had vanished. "Yet I will trust that you continue to guard the other well, and make no demands of reparation. So tell your king. I will watch more closely, but that is all. And I will also watch how you deal with this human, whom you have to thank for my inclination to mercy."

The dwarves threw themselves on the ground; the dragon withdrew into the fastnesses of air. They looked up when it had gone, and scrambled to their feet.

"We've you to thank," their leader said. His mouth twisted, then he smiled. "Well, that's fair, I suppose. And what do you want of us, then?"

"N-nothing," Ker said. His knees felt shaky again.

"That won't do," the dwarf said. "Sertig knows we're not as rulebound as our cousins of the Law, but no one can say the brothers are mean enough to take such a service as you did us and give no gifts in return. And it's not for the dragon's sake, either," he said, glaring up at the leaf canopy overhead. "I need no dragon to teach me generosity." A bubble of light rippled through the dell, and he paled but shook his head. "No, and again no. We're in your debt, a debt we can't pay, but we can gift you with what we have." He looked around at the others. "Come now, lads, let's get busy."

Before Ker quite realized what they were about, the dwarves had picked up the bundles he and his mother had carried from the village the day before.

"Where was it you were going, ma'am?" he asked Ker's mother.

"I—I have family in the hills west of here," she said. "Swallowbank…"

"Swallowbank, yes. A difficult road, ma'am, and a hard three days' journey, if you'll pardon me saying so. Would you consent to travel an easier one?"

"I—" she looked at Ker. "I—I suppose so. What road?"

"Ours," the dwarf said. He turned to Ker. "We will take you on our road, smooth and straight and safe underfoot and overhead, we will carry all your burdens, and we will set you down safe and rested in sight of Swallowbank with all that you desire," he said. "If you will accept our gift."

"I thought—maybe—with Tam gone, and the dragonspawn—we could go back," Ker said. "Rebuild our village—" Surely they were not all dead, all the people he had known; surely the dragon would not have killed them all.

The dwarf shook his head. "No. I'm sorry, but what the dragon deals with cannot be changed. For all they are great healers in their way, they are also great destroyers. That land will not accept humans for a span of years; the dragon would have made sure of that. You must find a new place, and a new life."

"Then—I accept your offer with thanks." Ker picked up the walking stick, half-expecting to be dragged a league away with his first step, but it remained a bark-covered stick.

The dwarf led them back up the way Ker had come down with firewood, to a rock fence smoothed by falling water. The rock opened suddenly, like a door, and they passed into a dark tunnel, smooth all around. At once, the walking stick burst into cold flame, lighting the tunnel in blue radiance. Ker stared at it, but it did not burn his hand, so he held it firmly and walked on.

GRAVESITE REVISITED

The old woman held out her hand. Carver froze, crouched over the grave, the reindeer pendant still swinging slightly on its chain of carved bone.

"You know you can't put that in with her," the old woman said.

Carver scowled. "She liked it. She should have it."

"You can't. It's not permitted." The old woman glanced back over her shoulder, and the old man, Longwalker, nodded, emphasizing his agreement.

Carver clenched his fist on the pendant and chain, furious. "I don't understand. She wasn't Wolf Clan…. How could it unbalance the world to carry her own clan sign along?"

"It's nothing to do with the hunt's balance," the old woman said. She reached for Carver's hand, and pried up his fingers, then prodded the pendant and chain. "It's this—this chain. The latepeople will see this and think. We don't want them to think."

"The latepeople?" Carver had lived in Molder's family for only four years; he knew there were many secrets they had yet to share with him. By her father's clan, her seedclan, she was Reindeer, but her mother's clan, her bloodclan, was Ash, godtalkers. And the old woman, whose name he had never heard, being an outsider and only Molder's chosen childfather, she was Ash. She had foreseen Molder's death in a fall, and had withheld warning, for she was Ash, and spoke warnings only at the gods' will, though she saw (Molder had told him once) all things that would come until the end of the world.

"The latepeople, those who will come when the times change," the old woman said. "The latepeople find our bones, and our graves—"

"They dig up graves?" Carver was shocked. Animals dug up graves, but only because they were the Elder People, and had rights humans did not share.

"Yes, indeed, they dig up graves. And when they find what they want in a grave, they travel backwards until it is new, and rob it."

"Backwards? In time?"

"Yes. As I see forward, which is proper for an Ash, and a gift of the gods, they see backwards, and travel backwards, by witchcraft."

Carver shuddered. The past was past; he had been taught that the past was unbreakable, the foundation of time. Mistakes could not be unmade, so all acts must be carefully considered, but anything done rightly was as safe from error as a mistake from correction. To travel backwards, to tamper with the past, was obscene. The old woman nodded at his expression.

"They are witches," she said. "Empty hearts, fearing their future, looking for treasures to rob in the past." She smiled without humor. "We give them nothing to think about, nothing to rob."

"But her spirit—" Carver's people made better graves, he thought. Had thought before, and had not said, being a stranger among Molder's people. It was discourteous to criticize the wife's family. But his people laid food and tools with the dead, on a nest of flowers (in spring and summer) or fur (in winter), and a gift from each person close in relation or in feeling. He had grown up knowing that the dead lived in the shadowed lands, yet hungered for mortal food and the love of mortals. If not fed or gifted, they might come back as haunts, angry spirits who stole away children or even sprinkled death pollen over a whole encampment, so that sickness bloomed in terrible shades of red and white.

The old woman grimaced, and gestured him away from the grave, the sad little hole where Molder lay curled on her side, nested on nothing but the old piece of hide she had liked to sit on while she worked, the wound in her head against the damp soil. Carver moved stiffly, still angry and worried. Finally the old woman stopped, crouching under a bush, and gestured for him to sit down. He lowered himself slowly to the ground.

"I am an Ash," the old woman began. Carver shivered; her voice had the tone and cadence of the nightfire chants. "Ash are the godtalkers, and the gods gift Ash with vision of times to come. Days and days, and seasons of days, winters and springs more than anyone's life, and the latepeople, the witches, will be born."

"There are witches now," said Carver, very politely. "Are the latepeople born to the witch clans?"

"We have no witches now!" the old woman said angrily. "No witches!" Carver sat stunned. All his life he had heard of witches. His father's older brother had been killed by a witch, tranced into sleep in a storm, and frozen: that was true. His father had demanded a callsong, and a visitor from another camp had come, answering that call, and been speared by all the men, and hung from a tree. A witch, his father had told him, and yanked him back from touching any of that dangerous blood. The other tribe had never complained, which meant they had known they harbored a witch—but killing a witch in the tribe was harder than letting another do it.

"My father's brother—" he began, but the old woman stabbed a finger at him, and he clamped his mouth shut.

"No witches like the latepeople will be," she said. "Now we have one or another who makes a bargain with the wrong gods. One person may be killed, perhaps two or three. But it is all water running downhill, as water should do. Your father's brother—I know about that. He boasted to that witch about his skill in foreseeing storms, and more shame to him that was no Ash, but a Mink. What does a Mink know about storms? So that one gave him drink sweetened with wild honey, and he drank more than he should; and slept on a night when the moon was ringed by cloud, and snow came. Is that witchery? No, you could do that, if you wished."

Carver could not imagine it, giving death in the drink of welcome.

"He didn't mean to kill your father's brother. He thought to have him boast more, and then waken to snow in the camp, safe but shamed. But your father's brother quarreled with another, and walked out into the darkness, and no one would follow. There he died, when the snow came. The witch came to your father's callsong, yes, but he already knew he must die."

"But he was a witch—"

"No. Not like the latepeople. Listen, Carver, and I will tell you. But this is a secret, and you must not tell others." He touched his hand to his own clan emblem, and she went on.

"It was in my mother's day that we first noticed it. Like your people, we made comfortable graves for our dead then: nests of soft grass or fur, and grave-gifts to comfort them in the shadow lands. Even the winter graves had flowers, for we dried the yellow lilies of the swamps, and saved them, so that all the dead would have color and light in the darkness. And we did something else, which no other people I know of tried to do. When we could, we buried our dead with their kin: bloodclan with bloodclan, in joined graves, then linked head to foot, so that the Eldest could be honored by their descendants.

"My mother told me that she was just swelling with her first child when the people returned to their summerlands one year and found all the graves open. Freshly open."

Carver stiffened, and the old woman nodded.

"Yes, it was shocking. At first they thought a plague of bears or wolves had torn the graves open, or the earth itself had split, but the best hunters looked carefully and said no. There were prints enough in the ground: some of people with strange clothing on their feet, some of animals with no feet at all, a pattern like this—" And the old woman scooped the reindeer pendant from Carver's hand, and pressed the chain into the ground, then again beside the first print, leaving an odd pattern that looked like nothing he had seen.

"*People* had robbed the graves," the old woman went on. "They had taken the bones of the dead, and all the grave-gifts in the most recent graves, those of the year before." She paused a long time. Carver sat thinking about it, what they must have thought, coming on those graves all open to the sky, as Molder's was now. He would have been terrified of the spirits, sure that the air was full of death pollen. But these people had the Ash Clan with them, the godtalkers, so they may have felt less fear.

"My mother told me that everyone went a day's journey away to camp, walking all night. They were frightened of the dead, and of the people who had taken them. But a man of Ash, and three hunters, went back very early the next day. And what do you think they found?"

"The latepeople?"

"No. Worse. The next day, they found the graves still open, but open for a long time. Deserted, empty, weathered: the hollows nearly filled in the older graves, grass and moss growing all over." She peered at Carver's face, intent on something he could not imagine. "You don't understand?"

"No." Open graves weathering overnight? It had to be witchcraft, but nothing he had ever imagined. Why would a witch do that?

"It had been years—*years* since the graves opened. Years in a night. The man of Ash then burned sweet woods, and spoke in a way we know of, we of Ash, and the gods answered. By their wisdom, he could see that it was the latepeople. Far in the future, in their own time, they found one grave. In it was that which made them search for another. And by witchcraft then they walked back in time, just as a man might walk upstream to find the place where berries grow, if he sees one float by in the water. And they found our gravesite, and robbed it, and then came back earlier, and robbed it again, in what was to our people a day and a night, at most."

"Did anyone ever see them?"

The old woman looked away. "Some have said so. Some say they take the children who disappear—that it is not *our* witches, but those latepeople witches. I have not seen them myself. But I know what they look for, and where. If our dead are to have any comfort, and be safely housed until the gods turn the world over, we must leave them nothing to interest the latepeople. I have seen graves opened, and left alone, when no treasure was in them. Now. Give me that pendant."

So compelling was her voice that Carver had opened his hand again before he thought. The old woman took the pendant and chain, and led him to a small tree growing nearby.

"The young trees are best, Carver. Old trees may die, or blow down. Choose always one too large for the reindeer or other horned ones to break when they clean their antlers, but one small enough to live long." With her best blade, the old woman slit the bark, lifted a section, slipping the blade underneath as a skilled hunter skinned game, and pressed the pendant and chain under it. "We never place more than one gift in a tree. Some things can be buried under a live root, where the root will grow over it. The dead are not like us; they can reach their gifts even through the wood of trees, or the roots. As long as we give them clues." Now she twisted off a twig of that tree, and took it to the grave, where she dropped it carelessly onto Molder's folded body. Carelessly? Carver looked up as another twig fell along Molder's cheek, and saw the old woman nod toward another tree. One by one the family came, each dropping a twig—in one case a pebble—beside the dead woman. And then they closed the grave, piling stones more carelessly than Carver's people—or more carefully, he finally thought, watching the caution with which they chose stones and placed them.

"She will sleep long, and waken without pain," said the old woman. "When the gods turn the world over, she will have her other children."

"It's got to be climate." Ann leaned on the counter and squinted at the computer screen. Her new glasses were driving her nuts; bifocals were not the answer. She wanted the new surgery. Maybe next year, if the bigger grant came through.

"Invasion," said Chris. He was being difficult, as usual.

"Climate. It matches with the onset of the interglacial—"

"You think you take four lousy trips backtime, and you know everything."

"I know four trips more than you do." She knew he thought she was being bitchy, but she did have four trips back to Stone Age Europe, and he had yet to be cleared for one.

"You never even *saw* them. You just robbed graves. You can't be sure of anything just from the graves—"

"Chris, you're never going to get clearance for backtime research if you stay an interventionist. No one is about to let any of us make actual contact with the primitives." Ann punched up the climate data again. The match wasn't exact, but then the climate data were approximations from pollen analysis—old dates, not direct measurement. They couldn't leave a team onsite in the past long enough to do climate studies, much as she'd have loved it. The match was close enough. Warming climate had sent the prim's main prey north, had changed their society, and that must be why their grave customs changed, from the lavishly decorated and prepared graves of the previous centuries to the plain, stark burials she'd found recently.

Chris leaned over her shoulder, peering at the screen. "That stuff's outdated. Pollen analysis! If you'd put a team down for even one week, real time, in decent weather, and let them do an astronomical scan—"

"Interference."

"Who cares? Those old stone-carvers? Ann, what if they do see a team? They won't know what it is. They're savages, primitive, superstitious—they'll just call 'em gods and run away. Didn't you say you'd found contemporary tracks at Site 402?"

Ann pushed her chair back slightly and bumped into his knees. Site 402 still scared the hell out of her. They'd gone in, found a couple of six-month-old graves, still untouched, and some other obvious graves nearby. They'd done a bounce-scan and decided to drop back fifty years, then another fifty: a fast in-and-out each time, plucking the graves clean. Then a final stop at the first time, maybe a day later real-time, and they'd seen tracks. Human tracks, recent, clear evidence that some of the primitives had arrived just after the first sampling. How long after? Ann still wondered if they'd come before, or after, the older graves *changed*. And had the graves changed *then,* at the theoretical fork in time, or along the main line back when they'd been opened?

She mentioned that chilling possibility. Chris shook his head.

"Ann, they can't think—not like we can. They won't be able to reason anything out. And if they did figure it was people from the future, what could they do?"

"I don't know." It was the not knowing that was worst. Would they fumble around for a new set of words to express that concept? Would they migrate away from the place where their graves had been robbed? What could they do, primitive hunters that they were? They couldn't change history, surely. "It doesn't matter, anyway," she said, pushing all that aside. "What matters is this paper for the meeting, and that means coming up with a reasonable explanation for the change in burial practices. Climate fits well enough. If you have to hunt different animals in the same place, or follow familiar animals to new places, you won't have time to accumulate the same quantity of grave goods, or build elaborate graves—"

"Behavior is conservative. I still think it's invasion— different people, with different customs. Look what you found this last time: twigs and pebbles in the graves, with nothing but a scrap of skin under the bodies. Stones carelessly tossed on top. If you'd brought back even one whole gravesite, we could have found evidence of a new culture—"

"It wasn't worth it. Chris, the body type's the same. Biochem sampling on the one indicates it's the same genetic type, same everything… they just aren't putting any cultural goods in the graves, and it has to be because they can't afford to, they don't have enough. An impoverished culture, struggling to maintain its way of life—"

"*Twigs!* Dammit, that's a different religion." She was fascinated that the change from carved bones to uncarved twigs could excite him on religion, but the possibility of a resurrection myth didn't move him at all. "Ann, think about it. They used to bury their dead with carved bone and wood: animals, mostly. Bits of stone, yes, but carved or shaped into ornamental items. Carved bone buttons, awls, that amber whatsit from Site 327, fancy leather items. Animals, dammit. Not twigs, not plant life. Maybe it's not an invasion, but something's made them start worshipping trees instead of reindeer and wolves."

"A climate change could do that. Forest expanding, with higher temperatures, or—"

Chris leaned against the wall, and she could tell he was thinking about it. She considered the possibility herself. A change in religion leading to tree worship? Certainly there was tree worship later in Europe, on the edge of historical time.

Trees hung with offerings to forest deities, trees in sacred groves. But would people really change from worshipping animal totems to trees just because the forest was expanding? She tried to think herself back into a primitive mind…would they see it as trees chasing the animals away? It didn't make sense, but then primitives didn't have to make sense. They were primitive, nonrational, that was the whole point….

Two summers later, Carver saw that Molder's grave had not been disturbed. The bulge of his gift was hardly noticeable now beneath the bark of its tree. He plucked a twig from it, and dropped it on the stones piled not-quite-carelessly atop Molder's grave. They had had good luck, the past seasons, and he wished he could share more with her spirit. But the others agreed that their luck lay partly in the quiet rest of their dead… a rest that depended on fooling the witches of the future. He still found it hard to think about, the way they could walk backwards through time and change the past. Why would they rob graves, when they could gain more power by undoing their own mistakes? He thought what he could do with such ability—prevent Molder's fall, find where the herds had gone when they didn't appear in the usual ranges, know which trail he should have taken, and what had happened to those who disappeared. He would not bother to find old graves and rob them. Unless the dead had more power than anyone had believed until now, more power even than the spread of death pollen.

But they had fooled the latecomer witches. This tribe, at least, was safe from them, its dead resting peacefully and properly gifted throughout time. Once he believed, he'd wanted to tell the others, at the trading sites and hunting conclaves, but the old woman of Ash had forestalled him.

"We must first protect ourselves," she had said. "If the witches find no graves' goods to rob, they may rob bare bones or search the trees for gifts, and leave us to the wrath of our dead. Other tribes have godtalkers of their own—if they listen truly, they can learn for themselves." And she had bound him with terrible oaths, so that he could not tell even his mother's brother, when they met at the rapids of the river where the fish leaped into their basket, answering their need.

"Climate," Chris finally agreed. "It's spread through the whole region, and no invaders could move that fast. There wouldn't be that many of them, anyway. But I still think it was a change in religion, not just cultural impoverishment from the climatic change. Some weird superstition, maybe like the Ghost Dancing thing in the American Indians."

"Wish I knew how it started," said Ann. Now that he agreed it was climate, she found herself looking for something else. "A big storm, or bad year, or what?"

"A god came out of the sky and told them to put twigs in the graves instead of tools," said Chris sarcastically. "It could have been anything. Primitives don't think—they just react."

"Whatever. We might as well cancel the rest of the series. It's not worth it, spending all that money to find scraps of deerskin and twigs. We already have enough botanical samples; we need more artifacts. And since they've quit putting the graves in clusters, it's getting damned hard to find one at all. We can come all the way up to Neolithic, and get a lot more for our money."

Carver sat nearest the fire, an honor due his age and position in the tribe. He sang the Year Dance, and it was to him that the godtalker spoke of plans and seasons. His sons and daughters carried his seedclan here and there across the hunting grounds. And this night he had proclaimed the good news: the Ash Clan reported from all the campfires that the latecomer witches had departed from their graverobbing. In less than three lifetimes of men, they had come, and robbed, and departed, fooled by the wisdom of the godtalkers and those who loved their dead enough to send them bare into the afterworld. For three more lifetimes, the Ash decreed, they must leave grave gifts only in secret, outside the graves, but after that it would be safe to restore honor as it had always been. He thought, himself, that this was needless: if the dead were happy enough with their grave gifts in trees and roots and hollow stone, why not continue that way? It hadn't hurt the trees any.

He wondered, in the sleepiness that often overtook him now in the long firelit evenings, what the latecomer witches had thought when their luck ran out and the graves held no treasure. Had they returned to making their own tools and tokens? Had they spent the gift of time-walking on better things? Had they finally learned that walking backwards was wrong, that the power of the dead could not be used well by the living? The Ash would not say, for the gods had not commanded that song.

SWEET CHARITY

Krystal Winterborn eyed her lumpish fellow members of the Ladies' Aid & Armor Society, and sighed. There they were: the brave, the bold, the strong… the plain.

She was tired of being the butt of their jokes, just because she paid extra on her health-care plan for a complexion spell to keep her peach-blossom cheeks and pearly teeth. They laughed at her herbal shampoos, the protective grease she wore on summer maneuvers. They rolled their eyes at her fringed leather outfits, her spike-heeled dress boots.

Well, this year's Charity Ball would show them. No more laughing, when she was Queen of the Ball, and raised many times more for the orphaned daughters of soldiers killed in the line of duty. She would never have to hear their condescending "Shut up, Krystal" again.

When the chair asked for volunteers, Krystal surprised everyone by signing up for Invitations.

Harald Redbeard had come to the city in the character of an honest merchant. Downriver, on the coast, everyone knew he was a Fish Islands pirate. The coast patrol had almost trapped him in Hunport, but instead of making a break for the sea, he'd come upriver with his crew, until things quieted down.

It was nigh on midwinter when he reached the kingdom known to its downstream neighbors as the Swordladies' Domain. He grinned at that—most of the mountain kingdoms had a reputation for fierce warrior women. But the only warrior women he'd seen had been bouncers at Gully Blue's tavern in Hunport. He'd tossed both of them into the harbor.

An icy wind blew from the mountains, and lowering clouds promised snow as the crew offloaded their cargo; Harald sent old Boris One-eye off to find them an inn. One-eye reported that he'd found rooms at the Green Cat, and he'd seen some warrior women.

"Like soldiers, they are, in uniform."

"Not a problem," Harald said. "If they're part of the city guard, that'll make it all the easier for us."

"How?"

"City guards are city guards the world over," Harald said, rubbing fingers and thumb.

That night in the Green Cat's bar, Harald kept eyes and ears open. One particular corner table caught his interest. A cute perky blonde wearing fringed black leather and polished brass pouted at the louts around her, who were all clearly ready to do anything for another glance down her cleavage.

If that was an example of local women warriors, he and his men had nothing to worry about. She was too pretty, too smooth-skinned and full-lipped, to know what to do with the fancy little dagger at her belt, let alone a real sword. Her followers, big and muscular enough, wore fashions he'd seen only in the grittier port brothels, but no visible weapons.

When the blonde pushed back from the table, he saw that she actually had cute little muscles in her arms. She glanced over at him, and he grinned, raising his mug appreciatively. She stuck out her adorable lower lip; one of her followers turned to glower at him. Harald shrugged, unperturbed. He watched as she undulated across the room. Every part of her—many visible through the long black fringe—suggested unspeakable delights.

Harald turned back to his ale, as she flounced out the door, to find that the burly fellow with the bits of metal through his ears and nose was now beside him. "She's beautiful," Harald said. Under the table, his hand slid down to the hilt of his boot knife. "You can't blame a man for looking."

"S'long as you're respectful," the man said.

"Oh, I am," Harald said. "But such beauty cannot be denied."

The burly man grinned. "Since you appreciate her many qualities, perhaps you'd like to make her acquaintance a little closer?"

What was this? Was the woman a high-priced whore, and this her pimp? Did they think he'd been born under a rhubarb leaf, and still had the dew on his backside?

Harald brought the knife up in one smooth motion, and laid the tip in an appropriate place. To his surprise, the burly man neither flinched nor changed expression.

"No need for that," he said. "I just wanted to invite you to the Ladies' Aid & Armor Society Charity Ball. Being as it's midwinter, and cruel dull for a stranger in town otherwise, with all the taverns closed for three days—I thought you might enjoy it."

"The Ladies' Aid & Armor Society? What's that, a bunch of women in bronze bras and fringe playing with toy swords?"

The man laughed. "Not exactly. But they clean up nicer than usual, for the Charity Ball for the Orphans' Fund. There's this contest, for queen; everybody who goes can vote. Thing is, the other cats pack the place with their supporters, so although our Krystal is far and away the most beautiful, she never wins. This year, we're changing that. All I want from you is a vote for her. We'll pay the donation and everything."

These upriver barbarians had strange customs. Collecting money to support girl orphans, when girl orphans properly managed could support him? Taverns closed three days? His crew would go crazy and start breaking open barrels on their own; he couldn't afford that. This ball now—fancy dress, jewels, money—looked like fun and profit combined.

"Tell you what," Harald said, slipping the knife back into his boot. "My friends wouldn't like it if I went and they had to stay here with nothing to drink. If you can get us all in, that's more votes. How about it?"

"Great. My name's Gordamish Ringwearer, by the way; you can call me Gordy. I'll need all your names for the invitations—nobody gets in without one."

Mirabel Stonefist scowled at the stacks of invitations. Every year, she tried to argue the Planning Committee into hiring a real scribe to address them, and every year the Committee insisted it was too expensive. They had to have money for decorations, for the orchestra, for the food, and of course the drink. Which meant that each member of the LA&AS had to address a stack of envelopes herself, in whatever scrawly, scribbly, crabbed and illegible handwriting she possessed.

Primula Hardaxe, chair of the Committee, always made some remark about Mirabel's handwriting. *I never claimed to be an artist,* Mirabel thought, stabbing the tip of the quill into the ink-bowl. *Not with anything but a sword, that is.* She looked at the list she'd been given. Naturally she was not entrusted with the invitations to important persons. She hadn't been since the time her version of "Lord Pondicherry and Lady Cordelia" was misread as "Lard Pound and Laid Coldeels" and delivered to the butcher's.

She was halfway through the list when her old resentment cleared and she noticed the names. Harald Redbeard? She'd heard that name before, surely. She shook her head and copied it as carefully as she could. Skyver Twoswords? Again, something tickled her memory then withdrew. Gordamish Ringwearer? Probably the cavalry units; they recruited all sorts of people, not just the solid peasants and smalltraders' children who ended up in the *real* army.

She realized she'd just left the "g" out of Ringwearer, and muttered an oath. That's what thinking did for you, caused mistakes. It wasn't up to her to decide who got invitations; all she had to do was address the blasted things. She struggled through Piktush Drakbar, Zertin Dioth, Badaxe Oferbyte, and the rest.

At last, she had her stack finished—smudged with sweaty thumbprints, slightly rumpled, but finished. She put them in the basket (noting that it was now half full) and stirred them around. With luck, Primula wouldn't know who had done which. She hoped that every year.

Three days before the ball, Mirabel tugged at the bodice of her green ball gown. Her armor still fit; what was the matter with this thing?

Of course she could wear a corset. She hated corsets. Just something else to take off, the way she looked at it. She tugged again, and something ripped.

Perhaps she could get through the ball without raising her arms. No. She liked to dance, and she liked to dance fast. She pawed through her trunk. The old copper silk still had that chocolate stain down the front where she'd jogged someone's elbow, and the midnight blue had moth all up the front center panel.

Time for a new gown, then; after all, she'd worn this one four years.

Strictly speaking, it was not a costume ball. But it had become customary for guests to dress up in whatever fanciful outfits they chose. Thus the appearance of a crew of pirates (striped loose trousers, bucket boots, eye patches), several barechested barbarians, and someone clad mostly in chains and other bits of uncomfortable-looking metal attachments provoked little comment. They had invitations, surrendered at the door to a little girl wearing the red cloak of a Ladies' Aid & Armor Society ward, and that was all that mattered.

Sergeants Gorse, Covet, Biersley, Dogwood, Ellis, and Slays, all resplendent in dress blue, were not so lucky. They had attended the ball for years; the Ladies' Aid & Armor Society knew better than to exclude sergeants. This meant nothing to the stubborn nine-year-old who had been told to let no one through without a card. Last year she'd been banished to bed after singing "Sweet Sword of Mine" with the orphan chorus, and she was determined to prove she was old enough for the responsibility.

"They just forgot to send ours, or it got lost," Sergeant Gorse said. "We're *sergeants,* Missy. Sergeants are always invited."

"Miss Primula said no one can go in without an invitation, no matter what they say." The nine-year-old tossed her butter-colored braids and glared up at them. The sergeants shuffled their feet. Any one of them could have tucked her under one arm and had room for a barrel of beer, but she was an orphan. A soldier's orphan.

"Suppose you call Miss Primula, then."

"She said don't bother her," the nine-year-old said. "She's busy."

Sergeant Heath strolled up behind the other sergeants, also resplendent in dress blue. "What's going on here? Why are you fellows blocking the door?"

"They don't have invitations!" clashed with "This child won't let us in, and we're *sergeants.*"

"Decided not to invite you lot this year, eh?" Sergeant Heath smiled unctuously at the child, and reached past Sergeant Gorse to hand over his card. "Remember your antics last year, do they? That bit with the tropical fruit surprise not quite so funny on second thought?" He strolled through, exuding virtue. The others glared after him, then at Sergeant Gorse.

"It wasn't my fault," Sergeant Gorse said. "It was really Corporal Nitley, and I know *he* got an invitation." He looked around and spotted a familiar figure hurrying along the street.

"She'll take care of this," he said confidently. She was, after all, in his unit.

Mirabel Stonefist discovered that no one had time to make her a gown, or even repair the old one. She tried the plastic wizard the Ladies' Aid & Armor Society had on retainer, but he was overbooked, without even a spare six-hour reweaving or banish-stain spell.

She couldn't possibly mend it herself. She was even clumsier with needle and thread than with a pen. That left only one possibility, her sister Monica. The Monica who was still angry with her for not rescuing Cavernous Dire from a dragon. Hoping for the best, Mirabel knocked on her sister's door and explained her problem.

"You have a lot of nerve," Monica said. "You didn't even invite us this year."

"I put your name on the list," Mirabel said. "I always do."

"I'm sure," Monica said, in the tone that meant she didn't believe it. "But when you need something—at the last minute I notice, never mind my con-venience—here you are. I'll fix it for you all right!" Monica grabbed the dress, and ripped the bodice all the way to the waist. "There!" Then she slammed the door in Mirabel's face.

Mirabel turned away from the door. That was it, then. She would just have to go in uniform, and be laughed at. As she trudged down Sweet Street, someone hailed her.

"Why so gloomy?" Dorcas Doublejoints asked. Dorcas, an exotic dancer, had maintained her friendship with the LA&AS ever since they'd solved the mystery of her missing belly.

Mirabel explained, and displayed the torn bodice.

"Oh, that's not a problem." Dorcas eyed her. "You won't fit my clothes, but we have lots of clothes in my house. Come along with me."

Mirabel stood in Dorcas's suite, with a flutter of lovely girls around her, all offering their best gowns. She noticed that they all called Dorcas "Miss Dorcas, dear" and drew her own conclusions. Somewhat to her surprise, she found that the strumpets' best gowns were fine silk of the first quality.

Her fashion advisors settled on an apricot-shot silk with shimmering highlights. It hugged her body to the hips, then flared into a wide rippling skirt. Three-puff sleeves ended in a drape of ivory lace. A small scrap of the same lace peeked from the depths of the décolletage in front. Mirabel had always liked low-cut gowns, but this one—she peered at herself in the mirror, wondering if she dared.

"Of course you do," Dorcas said, and the girls murmured agreement and admiration. "You have a beautiful back, and quite sufficient cleavage. Enjoy it while you can." Mirabel grinned at her image, thinking what her sister would say. No one had mentioned "corset," either.

The girls put up her hair, sprinkled it with something glittery, then painted her face. Ordinarily Mirabel didn't use cosmetics, but she liked what she saw in the mirror. A shy redhead offered her dangling emerald earrings, and a luscious brunette contributed an emerald necklace so spectacular that Mirabel knew it must be a fake. At last Dorcas handed her a fluffy shawl, refused her offer of payment for the loan of all this finery ("Don't be silly, dear; we're friends.") and ushered her out the back door.

So, in the gathering gloom, Mirabel Stonefist found herself going to the ball in the most gorgeous outfit she'd ever worn. Although it was a cold evening, and so much exposed flesh should have chilled her, she felt warm through with excitement. She would be careful with her borrowed glamour, she told herself. No jogging elbows, no tripping, no catching the lace on someone's belt buckle. She'd take everything back the next day, safe and sound.

"Hey—Stonefist!"

She looked up, and there were the sergeants—six of them anyway—in their dress blues.

"Yessir?" Even on Ball Night, she couldn't avoid calling them "sir," at least once.

"Did you write the invitations this year?"

"Some of them," Mirabel said cautiously. "Why?"

"We didn't get ours," Sergeant Gorse said. "Didn't you notice we weren't on the list?"

"I didn't do all of them," Mirabel said. "Everybody helps. Are you sure they didn't just get lost? What did Primula say?"

"We can't ask Primula," Sergeant Gorse said, "because that child at the door won't let us in without an invitation, and she won't call Primula to the door. Get this straightened out."

"Of course," Mirabel said. She paused. "Are you sure it didn't have anything to do with the tropical fruit surprise?"

"Yes!" they all said. Mirabel shrugged, and turned away to the door.

"Good evening, Miss Mirabel," said the child. The flaps of her red felt cap liner almost reached her shoulders; the little bronze cap with its tiny spike glittered in the torchlight. "I'm being really careful about the cards."

"Good for you," Mirabel said absently, looking around for Primula. Stalls offering the orphans' handiwork filled every alcove; guests were expected to buy patchwork pigs, lopsided clay bowls, and other useless items to swell the Orphans' Fund. Primula—wearing the same stiff black bombazine trimmed in purple bobbles that she'd worn for the past millennium—leaned over the piecework table. Mirabel threaded her way through the crowd, nodding to acquaintances, and heard the last of the lecture.

"—Now remember—you curtsey and say 'Thank you, kind sir' or 'kind missus' as the case may be, and hand them the purchase first, then the change. Is that clear?"

"Yes, Miss Primula." The freckled girl in charge of this stall was older than the doorkeeper—old enough to be allowed to handle money. Primula turned away, and caught sight of Mirabel.

"My dear! A new dress after all?"

"In a manner of speaking." Mirabel let the shawl drop, and Primula blinked. "Is it that low in back?"

Mirabel twirled, to a chorus of wolf whistles.

"Well," Primula said. "I must say I'm surprised. I thought you'd be wearing that old green gown forever."

Mirabel ignored this. "Did you leave the sergeants off the list on purpose?"

"The list?"

"Invitations. Sergeant Gorse didn't get one. Or Sergeants Covet, Biersley, Dogwood, Ellis, and Slays. They're all outside—they were sure you'd *meant* to invite them—but little Sarajane at the door wouldn't let them in, or call you."

"But of course they're invited," Primula said. "Though I did think that tropical fruit surprise trick wasn't funny. Now who was it, who should have had their names... ?" She closed her eyes, evidently trying to remember. Mirabel touched her arm.

"Thing is, they're out there in the cold now. Don't you want to let them in?"

"Oh. Of course." She bustled away. Mirabel let the shawl drop again and looked around for people she knew. An eye-patched pirate with a red beard and moustache appeared in front of her, his visible eye twinkling.

"My dear, I am tempted to live up to my costume and carry you away into tropical captivity—you are delectable."

She didn't recognize his accent, or his face, but what did that matter? "Sirrah, I fear you admire only my jewels, and not my face—"

"T'would be useless to deny the beauty of your jewels, but you—" His eye raked her up and down, and his hand stroked his moustache. "You are the pearl beyond price, compared to which your emeralds are mere baubles of colored glass."

Mirabel blinked. With that glib tongue, he ought to be a horse trader, but she knew all the horse traders in town. "I fear, sir, I know you not."

"I'm Harald Redbeard," he said.

"I wrote your invitation," Mirabel said. "I've been wondering who you are. Shall we dance?"

"With a will," he said, and offered his arm.

In the course of the first two dances, Mirabel discovered that Harald suited her perfectly as a dance partner. Tireless, nimble, quick-witted, familiar with all the standard dance patterns and variations… and with unflagging appreciation of her charms, which he described in terms that made her fantasize about the latter half of the ball.

She would happily have danced more with Harald Redbeard, but Nuttin Broadaxe tapped her firmly on the shoulder at the end of the second, and she remembered that she'd promised him a dance last week.

"Excuse me," she said, giving Harald a last squeeze of the hand and significant glance from under her lashes. He bowed.

Nutty was, after Harald, a letdown. A competent enough dancer, he felt no obligation to flatter someone he already knew beyond, "Gosh, Mirabel, this dress doesn't have any back at all!" and "Good thing that necklace isn't real; some thief would have it off you in no time." Instead, he regaled her with a description of the Queen's emerald necklace: "a lot like that paste thing you're wearing, actually, but of course hers is real." The last thing Mirabel wanted to hear about was the Queen; the Queen didn't like women soldiers in general, and Mirabel in particular.

Mirabel parted from Nutty at the end of that dance, pleading a need for something to drink, and went in search of Harald. Before she was halfway to the drinks table, Primula had caught her by the arm. "Mirabel, didn't you have Sergeant Gorse in your list of names?"

It took a moment to think what Primula was talking about, and then she shook her head. "No—I'd have remembered. At least half mine were people I'd never heard of."

"Oh." Primula let go and wandered off. Mirabel made her way to the drinks table, handed in her chit for a free drink, and spotted the chancellor, Sophora Segundiflora, chatting with two ministers of state, and a banker. Mirabel edged that way, keeping an eye out for Harald.

"Mirabel… what a lovely gown," Sophora said. "And necklace, too. So like the Queen's, did you know that?" Her voice had the slightest edge.

"No… it's borrowed."

"Ah. I'm glad you didn't wear it just to annoy her. It's amazingly good—it hardly looks like paste at all."

No one ignored Sophora's hints. "Do you think I should take it off?"

"Perhaps—oh, dear." Sophora looked past Mirabel and then murmured, very fast. "It's too late, be sure you tell her it's a cheap imitation and that you borrowed it." Then, in her usual ringing tone, "Good evening, Your Majesties. What an honor to have you at the ball."

Mirabel turned. The Queen's face squinched up as she recognized Mirabel—then paled in fury as she recognized the necklace.

"Where did you get that?" the Queen demanded. "What are you playing at?"

Mirabel looked at the Queen's necklace—as like her borrowed one as if it were spell-doubled, except that the emeralds seemed somehow diluted of their rich green color. Perhaps that was because of the taupe gown the Queen wore, perhaps the colors cancelled out or something. "I'm—I'm sorry, Your Majesty," she said, attempting a curtsey. "I just borrowed this—I didn't know—"

"Borrowed! From whom, may I ask?"

"A—a friend." Instinct, racing ahead of thought, warned her not to give a name. "A—a dancer. It's only paste, Your Majesty, and I didn't know it was a copy of yours—"

"A likely story," the Queen sniffed. She turned to the King. "You promised me mine was unique. No other like it, you said, an exclusive design. And now I see it around the neck of a muscle-bound swordswoman who got it from some bawd. What do you say to that, eh? I demand that you take this up with the Royal Jeweler; if he's selling copies on the sly—"

Mirabel glanced at the King, who looked paler than the Queen. He patted the Queen's arm. "It's not like that—" he began.

"Not like what?" the Queen asked. Her brow furrowed. "Did you *know* about this? Did you intend for me to be humiliated in front of everyone?"

Mirabel edged away from what promised to be a royal spat of epic proportions, and bumped into a large well-muscled man in barbarian costume of fur and leather, who leered straight down her cleavage. She vaguely recalled seeing him with Krystal, but couldn't think of his name.

"You're... stunning," he said, dragging his gaze back up to her face, but only momentarily.

"Who are you?" Mirabel asked.

"Skyver Twoswords," he said.

Another one whose invitation she'd addressed, and wondered about. "You're a friend of Krystal's, aren't you?" she asked.

He gulped, blushed, and said, "Well, sort of. More than, actually."

Mirabel eyed him with more interest. "Sort of?"

"Well, she's... you know... she's different."

Different was not the adjective Mirabel would have chosen. Just then the band struck up "Granny Morely's Wedding," one of her favorite pattern dances, and she smiled at Skyver. "Want to dance?"

"Er… I'm sorry… Krystal told me to stay here."

"Do you always do what Krystal says?" *It was on a bright May morning… when Granny Morely came…* Her foot tapped the rhythm.

"Well… er… yes. I'm supposed to…"

…With all her friends and relatives… to change her maiden name… Skyver looked glum and embarrassed all at once, and Mirabel didn't want to miss the dance. She looked around for another partner.

"There you are!" Sergeant Gorse said. He beamed at her, not his usual expression. "May I have the honor?"

They set off into the pattern: *She had pink ribbons in her hair… she had them on her shoe…* and Sergeant Gorse inserted his words where he could. "I wanted to thank you… for getting us in. Some mistake… just as we thought…"

"My pleasure," Mirabel said, ducking under his upraised arm twice for *She turned herself about again, as shy maids often do,* and caught sight of Krystal in the middle of the next row. She was dancing with Harald, and Mirabel almost tripped to see the same look given to Krystal that he had given to her. Then she shrugged—what did she expect from a smooth-tongued stranger at the ball? She continued the figure with her usual enthusiasm, all the way to *And so you see, dear children, was never such a sight, as Gramps and Granny Morely, upon their wedding night,* which ended with a whirling embrace.

"You dance as well as you… er… look," Sergeant Gorse said.

"My turn, Quill," said Sergeant Dogwood. He bowed to Mirabel. "If I might have the honor."

Mirabel spent the next five dances with the sergeants, one after the other; by then she wanted a rest. Though the sales booths hid the alcoves, she managed to squeeze in behind the patchwork animals, where she lounged sideways on the bench with her feet up. The freckled girl looked at her.

"I don't know if you're supposed to be here. Miss Primula said—"

"Miss Primula hasn't been dancing with six sergeants, child; my feet hurt."

From her vantage point, she could peek over the pile of patchwork animals and see the dancers. At one side of the ballroom, the King and Queen sat on a dais, pointedly not looking at each other. Sophora had collected another two ministers and the Duke of Mandergash. Then she spotted Harald by his red beard, and next to him Krystal.

Krystal leaned gracefully against a pillar, her followers around her… two barbarians, a man dressed in leather straps and chains, half a dozen pirates, and someone wearing a long plaid skirt with his face painted green and a green target painted on his naked chest. Krystal herself wore a gown like nothing Mirabel had ever seen—it might have been painted on, glittering silver mesh slit up the side to reveal her tall dress boots. She was, Mirabel had to admit, incredibly beautiful.

"Mirabel Stonefist, what *are* you doing back there lounging at your ease while the rest of us—" Primula glared over the stack of stuffed animals.

"I tried to tell her, Miss Primula," bleated the freckled girl. "She wouldn't listen."

"She never does," Primula said to the girl. Then to Mirabel, "Come right out of there; I need to talk to you."

"My feet hurt," Mirabel muttered, but she knew it would do no good. She got up and squeezed back past the corner post of the booth.

"I had to go to the office for my master lists," Primula said, "I have them here." She waved a sheaf of papers.

"And now, majesties, lords and ladies, gentlemen and women of quality, it's time to vote for the Queen of the Ball—" That was Lord Mander Thunderblatt. *"We honor the Ladies' Aid & Armor Society, by choosing one among them to reign as queen for a night—meaning no disrespect to Your Majesty, of course…"*

"Will you pay attention, Mirabel! Quickly now—you say you didn't have Sergeant Gorse on your list?"

"No, I told you."

"Do you remember who you did have?"

Mirabel thought about it. "Corporal Venturi, Corporal Dobbs, Granish the greengrocer, Stebbins the headgroom of the royal stables…" She noticed Primula ticking these off on the master list. "Er… Harald Redbeard, Skyver Twoswords, Gordamish Ringwearer, Piktush somebody… I can't remember any more. Someone named Overbite or something like that."

"Just as I thought!" Primula looked simultaneously triumphant and furious. "Those are not on my list at all."

"All of them?"

"No, the last four. Who gave you your list?"

Mirabel blinked. "Krystal, of course."

"Now you remember the rules," Lord Mander said. *"Nominators contribute a gold piece to the Fund; voters contribute ten silvers. Ladies of the Society may not nominate themselves—not that any of our hostesses would—but may nominate another Member, as well as vote…"*

"That scheming little tramp!" Primula said. "I see it all now—"

"I nominate Krystal Winterborn!" someone called.

"She's wanted to be Queen for years," Primula said. "And now she's cheated—"

"Huh?"

"She stacked the lists," Primula said. "Erased some of the names she knew would vote against her and added her friends." Primula tapped her own sheaf of papers. "I'll soon put a stop to this nonsense—"

"I nominate Cabella Ironhand!" called someone else. Cabella had been Queen

of the Ball for the past three years; as a sergeant herself, she could count on the sergeants and corporals to vote for her.

"*I nominate Sophora Segundiflora*," yelled another.

"I refuse the nomination," Sophora said. "But thank you."

Across the floor, Harald Redbeard met Mirabel's eyes and grinned; then he winked. "*I nominate Mirabel Stonefist,*" he said loudly. Krystal whirled and glared at him; Mirabel felt as if she'd just had the wind knocked out of her. What did he mean? She'd never been a candidate for Queen of the Ball.

"What are you up to?" asked Primula.

"Nothing," Mirabel said. "I had nothing to do with it."

Primula glared at her, but apparently decided Krystal was the bigger game, and started across the floor.

"Nominators, make your way to the Donations Table," Lord Mander said. "Voters, you may begin lining up to vote when the nominations have been verified. Nominees, come join me at the front of the room."

"Go on, silly," said the freckle-faced girl when Mirabel hesitated. "I didn't realize you were important—imagine being nominated for Queen of the Ball."

Mirabel made her way through the crowd, accepting congratulations and wolf whistles, until she joined Krystal and Cabella at Lord Mander's side. The room seemed full of eyes; she had never been shy, but she'd also never stood on a dais being stared at by a roomful of people while wearing a whore's dress and a necklace that annoyed the Queen. She could see over the heads of the others to the Donations Table, where Harald was just then handing over a gold piece to one of the clerks.

"Look 'em over, folks," Lord Mander bellowed past her ear. "Here they are, three lovely and talented Members of the Ladies' Aid & Armor Society. For those who don't know them well, let me introduce… Krystal Winterborn." Krystal twirled; her gown glittered in the light. Enthusiastic cheers from part of the crowd, including her barbarian followers. "Cabella Ironhand." Cabella, in a handsome rose brocade, smiled and waved at the crowd, to similar cheers from her supporters.

Mirabel felt like a stray cow at auction, not a candidate for Queen of the Ball. As far as she knew, she had only one supporter, and he had his back turned, leaning over the Donations Table. "Mirabel Stonefist," Lord Mander said, and she struck an attitude and did a swirling dance step. To her surprise, another storm of wolf whistles and cheers broke out.

Lord Mander looked at the Donations Table, got the wave he was waiting for. "All right, folks—all the nominations have been verified. You vote with your silver… form three lines, have your coins ready… you know the rules." He nodded, and the band began to play "Stillwater Faire" to cover the shuffling and talking.

Cabella turned to Mirabel. "Do you know what Primula's upset about? She cornered me to ask about the list of people I'd addressed invitations to... she's never complained before."

Past Cabella's shoulder, Mirabel saw Krystal's tense face. "I'm not sure," she said. It wasn't her place to embarrass Krystal in front of the whole group. "I thought it was just me; she complains about my handwriting every year."

"Well, whatever it is, she thinks it's serious. She's talking to our Chancellor—" Cabella nodded to the far corner, where Primula, gesturing and waving papers, had trapped Sophora Segundiflora.

"She thinks everything is serious," Krystal said, with an edge to her voice.

Harald Redbeard was relieved to find that aside from a few unarmed sergeants in dress uniforms the ball consisted of civilians in fancy outfits. Some costumes required weapons, to be sure—the barbarians had fake spears, and Gordamish Ringwearer had a peculiar looking knife that couldn't possibly work in a fight—but nothing he need worry about. No one had tried to relieve him or his crew of their pirate cutlasses, which were not fake at all, and with which he intended to make a clean sweep of the gathering's jewels and gold.

His nomination of Mirabel Stonefist—whom he did intend to steal away for later enjoyment—would generate more cash in easily snatched piles. He'd explained to Gordamish that it took fewer votes overall to win in a three-way split than a two-way split.

Now Harald leaned against the wall, arms crossed, waiting for his moment and wondering where the city guard was. He hadn't seen a guardsman all day. He imagined they were all carousing in some illegally open tavern barred to the public. This crowd now—he eyed them professionally. From royalty obviously self-indulgent to citizens full of good food and strong drink... easy marks, every one.

The only problem he foresaw was that necklace. Which one was real? Maybe he'd better snatch both. As the lines of voters thinned out, Harald glanced around and signalled his crew.

"And the winner is..." Lord Mander bellowed. Silence fell; the woman at the Donations Table pointed to one of the piles. "Krystal Winterborn!"

Cheers and groans from the crowd, a shriek of glee from Krystal, then a booming, "No, she's not!"

"Am *too*," Krystal said, stamping her foot. The crowd roared.

"No." Sophora Segundiflora made her way to the nominees' stand. "Some voters were not invited guests; Primula has explained how the misunderstanding occurred." She scowled at Krystal, who pouted back. "We are going to expel the wrongfully invited guests, and vote again." In a low voice that Mirabel could barely hear over the hubbub, Sophora said, "You're lucky, Krystal, that we care more about the reputation of the Society than you do, you naughty girl. Otherwise we'd expose you publicly."

"But Chancellor—"

"Shut up, Krystal," Sophora said. Then, more loudly, "As your names are called, please line up over there—" She pointed toward the band. "If your name is not called by the end of the list, you can simply leave and no questions will be asked."

"Oh, we'll leave now, if it's all the same to you!" Mirabel recognized that voice, but it took her a moment to realize that Harald Redbeard and the other pirates had surrounded the Donations Table, and the cutlasses laid to the clerks' necks were not decorative accessories. Two pirates were already scooping the piles of coin into the Society's brass-bound money chest. Another pirate was creeping up behind the Queen.

Even as she stared, Mirabel felt a sharp steel point at her back. "I'd come along if I was you," said someone behind her. "Cap'n's got a fancy for you, as well as them pretties you're wearing. Be a good girl now."

Mirabel's years of training took over, and she threw herself forward off the dais, tucked and came upright; she heard the pirate curse, the boom of his foot as he leaped after her, then the louder thud of his body as he hit the floor near Krystal. Sophora stood over him, his cutlass in her hand. "Here, dear—you're quicker." She tossed the cutlass to Mirabel. "Go save the Queen."

"I'll get you!" the pirate snarled at Sophora, reaching for the long dagger in his boot, but Krystal's accurate kick made him grab something else instead. Krystal took the knife and his life before he could move.

Mirabel whirled. The Queen screeched, hands to her neck, as the pirate tugged at her necklace one-handed, while fending off the King with his cutlass. Mirabel charged across the floor, but before she could intervene, the necklace broke. The pirate thrust it into his belt, and ran for the door. Mirabel followed.

Behind her, sergeants bellowed and corporals cursed. A good dozen of the members ran for the armory, where they could find weapons enough to deal with a mere handful of pirates, no matter how vicious, but in the meantime—Harald snatched one of the wards from her booth, and held a blade to her neck. His men did the same; one even had the child who had guarded the door, holding her by her braids, with the cutlass over her head.

"Now, now—you don't want me to hurt this sweet child, do you?"

The uproar sank to a growl, and Mirabel skidded to a stop just out of reach of Harald Redbeard. He winked at her. "Come on along, sweetheart—I'll teach you how to use that thing properly. I like a girl with spirit."

"Do you?" Mirabel said, and signalled.

The nine-year-old dropped abruptly to the length of her braids, then bounced up between her captor's legs. Her little bronze cap hit his pelvic arch with an audible crunch. He shrieked and fell; she grabbed his cutlass and hamstrung the pirate next in line. As Harald turned to look, the girl he was holding sank her teeth into his thumb; Mirabel stepped to one side and ran her blade up under his ribs.

"I already know how to use this thing," she said, wincing as blood spattered her borrowed gown. The girl grabbed his cutlass, and passed it to another adult. Two of the other pirates dropped the children they held only to find that the girls were more dangerous loose, and all the guests knew how to use a cutlass when they had one.

"But you aren't *real* warriors," moaned the last survivor, cowering from the blows of three energetic orphans pelting him with misshapen pottery from the pottery stall. "Cap'n said so—"

"Your Cap'n might say something different now," Krystal said. "If he could." Her blade, already bloody, swung once more.

In the aftermath of the brawl, in the flurry of cleaning up, no one could find the Queen's necklace. Not until they stripped the pirates' bodies, and the shattered remnants were found in the codpiece of the pirate who'd been felled by Sarajane. "So the Queen was wearing paste…" Sophora said, and looked at Mirabel. Mirabel sighed. She knew where her duty lay, but how she would explain to Dorcas… first blood on the gown, then this…

"Here." She unhooked the clasp and handed it over. "Tell her you found it, and mine was crushed."

Sophora smiled at her. "Mirabel, you're finally growing up. I'm proud of you."

When the crowd settled down, Lord Mander collected Cabella and Mirabel and tried to call for a second vote, but a loud yell of "We already *paid!*" drowned him out.

Cabella took Sophora aside. "Look—I've been Queen before, and you don't want to give it to Krystal. Why not Mirabel? She's decorative enough, she fought the pirates, and she gave up the necklace."

Sophora looked at Mirabel.

"But I—but I never imagined—"

"Sounds like a Queen to me," Sophora said. She gave Mirabel's name; cheers rang out. Lord Mander put the tinsel crown on Mirabel's head, and a score of men stood in line to dance with her, bring her drinks, fetch her snacks, anything she wanted.

She could get used to this Queen business.

The King himself took her hand for the last dance of the evening. The King danced better than Mirabel expected, though his gloved hand wandered along her spine.

"About that necklace," he murmured in her ear.

"I borrowed it," she said.

"From a gorgeous brunette in Dorcas's house?" he asked.

"Yes..." She worked it out—if he knew that, then—for the first time she felt a pang of sympathy for the Queen. Over his shoulder she saw Corporal Nitley lurking near the wine punch, only to be collared by Sergeants Gorse and Dogwood. No tropical fruit surprise this year, then. Over his other shoulder, she saw Primula herding a sulky Krystal and her followers, loaded with dirty dishes, toward the kitchen.

"Thank you, my dear," the King said, "for getting me out of a very sticky situation. I will, of course, explain to the... er... young woman who had been... er... taking care of it. But is there anything I can do for you?" His hand wandered lower.

"No, thank you," Mirabel said, surprised to realize that what he could give, she didn't want. Not from him, anyway. "Only a donation to help our poor defenseless orphans."

A resounding crash came from the kitchen passage; Krystal stormed back into the ballroom. "It's not *fair*," she said. "Why should I have to do all the work? I killed *two* pirates."

"Shut up, Krystal," Mirabel said, in chorus with others.

WELCOME TO WHEEL DAYS

Murray and Steve were down under the floor, digging out last year's leftover flyers for the festival when the speaker clicked. I slammed my hand on the OFF button and continued what I was doing, calculating how many porta-potties we could afford to hire from Simmons Sewer Service. Our Ecosystems Chief Engineer insists that he can't let the festival crap (the technical term in this colony) run through the usual pipes, just in case some idiot visitor eats lead or mercury or some other heavy metal that would poison the weedbeds. So every year we have this problem. You just can't run a festival without porta-potties, and with the gravity gradient in LaPorte-Centro-501, that means three separate sets of them, sexed. We never have enough, and we always have complaints, chiefly from uptowners near the core, who go into jittering fits if some stranger in a hotsuit knocks on their door and wants to use the inside can. I will admit, low-grav mistakes are the hardest to clean up, but still you'd think they'd understand why the festival is so important. If LaPorte-Centro-501 continues to grow, we all benefit.

Murray crawled out with the dance flyers. All we had to do was change the year and the day; we were having the Jinnits again for lead band, and Dairy and the Creamers for backup. Some people complain about that, but Murray's old buddy Conway is the keyboard man for Jinnits, and they'll come here without a guarantee. We don't get soaked if a solar flare keeps everyone home. So far that's saved us a bit more than I'd like to confess, when we're talking here about a successful annual festival that draws crowds from all over the Belt. And Dairy's local; the Creamers play at Hotshaw's all year 'round, and everyone likes them well enough. The flyers looked pretty good; I nodded and Murray racked them into the correction bracket and went to work. Steve was still out of sight, but I could hear him scrunching around in the insulation.

That's when the speaker clicked on again, and I didn't get my hand on the OFF button in time. "Radio relay message," said the voice, and I sighed. Nobody I wanted to talk to was going to be calling me for another week. I punched for a hard copy, rather than voice, and watched the little strip of paper come zipping out the groove. It's not really paper, of course—paper is precious—but it acts like paper. You can write on it. I tore it off and crammed it into a pocket without looking at it. That was a mistake.

The parade flyers Steve had gone after were all unusable; something had leaked and frozen into them. We had the old master, and we refilled the crawl space with insulation, then set up the master for a print run. I crossed my fingers, assumed five percent more attendance than last year, and ordered another set of porta-potties. Next up were the day's parade and display entries.

I don't want to overdo this about how hard it is to do things in the colonies—that's not my point—but a simple little annual festival like you'd run with maybe fifteen or twenty volunteers back on a planet is not so simple on the inside of a hollow ball with a gravity gradient from zip to norm. Take parades. LaPorte-Centro-501 was built in two helices, like most of the cored colonies. The only way to route a parade all through town is rim to core to rim again in the other helix pattern, and that means everything has to go through all the gravity gradients twice. Ever try to design a float for variable gravity, not to mention spin? We keep the kiddy parades in near-normal gravity, all around the base of Alpha Helix one year, and Beta the next, and run the main parade from 0.25 to 0.25 through the core. That way the floats really float, but they don't have to contend with heavy stress.

Right now the parade entries were looking a bit thin. Central Belt Mining & Exploration would have a float: they always did. Usually it was something "pioneering," an adventure still-life. FARCOM would bring a communications satellite mounted on a robotic flying horse (they alternated that one and a float with two robots using tin cans and a string). Holey Bey, our nearest neighbor (and a nasty neighbor, for that matter), was sending two floats, they said. I scowled at that, and wondered if they were going to try to smuggle in another gang of ruffians. Four years ago they'd disrupted our parade with screaming youths in blood-red hotsuits who made off with parts of other people's floats. Almost cost us the whole profit of the festival. (I know, you've seen Holey Bey's brochures in the colonial offices: that fake beach, with luscious bathing beauties backed by handsome neo-Moorish arches. Forget it. Their chief engineer was a drunken incompetent who couldn't hook one helix with another, their plumbing leaks, and they're infested with mammalian vermin. Even dogs. I know; I took our float over there for "Back to Bey Days" and it was disgusting.)

Anyway, we had to have at least sixty entries to make the main parade work. Sixty full-size entries. No matter how you handle core, it's big, and a parade can look pretty damn puny out there, drifting across the very-low-gee gap. Back on Earth you get horse freaks to fill in the gaps with horses (at least I suppose that's why they're in parades, to fill up the gaps: they have that advantage of turning sideways to take up less room, or lengthways to take up more). But of course we don't have horses on LaPorte-Centro-501, and even Holey Bey wouldn't harbor big dirty mammals like that. I called up the parade file, added today's entries, and muttered. Thirty-nine, and five of those were small marching groups. I looked at the schedule for our float to see who might come.

That's how it works, of course. We send our float ("Miss LaPorte-Centro-501 and her Court… Rolling Along to Wheel Days") to other colonies' festivals, and they send theirs to us. Back to Bey Days. Rockham Cherry Festival (they don't have cherries, but it sounds good). Pioneer Days (two a year, one at each end of the settlement, and very different: Vladimir Korsygyn-233 is a Soviet colony). It's about like you'd see on Earth: every colony has its festival, and everybody sends a float. There are differences, to be sure. We don't actually *send* our float everywhere; the shipping fees would break us. We send a holo of the new design each year and hire a construct crew in whatever colony it is. Miss LaPorte-Centro-501 and her Court do travel to the nearer communities; beyond that we audition and pay standard rates to local talent.

You may wonder why our festival is "Wheel Days." I don't want to grab credit from anyone, but actually that was my idea. The whole Belt, it's like a big wheel, and the Settlement like a smaller wheel riding its rim. Our conviction is that LaPorte-Centro-501 will grow into its motto: "The Hub of the Industrial Center of the Solar System." You don't need to laugh… it could happen. Something will be the hub, and it might as well be us. We have talent, room to grow, resources, skilled labor, willingness to work… and most of all, we have *vision*.

That's how come we have Wheel Days, and nobody's laughed for the last nine years. We have the most successful annual festival for a community our size in the Settlement. And that's a big job. Everyone has two major assignments and half a dozen little ones, and of course we're all still employed, though some of our employers cut us some slack now and then. As for me, being junior vice president of Mutual Savings & Loan, I could spend pretty much my whole time on it, which is good because it took that and more. If you aren't a Chamber member, wherever you are, then you can't understand just how frantic those last weeks are. No matter how you plan all year (and if you don't plan all year, you don't have a good festival) something always comes unglued. Several somethings.

Our float came apart in a spin vortex at Rimrock, and we were charged with Insufficient Construction. (Luckily our insurance company's lawyers found we had a case against the designated construct company for fraud, and none of the young ladies on the float were hurt.) Still, the accident might deter some parade entries at our end. Simmons Sewer reported that they couldn't fill all the porta-potty order because they had just gotten a contract from Outreach Frames (the big shipbuilding firm). Conway, Murray's friend in Jinnits, broke up with his wife and threatened to leave the band; the band leader called Murray and said that if Conway left him in the lurch he wasn't about to do any favors for Conway's buddies. And so on.

It wasn't until three days before the opening that I wore the light blue zipsuit again, and heard something crackle in the breast pocket. I fished it out and found the message tape I'd never read. Now I read it.

In-laws are an old joke, right? That's because so many of them are just like the stories. My wife Peg is sweet, loving, bright, independent, and not half-bad-looking, either. But her brothers—! There's James Perowne, who's a drunk, and Gerald LaMott, who's probably the reason why James is a drunk, and then there's Ernest. Ernest Dinwiddie, if you can believe it, which I couldn't when I first met him, and I laughed, and he never forgave me. He suits his name, is the best I can say for him, and it isn't much.

The way Peg and I get along, you'd think I'd like her brothers and they'd like me, but that's not how it is. James will fling a half-pickled arm around my shoulders and breathe beery sighs at me about his lovely little sister while I hold my breath and try not to slug him. Gerald sits hunched behind something (table, computer, desk… a pillow if all else fails), staring at me with little bright eyes out from under his dark brows and expecting me to make an ass of myself. Peg says she never could play a piece on the piano (and she's good) when Gerald was staring at her. He has that way of looking at you, expecting you to fail, almost *longing* for you to fail, and then you do. And then there's Ernest.

Ernest is in middle management at Central Belt Mining & Exploration. He's told us about it, and about how important middle management is, and how important Central Belt Mining & Exploration is. Well, I know *that*. Anyone in finance in the Belt knows how important CBM&E is. He explained to Peg exactly why she shouldn't marry me, and to me exactly why I wasn't worthy of her, and from time to time he shows up to explain what we've done wrong between the last visit and this one. He asks detailed questions about every aspect of our lives, and gives the impression that he'd like to hire investigators to verify our answers.

Also he can't take a hint. Most people, if you tell them that you're going to be busy the weekend they want to visit, will shrug and say too bad and go on. Not Ernest. He showed up in the middle of our honeymoon, to see how things were going. He brought his whole family to help celebrate my fortieth birthday (when Peg and I had planned to spend a weekend alone, having farmed Gordie out with her best friend Lisa). For the past three years or so, we'd managed to avoid him by being "gone" when he came to LaPorte-Centro-501. This time we were stuck.

He was coming, the message strip said, on August 24, the day that Wheel Days opened, because he was *sure* we'd be there for Wheel Days. He was on his way in-system for a management seminar, with his wife Joyce and their three kids. They wanted to see us and would be there sometime during Dayshift. Even in hard copy from a radio relay, Ernest's usual accusing tone was coming through. And by this time they were four days out from Central Station One (the Company's own headquarters colony, as he made sure we knew), and there was no way I could stop them. That's what I got for not reading that message the month before.

I called Peg, and she reacted about how I expected. She's often said she married someone as unlike her brothers as possible. I held the earphone a foot away until she calmed down a little.

"We can hide out in the Wheel Days confusion," she suggested finally.

"They know where we live; they'll just camp outside the door."

"We could stay with Lisa…"

"Lisa's already having company, remember?" So were we, for that matter, and Peg and I both said, "What about the Harrisons?" at the same moment.

"I can't tell them not to come," Peg wailed. "I *want* to see them. We have *fun* together. Not only that… we won't have *room*."

"I'll find Ernest's bunch a room somewhere else," I said, but I was worried. We really haven't built our tourism industry up where we'd like to see it, Wheel Days filled the hotels—overfilled them—and by this time I doubted I could find anything but the most expensive suites still available.

"They are *not* coming here," Peg said, with a hint of Brother Ernest's heavy-handed determination. Then she hung up. Murray came to tell me that Conway had rejoined the Jinnits, but had gotten drunk in the ship on its way from Gone West and given his ex-wife two black eyes. She wasn't filing charges, but the ship's captain was, and wouldn't release him without a guarantee from an employer: the ship's captain was a Neo-Feminist, and wouldn't tolerate spouse (or ex-spouse) abuse. The band didn't count, because apparently the captain considered them a contributing influence, and had already fined them. And of course without Conway, the Jinnits wouldn't sound like the Jinnits, and our main stage attraction would be no attraction at all. Murray wouldn't meet my eyes, even though it wasn't his fault, and we both knew it. But everyone also knew that he was why we had the Jinnits at all.

By the time I'd straightened that out, it was six hours later and the last hotel room was long gone, at any price. I leaned a little on Bennie Grimes, manager of the Startowers, but he knew and I knew that the favors he owed me weren't worth kicking a corporate executive out of his room and alienating the entire company. And no one I knew—*no one*—had room at home. Everyone with spare rooms invited guests or rented them out; the last of the home-rentals had cleared the computer weeks ago.

That left the Campground, and I knew exactly what Ernest was going to say about that. You can't run a festival by turning people away, so when rooms were full we signed transients into the Campground… a vast, barren storage bay aired up for a week (it takes that long to get it above freezing), and divided into "campsites" with bright plastic streamers. For about the cost of a cheap room in town, we rent bubbletents, furnished with cheap inflatable seats and sleepsacks. Big tents, too—bigger than the rooms you'd get in most hotels, plenty of room to sleep the whole family. It's kind of a long walk from the Campground in toward the core, so we have some extra entertainment out there. A few clown/juggler acts, a little carnival with rides for the kids, that sort of thing. And we have one day of the games right next to the Campground: the penny toss, the ring-dunk, the disk golf tournament.

Some people even prefer the Campground, and reserve a favorite spot ("Aisle 17, lot D, next to the big bathroom with the sunken tubs") year after year. You can be sure you'll be next to friends. The traffic isn't as bad. It's less expensive than anything but the cheapest Portside hotels. One group of old-timers from Wish & Chips holds reunions there; they say it's like going back to the old days before the shells were built up, and they sit around singing sentimental pioneer ballads.

But Ernest in the Campground... we'd never live it down. Yet it was that or have him and his family crammed into our place with us and the Harrisons and only two toilets. The memory of my fortieth birthday, when instead of a long, relaxed bath and bed with Peg I ended up defending the right of independent investors to organize savings & loan associations, while Ernest's kids tore into Gordie's things and trashed his carefully organized Scout files, hardened my resolution. I reserved the best space I could find (Aisle 26, lot X), and paid the advance on a deluxe camping outfit so that it would be set up and waiting. I didn't figure that having a two-room inflated habitat with full cable connections would really soothe Ernest down, but it was the best I could do. I also recorded a message for him and left it in the Port message center. It would tell him where to go, and apologize for this inconvenience.

Then I went back into battle with Simmons Sewer Service. Our contract pre-dated the one they had with the shipbuilders, I said firmly, and they had no valid legal reason to back out. We went back and forth awhile, and came up still three complete sets of porta-potties short (eighteen units: three grav levels, both sexes) even after they said they guessed they could haul some on tomorrow's oreloader from Teacup 311, where they had just finished a contract. At least I'd originally ordered more than last year, so we weren't behind as far as it seemed.

Then it was only two days to go. By this time, of course, the main structure is in place. Anything that isn't is lost, and you can't change it till next year. Main Parade was still a little skimpy, a bare sixty entries with those seven (by now) marching units, but we usually picked up a few extras the last day, as people came in and saw the competition. In fact, we kept three or four blank floats set up in storage, ready for last-minute spray-painting and decoration as desired. The Kiddy Parades always had problems, but none you could anticipate, since any child who showed up at the beginning could join the parade: that was the rule. All the ribbons and trophies for the games had arrived on schedule.

The candidates for Miss LaPorte-Centro-501 were even now being interviewed by the judges for poise and personality; we had enough entrants for a good pageant, and plenty of contracts for the losers to ride floats representing distant colonies (which keeps losers happy; and unlike some colonies, we don't let outsiders haggle over our girls: we have them draw lots for the available contracts). The Scoutmasters had their assignments for traffic control and information booths. We've found that strangers will accept direction from a neatly uniformed kid when they'll argue with an adult cop. We started that about ten years ago, and now most colonies use the kids as traffic control and guides during their festivals.

Going through all this and checking what still had to be done took several hours, interrupted by calls from everyone who could find a line. Or that's what it seemed like, with people asking things like "When are the opening ceremonies?" (on the flyers, not to mention broadcast on video!) and "What are you going to do about the construction mess behind the middle school on Alpha Helix?" which had nothing to do with us, or the festival, and was the sole responsibility of the Alpha Helix School Board. It did look tacky, but it wasn't my fault. Peg's a Board trustee, not me. I gave that caller her work extension, and went on to someone who demanded to know why the official garbage pickup was two hours late.

Sometime after lunch the ship from Gone West docked, and my earlier fix of that band problem came unglued again. Seems that the Jinnits agent on board got into an argument with the captain about how much fine had been assessed to the band, rather than to Conway personally. By this time the captain was fairly tired of the Jinnits band, from drums to keyboard and back again, and she expressed this in my ear with some force, offering to space the lot of them if I didn't do something. Murray, of course, had disappeared as soon as he saw me mouth "Jinnits…" I swore up and down that the Jinnits did indeed have a contract engagement, that they had a good record on this colony and had never been in a fight that I knew of, that we would guarantee (how I didn't know) that they wouldn't cause any trouble for the ship's crew should the crew stay for Wheel Days. To which, of course, I lavishly invited them.

Somewhere in the next twenty-four hours, which you might think would be the worst, is a lull—never at the same point two years running—when for six hours or so everything seems to hang on a knob of time and wait. All the committee chairs were exhausted but triumphant. What could be done had been done, and we all looked at each other and wondered what we'd see four days later, when the whole thing was over. A hush settled over the Chamber offices. Peg and Gordie and I had a last quiet meal (no ringing phones!), and I even lay down with my shoes off for a brief nap.

Finally it was opening day, with two hours to go before the Chairman cut the ribbon for the official start of Wheel Days, and everything I'd worked for as President of the Chamber this past year was out there on the line. I had already been in the office for three hours, checking in that last shipment of porta-potties, and making sure that they got where they needed to go. Checking on the bands (Dairy and the Creamers were peacefully eating breakfast; the Jinnits hadn't come out of their suite yet). Checking to make sure that the Scouts had picked up their armbands (green wheels on a blue background) and directional flags (green arrows on blue). Taking a look into the low-grav storage bays where the floats constructed here are aligned for the parade start. Finding an emergency ground crew to help with someone's unexpected float being unloaded at the Port, and entering it into the parade as entry 62 (61 had come in overnight). Racing home when I realized that I'd never changed from my worksuit the night before, and had to be in some kind of dress outfit for the Opening.

I got to the opening ceremonies just in time, and was glad to see that Connie Lee (our veep this year) was standing by in case I didn't make it. Last year's Miss LaPorte-Centro-501 posed gracefully beside the large silver wheel tied with a bright green ribbon. First came the Colony Chair's speech (short: that's one reason we elected Sam), then my speech ("Welcome to Wheel Days"), and then he cut the ribbon and Lori Belhausen took a good hold on the wheel and shoved it into motion. And then I went on with the rest of the welcome: "Rolling into the future with the Wheel of Progress, right here at LaPorte-Centro-501, the Hub of the Industrial Center of the Solar System." And it doesn't sound a bit silly, coming over the speakers like that, with the silver wheel flashing in the lights and Lori grinning for all the cameras.

It was when the candidates for this year's Miss LaPorte-Centro-501 honors came out to be cheered and photographed, and to toss handfuls of little gilt wheels into the audience, that I remembered that I'd forgotten to include something in my message to Ernest. I hadn't warned him about the wheels.

It's nothing unique. Lots of festivals have visitor requirements of the same sort. If you don't carry a six-shooter (a paper cut-out is enough) at Gone West's Pioneer Days, for example, you'll be put in "jail" until you're ransomed. They have a cute little cage you have to stand in, just outside the Lily Langtry Saloon, and everyone giggles and teases until you can persuade one of the honkytonk girls (if you're male) or bartenders (if you're female) to accept a donation for a kiss. They make a big deal of being persuaded, too, and the hapless prisoner has to do more than wave some money out the jail's window. All proceeds go to the Vacuum Victims Fund, and most people take it as it's meant, a big joke and a good way to earn money for the Fund.

At Wheel Days, we "arrest" everyone who enters the central festival area without a wheel… a pin, a dangler, something in the shape of a wheel, a circle with spokes. Most people simply pin on one of the hundreds of free wheels tossed into the crowd at the opening ceremonies, or handed out by any of the Miss LaPorte-Centro-501 contestants. It's true that no one is told what the wheels are for, but most people know (or find out quickly). We're lenient—we let a Shakespeare-revival streetdancer get by with a ruff—but we make a sizeable donation to the Vacuum

Victims Fund every year. Anyway, I hadn't warned Ernest… and I knew his attitude towards "commercial junk." He would be the last person to pin on a cheap plastic gilt wheel for the fun of it.

I really meant to call the Port, but even before I left the platform a long snaky arm in cerise, fringed with silver, had wrapped firmly around my shoulders. "We got a problem, son," said the raspy voice of the Jinnits lead singer, just as the crowd realized who that was and started oohing. I hardly had time to gulp before the Jinnits, all of them, whisked me away and into the nearest doorway.

I don't pretend to understand musicians. I like music, sure, and Peg and I love to dance. But the way musicians think is beyond me. Murray's had us over when Conway was visiting, and I always felt a little uncomfortable, knowing that he's never sat behind a desk from nine to five in his entire life. Now I was surrounded by them, strange-looking people in bright, shimmery suits, with gold and silver fringe on arms and shoulders and hips and ankles. Cerise male and female, tangerine male and female, caution-yellow male and midnight blue male. All bright-eyed, all very alert, and all very upset about something.

As it turned out, they had three problems. Someone had put only two porta-potties in the cubbyholes off Main Stage, and they needed at least four (three M, one F) because they'd brought along a whole new stage crew, much bigger than last year. I gave myself a pat on the back for sequestering one set in the Chamber offices, and said I've have someone bring the others right away. That got me a nod from the female in cerise and the male in tangerine, but the band leader didn't budge.

There was this ship captain, he said. I had formerly heard all of this from the ship captain's point of view; now I heard it from the band's. Conway, they agreed (patting Conway, whom I hadn't recognized with this year's hair-color and a shimmering yellow catsuit) had gone a little overboard with Zetta (the ex-wife), but it was mostly Zetta's fault. She'd threatened to leave him for a fat-cat management type at Central Belt Mining & Exploration, who was going to get her a permanent position there. So Conway had put the moves on a corporate wife, being hurt and lonesome and willing to make some CBM&E husband unhappy in return, and then Zetta had had a row with her new lover and come tearing in to find Conway embracing what'shername. Some brunette with plenty of miles, the cerise female said admiringly, but a lot of horsepower under the hood. Conway nodded, at this point, and said she was made for more than a middle manager's wife. No one said a word about the corporate wife's *husband*. I thought of Peg, who in a hotsuit and hood could pass for twenty, and decided to keep her far away from Conway.

Zetta had already filed for divorce, but apparently she still considered Conway her property, because she had sent the brunette away in tears. Then on the voyage across, she had started a row with Conway in the ship's bar, expressed herself in highly colored terms on the subject of his ancestry, his anatomy, and his eventual destination, and finally had thrown his own drink in his face. That's when he hit her, but actually it was Shareen (the tangerine female) who blacked her eyes, because Zetta had elbowed Shareen in sensitive places and said "nasty things" about Shareen's lover, who worked backstage. "Zetta deserved it," said the band leader, and everyone else nodded.

"I was drunk," said Conway, sadly.

"She deserved it anyway," said the band leader, and everyone nodded again. "But this damn captain…" Seems the captain, as a Neo-Feminist, considered any female who wouldn't file charges when assaulted to be in need of protection at best and permanent reeducation at most. She wouldn't believe that Shareen had blacked Zetta's eyes, and assumed that Shareen was another of Conway's lovers, trying to take the rap for him. Zetta didn't like being hit, but she liked even less being treated like a nincompoop. Shareen was furious because she'd never had an affair with Conway— she was gay, and proud of it. And now the captain was going around LaPorte-Centro-501, telling everyone that the Jinnits were a sexist band that no self-respecting Neo-Feminist would listen to, and the band was under a peace bond order (guaranteed by the Chamber, as their employer) and couldn't fight back.

"I could kill that bitch," said Shareen, looking me straight into the eye until I nodded agreement. "But it would break the bond, and our contract both, and you'd have no lead band, and we'd have no gig."

And besides (third problem) there was Conway, who was depressed and miserable, and needed a girl to cheer him up so he could do his best. Nothing else would do, and brunette was preferable. Somebody (they all looked at me, intently) had to do something to stop that captain from ruining their reputation and their business, and somebody had to get Conway cheered up so he could play. Then they patted my arms and told me they'd be in their suite when I got it all straightened out.

I started by calling the Chamber offices and arranging to have the porta-potties moved. The captain hadn't sounded very understanding on the radio, and I wasn't at all sure how I could deal with her. We do have laws about libel, and also about inciting a riot, but what with the way colonies depend on spacers, you just can't afford to alienate the people who run the ships. And for all I knew she'd claim it fell under religious freedom or something. I looked up Sarah Jolly Hollinshead, the Chamber's top lawyer, on the schedule. She had volunteered to handle Campground registration this year. This was too important for a call: I'd have to go myself.

The Campground was already filling up. Colorful bubbletents sprouted from the storage bay floor. Sarah had a line maybe seven families long, and I knew better than to break in, even though she caught my eye and nodded to me. Justice must be *seen* to be done, as she keeps telling us. I stood there catching my breath after the droptube ride, and admired Sarah's organization. She had two gofers with her, and really kept things moving along without seeming to hurry anyone. I moved up behind the family in front of me (by their T-shirt designs, recently from Teacup 311's "Tea for Two Days").

It wasn't until I heard Joyce's voice that I realized she was two families ahead of me in the line. I peeked. There was the back of her smooth dark head, looking very much as I remembered the back of her head looking, and there were the three kids (one niece, two nephews), some inches taller. They all held small travel bags. She was asking Sarah where to find Aisle 26, Lot X, as they had a reservation (which Sarah checked, before handing them a map), and then she asked where she could find me.

"Mr. Carruthers?" asked Sarah, as if she hadn't heard that name before, but she said it loud enough for me to hear, in case I wanted to.

"My brother-in-law," said Joyce. I started to back up and bumped into someone behind me, someone who turned out to be large and solid.

"Andrew Carruthers?" asked Sarah. I think she was trying to give me time to escape.

Joyce said, "He's the President of your Chamber of Commerce," in a tone of voice that implied Sarah was too far down the list to know that, and I saw Sarah stiffen.

The giant behind me read the name off my presidential seal and said, all too loudly, "I think someone's looking for you, Mr. Carruthers." And grinned at me. His gimme cap was from Holey Bey, and that figures. Troublemakers, that's what they've got over there. Perverted humor.

I stepped out of line and went forward as if I hadn't seen Joyce. When she turned around, I had a big smile ready.

"You came," she said, as if she really wanted to see me. "I didn't know if you'd find time…" But for once it didn't sound accusing.

"Had to check on you," I said genially, trying a smile on the kids. The girl, Cynthie, was looking around with some interest.

"What is this place?" asked the older boy.

"It's a storage bay," I said. "We make it a campground for Wheel Days."

"It's big," said the girl. "We don't have things like this in Central Station One."

"We're all built up," said the boy. "This is great. I hope our tent is a long way across." He pointed. Harris, that was his name, and the younger one, presently examining his toes, was Elliot.

"Andy, I hate to bother you," began Joyce. "It's about Ernest…"

"I'll be with you in a second," I said, "but I have to ask Sarah about something first—just came up on the way down." Joyce nodded, collected the children, and moved off a few feet. Tactful of her, I thought, and then launched into a very fast précis of the Jinnits problem for Sarah. She folded her lip under her upper teeth, and hummed… a sound known to strike terror into the hearts of opposing attorneys. When I finished, she nodded once, and pushed back her chair.

"I'll take care of it," she promised. That was that. One did not ask Sarah *how* she planned to do things; she was not a committee sort of person. I went back to Joyce and the kids, and (for no good reason other than the manners I was brought up with) picked up her travel bag and led them toward their bubble. I *should* have been somewhere else, but what could I do?

To my surprise, the kids continued to show a livelier interest in the Campground than they ever had in our place. A strolling juggler chucked Cynthie under the chin and gave her a momentary crown of dancing colored balls, then moved on; she was delighted, and flushed, and altogether not the same girl who had demanded a different brand of breakfast cereal and insisted that our house smelled funny. Harris came to a halt outside one of the bubbletents, eyes fixed on the logo hanging from a snatchpole.

"That's... that's John Steward's First Colony badge," he said, breathless with adolescent awe.

"Some of the pioneers hold a reunion here," I began, but he wasn't listening. Steward himself had ducked out the door of his bubble and paused, finding himself impaled on Harris's gaze. He nodded to the boy, gave me a half-wave, then ducked back inside. "He doesn't talk to strangers much anymore," I said, softening the blow. Harris didn't notice.

"He nodded to me. Mom, he *nodded* to me. John *Steward!*" Then he turned to me. "You know him?"

"Not really," I had to admit. "The oldtimers stick together pretty much. But I've listened to him at the Tall-Tales contest, and bought him a drink once or twice."

"I didn't know you knew *John Steward*," Harris said. "I wish we came here more often. Does Gordie know him?"

"Probably better than I do," I said, relaxing. The kids weren't as bad as I'd thought. "John does a program for the Scout troops every year."

Harris subsided, newly impressed with his cousin. Elliot had acquired a spring in his step, which indicated that things weren't too bad for him, either.

"About Ernest," Joyce began again. I tensed. "He's in jail," she said. "And I wondered..."

"I'm sorry," I said, and started explaining about the wheels and the festival jail.

"I understand," she said. "But it's not that jail. It's a real jail."

"Ernest?" My mind fogged.

"It's—I hate to explain—" She looked away. I glanced around, and saw that we were nearly at their bubble. Pointing it out and settling them into it distracted us both. Then she sent the kids to the nearest foodstand for a snack, and went on. "It's not what it sounds like," she began. "I met this musician..."

Lights flashed in my mind. "Conway?" I asked. "Of the Jinnits?"

She blushed. "How did you guess?" she asked. I couldn't have explained, and nodded for her to go on. "Well, anyway, he was sad and lonesome—his wife had just run out on him with another man, he said. And I suspected that Ernest was having an affair."

"With—?" I had a glimmer, but it seemed wildly improbable.

"I didn't know, then. Someone younger, blonder, whatever. I thought maybe I could make him jealous, and Conway was so sweet, so... pathetic..." Her lashes drooped, and I felt a rush of sympathy. "Then... we were just relaxing together, there in the sauna, and in rushes this blonde viper!" Joyce's voice had thinned and hardened; I could imagine it making holes in steel. "She grabbed my arm and *threw* me out, and screamed the most terrible things at us... threatened to tell Ernest..."

"Did she?"

"Not that I know of. Anyway, I went home, and Conway shipped out that night. And I was glad we were coming here, because I knew the Jinnits would play, and I might see Conway. Not anything serious, but... but he doesn't think I'm too old..."

"Of course not," I said gallantly, but worriedly.

"So when we got here, Ernest was—well, frankly Andy, he wasn't too happy with this—the idea that you'd stuck us out here in the Campground. I tried to tell him you'd probably done it for the children—much better than a crowded hotel, where they wouldn't have many people their own age. He kept insisting it was only because you hadn't bothered to find us a place until the last minute." I tried to look innocent as she glanced at me, then she went on. "We stopped on the way down to have something to eat. That's when I saw the blonde—Conway's friend or ex-wife or whatever she is—sitting up at the bar with two of the biggest black eyes I've ever seen. Frankly I was glad: she left bruises on my arm when she yanked me around. I wanted to hurry Ernest out of there, but he caught sight of her too... and he left me sitting there, just walked off, to go up to her."

"Mmm." Joyce had tears in her eyes when she looked at me.

"That's right, Andy. *She* was the tart he was having an affair with. Ernest demanded to know who had blacked her eyes, and a spaceship captain across the room yelled 'That bastard Conway,' and Ernest—" She paused, looking down. "You know, Ernest really doesn't get along with lots of people."

"Who hit him?" I asked, not surprised at that revelation.

"He told the captain to mind her own business—he really doesn't like women in authority—and she said it was her business since it happened on her ship. By this time she'd come up to the bar, and she said that the blonde—whatever her name is—"

"Zetta," I said.

"I never knew," said Joyce. "Anyway, that she— Zetta—was too enslaved to admit it was a man who hit her, and was trying to blame it on a woman. And Ernest said it was probably the captain, since she looked like the type, and she swung first, but he got in a couple of blows before he fell down. She filed charges, and he filed countercharges, and they're both in jail."

"Oh," was all I could think of to say.

"I'm sorry," said Joyce. "I guess I knew we shouldn't come. We always seem to be in your way, somehow, and you're awfully busy. I know you have important things to do. It's just…"

"Oh, that's all right." It wasn't all right, but for some reason the tight knot of apprehension that had bothered me since I read Ernest's note was loosening. Ernest in jail—a real jail, and for brawling in a bar—was something I felt I could handle. Suddenly I wished Peg were there with me. I wanted to see her face when she heard that holier-than-anyone brother Ernest had started a fight in a bar.

"I'm really sorry," said Joyce again. "I know we're causing you a lot of trouble, and at the worst time. If it hadn't been for me wanting to see Conway again…"

"Don't see why not," I said, suddenly reckless. Running any festival is a matter of dancing tiptoe on a tightrope with people throwing waterballoons at you. Crazier ideas than the one that came to me then had worked for others. "I can't get Ernest out immediately," I said, "not if he's really assaulted someone. And in the meantime, the Jinnits tell me Conway isn't playing up to his level because he's lonesome."

Her eyes began to sparkle. "I couldn't… I mean, to seriously—"

"No, not seriously, but you certainly could go to the core dance tonight. After maybe eating dinner with the band. Couldn't you? It would solve a big problem for me."

"But the kids—"

I grinned at her. "Harris is crazy about oldtimers, right? I'll bet he'd be glad to sit in on the first round of the Tall-Tales Competition, which is just three aisles over, where that big teepee is."

It was not really that simple, of course. It never is. But anyone who can organize the annual festival of a growing community which is going to *deserve* to be called the hub of the industrial center of the solar system can finagle or squinch or maneuver his way past a few difficulties. With Joyce radiantly at his side (in a silver-lamé suit she'd borrowed from Zetta, after a tearful reconciliation), Conway didn't even glance at Peg when she and I whirled past the Main Stage, with every curve of hers showing in her new scarlet hotsuit, Jinnits had never sounded better… and they'd already renewed their contract for next year, because, as the lead singer said, "I guess Murray's not the only friend we've got on this colony." Ernest would be out on bail the next morning; he had been pitifully grateful for my visit and promise of help, once he found that his Company legal insurance wasn't good in our jurisdiction. And when we finally escorted Joyce back to the bubbletent, in the short end of Nightshift, we found four cheerful and excited youngsters—her three and our Gordie—who had been invited to share snacks with the oldest of the oldtimers, John Steward himself.

If I do say so myself, it was a good start to Wheel Days.

SAY CHEESE

"They cheated us!" Stavros Vatta glared at his younger brother Gerard. "They cheated us and you didn't catch them." He gestured at the open canister. Under a double layer of expensive—very expensive—CraigsHollow Premium Choice cheese shaped into neat round wheels, seven per layer, were irregular, messily wrapped lumps of very cheap and very smelly Gumbone cheese, already demonstrating why no shipper would handle it unless it were flash-frozen at source. That rendered it stringy, but at least it didn't stink.

"All the telltales were good," Gerard said. "I used the sniffer, everything—"

"Everything but your brain," Stavros said. "You didn't unpack every carton." He transitioned from glare to glower.

"You didn't want to wait, remember?" Gerard glared back. "You didn't want to risk missing that early-delivery bonus on the run to Allray. I'm not taking all the blame. It's as much your fault as it is mine." He swatted idly at Moro, the ship's cat, whose fascination with the containers in question had led to the discovery of fraud. "And these CraigsHollow cheeses, we've got to move them to separate containers and hope the mold or whatever it is hasn't gotten into them."

"I'm sure it has, after five days." Stavros chewed his lower lip, then sighed. "Better try, though. Get Arnie to help—"

"Me? There's forty containers—why not you?" It was not the first time Stavros had expected him to do all the cleanup by himself.

"Because I'm captain, remember? And I have other duties, such as figuring out how to make a profit on this run even though we've just found out our private cargo—that *you* chose—is worthless." Stavros turned away. Gerard glared at his back, but wasted no time calling Arnie, their senior cargo handler.

Arnie Vatta, older by decades than Stavros and Gerard, shook his head as he came into the hold. "I told you, young sir—I told you to watch out for last-minute bargains."

"Yes, you did," Gerard said, as graciously as he could. Arnie, like the rest of *Polly*'s experienced crew, had offered far more advice than he wanted; by the time they'd reached Gum, he'd been tired of being treated like an apprentice. Arnie being right was worse than Stavros being angry. "You're right; I didn't watch hard enough. Now, though—"

"That stuff really does stink," Arnie said. "Best tell Baris, in Environmental, before any spores get into the cultures. She'll want special filters… "

One thing after another. He could just imagine Baris's reaction; she had little patience and a formidable temper. Gerard called her, with the result he expected. She cut off the intercom before he'd finished explaining the problem and was at the hold hatch in less than two minutes.

"What have you done—oh, spirits of space, you idiot. That stuff's just this side of toxic!" She smacked the hold's environmental control panel and shut off air circulation. Immediately the smell intensified. "There's enough oxygen in here for you to work six or seven hours—I'm not turning circulation back on until you have that stuff under wraps again. And I strongly suggest a hard vac or flash-freeze."

"But Baris—it's getting thicker. Can't we—?"

"No. Put on masks. Or suit up, if you want to; I don't care. I'm not having that stench—or more of it—all over the ship. And don't open the hatch until you're done." With that she was gone, shutting the hold hatch behind her as forcibly as the mechanism allowed. Gerard looked at Arnie, who shrugged and turned towards the hold lockers.

"I'm suitin' up, Gerry. If I stay in here with no circulation, I'll be pukin' in no time. And the smell will be in my clothes and hair and… "

Gerard sighed and got another suit from the lockers. This was not the way he'd imagined his first real trading voyage. He didn't mind having his older brother as captain and his boss; Stavros had always taken the lead when they were children. Handling backup, any pesky details, had always been Gerard's job. He'd expected to do the same this time. After all, he'd negotiated several tik-production contracts under their father's supervision. He'd thought he would make a good cargomaster.

And now he'd failed. Not just failed, but put Stav's future as a Vatta captain in doubt. Coming home with a contaminated ship, unsalable cargo, in the red? That promised to keep both of them off the list for a long time. "Let's get at it," he said, once he'd sealed the protective suit. "Any ideas for how to clean up the good stuff and store it so it'll be salable?"

"Get it all out fast and into fresh containers—we got any empties?"

"Er… no," Gerard said. Traveling with empties made no profit. Gerard had made sure they were all full.

"Mmm." Arnie was unsealing canisters as he thought; Gerard followed his example, pulling out the good cheeses and then setting the lids back on to contain—at least a little—the stinking mess below. Twice, Gerard had to pull Moro out of a canister before he could put the lid on.

"We could move the Gumbone too, pack containers tight-full of it, and that would give us some empties for the CraigsHollow—"

"Canisters'd have to be cleaned, Gerry. I dunno what would get this stink out of 'em." Arnie popped another canister lid. "I guess it's better than nothing, though."

Gerard started reopening lids he'd set back, stuffing Gumbone lumps into the space left by CraigsHollow wheels and then resealing the canisters. Even through the suit filters, he could smell the Gumbone.

"Why would anyone even make this stuff?" he said. "And why does the cat like it?"

"Dunno," Arnie said. "What I heard is, the people back there eat it before it stinks so bad and they say it's really good. Cats—can't ever tell with cats why they like some smells. You're lucky Moro likes you and the captain. He don't like everybody, and if he don't like you, he leaves marks."

"Moro? Bites people? Scratches?"

Arnie chuckled. "There's that, but there's worse. Years ago, we had this young captain. The cat we had then, Sally, hated him. He was a difficult sort, we found out, but Sally was hissing at him and peeing on his bed before he'd done anything. Puked in his shoes, used the captain's chair for a toilet. He hated her as much as she hated him; he finally threw her out the airlock—"

"Really?"

"Yes, really. Not a nice young man at all."

"Who is it? Is he still around?"

Arnie looked around, then shook his head. "I don't like to say. Not good to start rumors."

Gerard changed topics. "I was thinking… if Moro likes the smell so much, maybe we could market it—"

"As a cat-finder? For what you paid for it?"

"Cat food, Arnie. I know it's not hard to find cats…"

"You don't know it wouldn't make cats sick."

"Right." Gerard pushed Moro out of the way again. "It's interesting he's not trying to get into the CraigsHollow cheeses, even though they must smell a lot like this stuff by now."

"To us, maybe. He's a cat."

"Has anyone ever analyzed Gumbone? Seen if it has anything… you know… salable in there?"

"Not that I know of. It doesn't travel well, you see…" Arnie snickered.

Gerard repressed a desire to throw a lump of Gumbone at his back. He was an adult now, a cargomaster according to the personnel list; he couldn't give way to boyish impulses.

Finally the transfer of Gumbone produced enough empty canisters for all the CraigsHollow Premium, and they had sealed and double-taped the lids on the others, to Moro's annoyance. The stench hadn't diminished. Gerard called Baris. "We need to clean the canisters we've emptied of Gumbone, so we can put the good cheese in those. We'd only need to open the hatch for a minute; we can use the crew decontam just down the passage—"

"No, you cannot!" Baris said. "Decontam dumps watermass outside, and we're in FTL. No external openings, remember?"

Now he felt really stupid. He'd been on a ship before; he should have remembered that. "Well… where, then?"

"How valuable are those CraigsHollow cheeses? Really worth the trouble of saving them?"

"Yes," Gerard said. "If we can get even an ordinary price for them, it'll help get us out of the red."

"All right. In ten minutes, I'll have a stack of sealable bags outside your hold hatch. You're suited—unsuit inside, seal your suits, then bring your stuff out. Put it in the bags. Take it all to the big washroom, and before you repack it, wash the insides of the bags as well. Run your clothes through the vac unit. Use a sniffer—as long as you've been in there, your noses are probably saturated." She clicked off.

"Do we take the good cheese?" Arnie asked.

"Might as well," Gerard said. "We can at least rinse it down." They loaded the CraigsHollow into the empty canisters, put the canisters on a load-hauler, and moved everything near the hatch.

Gerard tried not to breathe as he unsuited, but he had to take several breaths… impossible to believe that anyone ever actually ate Gumbone. Soon they were out in the passage, moving the loadhauler upship. When they arrived in the washroom Baris was there.

"I could smell you coming all the way down the passage," she said. "I've already installed special equipment in the water system to handle any spores or anything."

Washing down the containers and the bags took another hour, because Baris insisted on checking every single one for residual contamination.

"And your clothes," she said, when they were down to the CraigsHollow pile. "No, not the cheeses… I'm still considering whether it's a good idea to rinse them off—"

"We have to do something about them—" Gerard began.

"Right now what you have to do is your clothes," Baris said. "Off with them."

Arnie was already half-stripped; Gerard ran a finger under the closure of his shipsuit, feeling like a little boy whose mother had found him wallowing in a mud puddle. Baris could at least leave them alone for this… but environmental security was her responsibility. Sighing, he handed over his clothes and walked through the scrubber. On the far side, he pulled a clean shipsuit off the rack and put it on.

"I'm worried that rinsing these cheeses could damage them," Baris said.

"They're wrapped," Arnie said. "We're not even sure the spores could get in."

"The wrapping could have sensors built in—change color if water touches them, something like that. I put in a call to Kerry, in Engineering; he's on the way with some specialized equipment."

Kerry and Stavros showed up together. "What's going on?" Stavros asked. Kerry crouched over the pile of cheeses.

"Trying to save the profit," Gerard said. Engineering hadn't been his strong point during his apprentice voyage; he had no idea what instrument Kerry was using. He focused instead on Stavros. "We have four canisters' worth of the CraigsHollow. If we can sell it at the next stop—"

"Allray? I don't think that's our best bet, not with so little. If we had forty canisters, I'd say yes. When we left Craigomar, the market price at Allray was fifty two five. You paid twenty five each for the forty—our net on just four would put us seven hundred ninety in the hole, not counting transport costs."

"Definitely sensors in the wrap," Kerry said, standing up. "Captain, I'd advise against any tampering, and that includes the use of water. There are at least five sensor suites in the wrapping of each cheese. Temperature, moisture, mechanical—that would be unwrapping or cutting the seal, a pH check, and one I'm not sure of. Quality merchandise, quality security."

"Which close contact with the Gumbone may already have compromised," Gerard said.

"If it hasn't," Stavros said, "there's a hot market—or was when we left—for exotic foodstuffs on Corland. CraigsHollow cheese was starred. Two zero six per canister."

Gerard felt a gleam of hope. Still in the hole but not as much, and maybe the price would have risen in the meantime. "And that's only thirty days station to station from Allray—"

"Since we're supplementary to the regular Vatta service, we don't have to do more at Allray than drop off the consignments and pick up anything that's shown up for Corland. We can be in and out in less than a day." Stavros grinned. He punched Gerard lightly on the shoulder.

"Of course," Gerard said, his mood dropping again. "We still owe for the transport of the Gumbone."

"We'll think of something," Stavros said. "Only 2.8 more days of FTL, thanks be. Kerry, Baris, do you think we should let the good cheese air before packing it away?"

"The packing instructions say in sealed, dry containers," Gerard said. "At least that way it won't be contaminated by anything else."

"When you get it packed," Baris said, "come by Environmental; I have filters for you to carry back to the hold and install in the intakes before I turn the circulation back on."

Gerard did not look at the CraigsHollow cheeses again until they were out of FTL flight, within a few hours of Allray Station.

The Gumbone canisters, the seals taped over, were as far from the CraigsHollow as possible. Gerard sniffed as he entered the hold. Air had circulated through the scrubbers repeatedly; he couldn't smell anything resembling the stench of aged Gumbone. He pried the lid off the first of the CraigsHollow canisters… and his heart sank. Their translucent wrapping had changed to opaque orange. The CraigsHollow seal, once metallic green, blue, and gold, had turned flat gray, with no logo.

Gerard pulled out the top layer of cheeses, hoping against hope that the others were undamaged, but no—all showed a color change in the wrapping and label. He took one and headed upship to tell Stavros the bad news.

"The seals changed," he said, as he came onto the bridge.

"What?" Stavros didn't turn, peering at the screen which showed *Polly*'s position on the inbound traffic lane. Another showed the current market for the goods they carried, and a list of cargo waiting shipment.

"This." Gerard held out the cheese. "The seals. Evidently there was something in the smell that could penetrate the wrapping and it set off the sensors."

Stavros turned, then, and grimaced.

"Damn. Now what? We can't sell it as CraigsHollow Premium if it doesn't have that seal. We might as well eat it ourselves."

They looked at each other. "We'll be eating dry bread and water if Father finds out how far down we are. So much for trade and profit," Gerard said. He peeled the seal off and unfolded the wrapper. It still looked like a CraigsHollow Premium round, the darker outer rind that should have a paler interior. "I can't really smell anything Gumboney now," he said, after a careful sniff.

"Well, the sensor could smell it," Stavros said. "Let's hope it's not too bad. I should make you eat it all yourself, but I'm a generous man—"

"You're in as much trouble as I am," Gerard said. "You know the rule: the captain is responsible."

"Mother should have had you first. Then you'd be captain, it'd be your responsibility, and I'd have had sense enough not to buy the stuff and cause you grief." Stavros turned back to the screens, highlighting for inquiry those whose mass and destinations would suit their schedule.

"You'd have walked over me to be captain, no matter who was oldest," Gerard said, prodding the cheese with one finger. "It looks all right. If it's not too bad, maybe we can feed it to the crew and sell some standard rations."

"Quit stalling. Go on and taste it, Gerry. I'm your captain; I'm ordering you."

"Bully." Gerard pinched off a crumb and tasted it. "It's not that bad," he said. "In fact... " The flavors suddenly expanded, layer after layer of complexity. Gerard had tasted CraigsHollow Premium once as part of his education, but this... this was more. Better. Vastly better. "Stav... you have to taste this."

"Why? I may be stuck eating it until we get home, but I don't have to start right away."

"Don't be an idiot." Gerard pinched off another crumb and held it out. Stavros took it, sniffed at it cautiously, then laid the crumb on his tongue.

"You're right, it's not so bad... in fact it's even... oh, *my*..."

"See what I mean?"

Stavros worked his tongue around in his mouth. "It's better than CraigsHollow. It's much better." He grinned. "Gerry, whatever was in the Gumbone that did this, however it did it—"

"Just sitting in the canister with the CraigsHollow for five days—"

"I wonder what it would do with other cheeses. If they tasted like this, we could make a fortune. We could start a new business—"

If they'd had cheese to try it on. If it worked on other cheeses.

"I don't see how we can sell anything made with it," Gerard said. "It's a food product—we have to show provenance. We don't have the Gumbone on the manifest at all—it was all supposed to be CraigsHollow. We can't sell the CraigsHollow itself because the label's degraded—"

"We could manufacture our own label." Stavros broke off another crumb and put it in his mouth. "Dear heavens. This is... incredible. Or maybe we just eat it all and die in ecstasy." Stavros reached for another crumb and Gerard slapped his hand away.

"Stop it. Profit first, if it's possible. The problem is, we have nothing on the manifest... no provenance. And we don't have a license for food production. No certifications—" Gerard had spent hours studying the Uniform Commercial Code, in hopes of finding exactly the right cargo to make their private stake.

"I wonder how picky Corland is about certificates," Stavros said. "I'll bet if they had a taste of this, they'd ignore the rules and pay... double what they were offering for CraigsHollow alone. There's got to be some way we can sell it."

"There's always forgery," Gerard said, half-joking. "If we could find a label we could copy—"

"Too easy to check up on us, unfortunately. It must've been great in the days before ansibles. Desperate rogues like us could get away with anything, just by skipping a few light years." Stavros grinned again. "Think of our es-teemed founder. But in these civilized days, I suppose we must not ruin the reputation of the firm. And these look entirely too much like CraigsHollow Premium—same shape, same color, same weight. Probably would test much the same, barring the flavor. Anyone can find out we were carrying some." He smacked his lips. "I could eat a whole wheel of this stuff... I wonder if it's re-ally addictive or just that good."

"Well... you mentioned other cheeses. If we could treat some other cheese... maybe mix some of this in with it," Gerard said. "For instance, back home... there's that place where Aunt Grace buys party supplies. Cheese rolls, cheese balls... roll it in chopped tik nuts and... What's that herb, the one she puts in sausage? Those things are expensive."

Stavros frowned. "I don't remember, but I think I know what you mean. Use the CraigsHollow as a base, or the Gumbone?"

"I'm thinking Gumbone as an additive. Everyone thinks it's worthless; no-body else is carrying it. We—well, the family—could have a monopoly on it, at least for awhile. If we take it home—"

"But we don't know it works with anything else. CraigsHollow is unique, that's why it has such a name."

"We'll be at Allray in four hours. Three hours to unload the consignment, three to load whatever you snag to replace it; we can be on our way in less than a day, even counting time for customs and such. There'll be cheeses for sale in dockside markets—we don't need high-quality cheese, just something edible, to test it on."

"Using what for money? You spent our personal allowance back on Gum; we're not allowed to use corporate funds, remember?" Stavros looked just as angry as when they'd first found the Gumbone where the CraigsHollow Premium should have been.

Gerard remembered now... they were *probationary* captain and cargomaster on this voyage. Only those with permanent appointments could tap into Vatta funds for trade capital. "Arnie might—" he said.

Stavros shook his head. "No. Only the captain and cargomaster can do it."

Gerard slouched deeper into the chair. "Well... there's got to be something we can sell to get some money." He thought through his own possessions: nothing worth much that he hadn't already sold off. "What about the early-delivery bonus? We're getting that, aren't we?"

"Goes to the company. We are well and truly in it to the earlobes, Gerry."

"Wait—that sapphire ring you bought for Helen—what about that?"

"You want me to sell Helen's engagement ring? You're crazy!"

"You can get her another—you're not actually engaged yet."

"I am not selling Helen's engagement ring," Stavros said, every centimeter the outraged lover. "I picked it out specially. She loves sapphires; they match her eyes. And I could afford a much better ring at Placer B than back home—"

"She won't mind," Gerard said. Stavros lunged at him; Gerard dodged around the navigation console and kept talking. "She won't mind not having a ring nearly as much as she'd mind having you in disgrace, not getting your permanent status for another year, if ever."

Stavros paused, scowling.

"I'm serious," Gerard said. "We've got to do something to fix this mess, and it's going to take both of us."

"He's right, Captain," said Collins, the duty pilot, who had ignored them until now. Gerard glanced at him.

Stavros transferred his scowl to the pilot, then took a huge breath and let it out slowly. "All right. All right. We are partners; I understand. But the moment—the moment—we have a profit, I'm taking it and replacing this ring. Helen knows I'm going to her family when we get back—" For a moment his eyes unfocused, then he gave Gerard a sharp look. "And I'm buying the cheese this time," Stavros said.

"You can't," Gerard said. "You need to stay aboard if we're doing a short turn-around; you'll be arguing for a departure slot. Send Arnie. He's experienced."

Stavros nodded. "Fine. The ring's in my cabin, second drawer on the left, in a little red leather box. You take it to him."

Immediately after they cleared the Customs & Immigration docking, Gerard took over the unloading of the consigned cargo while Arnie headed off with orders to sell the ring and buy cheap, but non-smelly cheese, nuts, and herbs.

Then Stavros, wearing his best uniform and his captain's cape, came down to dockside, where Gerard had just finished the offloading and certification of the consigned cargo. "Trouble," he said, before Gerard could ask. "Arnie's been arrested. They claim he tried to cheat a jeweler."

"What?"

Stavros muttered something Gerard couldn't understand.

"Sorry, I didn't hear that."

Stavros grimaced. "I said, they said the ring was a fake. They weren't real sapphires. Arnie insisted they were, the jeweler called the police, the police took him and the ring—"

"But Stav—surely you checked—"

"Don't say it. Don't you dare say it." Stavros shook his head and lowered his voice again. "It was a reputable store. At least, it looked like a reputable store. I checked the directory, all the things Father told us to look at."

"Could the store here be lying?"

"I don't know. What I know is that Arnie's in custody, the ring is in custody, they're bringing in an independent appraiser to determine if it's a fake or not, and no matter what the result, we're facing a delay, extra costs that will have to go on the company account because we can't pay them, and gods know what else."

Gerard opened his mouth to list what else could go wrong, but changed his mind. Instead he said, "Don't worry, Stav. I know you can handle the situation there; I'll make sure the ship's secure and check that the on-delivery payment gets to Crown & Spears."

Stavros nodded. "Thanks, Gerry."

Gerard turned back to the ship.

"What's happening?" Collins asked, when Gerard arrived on the bridge. "Captain left in a rush—he wouldn't say why."

"If he wouldn't say why, I shouldn't," Gerard said. He called up their account at Crown & Spears. The on-delivery payment showed as *Pending Clearance*. Collins raised an expressive eyebrow. "You think I should?"

"It's not my place to say," Collins said. "But if you ask me—"

"Oh, go on," Gerard said. "I know you and the rest could run the ship perfectly well without us, and you're laughing your heads off because we got into trouble—"

"Not really," Collins said. "If you mess up too badly, it's bad for us, too."

"And you think we're bad enough to cause you trouble?" Gerard said.

"Actually, no," Collins said. "You've made some mistakes, sure. All the young officers do. But for the most part, the crew thinks you've performed very well."

"So you've discussed us, have you?" Gerard could imagine… stories about Arkady Vatta's boys would soon be all through the Vatta fleet, and they were bound to get back to Arkady.

"Well, of course," Collins said. "What do you think? It's part of our job with any young officers like you. Anyway, you've done well on the whole and we'd hate to see you fail."

"So… does the crew have ideas that might help?"

Collins grinned. "Since you finally thought to ask, we might. We all have a cargo stake, you know."

Within the hour, the crew had chipped in from their personal funds and sent Baris off to buy cheese and other supplies to implement the new plan. Stavros called back a little later, to report that Arnie had been cleared of charges. The sapphires were synthetic and worth much less than he'd paid for the ring.

"Sell it anyway," Gerard said. "You'll want genuine stones for Helen and besides, you now owe the crew."

"Owe the crew?"

"Get it done and come back; I'm not explaining on this line."

Arnie reappeared first, lugging two sacks. "I just happened by a market and saw Baris. She said to bring this back."

"How's Stavros—I mean, the captain?" Gerard asked.

"Fit to be tied. He's really upset about that ring. I told him—" Arnie didn't finish; he didn't have to. Gerard knew that Stavros, like himself, had been given more advice then he wanted.

"He told me it was a reputable jeweler," Gerard said.

Arnie snorted. "A *dockside* jeweler. No such thing as a reputable dockside jeweler. But lovesick lads have to find out the hard way. Now don't you tease him. He feels bad enough."

"Me tease him!" Gerard shook his head. "I wouldn't think of it."

"You. You're a younger brother. I know all about younger brothers. Was one myself, had one younger than me."

"So, did Baris find cheese?" Gerard asked, retreating from what promised to be a long family remembrance. Arnie started to speak, but Baris herself appeared at the hatch.

"I'm back," Baris said, peering into the bridge. "Somebody'll have to open up below. I got a great deal on the ingredients. And the outgoing cargo's arrived."

Something about her tone alerted Gerard. "Ingredients?"

"Ingredients," she said. "The cheapest cheese was too expensive when the captain's ring turned out to be fake. And it wasn't good enough. We didn't need more bad cheese."

Gerry's heart nearly stopped. "You didn't get cheese... What did you get?"

"I told you. Ingredients. What you make cheese out of, milk and coagulant and salt. The local cheese factory went out of business, some kind of legal problem; I bought up their raw materials for a lot less than cheese would've cost." She looked entirely too cheerful for someone who had clearly just lost her mind.

"But we don't know how to make cheese—"

"I have it all right here." She held up a data cube. "It shouldn't be hard at all. Environmental's all about cultures and cleanliness, right? If I can't make better cheese than was in the market, I'll be very surprised."

"Does the captain know—?"

She pursed her lips. "Well... not exactly. I didn't see any reason to worry him with the details. He's always said you were his detail man. Now if you and Arnie will just go down there and open the cargo hatch..."

Being the designated "detail man" meant that he was the one who had to tell Stavros they had no cheese, just the ingredients for making cheese.

"Baris said she could do it," Gerard said, watching his brother's eyelid twitch. He had insisted on talking to Stavros in the captain's cabin. One interruption by a helpful crew member and his brother might say something unfortunate.

"She seems very confident."

"Baris—" Stavros began. Then he dropped his head into his hands. "This is the worst voyage anyone ever made. Neither of us will ever make permanent captain—and Helen—"

"It's not over yet, Stav," Gerard said. "We have three ten-days before we get to Corland Station. Maybe Baris will make good cheese, maybe the Gumbone will give it the perfect flavor... or maybe we'll come out of jump in a star and never have to worry about anything again." That had been the final chance their father listed every time they'd faced a difficulty, from being lost in the hills behind Corleigh Town to a feeling of panic when faced with asking a girl to a dance.

Stavros snorted and shook his head. "Gerry... I could almost wish for that collision with a star, right now."

"I know. The thought of facing our father if we don't come back at least even-money scares me, too. But the crew's on our side. They're not stupid, even if we were—"

"I wasn't stupid... not exactly. I swear to you, it looked like a legitimate jeweler's. Everything seemed to check out. But really—cheesemaking on a spaceship? And we still don't have any certification. How can we sell a food product we're not licensed to make?"

"Ah," Gerard said. "That's the real question. We can't pretend we have the license; they'd find out. We can't pretend it's someone else's product; they'd find that out, too. So it's really a marketing problem."

They sat staring at each other a long moment. Then Stavros shifted in his seat. "Wait... What if it's something that's never been exported before? Experimental or something?"

Gerard felt the hair rise on his arms as an idea leaped into his mind. "Something that hasn't been exported—so it doesn't have to be on the manifest—because it's not for sale."

"Not for sale? But the point is to sell it—" Stavros looked confused.

"Oh, we'll sell it. But we'll have to be persuaded... we don't want to sell it—"

"Of course we want to sell it!"

"Wake up, Stav," Gerard said. He saw the whole plan now, clear as the figures in red and black. "We can't sell it legitimately—we have to have an angle. That's the angle. Call it our rations or something. Not for sale. But we let the right person get a taste of it—"

Stavros's face lit up. "Gerry, that's brilliant! If Baris can make the cheese—"

"We can make the sale," Gerard said. "And the profit."

Corland Station's Customs & Immigration team came aboard to check out the consigned cargo. "Something sure smells good," the inspector said, as Gerard signed the datapad to indicate that they had nothing further to unload.

"Lunch," Gerard said. "Want to join us?"

"I can't," the inspector said. "We're not allowed—but what is it?"

"Nothing special," Gerard said. "You know, cheese and sausage and bread."

"Mmm. Ever consider selling some of it, whatever it is?"

"No. It's just crew rations," Gerard said, shrugging. "Nothing to get excited about." Across dockside, he saw two men lift their heads and sniff, their reaction completely unlike his to the undiluted Gumbone.

"How long will you be here?" the inspector asked, sniffing again. "If I stopped by when I'm off-duty…"

"We have to wait for the local sales agent Vatta works with," Gerard said. "I think there's something for us to pick up here—at least, our captain's trying to find us cargo to replace what we're dropping off. *Polly*'s a nightmare to trim with the load this unbalanced. If we can't find cargo, we'll have to move things around…"

The inspector finally moved away. Gerard pulled out the platter of cheese, sausage, and bread Arnie had placed on a hotplate in front of the ventilation blower, and the two of them sat down to eat in plain sight of dockside traffic.

"When's the company agent coming?" Arnie asked.

"Another hour," Gerard said. "That went well, didn't it?"

"Baris is a genius," Arnie said, and took a bite of ship's biscuit spread with Baris's cheese roll mixture and a slice of sausage.

Gerard took a mouthful and nodded. Never mind the suspense of those days when it seemed the cheese wouldn't be ready in time or that Baris would never find the right proportion of Gumbone to the cheese she'd made. It had worked out in the end and the flavors in his mouth were proof of that. Better even than the fume-flavored CraigsHollow Premium.

Several of the people walking by paused, sniffing, turning to look. One of them, after a hesitation, came nearer. "What's that you're eating? Smells good, but nothing like I've had before—"

"Just lunch," Arnie said. "Why?"

"I'm off *Morroway*, Bissonet registry, dock seven. Where'd you buy it?"

"Didn't buy it," Arnie said, taking another bite. "It's off our ship. Rations."

"Vatta feeds you that well? That's got to be Gold Level—"

"It's not," Gerard said, earning a look from Arnie. The whole act was going as planned. "It's homemade."

"Can—can I have a taste?"

"Sure," Gerard said. Arnie shook his head.

"Better not. We don't know what you're allergic to. It's got chopped nuts in it, and dairy—"

"I'm not allergic," the man said. "Just a taste—"

Gerard and Arnie exchanged looks. "Well, if you fall over dead, don't blame us," Arnie said. He smeared a round of ship's biscuit with the cheese and laid a sausage slice on it. "There you go."

The man took a bite, and his face changed to the blissful expression Gerard expected.

"This tastes even better than it smells. Sure you won't sell us some?"

Arnie laughed. "And not have any for ourselves? You've got to be kidding."

With a last longing look at the platter, the man finally went away. Gerard stuffed another bite in his mouth, to have some reason for the triumphant grin he was sure was spreading over his face.

"Act Two," Arnie said. "Word's going to spread fast."

Gerard left Arnie lounging in the cargo hatch opening, and went upship to set the stage for their next visitor, this one expected.

"What is that heavenly aroma?" the sales agent said as Stavros led him past the galley.

"Just ship rations," Stavros said. "It's only a cheese roll." He glanced at the table, where a cheese roll, haggled at one end, lay on a cheese-smeared plate with an open tin of ship's biscuit beside it. "Gerry, weren't you supposed to clean up the galley after lunch?"

Gerard glowered. "Not my turn. Baris should have—"

"You sell them?" the sales agent said.

"Ship rations? No, of course not. Traditional food."

Gerard, watching this, admired, Stavros's tone of voice.

"But—but I must taste that—"

"If you want to," Stavros said, sounding puzzled. "Gerry, cut him off a piece." To the sales agent he said, "It's just a cheese spread thing."

Gerard sliced off a corner and put it on a plate. The sales agent took it eagerly, eyes alight. His eyes widened when the flavors developed in his mouth. "You—you don't export this?"

"Wouldn't be profitable," Gerard said. "Labor-intensive, expensive to make."

"Really…" The rep looked at the roll on the table. "That's—it's quite good. There might be a market for something like that."

"But it's our rations," Gerard said. He cut off a lump, pressed it on a ship's biscuit with his thumb, and took a bite. The rep shuddered slightly, but his eyes shifted back to the table. "Besides," Gerard said, around the mélange of flavors in his mouth, "it's not licensed provender. You wouldn't want to buy something with no provenance."

The man's hand twitched. Stavros cut off a slice for himself, spreading it onto the round of biscuit with a knife, as a captain should. "Go ahead," he said to the rep. "Help yourself. I always did say Auntie Grace made the best—"

Gerard nearly choked on the last of the biscuit.

"A relative made this?"

"Yes," Stavros said, draped in honesty. Gerard admired his skill even more. That statement was true in all senses, but yet, in the conversational context, it was a plain lie.

"She makes fruitcake too," Stavros went on. "And sausage." He nodded at the sausage, which had indeed been a gift from Aunt Grace, but they had no idea if she'd made it herself.

"She's a cook?"

Gerard inhaled a crumb the wrong way and had to cough.

"Not exactly," Stavros said. "It's more of a hobby with her. But she's good at it, isn't she?"

"If her fruitcake's as good as this cheese—" The sales agent cut himself another slice. "Look, Captain, we're hosting a summit conference between—well, I can't give the names. Hostile powers, let's say. It's very, very secret."

Gerard was tempted to tell him it was no secret on the docks; the loaders had talked about it as the cargo came off. Santanians and Berklundians. If they went to war and started throwing munitions at each other, four useful trade routes would be yellow-tagged for years, until someone cleared all the mess away. Instead, he licked the cheese off his fingers, playing hick to the hilt.

The sales agent went on. "We are tasked—I am tasked—with providing the food. It's politically inexpedient that they know where the food is from—trade agreements on produce are a major source of the hostility. Something like this—something unique—is exactly what I need. Of course it would have to pass analytical tests, including testing against their allergen panels—"

"Allergen panels?" Gerard asked, as if he'd never heard of them.

"Oh, yes. Our guests provide us with a complete panel of any known allergies, with detailed specifications of the allergens, so we can ensure that nothing they come in contact with will cause them distress." The rep cut himself yet another slice of the cheese roll, this time spreading it thickly on a ship's biscuit. "But you're eating it, and I'm eating it, and my implant's not flagged it yet. Now—are all the ingredients from your homeworld? Slotter Key, is it, or is that just the ship's registry?

"No, some ingredients are imported to our homeworld," Stavros said. "Each family has its own recipes, you understand. For instance, Aunt Grace uses a small amount of CraigsHollow cheese in the mix. And if she runs short of rutter cheese, she uses whatever light cheese is available. We're not primarily a dairy supplier."

Aunt Grace would skin Stavros alive, Gerard thought, if she ever found out about this. And she would find out, because she found out everything.

The rep's expression of gustatorial bliss mixed with intense cunning suggested the source of his next question. "Supposing I were willing to buy such a food product. Without a license of course I could not pay premium prices… how much could you supply?"

Stavros shot a glance at Gerard. "Well… I don't know. We'd have to be able to resupply here, and your prices are awfully high—"

"What about a straight trade, then? Kilo for kilo? This stuff is good, but surely you're tired of it by now."

"Oh, we never get tired of good cheese," Gerard said. "Would you get tired of this?" His implant rolled the figures past him. If they even-traded cheese rolls for Corland's high-priced foodstuffs, they could sell those somewhere else and still make a profit. Corland's station inventory included flash-frozen bloodbeast filets, Turnoy tigerfish steaks, spices from at least twenty worlds.

"Straight trade. No paperwork. If it passes our toxicology tests that's all that really matters. Private-label it."

"I don't know," Stavros said. "I don't want to get in trouble with your food safety inspectors."

"Look—110% by weight premium. Really. How much—"

"Well… " Stavros looked at Gerard; Gerard shrugged as if he didn't care. "I guess we could let you have—how much have we got left, Gerry?"

"A couple gross," Gerard said. "We could let them have ten or twenty rolls and still get home before we ran out."

"You have over two hundred—come on, you can survive part of one voyage without it, surely. I could use all that—"

"Crew's not going to like it," Gerard said. "But it's up to you, Captain."

"It's irregular," Stavros said, as if that were a problem. "But I guess… if you can guarantee we won't get in trouble with the authorities…"

"No problem," the rep said. He cut himself another slice. "No problem at all. I'll put it in writing. Special import, traditional native food of… Slotter Key, wasn't it?" Stavros nodded. "And listen—if you can get people to jump through the hoops and set up for export, I guarantee it'd be a profitable product…"

"I don't know," Stavros said. "We're just a transport company really."

"We'll need to rewrap it all," Gerard said. "You know how it is—" he indicated the wrapper, where the words *Not For Sale* still showed on the uncut end of the roll. That had been another of Baris's bright ideas. "I suppose you have plain dairy-quality wrap on the station—"

"How soon?"

How long would it take to make up that many cheese rolls if everyone pitched in? The biggest mixer in the galley had a capacity of only 3 kilos of cheese. That would make six half-kilo cheese logs… Gerard ran the calculations, the number of batches, the time it would take to mix in the right amount of flavoring, shape them, roll them in nuts and herbs, wrap and label them. Add a few hours for the inevitable problems. "Day after tomorrow," Gerard said. "If we get the wrapping today. We'll have to be careful not to knock off any of the seasonings."

"I could have that done for you."

Stavros shook his head. "No—nothing can leave this ship with *Not For Sale* on it... an inspector couldn't ignore that."

"Oh. Of course."

They had the signed contract within the next hour, and an hour after that, Baris returned to the ship with two rolls of dairy-quality food-product wrap. Gerard had already cleared out the galley and dining area to make a workstation. Someone had started the big mixer in the galley, and two batches sat in bowls ready to shape, with bowls of chopped nuts and herbs ready to go.

By the time they had two gross cheese rolls ready for delivery, the entire crew was exhausted, but they were ready ahead of time, and every lingering trace of the Gumbone additive had been scrubbed from the air. Only the lush aroma of Baris's recipe, now neatly wrapped, sealed, and closed with the newly printed labels *(Vatta & Co, Private Treaty Cheese Rolls, 500g)* greeted the sales agent on his return.

Homecoming meant docking at Slotter Key Station and facing yet another customs and immigration inspection. With the exception of the remaining Gumbone, now stored in crew quarters as private property, everything in the cargo holds matched the manifests. The last of the cargo from that Corland trade had been sold off two stops before.

Gerard did not expect to see his father standing outside the ship when customs cleared them and opened the dockside access.

"I'll just come aboard, shall I?" Arkady said, with a nod for Arnie. "Hi, Arnie. Talk to you later." He stepped into shipspace before Gerard could say anything. Gerard gulped.

"Father. Welcome aboard."

"We'll go upship," Arkady said. The arm he put around Gerard's shoulders was hard as stone and felt as heavy. No chance to warn Stavros... "I understand you've had an interesting voyage, Gerry. You and Stav both."

"We're in the black," Gerard said.

"Very nice," Arkady said, in a tone that did not match his words.

Someone had warned Stavros, because he met them in the main passage.

"Your cabin," Arkady said. It was not a request. Stavros, stony-faced, ushered them in and at Arkady's gesture closed them in. Gerard had the feeling that only one was coming out of there alive.

"I should knock your heads together," Arkady began. "Do you even have an idea how many laws you broke and how much trouble you could be in?"

"I don't think we actually broke any laws," Gerard said. "At least, not until we unload the—" His father held up a hand.

"I don't want to know about that until it's downside, behind odor-proof seals. It's your problem how you get it down."

"We're in the black," Stavros said. He glanced at Gerard.

"Trade and profit," Gerard said.

Arkady gave them both a long, hard look, then slowly shook his head. The rumble of laughter that meant danger was over followed after. "You boys," he said. "No, sorry, you men. You are definitely, absolutely, without any doubt, Vatta to the core." He grinned. "We will have to have your pictures taken, added to the database of permanent crew." He chuckled again. "You will have to say cheese," he said.